PRIVATE GOLLANTZ

*

Private Gollantz is the fifth volume in the Gollantz
Saga. Again the central figure is young Emmanuel.
Emmanuel who had settled in Italy and whose
galleries in Milan now rivalled those of his father
Sir Max, in London.

But a change was coming over the Italian nation
with the rise of Mussolini, and Emmanuel was
apprehensive. He realised that he had to return to
England, to his parents and his bitter, jealous
brother, Julian. No soldier by temperament, he
realised that he must join the army and fight.

Naomi Jacob

Private Gollantz

(Fifth of the Gollantz Saga)

ARROW BOOKS

ARROW BOOKS LTD
178–202 Great Portland Street, London W1

AN IMPRINT OF THE HUTCHINSON GROUP

London Melbourne Sydney
Auckland Johannesburg Cape Town
and agencies throughout the world

*

First published by
Hutchinson & Co (*Publishers*) Ltd 1943
Arrow edition 1971

*Made and printed in Great Britain
by The Anchor Press Ltd.,
Tiptree, Essex*
ISBN 0 09 004720 6

To
REGINALD HARGREAVES
Soldier, historian, writer
and
kindest of friends
MICKIE

Book One

Emmanuel sat with his chin propped on his hand, staring blankly before him. The world—that world which had once held so much warmth, beauty and happiness—had reached, it seemed to him, the final stage of madness. Again and again during the past years he had watched events, listened to opinions, studied political questions, and always tried to hope and believe that one day Italy would assert herself; protest against a system which, however excellently it might have worked in the past, was now rapidly turning into a monster of terrible proportions.

He had come to Italy when his life had been touched with tragedy; when he had, for his mother's sake, shouldered blame which should have rested on his younger brother Julian. His mother—that mother whom Emmanuel loved so dearly—had been gravely ill, and her doctor, Nathan Bernstein, had warned the whole family that she must never be allowed to suffer any shock. Julian was the best loved of Angela Gollantz's sons, so when Julian contrived to become involved in a particularly unsavoury business, Emmanuel took the blame.

It was an old story now; only at rare intervals did Emmanuel remember it. His father had accepted his story and insisted that Emmanuel should leave England. Only Viva Heriot, who was now Mrs. Tatten and had been Emmanuel's first wife, had refused to credit the story.

Emmanuel's grave, stern face softened a little as he thought of Viva. She had asked for her freedom when they had been married about four years. They had always liked each other, felt a certain affection even in their worst days and in the midst of their most difficult arguments; only as a marriage it had not been a success He had been too serious, too occupied, and—even then—he had known that Juliet

Forbes filled his heart. He had married Juliet when the divorce was through, and Viva had married that queer, likable little man, Toby Tatten, who looked like something between a jockey and Adolf Hitler.

Juliet—Emmanuel whispered the name softly. Lovely Juliet, even the fact that Leon Hast had called her that didn't hurt him now. That one year of marriage, of intense and complete happiness, the birth of their son—and Juliet's death. A death so sudden, so swift, that he shuddered now to think of it.

That little irritating cough, her saying, 'Give me a glass of water, Emmanuel,' and as he offered it to her, the sight of her slipping down in his arms. Months afterwards he had said to little Gilbert, 'I shall be mentally lame all my life, Gilly.'

Gilbert answered, 'My dear young man, many of us will be lame without Juliet.'

In those days he had found help from Gilbert, from old Simeon Jaffe, who took him into partnership, and finally left him the magnificent Galleries stocked with superb antiques, and from Guido Maroni. People like Toby Tatten, Viva, and even his own brother William, wondered what he could find in Guido.

'Oh, I know that he's a good fellow,' William said, 'but—well, he isn't your type, Emmanuel. He's so over-coloured.'

'So is Italy,' Emmanuel said, 'but you don't notice that when you've lived in the country. I've lived with Guido sufficiently long to know him—and love him.'

William Masters, his brother's godfather, was even less understanding. Bill Masters was growing old and short-tempered, intolerant and over-critical. Emmanuel was fond of him because he had been devoted to Juliet.

'Why in heaven's name,' Masters demanded, 'you want to surround yourself with friends who are positively fantastic, passes my comprehension. Louis Lara, his over-blown wife, this Guido, and all the rest of them.'

Emmanuel had smiled; he was always tolerant with Bill.

'And do you include the opera people in the fantastics?'

'They have at least the excuse that they are artists!'

Now, in his splendid room at the Gollantz Galleries, Emmanuel sat thinking, looking back. He was thirty-three, very

10

tall and slim, with hair which turned grey after Juliet died. Someone once described him as 'an old-young man'. His face was unlined, pale and handsome. He looked arresting and when he walked through the streets people turned to watch him. Like his grandfather—the Founder of the House —he was distinguised and somewhat eccentric in his dress. Admittedly, it was a carefully restrained eccentricity, but Emmanuel Gollantz, with his high black stocks, his ivory-topped cane, and his immaculate clothes, which had something about them of a past era, was a noticeable figure.

The family was of Jewish origin, the founder having been Fernando Meldola, an Italian Jew from Milan. Meldola had moved to Paris, where he had adopted his niece, Miriam Lousada. She married a Dutch Jew from Rotterdam, one Abraham Gollantz. There was a story told in the family that old Meldola had never forgiven his niece's husband because he had gone with the army of Napoleon into Italy as artistic adviser.

'Even then,' Emmanuel thought, 'there was a hatred of watching Italy suffer!'

The family had prospered; Abraham's son Hermann had left Paris for Vienna, and after his death his only surviving son Emmanuel—still referred to by his descendants as 'Old Emmanuel'—had moved to London and founded the firm of Gollantz.

Thus it came about that there were branches of the family in Vienna, in Paris, in Holland and Germany. From time to time they came to London—The Foreign Contingent— Laras, Hirsches, Jaffes, Moises, Bruchs—all connected by ties of blood or marriage with the original branch.

Emmanuel had been living in Italy ever since the scandal which he had allowed to drive him out of England. True, evidence had proved after several years that the blame did not lie with him, and he had let himself be persuaded to return to England. He was to work with his father, Max Gollantz, and his small son Simeon was to be brought up as an English boy.

It hadn't been a success. Both Max and his son had managed their own affairs for too long, and with too much individuality. There had been difficulties, and finally Emmanuel—with his small son—had returned to Milan and the Galleries there.

Life had been pleasant enough, Emmanuel thought, except when something or someone reminded him too vividly and too painfully of Juliet. He had learnt to meet people who had known and loved her, he had schooled himself to listen to music again, to go about among his fellow men and women, even to entertain in that rather elegant and lavish manner which was characteristic of his family.

He had travelled up and down the country, he had delighted in its beauty and in the friendliness of its people. He often thought that the loveliness of Italy, the sunshine and the easy laughter, had helped to heal his heart and mind. He had watched political events with distrust. With the occupation of Austria the families of Hirsch and Bruch had left Vienna. True, they had contrived to take much of their wealth with them, and were living comfortably enough in England. Then the murder of Dollfuss had shaken him, and he had believed that the Italian Government would assert its authority and fulfil its promises. He had read in an Italian newspaper of some standing, 'Europe is tired of having to live in an indescribable state of tension at the mercy of a handful of madmen.' He had been conscious of a feeling of satisfaction. Surely that sentence, and the phrases which followed, meant that the heart and soul of Italy were stirred. He had listened to the great Requiem Mass broadcast to all Italy which had been said and sung for the soul of the Little Chancellor. He had watched the evidences of emotion on the faces of the people who listened to the blaring radios; perhaps the people were not so completely under the heel of Fascismo after all.

Abyssinia and the territorial ambitions of Il Duce: there had been a first flare of enthusiasm from the people, then, as the war dragged on, as taxes rose, that had died; when Addis Ababa fell, when there were processions and rejoicings, he felt that they were less demonstrations of joy for the victory than expressions of relief that the war was ended. In May, 1938, Adolf Hitler had visited Rome.

His telegram, which had caused so many Italians to smile wry smiles, sent after the Abyssinian war, '*I shall never forget*,' was apparently forgotten by the Government. How

12

many stories there were regarding that visit! The mayor of Milan had telegraphed to Mussolini that if Hitler came to Milan he came at his own risk. They said that when Hitler's train drew into the station at Bolzano, the Duce whispered, behind his hand, to Ciano, 'I don't like this man!' They said, they said, they said . . .

What was it all? Wishful thinking? Complete incredulity that Italy could form such a close alliance with a nation so unlike herself? Was it made through fear—that alliance? Fear of what? Of whom? English diplomats had not been too wise, too skilful; they had bungled and bungled badly. How often had his friends said to Emmanuel, 'Why did you send . . . this or that man?' Again and again they had asked, 'Why did England not send . . . so and so?' Out of the visit of Adolf Hitler one thing alone appeared to give satisfaction to the Italians. They resented the money which was spent like water, they disliked the infiltration of German police, and their interference with foreigners in Italy before the visit—but they rubbed their hands when they heard that no matter who had received the German Chancellor, he had not been granted an audience by His Holiness Pius XI.

Again speculation ran riot, again there were stories, reports, inferences and insinuations.

The Germans returned to their own country, the triumphal arches were taken down, the Militia sent back to their homes. Emmanuel, watching, listening, exchanging ideas, realised that a new spirit was abroad. Again and again he heard the phrase used of Hitler, *'Il Duce del nostro Duce'*— the Leader of our Leader. The man who had risen so high was beginning to fall—slowly but surely.

Now, on September the first, 1938, Emmanuel Gollantz sat in his study and understood that the manifesto against the Jews, which had been announced in May, was to be enforced. The manifesto had caused little attention. No one believed that it was anything more than a sop to Hitler. There was a sense of resentment that Italy must—even on paper—fall into line, but no one believed that there was the least likelihood of the Jews being either banished or, still less, persecuted.

Now—it had come! Emmanuel spoke that word, 'Persecution,' and shivered. To this had Italy fallen. Italy, who

13

had befriended so many of the Jews from Germany and Austria; Italy, who—strong in her own Catholicism—had never enforced her religious beliefs. He remembered the English churches in Florence, in Merano, in the lakeside resorts; he recalled the new synagogue in Verona. There had been freedom for religious creeds—now that had been banished at the order of 'Il Duce del nostro Duce'.

He, himself, was only half a Jew. His mother was lacking in any Jewish blood; his own son, Simeon, could boast of only twenty-five per cent. All the Gollantzes were proud of their Jewish descent, though for many years they had ceased to practise the Faith in any way. Of the three sons of Max Gollantz only Emmanuel showed any trace of Jewish ancestry. In his pale, rather melancholy features and his dark eyes there was much which was reminiscent of his grandfather as a young man. Julian and William were both fair, and resembled their mother's family.

Knowing the Italians, Emmanuel doubted if this persecution would be carried out with any great degree of thoroughness. It might be nothing more than an attempt on the part of the Government to impose heavy fines, to confiscate money and investments with which to swell the—very depleted—exchequer. But . . . he sighed.

'But, on the other hand,' he said softly, 'this is not the time for me, or any other man with Jewish blood, to wait. However little of that blood we have, this is not the time to attempt to conceal or deny it. My grandfather used almost to boast of the pride of race possessed by his people. Well, thank God, that pride is still there!'

He pressed an electric bell on his desk, took a cigarette from a huge onyx box and lit it carefully. The door opened and Guido entered.

The time had been when Guido's love of 'English sports' clothes as interpreted by a cheap Italian tailor had set Emmanuel's nerves on edge. Now, Guido had learnt. Emmanuel had been his pattern, his model; in addition, in these days Guido earned quite sufficient money to go to a good tailor. He was a small man, who only preserved his waistline by violent and continual exercise. Guido played tennis whenever it was possible, though he preferred the game of rackets as being more English and more *individuale*. Although he was past thirty, he still retained his likeness to a cherub in a Baroque church. His face was round and beautifully shaped, his mouth full, and his eyes dark and of a melting affection. His clothes were supremely elegant; his light grey suit fitted him almost too perfectly, his tie was expensive and splendid, though restrained.

'I believe,' he said, smiling, 'that this is the tea hour. How English we become! In England there is a proverb, "Everything comes to an end for tea." Am I right?'

Emmanuel said, 'Sorry, Guido. It's not tea. Do you never read the papers?'

'Not if I can help it. What for should I? One paper belongs to Mussolini, another to Ciano, another to someone else. They all—to use your English expression—want to nourish me like a wet-nurse. Has something interesting happened?'

'The persecution of Jews in this country is to be made an official business,' Emmanuel said grimly. 'You're not a Jew by any chance, are you?'

'No—but I will become one if you wish.'

'Well, I am—half of me at all events.'

The soft brown eyes widened with horror. 'It is not true! It cannot be true. Emmanuel, there is no one in Milano, in all Italy, who would dare to—*Dio,* I cannot even speak the word in connection with you. My friend, my dear friend— you must fly, with Simeon and with me. I shall follow you to the ends of the earth. Let me collect the best jewels, money, securities, and we shall leave in an hour.'

Emmanuel shook his head. 'Bless you,' he said, 'don't fly off the handle. I'm not going to leave unless they make me. It occurs to me that I am one of the lucky ones. I am rich, I have many friends, and I am only half a Jew. There may be others . . .' He paused, and then said, 'I can speak frankly to you, Guido, I know that.'

'Frankly!' Guido exclaimed. 'Speak with rudeness or brutality, I can accept it on my chin!'

'There may be others less fortunate. I have the Galleries. There are various entrances and exits. I may be of use to— the less fortunate ones. You understand?' Guido, his eyes still round with interest, nodded. 'Now I am going to report to the Mayor.'

The little Italian sprang forward. 'No, no! This is impossible! Emmanuel Gollantz to report to the *podestà* like some malefactor. I shall go. I shall go with haughtiness, and speak to the officials, but with my eyes looking over their heads all the time. I shall say, "Kindly examine these papers, these passports. Name: Jewish. Name also: honourable. Do you mind if, while you make this examination, I sing to hide my embarrassment at this intrusion into the private life of the great Signor Gollantz?" Then I shall sing softly—but with clearness—*O bella libertà*! Let me go, I beg.'

Emmanuel laughed, and while he was busy unlocking one of the drawers of his desk, he answered, 'No, Guido. I can't have my best friend, my manager, flung into prison. Also, I happen to know the *podestà*, he's a very fine fellow. There —passport and credentials. I shan't be long, Guido.'

Emmanuel walked slowly through the Galleria and out into the bright sunny square in front of the great cathedral. He looked up at the great West Front as he passed. The intricate carving always pleased him, and the lovely tracery of the window delighted his eyes.

Strange that these churches stood while men quarrelled and fought over how their fellows should worship. He remembered a verse which he had learnt as a child, 'There shall be one fold, and one Shepherd', surely if that were to be achieved the first step would be tolerance. Persecution only established men's hold on their particular form of religion; not much chance of unity so long as cruelty and religious oppression lasted. At this moment, surely, the pride of every Jew in his race and faith were being re-established not only in Germany but in Italy too.

He reached the Town Hall and sent up his card to the Mayor. There appeared to be no change in the attitude of the various officials towards him. They wished him 'Good day', one of them thanked him for a donation which he had given to some town charity, another asked after Simeon. The messenger returned, the *podestà* was disengaged and would see him. He was ushered into the Mayor's office.

The thin, neat man who sat at the big desk rose and held out his hand, saying, 'My dear Gollantz, this is a pleasure. What can I do for you? Only last night my wife was asking why you had not been to dine with us lately. We might

16

arrange an evening now you are here, eh?'

'I shall be delighted. First—surely you know why I have come to see you? No? I have come to—report.'

The *podestà* raised his well-marked eyebrows. 'I don't follow you.'

'Let me refresh your memory. You remember the manifesto of July—against the Jews. Today is September the first —the contents of that manifesto come into force today.'

He leaned back in his chair and watched the flood of crimson which suffused the other's face; he saw the thin, well-kept hands clench suddenly, heard the quick intake of breath.

'My dear friend!' there was a hint of indignation in the tone, 'if this is a joke—forgive me—it is a very poor one!'

'No joke, merely conforming to the law of the country which has given me hospitality for so long.' He pushed his passport over the expanse of green leather which covered the desk. 'Please.' Unwillingly the *podestà* flicked over the pages, Emmanuel began to speak: 'I came to this city many years ago. My father, who lives in London, is entirely Jewish; my mother is an Englishwoman; she was a Miss Drew. My grandfather, Emmanuel Gollantz, went to England in 1869 from Vienna. Since I have lived here, in Milano, I have allowed my name to appear—as a benefactor —to most of your charities. I have a great affection for both the country and the people. My wife is remembered by the endowment of two beds in . . . My dear Casimero, what have I said to annoy you?' The *podestà* had closed the covers of the passport, and, with a movement which was almost epileptic in its intensity, pushed it towards Emmanuel.

'Annoy me! Nothing! Nothing! You make me ashamed! You are my friend, the friend of every good man in this city. You have always behaved as an example to us all. We shared your joy at the birth of your son, we mourned with you when your wife began her journey to God. Now this— this damnable business! And why? *You* know, I know, all Italy knows. No one knows how far this will go. No one knows what rules and regulations will be made for us. We are caught, held fast in a net. Once—once many years ago, we believed that we had found a solution. We needed dis-

17

cipline, we needed someone to say "do this" and "do that".
We were lazy, we refused to think for ourselves. We were
ready to become part of a machine—a machine which now
will grind us to powder! Take your passport. I have no
doubt'—and his sensitive mouth was disfigured by a sneer—
'that the gentlemen who have been poured into Italy to
guard "our Partner in the Axis" will have possessed themselves of a complete *dossier* of your life and activities.'

'Think no more of it,' Emmanuel begged, 'we are old
friends, you and I. We have trusted one another in many
circumstances. Tell me, there will be no need for me to
leave Milano? Now'—as the *podestà* showed signs of growing angry and indignant again—'no need to get furious. I
want cool, calm and well-considered advice. But there will
be Jews who will be—*advised* to leave?'

'I imagine so.' The words came sulkily.

'I too, imagine,' Emmanuel spoke very slowly, 'that they
might be glad of my help. You see, Casimero, relying on
our old friendship, that I trust you completely.'

The other man glanced up quickly, frowning nervously.

'Emmanuelo, don't get in bad odour with the Party!'

'No, no and no! I have always been in the good books of
the Party. And,' he laughed, 'thanks be to God, I am a rich
man.'

'Can you imagine how I feel to hear you say that of the
people of my country—my beloved country?'

'And a country beloved by me too, Casimero. Only when
followers see their leaders growing rich, they have an urge
to become rich too. It's inevitable. These small officials—
not very clever men, as I have often heard you yourself
admit—when they see an opportunity to make a considerable sum of money, the chance is too tempting. Documents,
sealing wax, forms, returns and so on have a bad effect on
stupid people! Then too, from being powerless, they have
power. They don't use it, they abuse it. And so, here we are
in this mess. Casimero, I must go. Put it on record, I beg,
that Emmanuel Gollantz, who is fifty per cent Jewish, came
to register with you on September the first.' He held out his
hand and the *podestà* took it, holding it firmly in his own.
'And if,' Emmanuel continued evenly—'if you should hear
of any Jews who would be wiser to leave Milano, perhaps

18

you would send me a note—asking me to dine with a friend of yours at some address, or to call there to meet you. I can leave the form to you—you're sufficiently intelligent. *Grazie, a rivederci, caro amico.*'

2

That evening Emmanuel took Guido home to dine with him. He had returned from the interview with the *podestà* apparently satisfied, with a little smile touching the corners of his well-shaped mouth. Guido sprang forward, his face almost twisted with anxiety.

'Tell me,' he begged, 'tell me, beloved master, what happened? Did Casimero Boccalini weep with shame? Did . . .'

'Almost, poor fellow,' Emmanuel answered. 'I felt sorry for him; it's not his fault that this monstrous order must be enforced.'

With one of those sudden flashes, which always astonished Emmanuel a little, Guido said bitterly, 'You are wrong. It is his fault. His fault, as it is mine, as it is the fault of each one of us. *Ma!* How again can we face the world! What of our art, our music? What of our opera houses? Who have been their greatest patrons? It is not necessary that I should tell you—you know, as well as I do.'

Together the two men walked back to Emmanuel's house, both silent, both conscious of the fact that they were watching the faces of the people who passed them in the crowded streets. Were those people, who recognised Emmanuel, thinking, 'There goes one of the Jews, marked—perhaps—for persecution'?

Giacomo met them, took his master's hat, gloves and cane in silence; when Emmanuel smiled and said, 'Don't look so gloomy, Giacomo!' the man seized his master's hand and kissed it.

'*Sarò sempre fedele,*' Giacomo said.

Emmanuel thought, 'How they love to dramatise themselves!' Aloud he said, 'Faithful, but of course you will

19

always be faithful. You have been that for so many years it has become a habit of which you cannot break yourself, Giacomo.'

In the huge splendid room Simeon was waiting for them. He was a well-built, good-looking boy, tall for his age, and with bright brown hair and blue eyes. Emmanuel knew that he was so like his dead mother that at times the likeness was almost painful. His character was like Juliet's too, warm and generous.

'Papa,' he cried as Emmanuel entered, 'have you heard the news? Pierrino tells me that all Jews are to be murdered in the streets. Hadn't we better do something about it? Hadn't we, Guido?'

He showed no fear, rather, his father felt, a queer kind of suppressed excitement.

'At the risk of appearing to doubt the veracity of your friend, Simeon,' Emmanuel said, 'I feel that he is giving you a slightly over-coloured version of the truth.'

Simeon chuckled. It was an old joke between them that Emmanuel used the longest possible words, the most formal style of speech, when he was really being humorous.

'I told him so,' Simeon said with satisfaction, 'only some of the boys were very concerned. Bruno shook my hand when he left me at the corner and said that he hoped death would not be too unpleasant! I said, "Pooh, my father will make an arrangement!" Have you made an arrangement, Papa?'

'I think that you may rest easy in your bed, Simeon. I have seen the *podestà*, and he appeared completely satisfied.'

'I knew that you would. After all Uncle Casimero could scarcely order anyone—even Germans—to kill you, could he? You and he are such friends.'

'And I hope always will be. And now, I am afraid that Guido and I must—regretfully—dispense with your company; we have business to discuss, and might I remind you that you have preparation to do. Come down for dinner, won't you?'

That night Emmanuel and Guido Maroni sat late, talking and making plans. There must be care, Emmanuel insisted. Once the authorities, many of whom were already strongly

20

tinged with the beliefs of Nazism, became suspicious, the game would be up. There was only one thing to counteract suspicion—bribery. Bribery once begun meant increasing the bribes, with every future hint of danger.

'I do not wish to plan anything spectacular, Guido,' Emmanuel warned; 'don't imagine yourself as a kind of modern "Scarlet Pimpernel". Don't look conspiratorial. Be your ordinary, delightful self, but keep those very sharp ears of yours open and bring back accurate stories to me.'

During the months which followed some strange people visited the Galleries of Gollantz. They brought with them antiques, pictures, jewels and carvings. Some were of great value, many were worthless. Emmanuel, in his study, seated at his great desk, listened to stories which were sometimes tragic, often pathetic, and occasionally capable of rousing him to anger.

To old people, uncertain and frightened, he was very tender. Carefully he explained to them what the position was, very exactly and precisely. With great courtesy he inquired into their financial position, investigated their assets and liabilities. He bought their antiques, paying a small amount in cash, far less than the value of the article. The remainder was 'arranged' to be paid into banks in Holland, Switzerland, England and France. Money would be waiting for them when they arrived. He entered large sales in his books, sales of things which existed only in his imagination, and after deducting the correct amount for Italian taxation, he transferred the monies to his English bank. It was a difficult and complicated business, one which caused Emmanuel and Guido long and tedious evenings when they made up the books, and satisfied themselves that their plans could evade detection.

For long hours he remained in his room, talking to people who wished to leave the country which they had believed would always give them a refuge and a home. Old people cried, telling stories of their families, of how they had come to regard Italy as their own country; they were bewildered, heartbroken. Young people, some recently married, who had planned a life which should be well ordered, active and prosperous, came to him, and he gave them advice and sympathy.

21

Only when he doubted that he was being told the whole truth did his face harden.

'And these are all the jewels your wife has, Signor Grabbo?'

The little dark-faced man before him spread his hands in a typically Jewish gesture.

'But I have said so, Signor Gollantz!'

'I know that you have. I asked you if these were all the jewels your wife possesses.'

A shrug. 'Maybe that there are still a few unmounted stones!'

'Ah! And the gold—what of that?'

'There was very little . . .'

'And the gold cups, and plates of which you were so proud, which I saw once when I visited your house in the company of Signor Farinuchi?'

'Oh, that . . . that is . . . well, what I wish to tell you . . .'

It was at such moments that Emmanuel rose, looking very tall, as he stood with his finger-tips resting on the desk and stared down at the dark-faced Italian Jew.

'Please go. I find that your presence makes the air unpleasant for me to breathe. Get out of Italy as best you can. I have no intention of helping you. You are going to make the mistake of so many stupid Jews who pretend to be clever. You are going to underrate the cleverness of your adversary. Do you know what will happen at the frontier? The same thing that happened to Manrico Corda! He was so clever with his mudguards, and his stuffed cushions, and his wife's maid, wearing the Corda emeralds and pretending they were trash from the U.P.I.M. Allow me to wish you "Good day" and a safe journey—though I doubt that very much indeed.'

After such interviews Emmanuel would emerge white-faced and angry, to pace up and down the Galleries, his lips compressed, his eyes cold and furious.

He had other worries too. The future of Simeon occupied him very much. Simeon was thirteen, he was attending one of the big day-schools in Milano. The education given there was good, and the boy learnt easily and worked hard. His English was perfect if at times a little stilted; his Italian was that of a native of the country and less formal than his

22

English. He spoke French easily, and German deplorably. He played football, cricket he knew nothing of, he swam well, rode excellently. During the holidays Emmanuel took him to a lakeside town where there was a fairly good golf course, and where the English secretary gave the boy lessons.

Simeon was good, obedient and affectionate. Guido and he vied with each other as to who should give the greater measure of admiration to Emmanuel.

Someday the boy would grow into a man, a very wealthy man. He would have a considerable fortune which old Simeon Jaffe had left him; Juliet's money would be his too. Emmanuel himself was rich. Young Simeon might well be one of the richest young men in Europe. And what was Simeon going to be? An Englishman who had been born and brought up in Italy, who lived there because it was the country he knew and loved; or an Italian who lived in England, lacking an English education and the traditions which went with it, for ever facing rules and traditions of which by reason of his education he knew nothing?

Two years ago Emmanuel had taken the boy home for a short visit to his grandparents. They had been glad to see him, had made much of him, and Simeon had behaved charmingly. There had been difficulties. Julian and his wife Amanda still occupied the wing at Ordingly which had been old Emmanuel's. He lived extravagantly, and was constantly appealing to either his father or his mother to pay his debts. He had adopted the attitude of a chronic invalid; and had, as always, the trick of introducing a hint of pathos into his requests for money. His son, Max, was a few months older than Simeon. The contrast between them was very marked. Max was already at a public school, inclined to adopt an air of superiority towards his cousin.

'A day school!' he exclaimed. 'I say—I should hate that!'

Simeon asked, 'Why would you hate it, please?'

'Oh, I don't know, only no one goes to day schools.'

'Excuse me, there are nearly six hundred boys at my school.'

'Yes, but they're Italians!'

'Not all. Several are French, there are two Roumanians, and I, myself, am, of course, English,' Simeon explained.

23

Max said, 'I shouldn't call you English! You're not a bit like an Englishman.'

One day Emmanuel had taken both boys to Harrods'. Simeon was entranced; he stared at everything, exclaimed, 'Oh, *bella*!' at intervals. Emmanuel watched Max grow more and more rigid, less and less ready to smile.

On a stand was hung a striped flannel blazer. Simeon stopped to admire it. Emmanuel heard him murmur, 'Ah, *elegante*!' He said, 'Would you like to wear a blazer like that, Simeon?' Simeon beamed at him, 'Oh, Papa—will you really buy it for me?' Max cried indignantly, 'I say—you can't wear that. It's Harrow!' Simeon, imagining that his cousin was joking, answered, 'I know that it is Harrods', but if Papa buys it for me—it will be mine.' Max scowled, muttered something about 'foreign cads', and Emmanuel tried to explain patiently that he had meant to ask if Simeon would like to go to a school which would allow him to wear one of these beautiful striped blazers.

Simeon had seen the look of intolerant disgust on his cousin's face, and his expression suddenly reminded Emmanuel of Juliet's, when she had said something which had unwittingly annoyed Leon Hast in the old days. He longed to defy tradition, to ignore Max and buy Simeon every brilliant blazer he could find. Instead he continued his explanation as to how different schools had different colours which were regarded as their own private property.

'I understand,' Simeon said, 'I understand perfectly. Thank you, I am very happy in my own school, Papa.' Turning to his cousin, he said with considerable dignity, 'I did not understand, *ho fatto uno sbaglio*; please excuse the mistake.' Then quickly, 'Again, excuse—I forget that you do not speak any language but your own.'

To atone Emmanuel had taken his son to an excellent tailor, had spent a great deal of money on clothes for him, clothes of every description, even to a dinner jacket which Simeon called 'a smok-ing', to the tailor's discreet amusement. Emmanuel added a dark blue blazer, with the arms of Simeon's Milan school embroidered on the pocket.

'This, then,' Simeon asked, 'is correct, Papa?'

'It could scarcely be more correct,' Emmanuel assured him. Now, he worried over the boy. Was he doing the right

24

thing? One day Ordingly would belong to Simeon, he would have sufficient money to establish himself there and live in dignified comfort. Were these early years of his life going to make him unfit to take up the position which would one day be his? Would he always feel that Italy and the house in Milan stood for home, always regard England as a place to which he went for holidays—holidays which had not proved entirely pleasant?

He talked to Guido, who cried passionately that Simeon would break his heart if banished to England. 'In addition,' he added, 'consider, please, what it would mean to Simeon to live always in fog and darkness! Wet to the skin every day, *senza dubbio,* his lungs filled with a fog which Louis Lara assured me is bright yellow or brilliant and sinister green! Emmanuel, could you send your child to meet death at the hands of the English climate!'

Emmanuel said, 'Oh, it's not so bad as Louis makes out!'

'Louis told me,' Guido persisted, 'that summer lasted for two days only, and then everyone panted like dogs!'

He went to discuss the matter with Iva Alfano and her husband, an Englishman for all his Italian name, Paolo Mancini.

Iva shrugged her shoulders. 'Why worry? From all I hear, if Hitler insists Mussolini will go to war, and then you and Simeon will have to go to England. Oh, don't ask me with whom he will go to war! How should I know, when Mussolini does not know himself? He only waits for orders. When he hears—*la voce del padrone*—he will do as he is told! I should make the hay while there is still sunshine. Stay where you are; let Simeon be happy. There is sufficient misery waiting for us all, Emmanuel.'

Paolo said, 'I don't know, Emmanuel. You see, I was never at any school except an elementary one—or did I go to a secondary school for a few months? I forget. I have no traditions. I do not know if this is "done" and that is "impossible". I don't think that I disgrace Iva when we appear in public together, eh, *cara mia?*'

'But then I have no traditions either,' Iva protested; 'I am a singer, my father kept a little *drogheria—salumeria*—what do you call it—*gro-saire*. What a name! I am a peasant, or very nearly one. I can read and write, but it only matters that I can sing! Simeon sings too—he has a singing heart. Let it continue to sing, Emmanuelo.'

It was not possible to explain that neither of them would be asked to live in a huge and beautiful house, to administer considerable wealth. Iva made a great deal of money, she was one of the highest paid artists in Italy, but she hated saving, loved to live extravagantly and in luxury. Her husband, Paolo, was the son of an Italian who had gone to England with nothing in his pocket except a marvellous recipe for making ice-cream! Neither of them cared a rap for tradition.

The year drew to its close; wherever Emmanuel went he found Germans, heard Italians mutter, *'Fuori i Tedeschi!'* They hated the 'tourists', distrusted them and—feared them. They might whisper, 'Away with the Germans', might murmur that all Germans were *'porci'* and, even worse, 'dirty pigs', but the infiltration continued. He heard, too, stories concerning the hardships inflicted upon the Jews, though he always admitted that he had never contrived to trace any actual prosecution to its source. Still, the Jews were leaving Italy, and he was helping them to leave. In September there had been a bad scare. Everyone had held their breath, until the 28th, when the world heard that—there was to be no war. Italy listened to the announcement that Mussolini was leaving for Munich, and his old popularity flared up. The Duce could speak English; together he and Chamberlain would overrule Adolf Hitler. Italy, in common with the rest of the world, breathed again.

Louis Lara, visiting Milan with his incredible wife, Olympia, spoke to Emmanuel with deep apprehension.

'A breathing-space,' he said. 'Yes, for people such as my superb Olympia it may seem that this is peace for ever. They see only what they wish to see, these dear and beautiful women. They say, "Ah, Benito Mussolini has done it again!" or "Oh, this so-dear, so-upright Cham-ber-lain, with his piece of paper in his jacket pocket." Or, "This time Hitler has been frightened. He will not dare to break his promises —these are no pie-pastry promises." Pah! Listen, Emmanuel —England is not ready; France is r-rotten, like a bad apple! She has no statesmen, she has only scheming politicians. Who is ready? You know, I know, the world knows! Like children with cherry-stones—we say, "This year, next year, sometime!" I say—counting the cherry-stones—"This year" you, doing the same, cry "Next year"; Guido, maybe, says "Sometime"; but no one, unless a cretin, says never!'

In the New Year Chamberlain and Lord Halifax visited Rome, and Italy indulged in a storm of sentimental affection and admiration. Sufficiently genuine, Chamberlain made an instant appeal to them. He was ready to smile at small children, to bow and lift his hat to the people who cheered and greeted him. If Mussolini, in meeting him, did whisper behind his hand to Count Ciano—who cared? Chamberlain, they declared, was a 'gent-il-man'; the Duce—they shrugged their shoulders! The women wore little model umbrellas in their hats, the papers were flooded with photographs of Chamberlain smiling widely, and Lord Halifax looking depressed and melancholy. No one bothered much about Halifax! He made no appeal to the Italians.

Again the stories were in circulation. Chamberlain had called Mussolini 'my dear brother'; the Pope had wept because his doctors would not allow him to talk for many hours with *questo galante Cham-ber-lain*. Peace was established firmly between England and Italy—how could it be otherwise? There existed a traditional friendship between the two nations. What had Garibaldi said? How good had England been to this great patriot. Italy did not forget! Neither did she forget on which side she had fought in the great war.

On February the twelfth the country was stunned by the news that the Pope was dead. Simeon brought an illustrated paper to show Emmanuel, and with tears in his eyes cried, 'Look, Papa! The death chamber of Pius XI. How simple, everything so plain—and this was a King!' Hitler was forgotten, the prospect of a world war was forgotten, the eyes of all Italy were turned towards the Vatican, where Eugenio Pacelli was elected Pope on March the third. The bells clashed, people ran about the streets, through the Galleria, crying—many with tears streaming down their cheeks—'*Noi abbiamo un Papa!*'—We have a Pope.'

Again the stories: the new Pope was a great statesman, a great diplomat, he spoke eleven languages, he was versed in matters political. He had sent word to Mussolini—Musso-

lini had replied—Hitler hated Pius XII—His Holiness cared
nothing for Hitler.

In less than two months Italy marched into Albania on
Good Friday. Emmanuel, standing in the Galleria, listened
to a group of men talking. Some of the group were known
to him. There was Tolini, the lawyer; Rosteeno, a devout
Catholic; a man who was only known to Emmanuel as
'Chico', an ardent Fascist, and two more who were unknown to him. He stood, leaning on his ivory-headed cane,
his dark eyes turning from one to another of the group as
they spoke.

'Chico' said, 'The Duce pursues his victorious career!'

Tolini nodded. 'It might be well to hasten more slowly.'

Rosteeno added, 'Indeed, I think that you are right. The
day itself is a great pity. It has influenced the minds of many
people against this project. Don't you agree, Gollantz?'

'I am afraid so,' Emmanuel agreed; 'only this morning
someone asked me, "Why this day, when there are three
hundred and sixty-four others in the year?"'

The little Fascist stared at him impudently, his jaw stuck
out in imitation of his Leader. 'Ah,' he exclaimed, 'and tell
me, how does the day affect you, Signor Gollantz? Is the
entrance into Albania—peaceful penetration—as bad as
what happened *once* many years ago on Good Friday? On
the day your people did . . .'

Tolini interrupted him. 'There is no necessity to tell all
Milan, "Chico",' he said, 'this is not a public meeting.'

'Chico' scowled. 'Then let Signor Gollantz keep his criti-
cisms of Il Duce and the Italians to himself. What has it to
do with him, please tell me? A Jew!'

'Please, please,' Rosteeno begged, 'you forget yourself.
Signor Gollantz is respected by us all.'

'Signor Gollantz is a Jew, nevertheless. Jews are being
dealt with in Italy! Hitler has taught us a good and valuable
lesson. We have profited by it; we shall profit even more in
the future.'

Smiling a little, Emmanuel laid his hand lightly on Tolini's
arm.

'The air grows a little sultry,' he said. 'Would you and
Signor Rosteeno care to drive home with me and honour

28

me by taking coffee? I have some ivories which I think would interest you both.'

As they were moving away, 'Chico' rushed after them; he caught Emmanuel's arm and cried, 'And these ivories? Did you buy them from one of the Jews who were escaping justice?'

'No,' Emmanuel answered coolly. 'The man from whom I bought them was not escaping from'—he made the slightest possible pause, then added—'justice.'

3

Tolini and Rosteeno admired the ivories; they held them tenderly in their hands, touching the carvings with the tips of sensitive fingers, yet always their faces remained grave. They scarcely spoke while the coffee was being served, and when Emmanuel suggested that they should take some of his very fine old cognac, they thanked him without any of the pleasure which they were wont to show.

'There!' Emmanuel said, 'the best cognac in Italy! I do not allow myself to indulge in boasting, except about this cognac.'

Tolini sipped the amber liquid. 'It is exquisite.'

Rosteeno nodded his agreement.

'And now a cigar from Havana,' Emmanuel insisted. 'Allow me to prepare it for you, Tolini. There!'

He sat down and looked from one to the other, smiling a little.

'My dear friends, why are you both so grave? Not about Albania, surely?'

The Italians exchanged glances. Rosteeno nodded, and Tolini began to speak.

'Emmanuel, *caro mio*,' he said, 'we are both disturbed that you should have possibly made an enemy of "Chico". His name is Antonio Barach. He may be an Italian; I suspect that he is some half-breed jackal with mixed blood. Mixed bloods are bad.'

Emmanuel laughed. 'You can't be seriously disturbed

29

because that little *zanzara* buzzes round and tries to sting me!'

'He may be nothing more than a mosquito,' Rosteeno agreed, 'but I have known men become ill—to the point of death—through the sting of a *zanzara*. Gollantz, be wise, be prudent. Tolini and I know a great deal, so does Conte Boccalini. We are men who can keep still tongues; we respect you and what you are doing. It may even be that we —in our own way—are following the example which you have set us.'

'During the next weeks,' Tolini begged, 'be careful who you admit to your office. Watch your letters, be careful how you speak, and of what you speak, on the telephone.'

Emmanuel held out his hand, offering it to both of his friends. In turn they shook it warmly.

'Have no fear,' he said, 'I shall be very, very careful.'

It was during the following afternoon that Guido came in to ask if he would grant an interview to a certain Giobbe Gualtieri. The man was ushered in. He was a short, thick-set fellow with a heavy, stupid face and small, cunning eyes.

Emmanuel thought, 'I've rarely seen a more unpleasant fellow.'

The man was wearing a light suit over which was a thick and rather clumsy overcoat. The collar showed marks of grease from his over-long hair, but Emmanuel—his eyes searching for the usual Fascist button in the lapel of the coat —saw only a flattened ring of the material.

'So whoever he is,' he thought, 'he's removed his Party button before he came here!'

The man seated himself and began to pour out a pitiful story. He was a Jew, a professing Jew, a religious man; all his family had been brought up in the Jewish Faith, he had hoped that his eldest son might become a rabbi.

Emmanuel smiled. 'Ah, now I see it, Signor Gualtieri, you wish me to help you with money for the education of your son! Tell me more, please.'

No, it appeared that Signor Gualtieri did not want help for his son, he wanted it for all his family. They had been treated with terrible harshness by the Italians in Milan, his wife was terrified that at any moment her husband and sons might be set upon by the Black Shirts. Would the Signor

Gollantz help them to escape into a less barbarous country?

Emmanuel shrugged his shoulders. 'But how can I help you?'

Gualtieri leaned forward. Emmanuel drew back; his visitors breath was strongly impregnated with stale garlic.

'You can help me,' he said scarcely above a whisper, 'as you have helped so many others.'

'Helped others . . .' Emmanuel repeated. 'Oh yes, I suppose that I can admit that—being a fairly rich man—I have been able to help others. The wife of the Captain of the Fascisti when she was ill. I was able to give a little help there! To the hospital of the Holy Child—to the orphanage of the Blessed Virgin—oh, to this and that charity I have given. But to help you to get away? How can I do this? Surely,' his voice changed from being very quiet, it rang through the room so that Gualtieri started in his chair, 'as you are a member of the Fascist Party, they will help you! What made you remove the button from your coat when you came to see me? Please go—you are a bad actor, and a very stupid agent. I shall advise the Party to dispense with your services. Good day.'

'But I am a Jew,' the fellow spluttered. 'My name will tell you that!'

Emmanuel smiled pleasantly. 'Even bad actors have been known to adopt a—stage name. Even among Jews there are —bad Jews. Again—please go.'

There were other signs of a change in the attitude of some of the Milanese towards him. One evening, returning home late from a dinner party at Tolini's house, he heard quick, light steps behind him, and, as he swung round, a heavy stick—loaded, Emmanuel thought—descended upon his shoulder. He thought, 'If I hadn't been quick and side-stepped the brute would have got my head!' He had always kept himself very fit, his regular games of tennis and fives with Guido had made him quick on his feet, his muscles were strong and elastic. He thought, 'They may laugh at my "exerciser" in the bathroom, but here's the proof that it's been worth using.'

He caught the man who had attacked him by the collar, pressing his knuckles into the back of his neck until the fellow yelped with pain. Emmanuel caught the words, *'Il sporco d' Ebreo!'*

He laughed softly. 'A Jew, my friend, but I trust not a dirty one. Now march—and quickly. I don't want to waste time with you.'

'Where are you taking me?' the voice quavered suddenly.

'To the *questura*.'

At the police station he handed the man over to the officer on duty, who took down the particulars in his flowing Italian writing.

'It might be well, Signor Gollantz,' he said, 'for you to speak with the *commissario*.'

Emmanuel hesitated, then said, 'I am late already. Still'— he shrugged his shoulders—'if it is necessary I will see the *commissario*.'

'Grazie, signor.'

He was shown into the office of the chief of police for the district. A short, stocky man sat at the desk, his collar unhooked, his face badly in need of shaving. A cigarette dangled from his lower lip, a cigarette which he did not trouble to remove when Emmanuel was announced.

'Sit down,' he said, waving a hand with long and dirty nails towards a chair. When Emmanuel had seated himself, the *commissario* asked, 'What is the trouble?'

'Nothing for me, except that it will make me late getting home,' Emmanuel answered, and very briefly told what had happened.

The *commissario* listened, frowning, chewing the end of his pencil.

'The man attacked you?'

'He tried to do so, signor.'

'Have you any enemies in Milano?'

'Candidly—I know of none.'

'You are a Jew, Signor Gollantz?'

'Indeed, yes, and very proud to be one.'

The *commissario* stared at him; he had pale eyes—Emmanuel thought that they were like gooseberries—he pursed his full, thick lips.

'There are,' he said, 'too many Jews in Milano. You have registered?'

'On the first day that the manifesto was put into practice. I registered with the *podestà* of Milano.'

The *commissario* made a convulsive movement; he swept a small pile of papers towards him, and became very occupied in reading them. Emmanuel waited; the *commissario* did not look up from his paper. At last, after he had waited for several minutes, half annoyed, half amused at the little man's impertinence, he made a movement. The *commissario* glanced up from his papers.

'Yes?' he asked.

'Were there any other questions which you wished to ask me?'

Again the pale gooseberry eyes stared, and the thick voice answered:

'No—none. The case will be examined.'

'Then may I wish you a very good night?' Emmanuel said.

There was no reply. For a moment he waited, scarcely able to believe that any Milanese could behave with such discourtesy towards him, then, as no sound came from the man at the desk, he picked up his hat and stick and walked out of the room.

The police officer at the desk in the entrance hall wished him a 'Good night', and Emmanuel went out into the street. He was shaken and profoundly disturbed. It had been necessary for him to visit the *questura* many times; he had always been received with courtesy and consideration, and the latest interview had come as a shock. Was this Milano, the city where the people were reputed to have the kindest hearts in Italy? Was this man—the *commissario*—an Italian? That remark, 'There are too many Jews in Milano,' was something which Emmanuel Gollantz had never thought to hear directed towards him. What had happened to the city, to the country?

He walked home slowly, his face grave and clouded. Was he really awake, or was that attack upon him, and the subsequent interview with the *commissario,* an unpleasant dream? Back in his own home, he felt that he must have imagined it all. There was Tommaso, waiting in the hall for his return. Emmanuel thought sometimes that Tommaso never left the hall when his master was out, in case he should not be there on the instant when he returned. Tommaso took his hat and stick, smoothed out his gloves and laid them carefully in the drawer, then, smiling, asked if there was anything which Emmanuel desired.

'Nothing, except that you should go to bed, Tommaso.'

The smile widened. 'There is plenty of time, I sleep too much.'

'I wonder when,' Emmanuel said; 'early in the morning, late at night, I have never contrived to come home and find that you had gone to bed!'

Tommaso shrugged his shoulders. 'Would the Signor deny me the pleasure of welcoming him when he arrives home?'

The following morning Emmanuel chanced to meet Casimero Boccalini on his way to the Galleries. They walked together through the sunlit streets, where at almost every corner women were selling flowers.

'A nice city,' Emmanuel said.

Boccalini sighed. 'Sometimes. It *was* a nice city, my friend.'

'That reminds me, I have not told you of my adventure last night.'

Carefully, even amusingly, Emmanuel recounted what had happened. His friend's face was very grave, and, when he told of the *commissario* and his conversation, the *podestà* made no attempt to conceal his anger and distress.

'Let me come with you into your office,' he begged, 'I must have all possible particulars. This must be investigated —and immediately. I am still—for how long who can say!— *podestà* of this city.'

'Certainly, but don't annoy yourself, Casimero. The *commissario* told me that the case would be examined.'

'Let me tell you something,' Casimero answered with considerable heat; 'the case will be examined, so will the *commissario*!'

Emmanuel poured out two glasses of his fine cognac. 'There, drink that, and don't worry about it. Some petty thief, and an impertinent—but equally petty—official. Who cares!'

The days which followed were busy ones for Emmanuel; he was called away on business to Novarro, and when he arrived home again there was another call advising him to go to Venice, where the contents of an old palace were being sold privately. Nearly three weeks passed before he saw Conte Boccalini again. He was in his office when Guido entered and asked if Emmanuel would see the Conte.

Emmanuel rose and went to greet his friend.

'My dear *Podestà*, this is a great pleasure.'

Boccalini seized his hand, and said in a voice which was heavy with emotion, 'I am no longer *podestà*, Emmanuel. Let me sit down and I will tell you.'

Slowly he told his story, one which Emmanuel was to hear repeated again and again by other officials, who were deprived of their posts in the different cities.

Boccalini said, 'I sent for that impertinent *commissario*. I interviewed him, and dressed him down. I asked when the case against the man who attacked you was to be heard. He said that he did not know. He had reported it to the head of the police, who, no doubt, would attend to the matter in his own good time. I sent for the chief of police. He came—you know him, of course. Palumba, a thick-set fellow, with an immense jaw and a huge head with very little inside it. Our interview was stormy. The case had been dismissed. They had telephoned to you, here, and received the reply that you were quite unable to attend the court. Palumba said, "And so, if it matters so little to Signor Gollantz, why should it matter to us?" '

Emmanuel said, 'When was this, for I have been away? Let me ask Guido.'

'I asked Guido,' Boccalini said, 'immediately after this interview. He told me that he knew nothing about it. Someone telephoned to know if you could attend a meeting; Guido replied that it was quite impossible, as you were away. Whoever telephoned hung up their receiver immediately. They had given no name, no number. To return to my interview with Palumba—I was very angry, I declared that they had no right to allow foot-pads and thieves to go free. He made a gesture of indifference and added, "We have sufficient to do to protect our own people. These foreign Jews must take care of themselves." I replied that justice was still justice in Italy, and that the whole affair would be reported to higher circles, and also that I should recommend that both he and his understrapper, the *com-*

missario, were removed to some less important city than Milan. He smiled, suavely impertinent, and said that he had nothing to fear. He added that he was a good Fascist; the Party valued the work which he had done—and was still doing.' Boccalini's thin face worked with emotion; he paused, and Emmanuel could see that he was controlling himself with difficulty. He was a proud man, proud of his name, his ancestry, and the work which he had done for the town he loved. He sat there, twisting is thin, brown fingers, his jaw set so firmly that the bone showed white against his dark skin.

Very gently Emmanuel said, 'Yes, go on, *amico mio.*'

Boccalini nodded. 'Yes, yes, I will end my story. Last night there was a long-distance call for me from Roma. I was advised—mark that word—advised to resign my position as *podestà.* I said that I had no wish to do so. The reply was, "There are other wishes than yours to be considered, Conte." This morning came the official confirmation. It was considered advisable—again that word—that my resignation should be accepted. I heard from Tolini this morning: he has been the legal adviser to several large concerns. They have informed him that they are placing their affairs in the hands of that scoundrel Romice. Romice, who boasts that he thinks nothing too bad for any Jew, and that one German is worth five Italians! There you have the story, Emmanuelo.'

'And why, Casimero,' Emmanuel asked, 'have these things happened?'

'You know almost as well as I do. I have never been entirely with the Fascist Party; I have never regarded the Tedeschi as our friends. In the Great War we fought against them. In that war I lost two of my brothers, four of my cousins, and saw my wife robbed of her father and elder brother. Twenty years is too short a time to heal such wounds, Emmanuelo. I have never approved of the Manifesto against the Jews. I never approved of the territorial ambitions of the Duce. I watched young men sent to fight in Spain for a cause of which they knew nothing and cared less. I have never ceased to denounce bribery and corruption. I am no Communist, but I have grown to hate a bureaucracy which opens the way to such men as Palumba

36

and his friends. And so—I am dangerous. Whoever is dangerous—whoever dares to have his own ideas of what is right and what is wrong—must go! The next *podestà* of this town will be Ignazio Palumba.'

Tears stood in his eyes as he spoke, his whole body was shaking with the intensity of his feelings. He looked shattered, broken and heart-sick. Emmanuel, watching him, thought that this was how the present-day Italy rewarded the men who loved and served her. Either they must conform or they must be broken.

He rose and stood beside his friend, laying his hand on Boccalini's shoulder

'I am so terribly sorry,' he said; 'I know what it means to you. I know how well you have served this city, how many sacrifices you have made. You and I, Casimero, are no longer very young. We have both suffered, and it seems that you—and possibly I—will be called upon to face more trials. You remember what Dante says?

> ' *"Nel mezzo del cammin di nostra vita*
> *Mi ritovai per una selva oscura."*

'We have come to middle age, and we have found ourselves in a dark, a very dark, wood. But, if one walks for a sufficiently long time, one comes to the end of the wood, and the sun is shining or the rain is falling gently and kindly. Courage, my friend.'

Boccalini stood up, and faced Emmanuel. 'Thank you. Your sympathy means a great deal to me. Only, I have to ask you to listen to me. Be careful, Emmanuelo. Take no risks. Keep always very, very much on the right side of the law—or rather keep on the right side of the officials who are supposed to administer the law. If there are still poor people who need your help, be quite certain that they are genuine. Do not listen to tales from people you do not know. The eyes of the hunter must watch always, and the eyes of the hunted must watch also if they will escape capture—or death. There, I must not say more. I must leave you to your work. Good-bye, and let us meet again very soon.'

'Good-bye,' Emmanuel said, 'I am very proud to have your friendship, Casimero.'

During the weeks that followed Emmanuel knew that his disquietude was growing. Associations which had once been pleasant had become difficult. He had always paid his taxes regularly, he had gone himself to the officials and exchanged greetings, and even stayed to talk with them Now the men he had known were gone, and the new tax-collectors were curt to the point of rudeness. Their scrutiny of his various forms seemed to Emmanuel to imply distrust and suspicion. He had always left his car standing outside his house when he went home for luncheon. The street was a quiet one, and very wide. Now, only a few days ago, there had come a hammering at the door, and Tommaso came into the dining-room scowling and furious.

'Here is the *poliziotto,* signor,' he said, using the word which means not only policeman, but conveys a profound contempt for their whole order.

'For me—what is it?' Emmanuel asked.

'It appears that your car must not stand in the street, signor.'

'Pooh! He must be a new importation. I'll come and speak to him.'

The policeman stood waiting; the moment he spoke Emmanuel knew that he was not a native of Milan. Probably, he thought, the man came from Naples. He was beetle-browed and truculent

'Is that your car?'

'It is,' Emmanuel replied.

'Don't you know the law? Don't you know that you can't leave cars standing about in the streets unattended?'

'But I have always left my car there, while I come in to eat my luncheon.'

'I can't help what you have always done! The point is that you have no right to do it, and in doing it you are going against the law. Let me have your name.'

Emmanuel heard Tommaso hissing with annoyance behind him; he turned and smiled, saying, 'Patience, Tommaso, patience!' Then to the policeman he said, 'Your manner is not of the most polite, is it? My name is Emmanuel

Gollantz. Do you wish to see the papers which relate to my car? I have them here.'

The man wrote the first name, then demanded, 'How do you spell your surname? As Emmanuel spelt it, he looked up and stared.

'You're a Jew, eh? That's the reason for that luxury car, and this luxury apartment, eh? The reason why you imagine that you can treat the law with impunity, eh?'

Emmanuel answered, speaking with dangerous quietness:

'The reason for my luxury car and my luxury apartment —as you call hem—is that I like them and can pay for them. I think that there is no more to say.'

The man's eyes narrowed, he peered into the hall, and evidently noted the fine old furniture and pictures. He hesitated for a moment, then came nearer and spoke scarcely above a whisper.

'Perhaps you would like to keep this matter out of the court, signor. I have no wish to inconvenience you, you are probably a very busy gentleman. I am willing to make it easy for you—if you wish.'

The quietness had gone, Emmanuel Gollantz blazed at him with terrifying suddenness.

'I wish nothing except that you shall bring the matter of the car before the authorities. I have never yet evaded the law. Now—go!'

He had heard no more of it, but the memory had stung and rankled. He was conscious that his bank manager, a good friend of many years, was nervous and evidently worried when Emmanuel called to see him. The headmaster of the school to which Simeon went called, and, with much hesitation, asked if Signor Gollantz was quite satisfied with his son's progress, or if he would prefer to send him to another school.

'Frankly,' Emmanuel said smoothly, 'don't you really mean that you would prefer that I should remove my son?'

The schoolmaster protested. He did not wish to lose Simeon. He liked the boy. He was popular in the school. But —again he fumbled for words—he had been visited by someone, an official, who had warned him that it was not advisable to allow Jewish boys to mix with Christians.

'If he calls again, this *official*,' Emmanuel said, 'send him to me, signor. My son is only twenty-five per cent Jewish. That, I believe, is *allowed* by the law.'

No, the Italy he had known was changing. The laughter was dying down; the kindness, which had been the rule, was now fast becoming the exception. There was a sense of strain in the air, men were growing to watch one another with suspicion and distrust. The streets were filled with German 'tourists'; their huge cars filled the parking-places, they swaggered into restaurants and gave their orders with arrogance. True, the waiters hated them, the proprietors eyed them with obvious dislike, and were quite evidently delighted when they could protest—with truth—that there were no free tables. Photographs of Hitler—*Il Duce del nostro Duce*—were displayed everywhere; German officers filled the best seats at the opera and the theatre.

Guido reported that he had been looking at a collection of photographs of Hitler shown in a shop window; his friend had said, 'He's an ugly little fellow.' Guido added, 'The Duce is no Adonis, but he's the more pleasant of the two.' A plain-clothes man had stopped and warned them sharply that they had better be careful, or they 'would hear more of it'.

Emmanuel's depression grew with each day that came. Where would it end, what was going to happen? Had Italy forgotten Garibaldi, and that freedom which he had helped her to win? Were they ready to accept the German yoke which, it seemed inevitable, would soon be laid upon their shoulders?

4

Through the hot summer months anxiety grew. Emmanuel heard rumours. Bartolomeo, the lawyer, had killed himself because he was afraid that, being a Jew, he would not be allowed to practise. Old Alfredo Basili, who had taken part in the March on Rome, had denounced Fascismo in the council chamber, and then flung himself from the window to be dashed to death on the paving of the street below. On the heels of these stories came others. Il Duce was said to have declared that nothing would drag him into a war, that he was still master of the situation, still only longing for Peace with Justice for Italy. Ciano had said—Gayda had written—His Holiness had pronounced. On and on, interminable reports, scraps of gossip, tales which were fantastic, tragic, improbable.

Max Gollantz wrote anxiously asking for news as to what was the real situation in Italy. Angela sent immensely long letters which begged Emmanuel to come back to England. Even his brother, the completely level-headed Bill, hinted that 'life might be more comfortable here in England'. Emmanuel went about his business, growing thinner and finding it less easy to laugh, or even to smile, when he met his friends. He still had friends, many of them people who were sane and kind, who resented injustice, and watched the infiltration of the German 'tourists' with apprehension.

Emmanuel took a holiday with Simeon in August. Together they bathed and boated, fished and played golf. With blue skies above, the blue waters of the lake below, sunshine, the gentle sound of water lapping against the rocks, as the fussy little steamer disturbed the still waters, it was easy to forget all those things which had loomed so darkly on his horizon in Milan. He lay on the warm flat rocks, watching Simeon rushing here and there, flinging himself into the water, swimming to outlying rocks, where he sat singing in his high clear young voice.

Emmanuel thought, 'Lying here, I can persuade myself that all will come right. After all, nothing can change the fundamental nature of a nation. The Italian may be romantic, but with all his romance there is a strong strain of practicality, and—poor countries don't rush headlong into war. No, everything will blow over, and the Duce will be the saviour of Italy once again.'

That evening, as he sat with Simeon outside the *caffè*, a car drove into the little square. Simeon looked up from the *arancata* which he was sipping.

'Look, Papa! Uncle Casimero! There, in that car!'

Emmanuel saw Boccalini descending from the car, and coming towards them. Simon rushed away to meet him. The old fear tugged at Emmanuel's heart.

41

'Ah, Casimero, this is pleasant. You have come to spend a holiday with us?' he asked as he shook his friend's hand.

Boccalini sat down, and shook his head.

'Not exactly,' he said. 'I like fine weather for holidays, and I have been warned,' he stressed the word slightly, 'that the barometer will change within the next few days. Already it is swinging to—*variable*.'

Simeon cried, 'Oh, surely not, Uncle Casimero. Only this morning the waiter—the Head waiter—showed me that it was—set fair.'

Boccalini answered, 'Possibly, but even Head waiters make mistakes, and barometers change very rapidly—in these days.'

Emmanuel said, 'And so you advise . . . ?'

The other man shrugged his shoulders. 'Milano is very hot, but if the weather should break—well, one is better able to buy umbrellas and mackintoshes in a big town, eh?'

'You think that it will be a very bad storm?'

'I think that it will be the most terrible storm the world has ever seen, *mio amico*. Why not return tomorrow, we can travel together? Perhaps I can find a room for the night.'

They drove back to Milano on the following morning, Simeon still protesting that his friend, the waiter, declared that the barometer was set fair.

'Perhaps,' he suggested, 'your barometer is not correct?'

'Nothing would make me happier than to believe that,' Boccalini assured him.

That night Emmanuel discussed the situation with Guido. Things looked bad; it was impossible that England and France should tolerate Adolf Hitler's continued contempt for treaties, his disregard of promises, his acts of aggression.

'I remember,' Emmanuel said, 'that my grandfather—the Founder of the House—always referred to Turkey as the "storm centre of Europe". It looks as if the "storm centre" had moved north, to Poland.'

Guido shrugged his well-padded shoulders. '*Non fa niente!* How will it affect us? Italy will never fight. We are sick of war, tired of discussions and political arguments. The tourists, the hotels, these made up one of our chief industries. Where are the tourists?—except the Germans, and they spend nothing. The hotels are empty! No, we are practical;

the Duce is at heart a practical man. We shall never go to war.'

'You may be driven to war,' Emmanuel returned grimly.

The tension was growing. Emmanuel carried the thought of that tension about with him during all his waking hours. In London, men were going backwards and forwards to Number Ten. Chamberlain was discussing policy, preparing for eventualities. In Germany a restless man, restless and ruthless, was in conference with his advisers. In France politician was meeting politician, tempers were rising, words banded from one to another, while the French people consoled themselves with the slogan, 'We have the Maginot Line!'

On the second of September one word was on everyone's lips.

'Tomorrow!'

Palumba, the new *podestà*, met Emmanuel in the Corso. He stopped and stared at him insolently.

'What will tomorrow bring, Signor Gollantz?'

Emmanuel said, 'Does any man in the world know that?'

'I think that your Cham-ber-lain knows that England will plunge the world into war! He and E-den, and the rest!'

'Is it not possible,' Emmanuel asked mildly, 'that Adolf Hitler may also have—information regarding what will happen tomorrow?'

'If he has *in*formation,' Palumba returned, 'be very sure that he has also made—*pre*-paration. Have you?'

'You mean—have the British Government? I should think that it is exceedingly probable, *Signor Podestà*.'

Sunday morning, the sun shining into the big room. Guido sitting with clenched hands and bright, anxious eyes, Simeon, a little puzzled, stood looking from his father to Guido and back to the big Marinelli radio set. No one spoke, no one moved. Emmanuel thought that all Milan, all Italy, all the world held its breath. Then the silence shattered, and a voice, clear and distinct, made the announcement.

'The Prime Minister.'

Another voice, controlled, restrained, and lacking any tricks of oratory, began to speak. Then it had come at last! After twenty-five years, a quarter of a century, war had gripped the world in its clutches once more. It was almost, Emmanuel felt, a relief to know that the waiting was over, to know the worst instead of continually hoping for the best. England was at war!

The quiet, reasonable voice was silent. The declaration had been made. Guido had buried his face in his hands. Simeon whispered:

'Papa—it's war, isn't it?'

'I'm afraid so, Simeon.'

'Oh—with Germany. Not,' eagerly, 'with Italy?'

Guido was galvanised into action; he sprang to his feet. 'Never, never, never, Simeon *caro*! I, Guido, tell you. Only in February our late Holy Father expressed his dying wish. "*Pace, pace, Italia.*" Let the rest of the world do what it will —we shall remain outside this quarrel. Remember today what I have told you. September the third, 1939—Italy will not fight.'

Simeon said, 'I'm awfully glad about that, Guido.' Then, turning to his father he added, 'That's a great relief, isn't it, Papa?'

'I hope that everyone will be as wise as Guido,' Emmanuel said. That night he and Guido sat talking very late. Guido was excited, and hopeful. He made no bones about his hope that the French and British would end the war quickly, and —vanquish the Germans.

'Why do you hate the Germans?' Emmanuel asked.

'I hate them,' Guido replied, 'because they are unlikable to people of sensibility, also they hate everyone in the world. To gain their respect you must be—German. They persecute—it does not matter to them whom—so long as someone can be persecuted. Jews, Catholics, anything, anyone. They are'—he wrinkled his fine nose in disgust— 'stupid! And generally ugly. The backs of their necks are so thick, their women have such large behinds. No, no, if there is a very great deal more of this rubbish I shall beg you to leave for England; in fact we will all leave for England. We will take everything of value. Tomorrow I shall, with your permission, begin to pack. You, Simeon and I—how happily we shall live in England! Not even the fog and cold shall prevent me. After all, I have a very fine fur-lined coat, with a collar of astrakhan.'

44

'But my poor Guido, would you be allowed to go to England?'

Guido opened his beautiful eyes very wide. 'Allowed—what is this "allowed", please? Italy is a free country! Men may go and come as they wish. We are not slaves!' Then slowly the indignation died, and he stared at Emmanuel miserably. 'Or, maybe—are we slaves?'

During the days which followed Emmanuel worked feverishly. He knew that behind his wish to leave everything in order there was something more than the fear that Italy might enter the war. For some time he would not admit, even to himself, what this queer impulse was which sent him to the Galleries early in the morning, and kept him there, working at high pressure, until late in the evening. Again and again he assured himself that he was only preparing for possibilities which might never eventuate. Only when he read of the reverses at Narvik did he allow his thought to crystallise. Again and again he had refused to face a problem which he knew must intrude further and further into his waking hours. He had deceived himself into the superficial belief that his anxiety to have his business in complete order was no more than the reaction of an average man who understood the new and imposed conditions.

'One must be prepared for anything,' he had assured Guido.

'I must be ready for any and every eventuality,' he said to Tolini.

Letters from home had been moderate and discreet. His father wrote giving advice and suggestions regarding the safeguarding of the works of art in the Galleries. His mother wrote, affectionately and anxiously, but neither of his parents made any definite reference to his return to England. Bill had been in the Territorials in peacetime, and had been granted a commission immediately after the outbreak of war. Julian was miserable that he would not be able to join the Army on account of his health. There had been no hint as to where either his father or mother felt that Emmanuel's duty lay.

Now, as Emmanuel listened to the English news, or read his two-days-old copy of *The Times*, he knew that he must go back to England. He had no fierce wish to become a

45

soldier, he hated the ugliness and brutality of war, he believed it to be the most illogical and expensive method of settling quarrels and problems. Yet, reading of the losses in Norway, of Quislings, of shipping lost, of lives sacrificed, he knew—with quiet certainty—that he must go back.

He sat, that evening, in his study alone. With his fine hands clasped, his eyes staring into space, he talked silently, as he had done so often, to his dead wife, Juliet.

'My dearest, I've got to go back. I don't know whether I want to or not; I fancy not, but I have to go. I may not be much use, but I'm thirty-four, fit and strong, and surely they —whoever "they" may be!—should be able to find something for me to do.' He sighed. 'It's a wrench, not only leaving everything, but leaving the place which held all the happiness I have known. It's not been the same without you, you know that, my dearest, but it has held so many wonderful memories. Memories which at first were terribly painful. No, they're not really painful now. I haven't time to feel the pain, because I am so grateful that I have experienced those wonderful times with you. Do you remember my first little shop! Where you came to buy silks, and a chicken-skin fan? Of course you remember! Now I have the Galleries! Do you remember Guido's awful clothes, and his wild attempts to speak English? He speaks it quite well now. What a good friend he has been to me! So I'm going back to England, Juliet. Simeon and I. Not for always—oh no, I shall come back. One day the world will be sane again. Not yet, I'm afraid. Be with me in England, my dear, as you have been with me in Milan. Never leave me. I'll do my best. I won't let you be disappointed in your husband—your lover. There, I must go and talk to Guido. Poor Guido, he'll be so unhappy. Help him, Juliet, as you've so often helped me. Good night, my dearest, good night.'

Calmly and very kindly he told Guido of his decision. He watched the large eyes widen, saw the tears rise in them and slip down the smooth cheeks, noticed how the full lips trembled, how the colour drained from Guido's face.

Almost pleadingly, he asked, 'You do understand, Guido?'

The muscles of Guido's throat worked spasmodically. He struggled to overcome his emotion, then said, 'I understand —as I have always understood—that whatever you do is of

46

necessity right and noble. No, Emmanuel, my master, my friend, let me speak. If in your heart something says that you must go—that is right. For me—it is end of the world. For many years we have known each other. At first I was almost gigolo, I was slipping down with every day. Very soon I might have been—what do you call it? nancy man. Very nasty, bad, dirty boy. One who runs about from first one to then another. Not real sentiment, only affection. I'm not a very hot fellow to say prayers.' He shrugged his shoulders. 'I am—sceptic. Maybe it's all O.K., maybe it's just—tales. Jabber, jabber, jabber don't get a fellow anywhere. But,' his voice shook, 'to watch Emmanuel Gollantz, to notice how he behaves, works, thinks—that gets a fellow a long way. I get a hellova long way in these last years. Now, when you go to England, for first time I say prayers—prayers from the bottom of my heart. Our Lady, Saint Antonio—ask him "please find peace for the world . . . Saint Francis, all saints in the calendar. Peace for the world, if you please!"' He came forward and seized Emmanuel's hand in his. 'Do you understand?' he said urgently. 'Do you know that if you go to be a military, and if Italy come into this dam'-fool war—you and I are against one another? It is not possible! Enemies with you! To raise a gun loaded with killing bullets to point towards the breast of Emmanuel! *Dio mio*—first it will be turned on the breast of Guido.'

Then bursting into tears, sobbing as a lost and frightened child might cry, he said, 'Take me with you! You are clever, you can make plans. I will walk to England. I will live only to work for you. When you are high-up military soldier I will be soldier servant to you. Emmanuel, do not leave me here to die of a broken heart.'

Gently Emmanuel said, 'Guido, we shall never be enemies. Whatever happens. Even if Italy comes into the war, not even then. I'm English, you're Italian. We both love our country, and if she needs us—we've got to serve her. Hate could never come into it. I can never hate your country, and you will never hate mine. It's only—duty, Guido. I can't take you to England, it wouldn't be possible. Maybe I wouldn't even if I could. Perhaps it's your duty to stay here. I'll come back—one day.'

'Duty! What duty have I to a country which has joined

her hands with the Germans? I have no duty to this country. If we should enter the war, it will not be the voice of
Italy commanding us to do so; it will be the voice of *Il Duce
del nostro Duce*!'

Laying his hands on Guido's shoulders, Emmanuel said,
'I don't know. There might be other voices—voices which
reached the people under the tones of the Duce. The voice
of Garibaldi—even now there may be other voices ready to
speak to the people. They may be forced to speak softly,
Guido, but if you listen intently you will hear them.
Courage, my brother! Courage!'

Painful days followed, days when again and again Emmanuel's strength almost failed. It would have been so easy
to stay in Milan. He still had sufficient influence to smooth
the path which would lie before him. Conte Boccalini shook
his head, looked at Emmanuel with great sad eyes, and nodding said, 'Yes, you are right, you must go.' Paolo Mancini
came to see him in his office.

He cried, in his thick, husky voice, 'I'm going back. I'm a
British subject. Iva must come with me! I want to be in it
too.'

'But Iva is Italian, Mancini.'

Mancini flung back his head. 'A wife takes the nationality
of her husband!'

Emmanuel smiled, 'Yes, and a great many complications
ensue!'

'I can't leave her here when I go, can I?'

'I don't know what you can do,' Emmanuel said, speaking
slowly, almost regretfully. 'That's something which only you
and Iva can decide. Women like the Alfano have no
nationality. They are artists, and art is and always must be
—international.'

'She has a duty to me,' Mancini protested.

'There is a mutual duty,' Emmanuel said. 'There must be
some adjustment. There can be—given goodwill and love on
both sides.'

Half sulkily Mancini flung himself into a big chair. 'I have
listened to storms and arguments, watched tears, and had
recriminations hurled at me for hours. Iva is wonderful, but
she is unreasonable. I adore her, you know that. But I can't
stay out here while even my brother, whom I detest, is fight-

ing. I hoped for sympathy, Emmanuel, understanding . . .'

'I do understand. But I do sympathise with both of you,' Emmanuel protested. 'That's what makes it so difficult. But,' more lightly, 'don't go home and hold pistols to Iva's very charming head. Don't hurl ultimatums about and say "either" and "or". Iva isn't accustomed to thinking, except about her work. She's been working tremendously at "Norma"—but she never thinks about anything else, except' —his smile widened—'the man she married.'

Mancini shrugged his shoulders. 'I suppose you think that I should give in, eh?'

'I think that you should go home and read *Hamlet*. It's a very good play, and let me commend to you a certain old gentleman called Polonius, Mancini. Shakespeare has solved the problems of quite a number of people. There, get along home to Iva—who is probably crying bitterly—it's so bad for her voice too!—and be wise and be kind. My compliments to her as always.'

The following afternoon Iva Alfano visited him. Emmanuel, working hard, heard her voice and that of Guido outside in the Gallery.

Guido's voice was raised in admiration; Iva's in reply seemed gratified at his compliments. Emmanuel caught the words, *'Diva . . .' 'Prego, signor Guido . . .'* On and on, compliments and protestations that Guido was too kind, too polite, too *'gentile'*. What children they were, with their play-acting and exchange of compliments!

Emmanuel rose and opened the door. 'Ah, Cara Signora Mancini!'

'Emmanuelo!' She rushed forward with outstretched hands. 'I must speak with you. Yes, Guido, and with you! Both my friends—good friends. All is arranged! I am English lady, and proud of it. What does it matter? Italy and England have a historic friendship. Nothing can break it. If Italy fights it will be as she fought in the Great War—*Il Grande Guerra*—beside the English. Paolo is to be an English soldier. So clever he is! In all probability he will be *generalissimo* very quickly. I shall want a house, Emmanuelo. At first—the Savoy, but later a house for my warrior to return to after his fighting and victories. What a life! Poor Guido, don't look so sad. Soon we shall all be

49

back in Milan, Emmanuelo and Paolo hung with laurel leaves, acclaimed as saviours of Freedom. There will be a gala performance at La Scala, I shall sing "Norma". You will all be seated in a box, covered with decorations!'

The end seemed to come with startling suddenness. They were leaving. Simeon was excited, Emmanuel thought that he had never known such depression. Guido was in tears, the servants crowded round to shake his hand, to embrace Simeon. The women weeping bitterly. Tolini arrived, grave and dignified; Conte Boccalini drove up and standing with one hand on Simeon's shoulder, watched Emmanuel with unhappy eyes.

'You take our hearts with you, Emmanuel,' he said.

'And in exchange I leave most of mine with you all.'

'We will write to you—but with a certain amount of care, *caro mio*. One must be wise in times of war.'

'Certainly. My dear friends, I shall come back to you very soon.'

The long station platform, Simeon going on ahead to find the carriage, Guido walking beside Emmanuel, silent and white-faced.

'You will attend to everything. Consult Tolini in any difficulty. There is plenty of money in the bank; live comfortably in the flat and eat well. You must not grow too thin, Guido, it does not suit you. There, once again courage, and it will soon be over.'

'If I can live through this separation!'

'You must,' Emmanuel said. 'I need you and your wonderful friendship so badly. There, and may the God of my Fathers bless and keep you.'

He thought afterwards how strange it was that he, who had never practised the Jewish faith, should have reverted to that formula at the moment of parting.

Guido, with a great effort at control, said, 'I shall pray too, always for your safety, your happiness.'

5

Paris at last, Emmanuel sighed with relief. He felt that he had been allowing his speculations, his regrets, his apprehensions for the future to take possession of him while the train went rushing north through the night. Paris would mean distraction, Simeon would ask a thousand questions, and Louis Lara would be there, with his magnificent, if slightly overblown, wife, Olympia.

Simeon said, 'Ah, Paris, Papa. I am interested to see Paris. Didn't the Germans once get to Paris—in another war, a history war?'

'They did indeed,' Emmanuel told him.

'But they can't get here this time, can they, because of the Maginot Line, eh?'

'We must hope that they never will.'

Louis Lara was waiting for them as the long train drew up at the platform. Exquisite as ever, wearing so much jewellery that, for a second, Emmanuel frowned. Strange that a man possessing such good taste, such appreciation of beauty and art, should be so lacking in the ability to dress with reasonable restraint.

The moment Louis caught his hand, the moment he saw the kindness in his dark eyes, Emmanuel blamed himself for being over-critical. What did it matter how Louis dressed? Louis and Guido were laws unto themselves! All that mattered was that they gave him their completely generous friendship, that they had been loyal to him, when the rest of his world believed him to be foul and utterly unworthy.

Simeon, proud to display his knowledge, said, 'How is the Maginot Line today, Uncle Louis?'

'It is in the best of health,' Louis answered, 'and it asks me to bring a message to say that it hopes that you are the same.'

There must be no going to hotels, Louis protested. His apartment was large enough to accommodate them easily, they must not rob him and his wife of the rare honour of entertaining them.

Olympia beamed on them; she had grown stout with the

years, but it was evident that Louis adored her, and she still had the airs of a famous, almost world-renowned, dancer.

'Pah!' she said, 'tell me, if you don't mind, why anyone should fear the Boche? France is still France, and Frenchmen can still fight like tigers! I tell you somet'ing—this war will be very short and most terribly boring. Now, we will speak no more of it, if you please.'

But Emmanuel and Louis sat long into the night talking, and their talk was of the war. The moment Olympia left them, Emmanuel watched Louis's expression change. Before he had laughed, smiled, shown his beautifully white teeth very often, because he seemed to find life such an amusing affair. Now, with his chin on his hand, he stared at Emmanuel unsmiling and very grave.

'One plays a part,' he said. 'It is necessary—particularly with women and children. They must not know—yet. One day they will *have* to know, but that day has not arrived. I dread the day when I must tell Olympia that I shall leave her, to become a soldier. Very soon now, Emmanuel. Very soon. And you—what will you do?'

Emmanuel said, 'Join the Army, I suppose, unless they find me more useful doing something else. We're all in this, Louis, we've all got to do something, eh?'

Louis nodded. 'Indeed, yes. And we shall every one be needed. All things are not marching well, Emmanuel. I move about, I hear men speaking, men who have knowledge and authority. In Germany the machines are roaring day and night, everyone is working, working, working with one common thought. Mark that—one common thought. That is what we lack! Yes, I tell you, we have no unity, and without complete unity there can never be complete strength. France will be tried in the furnace—will she survive that trial? I don't know. There are men who love money and power far better than they love France. How many men will England send here to fight with us? Will there be enough? Are there sufficient aeroplanes, ships, guns—big, heavy guns; are there men who know sufficient about the new methods of warfare to lead us forward to victory? And if there are all these things, will they be strong enough to fight against treachery, decay, decadence and—greed?'

Emmanuel listened. He could scarcely believe that this

52

grave, unhappy little man could be Louis Lara. Louis, who had never been depressed except through some love affair which had gone badly! Nothing else had ever reduced him to this state of doubt and despondency. Slowly Louis unfolded the whole story as he knew it. He had noticed this, he had heard that; he knew that this Minister had lost the confidence of the people, he knew that that General relied on methods which were years behind the ways of modern warfare. Contractors were making too much money, and giving inferior goods and equipment in exchange; the army lacked so many things which were vitally necessary for them and their efficiency.

With tears in his eyes, Louis said, 'The people are still— the French people. They have high courage, but—Emmanuel—courage can be drained away, spirits may be broken, hopes turned to fears. Workmen must have tools, soldiers have their tools with which to fight. Rob them of these, let them realise that they have been tricked, fobbed off with bad material, inferior boots, old, worn-out rifles, inaccurate maps—or maybe no maps at all—and then what happens? In less than two weeks I shall be one of those soldiers. I shall be an officer, because I have done military training and was considered clever. I was clever in the class-room, I could draw most beautiful maps, and learning came easily to me. How good shall I be now in these days? I don't know! I was taught by men who understood war in the Great War. How much will they know of this war, with its new ideas? How much shall I know?'

Emmanuel said, 'This all sounds very grave, Louis, unless you are taking a view which is unnecessarily gloomy.'

'Gloomy!' Louis exclaimed. 'How can one pretend in the middle of a very dark night that the sun is shining brightly!'

Trying to speak lightly, Emmanuel said, 'But in all probability the sun is shining brightly—somewhere.'

'I am only concerned that it should shine for France and her allies, my friend. Believe me, there is very little sunshine here!'

Two days later Emmanuel and his son crossed to England. He knew that his own depression was becoming deeper. Not only when he remembered all that Louis Lara had said, but because he knew that life in England would be difficult. He had never doubted that his mother loved him, he had always felt assured that his father had a real and deep affection for him; but both Max and Angela had given the greatest share of their love to their son Julian. Whatever Julian had done in the past, they had forgiven him, and after his accident in Milan, when he had injured his back, they had conspired to do everything in their power to atone to him for the loss of a career which had been so promising.

That accident, which had happened in Emmanuel's Galleries! How clearly he remembered it! Julian coming there, talking to Guido, and hinting, so carefully, scandal regarding Juliet. Guido, at first flattered that Julian Gollantz should talk so pleasantly to him, had listened, smiled, and only half understood the imputations. When realisation came, he had rushed forward, swearing that he would kill the man who spoke evil of either Emmanuel or his wife. Julian had slipped on the marble step, had clutched wildly to save himself, and a huge vase had crashed down on him. At first the doctors thought that he would never walk again. They had been wrong; Julian walked well enough, though he complained of attacks of pain. More doctors were consulted, they argued, discussed the case, and shook their heads. The pain was 'mysterious', it was difficult to find the real seat of the injury.

'Take it from me,' Bill Gollantz had said to Emmanuel, 'There's nothing much wrong with Julian! The world lost a great actor when our delightful brother decided to take up a political career!'

So Julian had continued to live at Ordingly, where he occupied, with his wife and son, a magnificent suite of rooms, indulged in every whim, and led a life of considerable luxury and extravagance. At intervals there would be heated arguments with his father concerning debts, which Julian appeared to incur endlessly. In the end Max Gollantz always paid, and for a time peace reigned again. There were times when Julian appealed to his mother, and Angela—to prevent arguments and discussions—paid his bills herself.

Bill told Emmanuel, 'Father was talking about Julian the other day. He tried to convince me that they felt he had been robbed of his career—through that accident. I suppose that I looked doubtful. Father said, "Don't be hard, Bill. A

man doesn't easily relinquish all his hopes and ambitions."
I said that other men had continued to work even under a
physical disability. I quoted several. The Gov'nor only
sighed, and I know that he felt I was hard and unsym-
pathetic.'

Emmanuel knew that he dreaded meeting his brother.
They had never been great friends. Again and again Julian
had done his best to make mischief for his brother. Why?
What was it? Not jealousy, surely, for Julian was by far the
more brilliant of the two. He was more handsome, he made
friends more easily. Emmanuel frowned, trying to discover
why Julian had always been antagonistic.

Simeon came and stood beside him. 'Papa, there they are!
The white cliffs of Dover. They're interesting, aren't they?'

Emmanuel nodded. 'Yes, the sight of them has meant a
good deal to many people.'

Incredibly quickly it seemed that they were at Folkestone.
There was the usual bustle, augmented perhaps by people
who were returning and were experiencing a sense of relief
that they were in England again. The train to London, very
full, and the queer feeling of security which came to one
at the sight of the dining-car attendants, and the elderly
ticket inspectors. Simeon sat staring out of the window,
scarcely able to eat his luncheon because the landscape was
so new and strange. Again and again he called his father's
attention to this object and that. Only once he smiled, saying rather ruefully, 'It's cold, isn't it? It *looks* cold as well.'

'The plain of Lombardy can be the coldest place I know,'
Emmanuel reminded him.

The boy answered, eagerly, as if he wished to apologise
for having said anything which might seem to be derogatory
to England. 'Oh, yes, yes, terribly cold, indeed.'

London, and again bustle and porters rushing here and
there, and Angela's chauffeur standing waiting, tipping his
cap and smiling.

'Her ladyship sent me with the car, sir. She thought that
perhaps your heavy baggage could come on later. By Carter
or the railway company.'

'Her ladyship is well?'

'First clarse, sir, and 'ighly delighted that you're 'ome.'

'And my father?

'Worried, sir. Mr. William left for France two days ago. Quite sudding it was.'

Simeon cried, 'Oh, what a pity! We were in France two days ago. We might have seen him.'

The man smiled. 'Indeed, sir. Thet's just too bad, isn't it?'

Driving to Ordingly, Emmanuel leaned back in the car, silent and thoughtful. Simeon was used to his father's moods of thoughtful abstraction. He never interrupted them, only sat upright, his eyes staring out of the window, waiting until Emmanuel should be ready to talk to him.

Ordingly—and the memories which it held. His grandfather's funeral, when he had seen Juliet Forbes with Bill Masters. The first time that he had seen her for years. He remembered how Max had taken her hand and said, 'My father would be very much pleased to know that you are here.' With the memory of her came that painful rush of emotion which was almost physical pain. Then he felt his throat and chest contract, and again realised that if it were not for Simeon he could never have remained in the world without her. Simeon—his son, Juliet's son—who was going to begin a life which would be strange, and probably difficult. Had he armed the boy sufficiently, or had he allowed him to become so used to Italian ways, manners and speech that life would be more complicated than necessary for him?

He frowned and turned to his son.

'Simeon . . .'

Simeon turned from staring out of the window. 'Yes, Papa?'

'Listen; you've come to England and you've got to be an English boy.'

'But, Papa, I am an English boy!'

Emmanuel smiled. 'Not quite; you're an Italian translation of one.'

Simeon chuckled. 'That's funny! A translation!'

'You always have the power to flatter me when you laugh at my very mild jokes,' his father said. 'I only hope that you'll never abuse it. Listen, you are going to meet your cousin, Max. Max is completely English. In moments of annoyance he may call you an "I-ti". Don't allow that to disturb you. But I think if you could remember to call me

56

"Father" and not "Papa" it might be a help. Don't slip into Italian phrases. Talk it with me if you like, but guard against it with your cousin. Simeon, we—you and I—must not be different. We must be the same, we must conform. Do you understand, I wonder?'

Simeon laughed. *'Si, si, papa, e tante grazie. Per l'ultima volta ... papa!'*

'Thank you. Now there is Ordingly. The drive which was your great-grandfather's pride. He used to say they were the finest chestnut trees in England.'

As they drove towards the house which Emmanuel had always loved, he remembered that some day this splendid house, these magnificent trees, this land would belong to Simeon. His own love for Ordingly had always been very great, and now—bringing his son home—he must teach him to love it too.

'It's a fine place,' he said, 'a place of which to be proud.'

Simeon, leaning forward, his hands on his knees, breathed deeply.

'I am proud of it, Father,' he said.

The long cream-coloured house, with its portico and pillars in the style of Palladio, the rows of windows with their decorations and essentially restrained dignity, its formal terrace and Italian garden, now lying cold and rather grey in the light of a February afternoon, lay before them. The car drew up; with mechanical precision the front door swung open, and servants came running out. Emmanuel got out, and stood for a moment in his long, straight travelling-coat staring at the building. The curtain was rising on another act of the play which was his life.

'Her ladyship asked that you would go directly to her room, sir.'

Emmanuel said sharply, 'My mother is not ill?'

'No, sir. Only her ladyship dislikes the cold.'

Together he and Simeon mounted the wide, shallow stairs. How strange it was to be home again, not for a holiday but for the duration of the war.

Angela's voice crying, 'Come in, come in!' and they entered the warm, bright room. Emmanuel walked forward, his hand on Simeon's shoulder. He sensed that, for all his gaiety, the boy was nervous. He was afraid that he might

57

make mistakes, might not be able to impress upon his grand-mother that he was really quite an English boy. Angela, older, her hair turning grey, rose to greet them. She held out her arms to Emmanuel. He folded her in his.

'Mother—I'm back.'

'My dear, dear boy.' She kissed him and, still held in his arms, turned to greet her grandson, holding out her hand to him.

'And Simeon . . .'

The boy took her hand and raised it to his lips. 'Dear'—there was the faintest possible pause—'Grand-mother.'

Simeon glanced quickly at his father, half dismayed, as Angela said, 'Oh, darling, not Grandmother—that is so for-mal. Call me "Grannie".'

Emmanuel and his son laughed. She looked from one to the other in surprise. 'What is it? Have I made a joke?'

Emmanuel said, 'Darling, no. You never made a joke in your life! My instructions were, "No Italian greetings". Simeon has prepared "grandmother" with great care, and now—he must learn another word!'

She twisted away from Emmanuel and turned to the boy.

'Tell me, what would you have said if your father had not given you instructions?'

Simeon answered gravely, *'Ah, cara nonna, tu séi bella.'*

She nodded, then said to Emmanuel, 'He's a charmer! Now, come and kiss your grannie, Simeon.'

Tea was brought, and she began to talk as she had always done. Her words came crisply, her ideas were ordered and arranged.

'How old are you, Simeon?'

'I am nearly thirteen, *non*—Grannie.'

'And school? What about that? You've been to school, of course. I can see that you are clever. Oh, yes, it's obvious.'

Emmanuel said, 'Darling, of course he has been to school. Do you think that we have lived in Darkest Africa? A very good school, and he has done—yes, I think that I may claim that—very well.'

'And now? I have been thinking of this schooling ever since you came home. He must go to a very good, first-rate prep. school. We will send him to a public school next year. Max is nearly a year older. He is at Tellinghurst. He will go

58

to Harrow. For Simeon—well, we shall see. I don't'—thoughtfully—'think—Harrow for him.' She turned her still dazzling smile on the boy. 'You'll trust me, trust your grannie, won't you?'

Simeon nodded. 'With everything, what you say will be right.'

Later, Emmanuel said to his mother, 'You've made another conquest. My son is ready to adore you.'

'I am ready to adore him. Ah, how like Juliet he is! The same smile, the same trick of standing listening with absorbed interest.' With a sudden movement she laid her hand on Emmanuel's. 'Dear Juliet! Did you hate leaving very much, dear one?'

Sombrely he answered, 'One half of me was heartbroken. The other—knew quite clearly that there was nothing else to be done. If I were to retain my self-respect—I must come back to England.'

'To—fight?'

'If that is the most useful work that I can do—yes, to fight.'

'You and Bill . . .'

His voice hardened a little. 'And Julian?'

'Ah, my dear, poor Julian. He is eating his heart out. He sits and thinks what he could do, and always comes back to the belief that a man who is not quite fit, whose health is not completely reliable, is a liability to any organisation, never an asset. Amanda is going into the A.T.S. Julian's interest in all her plans is almost pathetic.'

She sat and talked to him, the light from the bright wood fire shining on her face, touching her grey hair, making her seem, to the son who loved her so dearly, illuminated and entirely delightful. He felt that the years had slipped away, and that he was back living at Ordingly, delighting in his mother's kindness and sympathy. She might—did—love Julian the best of all her sons, but she had always been able to talk to and discuss things with Emmanuel. He, on his side, had always loved her better than anyone in the world, except Juliet. He forgot when he was with her that she was not and never had been a very clever woman; he was only conscious of her charm and a certain innate wisdom which was hers. She had always been able to make him talk, to

59

open the doors of his heart, and to overcome that faint distrust of people—however well he knew them and however much he loved them—which was the result of the experiences which life had meted out to him.

Again and again as she glanced at his grave face, noted how his hair was greying at the temples, saw the new lines which the last two years had engraved on his clear, pale skin, she felt her heart contract. Julian might have suffered physical pain and disability, but Emmanuel had known mental torture and great loneliness. She stretched out her hand and laid it on his.

'Emmanuel, we must make you happy, my dear.'

'I must learn to make myself happy,' he said; 'happiness is a thing you find alone—in yourself—or with one other person. Even then, the two of you walk along together. There can't be any chance of other people—making happiness for you.'

'Darling, you're too young to talk in that way!'

He smiled, and she felt his fingers close over hers.

'I have often felt that was one of my legitimate grudges against Fate.'

The door opened and Max Gollantz came into the room. He stood for a moment, very tall and thin, his face grown more haggard with the years. His hair had thinned a little, and the healthy pallor of the Gollantzes had changed to the colour of parchment. Max had never been a handsome man; he had been pleasant to look at, he had always been attractive, and his essential kindliness had shown in his expression. He came forward holding out his hand.

'Emmanuel, I am very happy to know that you are home again.'

Immediately he turned to his wife. 'You're all right? Not felt the cold too much? Ah, how good it is to be home again! I have only been away since this morning.' He laughed and said to Emmanuel, 'I always feel like a returned wanderer. Where is your boy?'

'He went off to wash, unpack and make various explorations.'

Max nodded. 'Pity that Max is back at school. We must make arrangements for Simeon. And you.'

'The Army, I suppose. I'm too old to fly.'

He saw the look of relief on his father's face.

'Good. We must see what can be done. You've seen Julian, No? He's breaking his heart, poor fellow.' Max sighed. 'It's very sad.' Then with an effort at regaining his interest, he said, 'Doesn't it strike either of you that I should like to see my grandson—and also that I should like some tea?'

6

His first dinner at Ordingly as a resident there. Before, when he had visited his family, every dinner had been an occasion which offered to invite those numerous friends of Max and Angela. This evening he had to face a family dinner. Why did he dread it so? His mother had been adorable, his father had been kind, and yet he felt a sense of oppression at the thought of a family dinner. He liked Julian's wife, Amanda; the only person who presented difficulties was his brother Julian.

As he dressed, tying his elaborate evening stock with the care which was habitual to him, Emmanuel frowned at his reflection in the glass. How stupid it was! The time was past when Julian had the power to hurt and wound him. He had made his own career, lived his own life, he depended upon no one. Julian could never hurt him again. If his brother's remarks were bitter, even offensive, surely Emmanuel Gollantz was sufficiently a man of the world to know how to deal with them suavely and easily.

He went down to find his father drinking a glass of sherry in the drawing-room, looking taller and thinner than ever in his severe black and white.

'Ah, Emmanuel, a glass of sherry? You don't—I hope—prefer those abominations—cocktails?'

Emmanuel laughed. 'No, I like sherry. You have to give Italy credit for that. They do not affect—to any extent—the cocktail. They still refer to them as "cocktail *inglese*".'

'*Inglese!*' Max cried indignantly. 'The wretched things are American pure and simple!'

'Both the purity and simplicity are questionable,' his son said.

Max nodded. 'I agree.' Then, raising his glass, 'Glad to know that you are back. I said nothing in my letters, but I knew that you would obey the dictates of your own heart—and that would never lead you very far wrong.'

'That's one of the nicest things you have ever said to me.'

Max became immediately embarrassed. 'Nonsense. Truth, nothing more. Pleasant room this, eh? I disliked those portraits of you all as children, but I've grown to like them. Of course, the gem of the place to me is Sargent's picture of your grandfather in the dining-room. Queer how it dominates everything. There have been times when we've had young people here, rather silly young people, who think that it's clever to drink too much wine after half a dozen of those infernal cocktails, and I've felt positively uncomfortable. Why? Because I felt that my father was watching and—disapproving. Queer, how he still seems to permeate the house with his character.'

'I hope that he'll go on—watching,' Emmanuel said gravely.

The moment they entered the dining-room he knew that his eyes turned towards the portrait. They found it, and rested on it with a sense of pleasure, and a realisation that he longed for that old man to approve of whatever he did. For many years Emmanuel had indulged in a kind of superstition. He had believed that should he break any of those unwritten laws, by which Old Emmanuel had governed his life, those eyes would turn away from him.

The splendid old face, with its keen eyes and fine aquiline nose, the beautifully kept white hair, and the mouth which was so strong but never hard, looked down at him. He saw the elaborate stock, with its great black pearl pin, the slightly outdated clothes which Old Emmanuel had always affected; the sensitive hands which held the ivory-topped cane; and the one magnificent ring, which had been the envy of half the collectors in England, on the little finger of the right hand.

Angela, entering, stood for a moment looking at his rapt and attentive face, then came forward and laid her hand on his arm.

'There he is,' she said gently. ' "The Founder of the House"—my dear first Emmanuel. You're growing so like him.'

He looked down at her and smiled. 'I shall never have his *panache*.'

The sound of voices at the door made them turn. Julian was coming in with his pretty American wife. Angela felt Emmanuel's arm stiffen slightly, but his voice was under complete control as he walked forward and said, 'Amanda, how nice this is! Hello, Julian, glad to see you again.'

Amanda said, 'Well, Emmanuel, if this isn't grand! My, how well you're looking!'

Julian, who leaned on a cane, said, 'Well, Emmanuel, so you've had to leave Italy after all. Did they try to persecute you?'

Making a great effort to speak pleasantly, Emmanuel answered, 'No, not at all. I came home fr-rom entirely personal motives.'

'And those were . . ?'

Angela interrupted, 'Might I remind you that dinner is waiting, and I, for one, am extremely hungry?'

During dinner Emmanuel watched his brother. How handsome he was, with his crisp fair hair, well-cut features and clear skin. His smile came so readily; he had the ability of listening to his wife, to Max or Angela, with an air which implied that whatever they said was of paramount importance to him. Once or twice Julian's smiling eyes met his across the table; the smile persisted, but still Emmanuel's sense of apprehension remained. Sooner or later Julian would turn on him.

With a cigarette in his fingers, leaning back in his chair, Julian opened fire.

'What do you want to do, now that you have come home?'

'The Army, probably.'

'I should have thought that the Air Force would have appealed to your sense of the—romantic!'

'It might, indeed, but I don't imagine that I should appeal to them. I'm over thirty, you know.'

'Not going to get exemption and go into the shop?'

Max said, 'Julian, you know how much I object to that expression.'

'Sorry, Father. But then, you see, I'm a democrat. I see nothing objectionable in keeping a shop.'

Sharply, Max returned, 'Probably not. I object to the expression. Oblige me by not using it.'

Julian turned to his brother. 'What do you call your— place?'

'Mine—Galleria Gollantz.'

'Of course, stupid of me. If anyone should remember the name of the place—I should!'

Amanda said, 'Now, honey, don't let's think of anything painful.'

'A little difficult not to! Oh, I saw Aunt Beatrice today in town. She tells me that Viva is going into the Women's Transport or some such thing. Toby Tatten's gone back to his regiment.'

Mechanically Emmanuel said, because he must 'keep his end up', and refused to show either annoyance or embarrassment when the name of his first wife had been mentioned, 'I should think Tatten's a good soldier. A very nice fellow.'

'Viva is a nice girl,' Angela added.

'Ver-ry nice,' Emmanuel agreed.

Julian grinned. 'Never know your luck, Emmanuel. Toby might get in a warm corner and—not come back, eh?'

Refusing to be drawn, Emmanuel said coldly, 'I sincerely hope not.'

Julian turned to Angela, smiling delightedly. 'He ought to have gone into the Diplomatic, darling, don't you think?'

Altogether an uncomfortable dinner, and Emmanuel went to bed that night determined that, no matter how much he loved Ordingly, he must find work which would take him away from it as quickly as possible.

The suggestions that Toby Tatten might 'not come back', and that he 'never knew his luck', had sent the blood drumming into his temples. He had forgotten Julian's ability to plant darts and barbs in one's heart. He had lived so long with people who knew what his marriage to Juliet had meant—little Gilbert, Guido, Louis Lara and the rest—who had never allowed anything to be said which might hurt or

64

wound him, that he had become soft and vulnerable. For so long as he remained at Ordingly he must watch and see that Julian was never allowed to find the chinks in his armour. At the risk of seeming tedious and boring, he would, in future, direct the conversation, and make it impossible for his brother to indulge in his favourite pastime of 'baiting'.

The following morning Max asked Emmanuel if he would drive to London with him. Simeon, hearing, asked if he might come as well, and his grandfather, after a moment's hesitation, nodded assent. Max had grown very silent, Emmanuel noticed. He rarely spoke unless necessity demanded it, and seemed to prefer to allow the conversation to flow round him, but never to draw him into it. Driving to London, with Simeon seated beside the chauffeur, Emmanuel, watching his father, wondered if Max Gollantz were not growing very tired. He was younger than old Emmanuel had been even when he began to admit that he was an old man; yet now it seemed that Max had grown old as his father had never done. Max was barely sixty, and Emmanuel felt that all 'the machinery had begun to run down'. His movements were slow, he spoke slowly and grew querulous quickly. Emmanuel thought, 'This war is going to make him old very soon. Poor Father! Two wars are too much for any man. He's been disappointed in me, in Julian; the only one of us who has been entirely satisfactory is Bill—and he's out in France.'

Speaking slowly, as if he weighed every word, Max said, 'Have you any idea what you are going to do, my boy? I want to tell you that if you come back and join me, I shall be pleased—very much pleased. I don't know why—for I am not an old man—but I get tired easily; frankly,' he laughed, 'I should be glad to shift the burden on to your shoulders.'

'In ordinary times, Father, I'd have been glad . . .'

'In ordinary times,' Max answered with some bitterness, 'you would have stayed in Milan.'

'Yes, I spoke without thinking. I've come home to see if I can be of some use . . .'

Again his father interrupted him. 'Then you don't think that the running of a great—an international—business is of some use?'

Trying to keep his voice even, fighting down his irritation, Emmanuel answered, 'No, no, you're getting it all wrong! Of course a business like yours is of gr-reat importance; only we're at war, and I believe every man who can must fight. I hate war, I loathe the idea of joining any of the Forces, but I'm afraid that is what I came home to do, and do it I must.'

'Then there is no more to be said.'

'I'm afraid not, Father.'

Even then Max Gollantz could not let the matter rest, and all the way to London he continued to refer to it. There were younger men who had not yet been taken from their civilian life; Emmanuel was no longer very young, surely he could wait until the Government ordered him to go; the arguments against his joining the Forces went on and on, until Emmanuel's nerves felt raw and jangled.

It was a relief to reach Bond Street, and, with Max going first while he followed with Simeon, to enter the familiar offices.

Hannah Rosenfelt came to meet them. She had grown enormously stout, there was something almost grotesque about her short, massive figure.

'Good morning, Sir Max, and . . .' She held out her hand, and, as his eyes met hers, Emmanuel felt the kindness of her glance, and knew that his irritation was vanishing. Dear Hannah, how good she had been to him when he felt ostracised and bereft of everything.

'Splendid to see you, Hannah. And looking so well.'

She wheezed a little as she spoke. 'Very good to see you again, and the little boy. Simeon, isn't it? Yes, to be sure. And grown so big, already.'

She bustled away to Max's office, leaving Emmanuel standing there feeling suddenly forlorn and unwanted. The place was so familiar; here he had worked for years, enjoying the bustle, the activity, the opportunities for accumulating knowledge, and securing treasures. How well he remembered when he believed that he had found—and bought—a Bellini for some preposterously small sum. He could still hear Old Emmanuel's gentle, half mocking and yet completely kindly criticism. He had given him a little lecture as to what the picture might be, ending, 'But neffer, neffer, my dear Emmanuel, a Bellini.'

Even when he was dying, he had referred to it, when Emmanuel entered his bedroom.

'Haf you found anot'er Bellini today?'

Hannah Rosenfelt came hurrying back. 'Sir Max would like to speak with you, Mr. Emmanuel, and he asked if Simeon would care to walk round the Gallery while he is waiting. Only,' she held up a stumpy forefinger, 'you must not touch anything.'

Emmanuel laughed. 'Don't be afraid. Simeon is used to a gallery.'

Simeon said eagerly, 'Yes, in Milano my father has the finest gallery in the world! Old masters and china, statues—though he does not care very much for white marble. Do you, Father? He once,' he assured Hannah gravely, 'refused to admit a Canova.'

'Go and see if you can see anything in these Galleries that appeals to you very much. I am sure that you will.'

Simeon left them, and Hannah, watching him go, said, 'Will he follow you, Mr. Emmanuel? Will he be the sixth Gollantz in the business?'

'How can one tell, Hannah? He is thirteen, and—who knows how long the war may last, or how many people will want pictures, and china, bronzes and statuary when it is ended? There, I must go to my father.' He added, 'Let me see you sometimes, Hannah. I want to talk to you. You've helped me so often in the past, you'll have to help me again.'

She answered soberly, 'I'm always there when you need me.' Max was seated at the huge desk which had once belonged to Old Emmanuel. He looked up as his son entered, his fingers held an old silver paper-knife.

'Sit down, Emmanuel. Well, as, during our drive here this morning, you made it plain that my business, my interests, have no interest for you, I can only apologise for bringing you up to town on a fruitless errand. Rather naturally I am disappointed, but I am used to disappointments. What are your plans?

The old sense of being chilled, which had so often attacked him when Max spoke to him, crept over Emmanuel. He felt suddenly disillusioned, lonely and unhappy.

'I'm sorry, sir. Desperately sor-r-ry. Only, won't you remember that if I had not felt it my duty to come home, I might have stayed on, doing my own business in Milano?'

Max said coldly, 'We call that city Milan in England.'

Emmanuel tried to smile. 'Milan then.'

'You might, of course, have stayed; but you know, as well as I do, that Italy will fight the moment she receives her orders from Germany. Also, from what I hear, Jews are not popular in Italy.'

Losing control for a moment, Emmanuel retorted, 'In other words, you believe that I came home to save my skin!'

'I did not say so.'

'You inferred it!' Then with a violent effort he regained his temper. 'Father, don't let us begin by misunderstanding one another. I can't bleat about "duty" and "defending my country"; you'd hate it if I could and did. Just try to believe that I want to do what I think is right and decent. Bill's gone, thrown up a career, and I can't let him do what I'm not ready to do myself. You m-must see that! Only, p-please don't let us get across one another.'

Confound it, he was stammering as he had not done for years! Doubling his 'r's' too, making what he said sound a little foreign. He knew that his father noticed it too, and saw the faint shadow of annoyance cross his face.

'Quite. Yes, I see your point. Now, to return to my first question. What are your plans?'

'I am afr-raid that I have not made any, sir.'

'I presume that you will—enlist. Do you wish me to use any small influence I may have to get a commission for you?'

'No, thank you, Father.'

'May I ask why?'

'Because if I am to get a commission I should prefer to work for one.'

'Then I think that I need detain you no longer.'

Emmanuel walked out; he did not attempt to speak, he knew that he was fighting down a wild desire to beg his father to listen to him, to ask what he held against him, to try to discover what there was about him which Max so obviously found antipathetic. He went back to Hannah

Rosenfelt's office, and sat down near her desk, resting his head on his hand.

'It's no use, Hannah,' he said. 'I tried, but—well, it just didn't work. I doubt if my father will ever do anything but dislike me.'

She made a clicking noise with her tongue, 'Tech, tech—I hoped so much. It's so queer. He is the kindest, most just man, and yet here is a blind spot. The tragic thing is that he hates it! He would like to get along so well with you. There you are—water and oil both good t'ings, but they don't mix, and not'ing will make 'em. Poor young Emmanuel. T'is is where we need the Old Emmanuel. He had such wisdom, he would have taken all the strings, which are knotted and twisted, and unravelled them. Oi, oi, oi.'

'Never mind, Hannah. I'll make some plans. One thing is quite certain: I can't stay at Ordingly, neither can Simeon.'

'But your mother? She loves you so much. So often she has come here and talked to me of you, and of the little boy.'

He nodded. 'Yes, she loves me . . .' he smiled; 'though never quite as much as I loved her. There—here is Simeon back, and we must go.'

Simeon was excited, and as they walked along Bond Street together he chattered about what he had seen.

'A Moroni, Father, and—I think—a Dal Libri. The man there pointed them out to me. Some Venetian glass—old Venetian, of course—and a complete set of Cappo de Monti. Oh, there were some fine things. Old English furniture, and some beautiful French.'

'Shall we make you an antique dealer, Simeon?'

'I don't know. I should not like to commit myself, Father. You know I've not seen very much of other professions. You don't want to know immediately, do you?'

'No, I think that I can give you a few days to think it over.'

Simeon glanced at his father's face. 'You're making fun,' he said contentedly.

Emmanuel sat that afternoon and talked with his mother. Without trying to make his father seem harsh or lacking in sympathy, he explained how impossible it was that he should remain at Ordingly.

'You see, darling, I did try it before,' he said, 'when Simeon was a baby. It didn't work then, and it won't work now. My father and I have both grown too set in our own ways. Then again, he still looks on me as a boy, or at least a very young man. Our wills would clash continually.'

'But Emmanuel, what are you going to do?' He could hear the distress in her voice.

'Join the Army.'

'Then Simeon can stay here, surely; and surely you can come home, for it is your home, when you have leave?'

He shook his head. 'I don't think so. A visit of a few days would be sufficient for—for everyone except you, bless you. I can't leave my son here, where Julian would continually be sneering at his father, and drawing comparisons between Simeon—the Italian, and Max—the complete Britisher!'

'Emmanuel, my dear, don't be so bitter against Julian! I can't bear to hear it. He doesn't *mean* to be unkind.'

'On the contrary, that is just what he does mean to be!'

She held out her hand and he took it in his, he saw that her eyes were filled with tears. In some way her unhappiness made her look younger, as he had known her years ago, when she had come out to Italy to bring him home again to Ordingly.

'Oh, Emmanuel, what a mess it all is! It ought to have all been quite perfect. I married the nicest man in the world when I married Max. I have three wonderful sons, and I love them all. Where have things gone wrong, and why? I puzzle about it so often, and no amount of thinking seems to solve the problem. Max knows it too, that is what is making him an old man. Do you remember Ordingly as it used to be? The fun, the dinners and dances, the young people who came in and out all the time? Old Emmanuel living here like a king who has abdicated in favour of his son, and only issuing from retirement at long intervals. Those were "occasions", when he used to come down and meet his guests. He kept us together. Since he died we've—disintegrated in some strange way. There isn't so much money—not that it matters, we shall always have sufficient. What does matter is that there isn't so much—happiness, so much *family*. The glory and the grandeur that once meant The House of Gollantz are fading. It was grand—in the real and best sense—once upon a time.

'I don't often talk about these things, it's funny how I have always been able to talk to you, my dear. More than either to Julian or Bill.'

'Yet you love Julian best,' Emmanuel said gently.

She sighed. 'Do I? Yes, I suppose I do; or perhaps I loved best the Julian I hoped he might be. I wanted him to be big, to make a name as a man who was not only clever but— great. I ought not to blame him, it isn't his fault that he had to give up his career; what I do blame him for is that he might still have kept the quality of being—*great*.

'He's allowed himself to grow small, and—yes—petty. He is envious, envious of you, of Bill, and yet he does nothing to make himself enviable. Emmanuel, am I disloyal to talk to you like this? Ought I to keep it all shut away? Perhaps I'm tired of pretending. I pretend to Max, to Julian, to everyone that Angela Gollantz is a very happy woman. I'm a very good actress!

'It's strange how bitterness seems to be able to affect a whole family, even to spread to the friends and relations of the family. It's a sort of disillusionment, of rating everything at its lowest possible value. Poor old Bill Masters—disgruntled expresses him best; my dear Charles Wilmot, who used to be so gay, such an exquisite, has grown sour; even my poor Max is tired and sick of most things—except me! Viva has grown hard—oh, I think that she still loves "Toby" —but it's "after her fashion". Julian, and you, no, you're not bitter but you're harder, and there's a kind of queer resignation about you. Maybe we reached our height with Old Emmanuel, and now we're beginning to decline.' Then, with sudden energy, which reminded Emmanuel of what she had been long ago, she demanded, 'What on earth am I talking like this for! It's all so understandable! This war, which has been hanging over our heads for so many years—why, we scarcely had time to get over the last war before this threatened us. Of course, we shall all get right again—one day. We must, we shall! Ring for Tucker and we'll have a cocktail, even if Max does disapprove of them!'

7

For nearly a week Emmanuel had worried and tried to make plans. The tension between himself and Julian had grown; last night during dinner he had thought that it must snap, that his control must break. He had tried to remember that he had learnt how to keep his temper and regain his dignity with such men as Palumba, Barach, and Gualtieri; he had been taught that it was unpardonable to indulge in recriminations and vituperations before women—he must remember that his mother and Amanda were present. He had watched Julian's smiling face, had listened to his insolent tone, and been conscious that Julian was enjoying himself tremendously.

'Queer,' Julian had said, 'that you still have difficulty with the letter "r". Gives you almost a Germanic tone, eh?'

Angela said, 'I like it. Emmanuel gets it from his grandfather.'

'Ah yes, I remember—vaguely.'

'You weren't so very young when he died,' Emmanuel said.

For a second Julian's face changed, his lips tightened, his eyes looked suddenly nervous. Emmanuel thought, 'I remember too—that Julian is terrified of death or illness. He can't bear, even now, to think of the time when Old Emmanuel died!'

Julian recovered himself. 'What will happen to all your Wop friends when Italy begins to fight? How will you feel, if you're in the Army?'

'Candidly, I don't believe that Italy will fight.'

'Inside information?'

'None.'

'Ah, not that it will make much difference on which side they fight. They'd be a greater liability than asset for the side they were fighting for.'

As if making a great effort to enter the conversation, Max said, 'I heard, in the last war, that some of them fought very well. Their engineering feats were stupendous, I believe.'

'Really, sir,' Julian smiled courteously, 'I don't think that opinion was shared by many soldiers who were actually on the same front as the Wops.'

Max said, suddenly testy, 'I dislike these nicknames for foreigners. It's undignified! Jerries. Heinies, Wops and the like! Pah!'

Now, tonight Emmanuel was going down to dinner able to tell them that he had made his plans, and that he was leaving Ordingly as soon as possible. He had told his mother that he must go; she had listened, sighed, and cried a little, but he was certain that she felt considerable relief.

Only that morning he had called at the Savoy to greet the Mancinis. The sight of Iva, lovely, generous, with her exclamations, and her obvious delight at seeing him, had induced Emmanuel to confide in her and her husband.

Iva had cried, 'The so-dear little Simeon. If you enter the Army, and Paolo also, then Simeon will come to me. I shall have a nice little house, a nice maid—two nice maids, and a man-servant to keep away burglars, and Simeon will go to the school every day.'

Paolo said, 'To school for part of the day, angel, and be spoilt by you for the rest.'

She was indignant, she told him that he was heartless, that he was unwilling to help his friend. 'Don't you remember,' she asked, 'that but for Emmanuel Gollantz you might not be married to me at this moment! Ungrateful one that you are!'

Paolo Mancini might have had an Italian father, but he was the son of a Yorkshire mother, and his practicality asserted itself.

'Listen, Emmanuel,' he said, 'the fact is that for days you've been worrying over this business, and you've got more and more fogged and puzzled every day. Prima Donnas are wonderful people, Iva is the most wonderful of them all, but they are not sufficiently placid for young children. Simeon wants some kind, elderly woman. I'd suggest sending him to my own mother, only she's growing old, and I don't believe in children living with very old folks, however kind they are. Don't you know a really kindly, elderly woman?'

Emmanuel frowned, then his face cleared. 'Paolo, I believe you've given me the very idea! Iva, thank you—

thank you both. When you have your house may Simeon come and see you on half-holidays? Sing to him sometimes, won't you? Paolo, let's try to get into the same regiment, shall we? There, I must go and begin to put Paolo's ideas into action.'

He went to the Bond Street Gallery, and sought out Hannah Rosenfelt; she greeted him warmly, begging him to sit down and talk to her.

'That is exactly what I have come to do,' Emmanuel said.

'Then you come at the right time. Sir Max left early to go to value some antiques for the Red Cross. Oh, how people give! With both hands! Your father is giving so much too. T'is a generous man. Now, what was it you wanted to ask me?'

He sat smiling at her, looking, she thought, tired and older than he should have done. She had always loved him, he had awakened all the maternity in her. She was completely loyal to Max Gollantz, but the whole strength of her love and devotion was given to Emmanuel.

'Tell me first. Do you still live in your house at Northwood?'

She stared at him through her strong glasses. 'Still live there? For the moment, but I am tired of it. To tell you the truth, I am not so young as I was once, and I have grown to dislike the journey backwards and forwards to London. Sometimes,' she leaned forward and spoke softly, 'I think that I should like to retire. I have saved, and I have worked for a long time. I have known four generations of Gollantzes. I should like to have time to read, to hear music, to see plays—I love the theatre! But why do you ask me t'is, Emmanuel?'

'Because, Hannah, I am going into the Army. I am going to a recruiting office tomorrow. I wanted someone to take care of my son. My friend, Paolo Mancini, told me that I wanted—someone like you. So here I am to ask.'

She chuckled. 'Someone like me, eh? Old, fat, not what is called—a lady. An old Jewish woman!' Then more seriously, 'And you wish me to stay at Northwood to make a home for Simeon? Why, of course. There is no need to ask.'

'No, no. I'll get a house for you, in town here. Or an apartment—a flat, as you like. You must go on working as long as you wish, not a moment longer. Have you a servant? If not I will arr-r-range for one.'

'My old Rachel would die! Rachel is the best cook in England, clean and kind and—oh, dear, so *froome*! No, no, she must come with me, we have grown to be as Ruth and Naomi.'

He spoke, and Hannah heard all the old eagerness in his voice.

'Whatever you wish, Hannah—wherever you wish. All that I ask is that you will take my boy to live with you, and bring him up in your own way.' Then suddenly his voice lost its eagerness and became very grave. 'But, Hannah, no hate. Not hate against anyone. Against cruelty, dishonesty, brutality—yes. But teach him to know that there is no nation under the sun which is one hundred per cent evil. There may be nations which are easily led, which have turned towards that which is bad, wicked, criminal. A proclivity towards evil, if you like—but in all nations there must be potentialities for good. Am I asking too much? Will it be upsetting your life to have a small boy living with you, possibly making a noise, asking for this and that, chattering when you wish to be quiet? If so—please tell me, and I shall understand.'

Hannah leaned forward and laid her fat hand with swollen veins on his.

'Emmanuel, I could wish for nothing better. Always I have loved you, longed to be able to help you in some way or another. Now—I have been patient for many years—the chance has come. Your son shall be given the best. By that I do not mean only food, warmth, attention; I mean that all t'ose t'ings which I have learned from your grandfather, from your father, shall be passed on to him. They have loved beauty, and I shall teach him to love it too.' Then as if she gave herself a mental shake, her voice changed and became entirely practical. 'Now, the question of a house. We must decide if it shall be a house or an apartment. Give me three days, Emmanuel, and I shall have propositions to put before you.'

He went back to Ordingly that night content and infinitely relieved.

At dinner Angela smiled at him. 'Emmanuel, I believe

75

that you have some marvellous secret! You look so . . . content. Tell us.'

He answered, 'Tomorrow I shall go to the recruiting office, and hope that the authorities will find some use for me. I have arr-ranged to take a small house, where Simeon will live with Hannah Rosenfelt while I am in the Army. She is very pleased about it—and so am I.'

Julian, his glass half-way to his lips, said, 'What! Your son to live with old Hannah! My God, can't you ever come home without disgracing us in some way!'

Angela, startled and distressed, cried, 'Julian, I will not allow you to speak in that way to your brother. He has never disgraced us, nor anyone else—never!'

Emmanuel felt that they were all talking at once. Max asking for explanations, Angela expostulating, Julian growing vituperative, while he, himself, sat there allowing the storm to beat round and about him, feeling curiously detached and apart from it all. Amanda, wide-eyed, listened, turning her eyes from one to another.

'To send your son to live with Hannah Rosenfelt—one of the firm's servants!' Julian stormed.

Angela said, 'Hannah is an admirable woman. Perhaps it may seem . . .'

Max cut in, cold and apparently impartial, 'I should like to have your explanation, Emmanuel, as to why you do not wish to leave your son here—the obvious place in which to leave him.'

Emmanuel pushed his fruit-plate away from him. His face was white, and Angela, watching him, thought, 'My poor Emmanuel, life hasn't been very kind to him after all!' He spoke slowly, as if he chose his words with tremendous care.

'I shall be going away,' he said. 'I want some place where I can come when I have leave. Some place where I can be with my son. Some place where I know that he will be happy.'

'But, darling,' Angela said impulsively, 'surely he could be happy at Ordingly—with us?'

He turned his dark eyes towards her. 'No, Mother, I don't see him being ver-ry happy here. With you, with my father —yes, but there are other influences with which we must r-reckon.'

76

Julian cried, 'Upon my word!'

Emmanuel nodded. 'Yes—you, Julian. You and your son would conspire to make him feel—different, a stranger, a foreigner. I won't risk that. With Hannah he will be tr-reated kindly, given a home. A *home*. Now, I shall ask you to excuse me.' With his strange touch of ceremony, he bowed to his mother and walked out of the room.

The night, when he passed out into the garden, was dark and softly damp; there was no chill in the air, only a gentle humidity. Emmanuel stood, his hands clasped behind him, breathing the air, conscious that it held sweetness and the promise of spring. He was shaking a little, the scene in the dining-room had unnerved him. He still adored his mother, but he realised that, although she had always tried to be just to him, she 'belonged' to Ordingly. With the love which she felt for the place had come an almost inordinate respect for its tradition and conventions. Max had always tried to be just and fair, but he had never understood his eldest son, and—Emmanuel frowned—possibly the fact that he had once dealt very harshly with him still rankled in Max Gollantz's mind. Your completely upright, just man was like that. His own mistakes made him almost dislike the person most concerned with the results of those errors of judgment.

Emmanuel was not conscious of any sense of actual resentment. He had known from the first that he would never 'fit into' the life at Ordingly. He ought never to have come here. As a visitor, he would have been welcomed, entertained, and even Julian might have tolerated him. His mistake had been that he assumed that Ordingly would be his home and Simeon's. Julian had resented that from the outset, and Julian—Emmanuel thought with sudden bitterness—was the person who coloured the atmosphere of the place.

He paced slowly up and down the terrace in front of the house, trying to recover his composure. The night was doing its work, the quietness and stillness reached his overwrought nerves, and already he felt that his heart had ceased hammering against his ribs. He laughed softly. What nonsense it all was! He had allowed himself to be disturbed, hurt, to grow angry—and why? This was nothing new, this was something which in his inner consciousness he had

77

expected. He must make a life for Simeon—impossible to imagine the boy growing up in an atmosphere of criticism and disapprobation. He had never known anything except kindness and affection, and to think of his being subjected to Julian's sneers and the grins of young Max was intolerable.

From time to time he would meet his grandfather and grandmother. He would be a little restrained, and very careful to speak almost painfully correct English; he would watch, too, that he did not gesticulate unduly. When he left, Max Gollantz would sigh and give it as his opinion that Simeon was 'a very nice little fellow', and Angela would say with slightly over-done enthusiasm, 'Simeon's a darling! I adore him!'—and that would be that!

No, far better that he should live with Hannah. Hannah, who never spoke bitterly, who lived a life which might be a little restricted, but which was filled with kindness and the love of beauty. Emmanuel turned back to the house. There were two cars standing before the big front entrance. Involuntarily he frowned. Who had come visiting at this hour? He was in no mood for meeting strangers.

The hall was filled with voices, and Julian stood in the doorway of the drawing-room, with that slightly malicious smile on his lips which boded no good to anyone. As Emmanuel entered, Julian cried, 'Here he is, Viva.'

The woman turned, and said, 'Emmanuel! How nice to see you!'

A second later he was holding the hand of his first wife, and saying how delightful it was to see her.

She had changed, grown harder, her hair was lighter, her nails shone brilliantly scarlet, her eyelashes were artificially darkened and stiffened, her lips like a red wound. Even her voice seemed to have grown a little metallic, he fancied that it was pitched higher than it used to be.

'This is nice, Emmanuel,' she said, and meeting her eyes—in spite of all the artificiality and over-stressed 'make-up'—he thought, 'She's really the same—terribly kind and essentially honest.'

'How is Toby?' he asked. Damn it, he'd show Julian that he could carry off a difficult situation as well as anyone.

'Darling, he's at some awful place in France. I've sent him

78

out everything warm that I can find, think of, or imagine, but he says that he is still dying of cold! Imagine my poor little Toby shivering in a trench—and he does so love his comfort!'

Emmanuel said, 'It's quite obvious that the war needs reorganising.'

Viva flashed a smile round the group. 'There, isn't he sweet! I never knew anyone—no, not even Toby—so sympathetic as Emmanuel. Oh, Emmanuel—you must know almost the nicest woman in the world. Vivian—this is our'—again that brilliant smile which embraced everyone—'*our* beloved Emmanuel Gollantz. Vivian Mallet, Emmanuel.'

A woman even taller than Viva Tatten, with dark hair, and a very white skin. Her eyes, large and a very definite grey, met his squarely. When she said, 'How do you do, Mr. Gollantz?' her voice was unexpectedly deep and full.

'Not loud,' Emmanuel thought, 'but full, with a great deal of power behind it.'

A laugh from Julian made them turn. He was standing in the doorway, slim and elegant, his eyes dancing with amusement. Viva swung round scowling. Emmanuel thought again, 'I'd forgotten that she was Viva Heriot, and has the celebrated Heriot temper!'

'Something amusing you, Julian?' she asked.

He smiled. 'The whole scene—and the unstinted praise—given by you!'

Her scowl persisted. 'Not pretty and not clever. You're growing stale, Julian. You could have said something much more biting than that five years ago. I say, can't we go in and sit down, or do we have to hang about in the hall? Oh, and, Emmanuel, here are Freddie Southbroke and Gregory Wilmot. Now—let's go into the warmth!'

Emmanuel followed them. The tall Vivian Mallet, Viva and the two young men. Angela and Max had disappeared, so had Amanda. Julian lounged against the mantelpiece and surveyed them all with unfriendly, critical eyes.

Viva said, 'Aren't you going to offer us a drink? Ordingly isn't living up to its hospitable tradition!'

Julian nodded towards the bell. 'Ring, will you, Emmanuel?'

As they poured out their drinks, chattered and laughed,

Emmanuel felt that they were people from a world of which he knew nothing. They spoke with such certainty, they knew everyone, they had the latest news of everything. Southbroke, it appeared, was in the R.A.F., but, to Emmanuel, it seemed that Viva knew as much about this and that type of 'plane as he did. Wilmot was at the Foreign Office; Viva said, 'He speaks six languages perfectly!'

Wilmot corrected her. 'Seven, and two incorrectly but fluently.'

'Yes, but the two are ones nobody has ever heard of—they don't count.'

'They might—when the places to which they belong are heard of. There are going to be a whole lot of places put on the map before this war's over.'

'And taken off the map,' Southbroke added.

Julian smothered a yawn. 'If you'll forgive me, I'll get along.'

Viva said, 'That's all right, Emmanuel will see us out.'

They stayed a long time, or it seemed a long time to Emmanuel, who was tired and wanted to be alone to work out some of his ideas regarding the future.

Viva asked, 'What are you going to do, Emmanuel? I mean—in the war?'

'I don't know. Paolo Mancini and I thought that we'd try to enlist together. Only,' rather ruefully, 'he's considerably younger than I am.'

'Not as Tommies!' There was horror in her voice.

He smiled. 'I don't see what else . . .'

'My dear, it's criminal, with your abilities, languages. Don't be silly! Greg, can't you do something?'

They argued over his future; it must be the Air Force, it must be Intelligence, it ought to be this or that. They were all so certain about everything. Only Vivian Mallet spoke very little, and when she spoke Emmanuel knew that her deep, quiet voice came as a sudden relief. Viva was a darling; no doubt the two men were first-rate people, but how they chattered! It was difficult to conceal his relief when Viva said that they must go.

'Come and see me, Emmanuel,' she said; 'I live in that new block of flats in Park Lane. Comfortable and incredibly vulgar!'

They drove back to London as fast as they dared; they all went to Viva's flat, shouting with laughter at the gold and peacock-blue decorations in the hall, and the ornate lift. Her own flat was modern to the last degree.

Viva screamed. 'Isn't it *awful*! If you'd seen the lovely house I had with Emmanuel! That was perfect.'

Southbroke asked, 'You were married to him, weren't you?'

She nodded. 'Yes—he let me divorce him when I wanted to marry Toby.'

'Nice chap,' Wilmot commented; 'bit on the dull side, eh?'

'Dull!' She squirted soda into a glass which held whisky. 'Dull! There never was a more wonderful man in the world than Emmanuel.'

'I say,' Southbroke smiled, 'what would Toby say if he were here and heard you say that!'

She turned on him, her eyes furious. 'Don't be so damned common!'

'Sorry, Viva.'

When the two men left, Viva sat talking until very late with Vivian Mallet. Vivian had never seen her so quiet, so thoughtful.

'There's something wrong with Emmanuel,' she said. 'I expect that it's Julian again. How I detest that man! He's made trouble for Emmanuel all his life, and he'll go on doing it. And,' with anger in her voice, 'neither Max or Angela can see it!'

'You're still very fond of him?' Vivian asked.

'I always shall be. Oh, don't think that I'd leave Toby for anyone. Toby and I suit each other—completely. We're both half-wits. But Emmanuel . . . he's finer clay than we are, or ever could be. He's not had a great deal of happiness, except for the time when he was married to Juliet Forbes. Even when he married me, it was only because I caught him on the re-bound. He thought that he'd lost her. But afterwards he went back to her. Then she died. Oh, Lord, what a mess life can be!' She laughed. 'How he'd loathe this room! He'd stand in the doorway and raise his eyebrows—just a fraction. Neo-Tottenham Court Road! That's what he'd ticket it. And . . . he'd be right. It's awful—it's expensively cheap—like most things in this rotten world.'

Vivian said quietly, 'Emmanuel Gollantz seems to have put you out of conceit with most things tonight.'

'Maybe that was the trouble. I couldn't live up to his standard.'

'Which was . . . ?'

'Which *is*—only the best.'

Book Two

8

Bill Gollantz lay back in the big chair in his brother's sitting-room in Heber Square. He looked haggard and very thin, and his fingers, as they filled his pipe, were not quite steady.

Emmanuel watched him gravely. Bill looked up, met his eyes and smiled.

'Queer to see you, the exquisite of the family, wearing those awful boots, and that frightful tunic that doesn't fit at the neck! Still, you don't look half as awful as I did when we landed. Gosh, I wasn't even decent!'

'Do you want to talk about it?' Emmanuel asked.

'Not much. The papers can tell you all about it so much better than ever I could. Frankly, looking back on it, it all seems a bit boring. I've told it all to Father and Mother. She cried, he cleared his throat and tried to look as if it didn't affect him in the least.' Bill laughed suddenly, a queer bark of a laugh which held little or no sound of amusement. 'Julian was sick as hell.'

'Julian was? What on earth has it got to do with him?'

'His usual trouble. The green-eyed demon jealousy.'

'But even then I don't see . . .'

Bill grinned, his pleasant rather snub-nosed face alight with sudden amusement. Even then, Emmanuel thought, he didn't laugh. Probably men who had been on the beaches of Dunkirk had almost forgotten how to laugh.

'Don't you ever read the paper?' he asked with exaggerated patience; 'don't you ever look at the *Sketch*, or the *Mirror*? No, you poor benighted mutt, you read *The Times*! Always have done, always will do. That's how you come to miss the really important bits of news. Allow me to tell you, ignorant Corp. that you are, that during the picnic at Dunkirk someone, who must have had precious little to do, noticed a certain officer—and, of course, gent—behaving like a perfect bloody little hero. You know, doing all the things they do in books! Well, that little hero was none other than Handsome Bill Gollantz!'

Emmanuel sat upright. 'My dear chap, how splendid! Not that I'm surprised. Tell me, what did you actually do?'

'In strict confidence,' Bill answered, 'I had a flask of good French cognac, and some Balkan Sobranis. A Brass Hat passed, noted the flask and the Balkans, and . . . well, I said, "Your need is greater than mine, sir!" Curse him, he scoffed the lot. Had to make amends, and so—one morning soon H.M. wants to see me at Buck House or elsewhere. That's why Julian wasn't enjoying himself last night.'

'All lies, except the last part,' Emmanuel commented. 'I'm awfully glad, Bill. Let me find some cognac to replace that which was scoffed by the Brass Hat.' He rose and went out of the room, his heavy boots sounding strangely out of place on the beautifully kept parquet floor.

Bill lay back in the comfortable chair and sighed contentedly. Nice place Emmanuel had made of this little house. A friendly, welcoming place, with a grand atmosphere. It must seem strangely small after those huge rooms in his *appartement* in Milan. He never spoke about his life in Italy; only when anyone mentioned the probability that Italy might fight did he answer, 'I don't think for one moment that she will.'

Bill, his eyes half closed, wondered vaguely what it must feel like to Emmanuel to know that he might have to fight—and, if possible, kill—men who had been his closest friends. The queer, pleasant little Guido for example, Count Boccalini—he'd be too old to fight—Tolini and the rest of the people he had met when visiting Emmanuel in Milan.

Queer, complicated life Emmanuel had led. Julian always against him, then what amounted to banishment, marriage that went wrong, divorce, marriage again, and that—and, Bill suspected, his brother's happiness—ended by death. Not that Emmanuel was a pathetic figure. He was almost invariably gay—in his own rather quiet fashion—he knew plenty of people; when he came on leave the little house was invariably filled with friends.

The boy was a nice chap too. He thought that Emmanuel

86

had been wise to get him a private tutor before sending him to a public school. The boy wasn't quite English somehow. He was given to using his hands too much, gesticulating, and growing wildly excited over small things. He didn't speak English perfectly yet, used queer turns of phrase, and was apt to slip back into Italian when he couldn't find the word which he wanted in English.

The door opened and Emmanuel came back, carrying a decanter and glasses on a tray.

'Here is your cognac, and without wishing to extol my own drinks, better stuff than your general took from you.'

'No soda?' Bill asked.

Emmanuel, in spite of his queer, badly fitting battledress, looked suddenly very like his grandfather.

'My poor Bill,' he said, 'I shall be forced to think that the sights of Dunkirk have affected your brain. This is a Fine of 1847, "Comte de Béarn". One does not put soda with such a brandy. But if you wish I can give you something which will not be—offended by soda. Yes?'

Bill said, 'No, give me a mouthful of that, and I'll have an honest-to-God-brandy-and-soda afterwards.'

His brother replied, 'A mouthful! Nothing of the kind! About twenty sips, and please dr-rink it, for the glass is already warmed. Later you want—a br-randy-and-soda! Small wonder that you are referr-ed to as the brutal and licentious soldiery! There—and you ought to drink that upon your knees.'

During that evening, Bill watched his elder brother constantly. Changed into civilian clothes, Emmanuel looked like himself again.

Simeon, coming into the room, cried, 'Papa, how nice to see you without those horrible clothes! Oh, and, Bill, did you see his boots? They weighed a ton . . . but literally—a ton!'

How Emmanuel contrived to make an atmosphere which was acceptable to him! He had taken this small Georgian house and decorated it in accordance with his own faultless taste. He had installed Hannah Rosenfelt and her old servant Rachel. Dinner was served in the tiny dining-room, a dinner which Bill—who was a healthy and often a hungry young man—knew to be exquisite, but could have wished to be slightly more substantial. True the cream soup was excellent, the turnedos delicious. Emmanuel murmured, 'Rachel has mastered the art of Turnedos Rossini perfectly!' A cheese soufflé which was light as a feather; again Emmanuel said, in extenuation, 'Very good, I think—for what it is. Good cheese, in these days, is not easy to get.'

Yet, Bill thought, 'Although he will spend hours discussing a dinner, and later eat it with the greatest possible enjoyment, he is content to take what comes when it's necessary. I don't mind betting that no one in camp or barracks grumbles less than my brother.'

'Bit different from the Beaches,' Bill said, and grinned.

Simeon begged, 'Tell us about it, Bill, please.'

'Think of the nastiest thing you have ever known, multiply it by a thousand, add every kind of discomfort you can imagine, and constant tummy pains from sheer fright— that's Dunkirk. And yet, here, Emmanuel, we might still be living in the piping times of peace.'

Emmanuel raised his eyebrows. 'I hope that, in those times, I should have given you a better dinner, Bill.'

'Couldn't have done, and this wine—it's a marvel. Then the glass, linen, silver! No, you do yourself very well.'

'I do myself very well,' his brother repeated. 'There is nothing used wastefully here, the household bills are miracles of economy. As for silver, linen and the rest—well, I have them and why not use them? Now, I will make the coffee.'

Simeon went off to bed, and the brothers were left alone in the little sitting-room, drinking the coffee which Emmanuel had made.

'Care to go out, Bill?'

'No, thanks, I'd rather stay here. Got room to put me up?'

'Of course. Bill, I don't want to seem either melancholy or depressing, but, in the event of anything happening to me, can I rely upon you to look after Simeon? I spoke to Charles about it, and he's drawn up something—subject, of course, to your approval.'

'I'd do anything I could.'

One of Emmanuel's sudden smiles made his face look years younger.

'I knew that would be your answer. Thanks, Bill.'

Almost without warning, it seemed to Bill, the room was filled with people. The bell rang, Emmanuel called to Rachel, 'I will answer it.' Bill heard voices in the little hall, and then the crowd entered. Viva Tatten, shrill-voiced, saying, 'Bill—the hero! Lovely to see you! Look, I've brought Mother round. Nothing except the thought that you might recount the horrors of Dunkirk would have enticed her out at night. She hates the dark.'

Beatrice Heriot, one-time Gaiety girl, swept forward, her silks rustling, her jewellery rattling.

'Bill, me dear old thing. What a shockin' time you've had! I read some of the papers . . . me dear, they curdled me blood! Prevented me from sleepin'; yes, 'pon me word that's true. Give me a chair, Viva. Now, Bill, I want to hear all about it.'

He shook his head. 'Sorry, Auntie Bea. I remember nothing. Got a whack on the head from a piece of shell and —knew no more until I found myself walking into the Savoy —almost entirely nude.'

'Good God!' She shook her head with its elaborately dressed curls so that her long ear-rings rattled and swung. 'Feel any ill effects?'

'None, but my doctor warns me that I must not try to remember. It might be fatal if I did.'

'Tut, tut, imagine that! Hear that, Viva? Come here, you old ruffian. Come and greet yer god-son.'

Bill Masters limped forward. 'Hello, Bill. Glad to see you're back.'

'Thanks. sir. How are you?'

'Terrible. Life's not worth living in these days. Food's bad, this black-out nearly kills me. Let me sit down, Viva.' He sank into a chair, resting his lame leg on his stick. 'How d'you think the war's going? Badly, eh? Shocking muddle at Dunkirk. As usual nothing ready. Everything left to chance. If we pull through—and we shall pull through—it will be more by good luck than good management. Mark my words.'

Bill said, 'You make one feel glad and happy to be in the Army.'

Old Masters grunted. 'Doing your duty. That ought to give you a certain satisfaction.'

'Of course, and added to that your bright and cheery out-look makes life worth while.'

The old man grumbled, 'That's right, make fun of me.'

Viva said, 'I suspect that in private you make fun of your-self, old Bill. Now admit it!'

He grunted, and Bill thought, 'He's let old age catch up on him. He hates not being in the war; if he were he'd swear that everything was done, and was going wonderfully. Poor chap!'

Emmanuel stood by the piano, talking to Vivian Mallet. The sound of her deep, full voice soothed him. He found himself watching her hands, not very small, well kept, with sensitive fingers—fingers with spatulate ends.

Impulsively he said, 'You play?'

'The piano—yes. How did you know?'

He smiled. 'Pianist's hands. Are you going to play for us? It's a good piano.'

Something in his tone, when he said, 'It's a good piano,' touched her. He wasn't boasting, he was holding out the excellence of the instrument, as an additional inducement, to prevail upon her to do something which he wanted very much.

'But—the others?'

'Old Bill will adore it; Viva likes music too; Aunt Bea and Bill will listen quite attentively, provided you don't play a moment longer than they care for.' He smiled, and stepping forward opened the piano.

Old Masters grunted, 'Miss Mallet going to play, eh? Well, she did pretty well at the Wigmore Hall last week.'

Emmanuel said softly, 'Oh, you play professionally?'

'Just beginning—and beginning too late. I expect that I shall join the A.T.S.'

'No, no,' with greater urgency than she had heard in his voice, 'they'll ruin your hands. Couldn't you—couldn't you work for ENSA?—play for the troops, play for anyone, but —play.'

Vivian laughed. 'Wait until you've heard me.'

Lady Heriot shouted, 'Now, Viv—we're waitin'.'

Notes which fell liquidly, smoothly, melody which had ended almost before it began. The First Prelude. It ended, and Bill Masters stirred uneasily.

'Remember once when Angela, your mother—Bill—asked Gilbert to play it again. He said—so far as memory serves me—"No, you can't repeat perfection". You can't either.'

Vivian began to play again. Emmanuel was only conscious of the music, what it was he had no idea. It was sufficient that someone should be playing, filling the room with lovely sounds. He stood very still, thinking, 'Bill Masters and I, probably Aunt Bea—we all live in the past—we're ghosts. For ever looking back over our shoulders. The First Prelude—a summer evening when Gillie played and Juliet sang. The scent coming in from the garden. At intervals the cry of a bird going to sleep. It's always been like that—since then onwards. I'm always thinking, "This reminds me . . ." What's this—a little tinkling tune—it's a Minuet—whose, I can't remember. Ah! She's finished—it's over, and Aunt Bea is looking restive.' He said, 'I can't thank you sufficiently, Miss Mallet.'

Lady Heriot cried, 'This house gone dry, Manny? Cellar empty, or what's wrong? Bill and I can do with a drink.'

Emmanuel came forward, only his aunt called him 'Manny'; he might and did dislike it, but he never showed that he did.

'Whatever you like, darling.'

'Oh, mine's a B and S.' Turning to Masters she said, 'They tell me whisky's going to be short.'

Gloomily he answered, 'It was in the last war.'

'D'you know,' she continued, 'I can remember Tom Walls singin' something like this, "Now we're told that of whisky we're short, Scotsmen are somewhat alarmed at the thought, Though for the future supply is assured, What shall we do 'til the stuff is matured?" Damn' funny it was too. Thanks, Manny. Well, here's love.'

Viva had been saying very little; now she drew Emmanuel on one side. 'I want to talk to you. Have you heard anything about going abroad? No? Well, I should be ready for it. No, I can't tell you how or where I heard it. I *did* hear it, that's all I can say. Where? Oh, where would you be going? Candidly, I don't know. Would you hate it?'

He answered, speaking slowly, 'Yes, I hate it all. It's—too different. I'm getting used to it. I'm going to an O.C.T.U. very soon.'

Eagerly she asked, 'Would you like me to hurry that up? Then you might miss going overseas? I might be able to.'

'My dear, no and no and no! I want to take whatever is coming. Don't think that I'm being her-roic, Viva. I shall probably be the greatest coward, but—I couldn't slide out of it.'

'No,' shortly. 'I suppose you couldn't. All right, leave it at that.'

'It was kind of you even to think of it, Viva.'

'Oh, kind! Kind—nothing! Look, Mother wants to go— or is she merely indicating another brandy-and-soda?'

'I *think* another brandy-and-soda. Yes, Aunt Bea . . . *subito*!'

'*Subito,*' Masters said, 'that's Italian for "immediately", eh? You'll not have to speak Italian when Musso drags the Italians into the war! It 'ul be the finish of him, anyway, if he does.'

Mixing a drink for Lady Heriot, Emmanuel said, 'They won't fight. I had two letters this morning—one from Guido, the other from Boccalini, saying, "We shall never fight".'

With that queer coarseness which sometimes showed itself, Lady Heriot said, 'They'll do as they're damn-well told! They've sold their souls to the devil, and they'll need a blasted long spoon to sup with him, mark my words.'

Bill Gollantz was lounging half asleep in his chair, Viva was discussing some play with Bill Masters, only Vivian Mallet noticed how white Emmanuel's face had gone, and without speaking she walked to the piano and began to play again. The courageous Ninth Symphony of Beethoven. Emmanuel turned, the strain gone from his face.

He whispered, 'How did you know that this was what I— at least—needed just then?'

She smiled. 'It isn't right for a piano. I thought that I'd risk it. It's got such—stabilising powers.'

'Stability,' he repeated, 'it's not a beautiful word, and yet it's what we all want. Listen, my leave lasts until the twelfth. Will you dine with me one evening?'

'Here?'

'Wherever you wish but'—smiling—'there is a piano here.'

'I'm to play for my supper, eh?'—but her eyes were dancing.

'No, no, of course not.' How easy it was, Vivian thought, to embarrass him, and yet he looked to be a man of the world, very certain of himself. 'No, but it would be so very delightful to hear you play again.'

'Telephone to me, will you? Kensington 8872.'

'Any especial time?'

'Before nine or after five.'

'I will, and thank you.'

As they drove away, with Lady Heriot and Bill Masters on the back seat, Viva said softly to Vivian, 'I think that you rather like my Emmanuel, eh?'

Vivian laughed. 'Is he still your property?'

'No, and yet in one way he is. I learnt to understand him, and to do it pretty thoroughly. So well that I realised that we should never hit it off. He's too serious for me, too intent on what he's doing. I wanted to dance and rag about. Emmanuel has never "ragged" in his life.' She negotiated a difficult corner, swore gently, and then added, 'He's quite the best friend that I have—this Emmanuel. I'd never forgive anyone who hurt him.'

'Why should anyone wish to hurt him?' Vivian asked.

'Well, he rather asks for it, y'know. Queer, when I believe that he's really a hard-headed man in business. I always feel that he's so damned vulnerable. He's had a good many knocks, and maybe they've left him tender! You've met the other brother—Julian?'

'Yes, is he nice?'

'Just the world's complete swine and the apple of his mother's eye—of both her eyes! Julian Gollantz and my own brother are the two nastiest bits of work I've ever met. Walter, my brother, is dead, but I don't mind betting that he's still nasty.'

The next morning Emmanuel was called to the telephone and heard his mother's voice.

'This is a nice surprise with which to begin the day,' he said.

'That's sweet of you! Listen, darling, Bill's with you, isn't he? Your father wants to give a dinner to the Fighting Forces as represented by the Gollantz family. Yes, Julian's

93

got the job he wanted so badly. Oh, it's dreadfully "hush-hush", but it's something to do with intelligence. He's terribly excited. Went off to get uniforms and bits before the thing was really settled. So, may we call for you and Bill tonight and perhaps you'll give us a cocktail to begin the evening? Max hasn't seen your house—neither have I since it was really finished. At seven then! Lovely; good-bye, darling.'

Bill's comment when Emmanuel told him was, 'That means the Guvnor wants us all in uniform. Just a little bit of ostentation. Well, I suppose we must oblige. What a bore! My uniform's so beastly brand new! My old one! There wasn't an old one! There were a few dirty rags draping my manly form. And Julian's got his precious job, eh? Whew—won't he be mysterious and secret and terribly important.'

'Let's try to make a go of it,' Emmanuel said, 'to please Max and Angela.'

He did try; he brushed and pressed his rather shapeless battledress, scrubbed his hands into a state almost approaching normal, and when the cars drove up he and Bill grinned at each other.

'Enter the chap who is England's secret weapon,' Bill whispered. Max and Angela smiling, and obviously content to have their sons around them, Julian immaculate in uniform, and Amanda gazing at him with pride in her lovely eyes. Emmanuel busy with a cocktail-shaker said, 'Congratulations, Julian.'

'Thanks.'

Amanda said, 'I only hope that his health will stand up to it.'

Max frowned, his voice was irritable. 'My dear Amanda, of course it will. Don't look for trouble. Julian will, in all probability, be better than he has been for years.'

'Why, we'll just hope so.' She agreed doubtfully.

'Emmanuel, I want to see my grandson,' Angela said.

'Immediately, darling.' He opened the door and called, 'Simeon!'

The boy entered; he had grown and broadened since his arrival in England. Angela thought that his clothes might

94

have something to do with the change. Max watched him with satisfaction.

The boy's manners were good, possibly a shade too much 'heel-clicking' and 'hand-kissing'. Someone ought to tell him that English boys didn't kiss women's hands.

He shook hands with Julian. 'I say, Uncle Julian, don't you look . . .' he hesitated, 'look . . .'

Julian asked, 'Look—what exactly, Simeon?'

The boy still hesitated, staring at Julian, then said, 'Oh ; . . this word! *Leggiadro*—Papa. What is it?'

'Handsome, Simeon.'

'That's right—handsome.'

Julian flushed, but Bill knew that he was pleased and flattered. That fact made him even forget to give a slight frown at the foreign word. It was true enough, he did look handsome. His uniform became him far better than his brothers' became them. Bill was too short and stocky, Emmanuel looked strange and almost 'unfinished' in his rough suit. Julian, slim, and tall, his hair still very bright and golden, his skin clear and unlined. At the moment, throwing back his head and laughing at Simeon's unconcealed admiration, he looked far younger than either of his brothers.

'I'm delighted that I meet with your approval, Simeon.'

'But'—Simeon made one of his queer un-English gestures —'how could you fail to meet with the approval of every-one. Of course, when Papa—Father, I mean—has an officer's uniform he will look most admirable. At the moment—well,' he laughed, 'it is difficult for him to look elegant in those clothes!'

'I'm the only one who does not come in for commenda-tion,' Bill said.

Simeon flushed. 'Oh, Uncle Bill, your uniform will be enhanced by a medal for gallantry. You have already accomplished your act of glory, both my father and Uncle Julian have still to accomplish theirs.'

Some of the brightness died from Julian's face. Emmanuel noticed it and thought, 'Bill's right, he is jealous!'

'Not much chance of ribbons and the like for me, Simeon,' Julian warned him. 'I'm only an old crock; they've dug me up and given me a job, but there won't be much

95

glory, or gold, about it. I'm one of the less fortunate fellows.'

'You might land an O.B.E. or something of the kind,' Bill said roughly. 'Any old medal in a war! I say, isn't it time we were pushing off?'

9

The Savoy. Max had always gone to the Savoy for celebrations, and always would. When Bill or Amanda had suggested other, and possibly newer, hotels, Max always answered, 'No, no. The Savoy—for me. I know it, and it knows me. I'm too old to get to know the new places. Besides, they've such small dancing floors, and Angela likes to dance in comfort.'

Bill looked at the decorated table, watched the dignified waiter speaking to his father. Clever they were, these head waiters! They knew precisely the right manner to use, a kind of friendly deference. That smile, 'Ah, Sir Max, good evening'; and then a bow to Angela, 'And Lady Gollantz, this is a pleasure which you give us too seldom.'

Max had relaxed, his face had lost its usual gravity. He smiled. Was he remembering, Bill wondered, other dinners at the Savoy, when he and Angela were young, and was the memory very happy?

'I've brought my three sons, Charles,' he said, 'all serving.'

Charles beamed at them all in turn. 'Very nice,' he said, 'very nice indeed.'

'And now, the dinner which we arranged yesterday.'

They discussed the wine, there was a suggestion of cocktails, and Max frowned. 'Disgusting habit, Charles . . .' Then turning to the rest of his party, 'Do you want more cocktails?'

His wife said, 'Darling—quite firmly—yes.'

'Very well, Charles. Give me a sherry—dry.'

Emmanuel said, 'And for me also—dry.'

Decorated tables, a band playing, people laughing and talking gaily. Bill's mouth hardened. Didn't they *know*,

96

these people, what was happening? Had they forgotten so quickly the story of those ghastly days and nights on the Dunkirk beaches? And France? What did they know of France, with her badly equipped army, her outdated rifles, and her internal cancer eating away her strength, her faith and her honour? He shivered suddenly, and Julian asked if he were cold.

'Yes—that's it,' Bill said, 'cold—damned inexplicably cold.'

'Better dance with Amanda, that will warm you up.'

Bill nodded. 'Yes—dance with me, will you, 'Manda?'

They danced, Amanda chattered gaily. Wasn't it grand about darling Julian, what a success he was going to make! He was so happy too. As they passed the conductor, Bill caught a glance of recognition.

'Hello, Motley,' he said, 'nice to see you again.'

The immaculate man with his huge glasses stretched out a hand.

'Why, glad to know you're back, Bill. This is fine. I'd like it a lot if you'd have a drink with me during the evening— to celebrate your return. Wonderful show you all put up.'

'Come over to our table,' Bill said, 'love to see you.'

'Grand! I'll be pleased to.'

'Wonderful show you all put up!' Bill began to talk to Amanda, quietly and very quickly.

'Hear what he said? That's a nice man. It was a good show. The boats were a good show too. Those funny little boats. Anything that would float. Hundreds of 'em. There was a girl, with a rowing-boat. Came alone. Queer to watch them coming out. Cockle-shells that you'd not have taken out on the Serpentine! Gosh, how good they looked to us! Frightened—I know that I was. I kept saying, "O God, don't let Jerry sink any of the little boats." Somehow you wouldn't have felt so bad about liners, or big ocean-going ships. Those poor damned little boats. Yet—we laughed, you know. Oh, yes, screamed with laughter when anything unexpected happened. It's in retrospect you don't feel like laughing. This is all right—people danced the night before Waterloo—and we won that!—only we mustn't overdo it. There's more to it than this. Things aren't going right. 'Manda. Not us—but . . .' the music stopped and he stood looking at her, blinking his eyes, 'I've been talking a lot, haven't I? Sorry that you should have had to listen.'

She answered in her small, sweet voice, that always sounded faintly prim, 'I'll say that it was very interesting, Bill.'

He stared, then said, 'You're right—most interesting.'

At the table, Max was talking to Julian, while Angela, her elbows on the table, allowed her soup to grow cold while she spoke to Emmanuel.

The waiter brought the fish; she waved it away. 'I don't want any. Emmanuel, that's a dear little boy of yours. Don't you think that you ought to send him out of London.'

'Out of London, darling? Why?'

'The Germans may bomb London.'

'They might—but they might bomb anywhere.'

'The Government advises that children should be sent into the country. Max's school has evacuated to Cloften Castle in Yorkshire. Why not send Simeon away too?'

Emmanuel sighed, 'Poor little devil, just as he's settling down. It's hard luck on him, being moved about, making new contacts.'

'Yes, but harder if . . .'

He laid his hand on hers. 'Yes, yes. I'll arrange something before my leave is over. I promise.'

Doubtfully she said, 'He could come to Ordingly, you know.'

'No, angel, that's just what he couldn't do, and isn't going to do.'

'We should be good to him . . .'

'I know that, probably too good. No, he must meet other boys, we must turn him out to the proper and required pattern.'

'Don't be so bitter, Emmanuel.'

He shrugged his shoulders. 'Oh, bitter! I'm not really. Come and dance with me, we haven't danced together for years.'

The dinner ended, Max leaned back in his chair, and smiled at them all. He was relishing the content which had come to him. Bill—back safely from Dunkirk and soon to be decorated, Emmanuel going to an O.C.T.U. almost immediately—poor fellow, he looked rather dreadful in those

98

horrible clothes—and Julian having found work which he could do, work which gave him the right to wear a uniform. This might be Julian's chance, might mean the fulfilment of his hopes. A career might be waiting for him, something which would give him that interest in his life which had been lacking for so long. He had changed already; in spite of that slight limp of his he had danced with his wife, with his mother, and was now dancing—and doing it very well—with a particularly good-looking woman. The dance ended and Julian brought her back to the table.

'Mother, this is Cynthia Crawley, Cynthia—my mother. My father.'

As Emmanuel joined them with Amanda, he added, 'My wife, you know—and my elder brother, Corporal Gollantz.'

Amanda said, 'He isn't going to be a corporal for long, though ... Oh, Julian, come and dance this with me. It's one of our "special" tunes.'

Emmanuel turned to the handsome woman beside him. 'Would you care to dance this, Miss Crawley?'

'I'd rather miss this one, if you don't mind.'

She was a type which Emmanuel admired. Tall and dark, with hair which looked smooth and polished. There was an air of polish about her altogether. Her skin was very smooth and white, her hands, with long slim fingers, beautifully kept. Her voice was, perhaps, a little hard, but Emmanuel admitted that he was too critical about voices.

'You live in London, Mr. Gollantz?'

'I'm not stationed in London. I have a little house here. I installed my small son there, with an old friend of mine and of my family. Now,' he smiled ruefully, 'my mother advises me to send the boy away into the country. I find life full of complications in these days!'

'How old is he—your son?'

'Nearly thirteen.' He explained to her his difficulty in sending Simeon to a big public school; she listened, her chin propped on her hand, serious and attentive. Emmanuel ended with, 'And so you see that it is difficult to decide exactly—where to send him.'

'Send him to my father.'

'Your father? Has he a school then?'

She nodded. 'Indeed he has, and it is considered most

99

satisfactory. He likes teaching, enjoys it. His results are excellent, I believe.'

She told him her father, the Rev. Sir George Crawley, was installed in the family living, and found that Dimstoke Manor was too large, and that time fell heavily on his hands.

The parish was small, the stipend excellent; he had private means as well. The old place was adapted, improved, and the venture had been a great success.

'My father has first-class masters; the boys can ride, there is a swimming-pool, they have a good cricket pro., who also teaches golf. Only nine holes, but not at all bad.'

'How many boys?'

'Never more than twenty. Mind,' she laughed, 'it's an expensive school, Mr. Gollantz.'

'But I don't r-really mind, if it is a place where Simeon will be happy and learn well. Languages, these he must have. Might I go down and see the school? This will be far the best, I think.'

She thought what a good-looking man he was when his face brightened and his eyes lost their hint of melancholy.

'Come down with me tomorrow. It's only sixty miles. The train leaves from Paddington at 10.30.'

'Might I do that? Tomorrow. That will be admir-rable. Perhaps I might br-ring Simeon with me? I could see then if he felt that he would be happy with your father.'

'Why not?'

'Splendid!'

'Or, might it not be wiser to come alone for the first time, and then, if you like the place, bring your son down later?'

'Again—you're right. I shall be waiting at the station tomorrow. You have solved a difficult problem for me, if the school is as good as I am sure it is.'

Cynthia met his eyes, they were kind, and his gratitude was quite evident. Impulsively she said, 'But you're the kind of person one longs to solve problems for'; then, laughing, 'and what a terrible sentence for the daughter of a school-master interviewing a prospective client!'

The next morning he was down at Paddington very early; while he waited for Cynthia Crawley he bought papers and illustrated weeklies. Why, he didn't quite know, except that he had always bought them for women who were going on

100

train journeys, and he had come to regard a pile of maga-
zines and papers as being almost as necessary as a railway
ticket.

She came as the clocks marked the hour, her appearance
pleased Emmanuel. She wore plain, well-cut clothes, a small,
but very smart hat, and excellent shoes. She moved well,
gave her orders clearly and distinctly to the porter who
carried her luggage. When Emmanuel would have tipped
the man, she refused to allow him to do so.

'No, no—of course not. There you are, porter, and thank
you.'

Seated opposite to her, Emmanuel said, 'You're a very
independent woman, aren't you?'

'I suppose so. I've always done things for myself, made
my own plans, gone abroad alone. That doesn't prove that
I dislike being waited on—sometimes. Did you tell your son
that you were going to see a prospective school for him?'

'Yes indeed.' She noticed how his face brightened when
he spoke of Simeon. 'He was very much excited, and made
me promise to tell him all about it when I got back this
evening. He was a little nervous at first, because he was
afraid that it was a public school. But when I told him that
there were only twenty boys, his nervousness vanished. You
see, he has never been to boarding school before.'

She made him talk about Simeon, tell her of the boy's life
in Italy, of his friends. He added, 'I have always been afraid
of making mistakes with Simeon. It isn't very easy to bring
up a small boy. He was really only a baby when I lost his
beloved mother.'

'I thought that your brother Julian told me you married
Viva Heriot . . .' The moment she had spoken Cynthia knew
that she had blundered. Emmanuel's confidences ceased, the
momentary sadness, which had shown in his eyes when he
spoke of his wife, vanished. He looked older, harder, almost
forbidding.

'My brother was right, of course. Viva Heriot—Mrs.
Tatten—was my first wife. She divorced me—and I married
again.'

Cynthia said, 'I'm sorry, I didn't mean to make such a
stupid *gaffe*. Please forgive me.'

He bowed rather stiffly. 'Pray forget all about it.'

101

He passed the pile of journals over to her, took *The Times* and began to read. She felt irritated; how stupid to make such a fuss about so small a mistake! Of course, she should have been more careful, but she had offered an apology, and surely that ought to have been enough. For half an hour she turned over the pages of the illustrated papers, while Emmanuel remained hidden behind the sheets of *The Times*. Then Cynthia took out a cigarette, and asked him for a light. The newspaper was lowered, and he held out his lighter to her.

'Perhaps you will be patient with me, and allow me to explain. I was not annoyed because you mentioned Viva Tatten. She is a ver-ry good friend of mine, so is her husband, Toby. I grew angr-ry because my brother had been discussing me. Ah, please . . .' as she tried to protest, 'I know how much my br-rother dislikes me, and nothing will make me believe that he would say much to my cr-redit.'

'But, Mr. Gollantz, I honestly don't think that he said anything to your dis-credit.'

With a lift of his chin, as though he raised it above a high stock, Cynthia thought, he answered, 'Forgive me if I say that I r-resent the fact that my brother should discuss me at all.' Then turning to look out of the window, he said, 'How delightful the country looks. Here, among these trees and fields, it is difficult to remember that the countr-ry is at war.'

'You would prefer to forget it?'

'Ah, if it were ever possible—who wouldn't? You see, all my life I have loved and worked among beautiful things. I am an antique dealer, you know. When I first joined the Army, the ugliness of everything nearly killed me. Only the fact that I had with me my friend, Paolo Mancini, saved me from doing something—desper-rate.' He laughed. 'The ugly clothes, horrible boots—oh, I know that they are very good boots!—the food, and the hideous words men used! I am not thin-skinned . . .' he stopped; 'well, it may be that I *am* thin-skinned! The inanity of the swearing *bores* me. Always the same adjective—or at least one of three. I told Paolo that I would introduce a new word, a very bad swear-word. I said before everything *preso*. That is the past participle of the verb to take! I said, "Take this preso-ing bucket" or

102

"Give me that preso-ing brush." They asked me, "What's this 'preso', chum?" I pulled a face, "It's a frightful word, I said, "don't you know it? It's the worst old English swear there is." In a week they were all saying it—they said the other words as well, but "preso" became current coin.'

'But when you get your commission things will be better?'

'I think so.' He wriggled his toes in the thin shoes which he wore. 'Oh, the relief of wearing soft leather again, and smooth linen, and clothes which fit! You'll think that I am a Sybarite! If I am, we must blame my grandfather—the Founder of the House.'

'Tell me about him.'

For the rest of the journey he talked of Old Emmanuel. She listened to his stories, and comments, heard tales of the sale rooms, of his grandfather's friends—also of great dealers in pictures and antiques. As Emmanuel spoke, he painted a very clear picture for her of an old man who had been a great and outstanding figure. An impression of dignity, courage and complete integrity came to her. When he stopped, protesting that he must be boring her, she asked, 'And you're like him, aren't you?'

'They tell me so. In looks I may be—a little, not handsome as he was. There is a portrait of him, done for my grandmother when they first married, which makes Count d'Orsay look plain by comparison. Mentally, I have not his brain; in my business I have not his knowledge, neither have I his flair. No, you must believe that I am a very infer-rior copy of this astonishing man, Emmanuel Gollantz.'

He laughed. 'One thing about me is like him. I have difficulties with my "r's". I have tr-ried and tr-ried, and now I have stopped tr-rying!'

At Dimstoke station a car was waiting. Cynthia nodded to the chauffeur, 'Good morning, Hawkins, I'll drive. Get in the back, will you? How is my father?'

'Nicely, Miss Cynthia. Very taken up with some new plants 'as 'ave come this mornin'. Very taken up, 'e is.'

She drove well; Emmanuel leaned back and watched the landscape. Nice country, well wooded, and not too flat. Again the thought came to him, 'How far away, how incredible, the war seems!'

Cynthia turned the car in through a pair of tall, old iron

gates. 'There you are,' she said. 'Dimstoke School.'

Mellow red brick, a terrace where great stone urns held growing plants, a wide, smooth lawn, and a general air of care and constant attention. Emmanuel liked the place, liked George Crawley, and his evident pride in his school. Good class-rooms, well constructed and modern, were hidden by the house; they lay at the back and looked out on to the playing-fields.

'I like it,' he told Crawley, 'and I know that Simeon will like it. Twenty boys seems to me to be ideal.'

'Small classes, plenty of individual teaching, chance for the boys to develop their tastes and ideas. I hated my own school!—oh, I'm ready enough to grow sentimental over it now!—and made up my mind that one day I'd have a school which no reasonable lad *could* hate. Now, come along and we'll have a glass of sherry before Cynthia orders us to come to luncheon. Ask me any questions that occur to you. After luncheon we'll get Mrs. Rawson to show you the sick-bay, and all the rest of the place that comes under her rule.'

A big, dignified room, excellent sherry, followed by a good, if fairly simple, luncheon. Emmanuel knew that he was enjoying his visit. Cynthia drove him back to the station to catch his train.

'Good-bye, Mr. Gollantz. I hope that you really like Dimstoke.'

'I liked it tremendously. Next time you come to town do let me know. I *might* be on leave, and we could dance, if you cared to.'

'Of course. And I'll send you a note from time to time to tell you how your boy is getting on. Mrs. Rawson will do that too, but, as a "looker-on", someone who has no official position at all, I might be able to give you news that she missed.'

He held out his hand. 'That would be the ver-ry gr-reatest kindness. I should appreciate that more than I can say.'

'Good-bye, Mr. Gollantz.'

Simeon listened intently to all that Emmanuel told him. He was full of questions, and excited at the prospect of meeting boys of his own age, not only in school but out of it.

'Of course, Papa,' he explained, 'if you had still been at home, then I shouldn't have wanted to go so much. And I shall be very sorry to leave Hannah. But I shall be home for holidays, shan't I? And perhaps when you're on leave you'll come and see me.'

'Whenever it is possible I shall come.'

'I hope it will be possible very, very often.'

Hannah, sitting with him that evening, agreed that it was wise for Simeon to go to school.

'He's too well-behaved,' she insisted; 'time that he learned to make a noise, break a few window-panes, be less obedient. Oh, he'll come back a different boy—you'll see.'

'But do we want him so different?' Emmanuel asked. 'I'm very satisfied with him as he is.'

'It's not only what we want—it's what will make him best able to fight, make his way. He wants—hardening. That's been your trouble, Emmanuel, you never got hardened. Oh, you went to a public school, but you've always remained too vulnerable. As a little boy, I can never remember you being grubby, or smelling faintly of mice and stale apples. You never came to borrow money from me, never asked me to help you out of some scrape or other. Then you've gone on expecting other folks to be as upright and straight as you are. Of course you're disappointed—and when you're disappointed you get hurt and unhappy. If you had a streak of Julian in you, and he had a considerable streak of you in him—you'd be more content, and he'd be a nicer person than he ever will be.'

10

Emmanuel was completely occupied with taking Simeon shopping; he was determined that the boy should have everything which would make him feel content in his new environment. Twice he telephoned to Cynthia Crawley asking questions regarding Simeon's outfit. On both occasions she was charming, and apparently delighted to be helpful. On the third day she telephoned to him that she was coming up for the night, and would he come and dance.

Bill, hearing of the arrangement, raised his eyebrows.

'New for you, dancing and dining, eh?' he asked.

'I suppose it is. I've asked Iva Alfano and Paolo to join us. Care to come, Bill?'

'Sorry, I'm dining with Charles.'

Later, when Emmanuel was walking through Harrods with Simeon, he met Vivian Mallet. Only then did he remember that he had asked her to dine one evening, had promised to telephone and—had completely forgotten. He felt almost guilty, and in addition vaguely disturbed. Why had he forgotten? Not only because he had been busy with Simeon; there had been two evenings when he had done nothing but sit at home, talking to Hannah or Bill. He liked Vivian Mallet so much, when she had played to him he had realised how intensely he wanted to see her and talk to her. Her voice, her movements, her grey eyes, set so widely apart and meeting his so steadily, had delighted him. Yet for three days—more, four days—he had scarcely thought of her.

Tonight he was going to see Cynthia Crawley. Impulsively he asked Vivian to join them.

'I know that it is dreadfully short notice,' he admitted, 'but these things are always best when they are done quickly. Two very dear friends of mine are coming, won't you bring that nice fellow Wilmot? The idea of giving a party in London excites me. Please say that you will come.'

'I think that I should like to come very much.'

'Then—thank you, and the Dorchester at eight.'

Simeon said, 'How nice, Papa! She's a very nice woman, isn't she, Miss Mallet? All kinds of pleasant things are happening today. A letter this morning from Guido, his assurance that Italy is not going to fight—and now your nice party. Could I come, for a little while, do you think? I'd go home the moment you told me to, and I've scarcely seen the Alfano for weeks. Can I, Papa?'

Emmanuel said, 'Do you know, Simeon, I cannot find any good and valid reason why you should not add to the gaiety by gracing my party with your presence.'

Simeon giggled happily. 'Oh, I do think that you are most exquisitely amusing!'

The boy was bubbling with excitement when Cynthia Crawley arrived at the house. She looked magnificent, and Emmanuel felt a sense of satisfaction as he took her cloak from her and realised how handsome she was. She entered the room with him, and Simeon came forward to greet her.

She stared at the boy, and then turning to Emmanuel said, in a tone which was sharper than he expected, 'Is your son coming with us?'

'Indeed, yes,' Simeon cried: 'that is why—like Papa—I am wearing my smoking. Ah, I should have said dinner jacket!'

'I see . . . Yes, thank you,' in answer to Emmanuel's question, 'You will have a cocktail?'

'I am to dance also,' Simeon said; 'two of my dances are already arranged for. One with the Signora Iva Alfano, the other with Miss Vivian Mallet. I—what do you say?— booked them by telephone myself.'

Cynthia turned to Emmanuel. 'I didn't know that it was a party. I thought we were going to dine and dance.'

'But we are going to dine and dance,' he answered, smiling. 'Only, somehow, after you telephoned it developed into a party. Simeon and I have been quite excited about it all day.'

'Perhaps you will give me the honour of a dance, Miss Crawley?' Simeon asked.

She nodded carelessly. 'Very probably.'

Emmanuel said, 'Simeon, go and tell Hannah that you will be back here by ten o'clock. I'll send you home in a taxi.'

As the door closed, he said to Cynthia, 'What do you think of him?'

'He's a good-looking boy, isn't he? Well-mannered—it's a pity that his English is so stilted. I suppose with other boys he'll soon learn to speak—well—more colloquially. Do you often take him out to dance and dine?'

'No, that is why he is so delighted.' With sudden eagerness which made him seem younger, he added, 'I hope that you'll like him. It will make such a difference to him when he comes to Dimstoke if he knows you. That was why I wanted to bring him tonight.'

'Yes, I see. As a matter of fact I don't see a great deal of the boys, you know.' Then as she saw the light fade from his eyes, she said quickly, 'Of course, I'll see Simeon as often as I can. Didn't I promise to write to you about him!'

'Indeed, yes, and very gr-rateful I shall be.'

She laid her hand, very lightly, on his arm. 'I'm afraid that I must have sounded ungracious about your party tonight. Perhaps I was faintly disappointed. Very stupid of me—but forgive me all the same.'

Emmanuel smiled. 'If you were—to use your own word— ungracious, you have atoned most wonderfully by speaking as you have done now. I am more flattered than I can say. Ah, here is Simeon. Please will you see if the car which I ordered is there, Simeon?'

Cynthia watched Emmanuel greet his friends, wondering how the very English-looking young man came to have a name like Paolo Mancini, if the beautiful, but slightly over- blown, woman were his wife, and if so why she was intro- duced to her as 'Signora Alfano'. Was this the celebrated soprano? Who was Vivian Mallet, how well did Emmanuel know and like her? The man Wilmot was a recognisable type, cool, probably efficient and very sure of himself.

Simeon was begging for his dance. 'Carissima Alfano, will you please dance with me?'

She beamed at him. *'Vol scherzate!* No, I will speak Eng- lish! You are joking, Simeon. To dance with an old voman likea vot I em.'

'No, no, dearest Alfano. Please—it will give me such a . . .' he grinned, proud of a new word, 'kick!'

Paolo said, 'Be sure to dance very badly, Simeon, other- wise you will be putting my nose out of joint!'

Alfano answered, 'Paolo, what words! Who will touch your nozz?' She repeated slowly and painfully, 'Emmanuel, vot is nozz-outa-choint?'

Simeon had his three dances, and when Emmanuel said, 'Now, home, and get straight to bed,' he shook hands with everyone and bade them 'good night', going off smiling and content.

Alfano said, 'That boy is an angel!'

Vivian Mallet nodded. 'A darling. He tells me that you have had letters today from a particular friend of his.'

'Yes, our much-loved Guido,' Emmanuel answered.

Gregory Wilmot leaned forward. 'From Italy by any chance?'

'From Milan. Assuring me—if I needed the assurance— that Italy will not fight.'

108

'Do you believe that, Mr. Wilmot?' Cynthia asked.

'I don't think that I am giving anything away,' he answered, his eyes watching Emmanuel, and then turning quickly to Mancini, 'when I tell you that by tomorrow—the whole world will know that Italy is at war with England and France.'

The atmosphere changed; Cynthia felt the sudden tension. Mancini whispered, 'My God . . .'; she heard Iva Alfano draw a long sobbing breath, and press her hand over her heart; only Emmanuel did not move or speak. He continued to stare at Wilmot, his face white and very still. Cynthia thought, 'It looks like a mask!'

Wilmot added, 'Mussolini will make the announcement in Rome.'

Alfano said, her voice heavy with bitterness, 'Mussolini *will* make an announcement! *Dio*—the announcement came first from Berlin! *Il Duce del nostro Duce* has spoken!'

At last Emmanuel spoke. 'This is certain, Wilmot? Not merely rumour?'

'No, no,' he smiled; 'there will be a good many hotels short of waiters tomorrow night! Pah, it's disgusting, when France is so nearly down and out, when we ourselves have just sustained that frightful setback at Dunkirk. To choose this moment!'

Emmanuel said, his voice cold and temperate, 'But, in common fairness, surely admittedly war is all a disgusting business. Then, it is only natural to wait until your adversary is in the weakest position—then you attack. Isn't this natural?'

Wilmot said frigidly, 'That comment doesn't sound particularly good to me, Gollantz.'

'Gregory—please!' Vivian interjected.

He shook his head angrily, then turning to Mancini asked, 'Are you naturalised?'

'No—certainly not.'

'You realise where your precious Duce will have landed you, in common with others of your countrymen, don't you?'

Mancini smiled. 'But he never was *my* Duce! How can what he does affect my countrymen, please?'

Suavely Emmanuel said, 'You have made a mistake, Man-

109

cini is born British. Iva, dear, will you give me this dance?'

The singer stared at him with wide, tragic eyes, her lovely mouth quivered.

'*E tutto una sbagilo,*' she said. '*No lo credo.*'

Vivian whispered to Mancini, 'Poor woman. What did she say?'

'That it is all a mistake, that she does not believe it. I think it will be better if we go home, Emmanuel. Iva, come, my dearest.'

She nodded, 'Yes, that will be better.'

Emmanuel walked with them to the entrance; Iva was weeping without restraint; Wilmot lit a cigarette with elaborate unconcern.

Vivian turned to him. 'I'm ashamed of you, Gregory.'

'No need to be, my dear,' he answered coolly; 'there is such a thing as duty, y'know. I'm prepared to do mine. I don't say that I enjoy doing it, or should have chosen this way to do it. It's far better to warn these people . . .'

Cynthia, who had watched and listened intently, asked, 'These people—what do you mean, Mr. Wilmot?'

'I mean people who go about assuring everyone that the Italians won't fight, who boast of their letters from their "much-loved Guido", who talk Italian openly—who are fairly obviously pro-Italy, and to be pro-Italy means to be anti-Britain.'

'I see, and you think this of Mr. Gollantz?'

Half sulkily he answered, 'I think that it is kind to warn him.'

Vivian said quickly. 'My dear Gregory, I think that you are being well meaning and very, very stupid. Emmanuel Gollantz is in the Army, so is Mr. Mancini.'

He glanced at her sharply. 'Well—I'm at the F.O.'

She returned quietly, 'I said that they were in the Army.'

Emmanuel returned, he sat down and called to the waiter to bring him some iced water.

'Poor Iva,' he said gently, 'such a wonderful woman. It breaks my heart to see her so unhappy. And now I am going to ask a great favour. Will you come back to my house, and I will make coffee for you—or get anything else that you like—and might we'—he smiled—'have some music, do you think?'

Cynthia knew that she flushed with annoyance. For her the whole evening had been ruined. First the small boy brought with them, then the discovery that she and Emmanuel were not going to spend an evening *tête-à-tête,* and now, after that hysterical outburst by the Italian woman, they were to be invited back to Emmanuel's house to listen to music.

She had found Emmanuel very attractive; he had obviously enjoyed being with her, had made excuses to telephone to her, and had seemed delighted at the prospect of spending an evening with her. All her life she had been given her own way, she had gone where she pleased, done what she wished. Her mother had died when she was a child, and George Crawley was absorbed in his school, his parish and his garden. He had been only too delighted to see that Cynthia was independent, able to fend for herself, and make her own plans. From time to time various young men had come down to Dimstoke; Cynthia had ridden and motored with them, played golf, and gone up to London to dance with them. Then their visits had ceased, and when Sir George had asked, 'What's become of young Fosdyke?' or 'Where's that fellow—the one with the red hair—these days?' Cynthia invariably shrugged her shoulders, and answered, 'Oh, I began to find him a bore!'

She was nearly thirty, and was quite conscious that her good looks would not last for ever. Her skin was not of the kind to wear well, no matter how much care she bestowed upon it. She wanted to be married, and wanted to marry well. Emmanuel had seemed to be the ideal person. He was evidently well off, his looks were excellent, he was cultured and very charming. Cynthia had felt that she could develop a real affection for him. Everything had seemed to be going so smoothly, and now, thanks to a concatenation of unforeseen circumstances culminating in this announcement that the wretched Italians were going to enter the war, all her plans and hopes had gone for nothing. Instead of a long, intimate evening with Emmanuel, she had been with a crowd of people, and even now he was preparing to carry them back *en masse* to Heber Square.

She said, 'I don't think that I can, possibly. I'm staying

111

with my aunt in Hereford Street, and she hates me to come in late. Perhaps you could drop me.'

'Ah, that is such a pity,' Emmanuel said, and she fancied that she heard regret in his voice, and thought that perhaps she was wise to go back early to her aunt's, though the old lady would have been in bed for hours!

Wilmot was stubbing out his cigarette, nervously. 'I think that I ought to be getting back,' he said. 'I've some work to get through.'

Emmanuel smiled, and when he spoke his voice was both kind and persuasive. 'But I do so particularly want *you* to come back!'

Wilmot stared at him. 'You mean that?'

'But of course!'

'I don't know why you should. I'm afraid that I got rather offensive. I'm sorry.'

'Don't you think that all our nerves are a little on edge? Rather apt to—go back on us. Then, we'll drop Miss Crawley and go back to my house.'

'Is my cousin coming? You coming, Vivian?' Wilmot asked.

Emmanuel laughed. 'Of course she is coming. She is going to make music for us!'

Cynthia scarcely spoke as they drove round to Hereford Street; only when Emmanuel helped her out of the car, and stood waiting for her to open the door, did she speak to him.

'I'm afraid that I've not been a great success at your party...'

'I'm afraid that my party itself was scarcely a success.'

'I'm not awfully good in crowds. One evening when I'm up in town again we'll go dancing. I promise that I will try to dispel the bad impression which I must have made tonight. There. Good-bye, and enjoy your music.'

As he walked back to the car, Emmanuel thought, 'I like her for admitting that she hadn't enjoyed herself! Though how anyone could have enjoyed themselves, except for the first few moments while Simeon was still there, is beyond my imagination.'

In his own home, he busied himself with making coffee. Vivian sat down at the piano while he was out of the room, and called to her cousin. 'Gregory, come here.' He came over to where she sat, playing softly, his eyebrows raised. 'Yes, Viv?'

'You weren't very clever tonight, you know. If Emmanuel wants to talk to you—let him, and listen. That's a very nice man, Gregory.'

'I didn't know that you knew him awfully well.'

'I don't—but my judgment is remarkably good,' she laughed.

When the coffee came, Vivian said to Emmanuel, 'Put my cup here—you go on talking if you want to—and I'll go on playing. Yes, just anything that comes into my head. No, of course I don't mind!'

He sat down opposite to Gregory Wilmot, crossed his long legs, and lay back in his chair contriving to look astonishingly elegant. Wilmot, trying hard to hide his confusion, asked, 'Was Mrs. Mancini less—er—upset before she went home?'

'Scarcely. Iva's emotional storms don't end so quickly. You see, she's a peasant, and her emotions are always fairly near the surface, always ready to get out of control. Paolo is a Yorkshireman, and, as such, is sterner stuff.'

'I'm afraid that I made a fool of myself. I felt certain that with his name he'd be Italian.'

'His father was Italian, lived in England for years, was naturalised. His mother is from the West Riding. Paolo has, I should say, an entirely British outlook.' He paused, then said, 'You are quite, quite certain that the news which you gave us is correct?'

Wilmot nodded. 'I'm afraid there's no doubt about it.'

'Ah!' he sighed, 'but let me make my own position clear to you. Someone has said that I am pro-Italian. For all I know that idea is recorded in your secret files at the Foreign Office. I don't doubt that you have my *dossier*. I only hope that you have all the facts correct; if not you must not hesitate to ask me for them. I have lived in Italy for many years, I have been happy there, I have also been more unhappy there than at any other time in my life. I have watched Fascismo decline from being something which—at one point—might have lifted the nation very, very high. Now, it is worse than useless, except as a tool which can and will

113

be controlled by the Gestapo. I love my friends—whether they are Italians, English, Austrians—indeed I have Austrian relatives, also Dutch. "The foreign contingent" we—my family—have always called them. One of my best friends—and he also is a relative—is a Frenchman. I am cosmopolitan. I am not pro-Italian, German, Russian; what I am is completely and absolutely pro-Freedom, pro-Democracy. I might have stayed in Milan; the worst that could have happened to me would have been internment—and that possibly only for a short time. I came home because I believe in the Cause for which Britain is fighting. I never wished to be a soldier—nothing could be less suited to my nature. I have hated it all—I shall probably continue to hate it. Now, you may hear nonsense spoken about me, and about Mancini, even about poor Iva—and'—Wilmot saw his eyes narrow suddenly, his mouth harden—'I know at least one source from which these silly, damaging things might come. Will you do me a great favour? Will you trust me always to tell you the truth? Come to me, and say, "Gollantz, is this true? Did you say this? Have you expressed that opinion?" I shall answer you—on my word of honour.'

Wilmot nodded, 'Yes, I promise you that. How old are you?'

The mouth softened again, the eyes lanced with amusement. These nice young men, how crude was their method of attack! Good, honest people, clever too, but surely someone should teach them to be less violent.

'I am nearer forty than thirty,' Emmanuel said.

'Then surely you could have stayed out of the Army for a time?'

'I could do a great many things—that I don't do.'

'Yes—well, thanks for talking to me. You kept your temper marvellously, because I know that I got rattled. It was unconscionable of me. And'—with sudden shyness—'would you offer my regrets to Mrs. Mancini? I hated to see her cry.'

Emmanuel rose, and went to refill the coffee cups. 'Don't you think that it would be a charming thing if you sent her a note? Quite a short note, and—written in simple words,' he smiled; 'poor Iva reads English so badly!'

'Where does she live?'

'She has taken—they have taken, that is—a flat in Gorchester House in Park Lane. Some idiot once told her, when she was here at Covent Garden, that to live in Park Lane was to have the hall-mark of success stamped on you! And now,' going to the piano, 'I am not going to deny myself a moment longer. I am going to listen, and be grateful.'

Vivian asked, 'What do you want?'

'Bach, please, to argue with me that—everything is less bad than I am inclined to think. And then, if you are not too tired, a little Mozart to prove that one must be gay in spite of everything. A kind of duty to the world.'

As Gregory Wilmot walked home with his cousin, he said, 'You're right, he is a very nice man. I think that he likes you a lot, Viv.'

'Do you?'

'Umph, I do. Where does the Crawley girl fit in?'

'I don't know. For your private ear, Greg, I rather hope that she doesn't.'

11

Emmanuel woke with a sense of impending tragedy filling his mind. Wilmot's declaration that Italy would enter the war had caused him acute distress. True, he had known for months, years, the domination of Hitler over Italy, he had watched the infiltration of the German 'tourists' into that country, and noted these things with apprehension in his heart. Now, when it appeared that Italy was to enter the war on the side of the Germans, he knew that he had hoped against hope that a miracle might happen, and that the country where he had been so happy, where his wife lay buried, where he still had so many good friends, might be spared from having this dreadful thing forced upon them. He had no illusions regarding the Italians—there was no real aggressive spirit in them, they were not fighters. He remembered one evening as he sat in the Galleria with Boccalini that the latter had said, 'Emmanuel, we are not and never shall be a warrior nation. Only when we have a cause in which we believe fiercely do we fight well. For example, the cause of a Free Italy which Garibaldi led. And it may be that I am not unduly depressed concerning this lack in my countrymen. Might it not be of greater use to the world to have bred a Michael Angelo, a Leonardo da Vinci, Marconi, Galileo, Puccini and d'Annunzio, saints such as Antonio of Padua, Pius the tenth and Pius the eleventh?'

Emmanuel remembered how he had said in reply, 'And a Benito Mussolini, a Ciano, a Strarace, a Farinacci, Casimero!'

Now he tried to imagine what would happen when Mussolini declared war. He could imagine the blank puzzled faces of the Italian crowd, the shouts of the Black Shirts—*'Viva, Viva, Duce!'* They would turn away and return to their homes, shaking their heads, asking one another, 'But why . . . ?' 'What is the reason for this?' and 'War again—the sixth in modern times!'

Not a very clever people, perhaps, not even always strictly scrupulous regarding such things as 'changing money', or weights and measures, or even working hard for a long time. People who accepted poverty, monotonous food, low wages with a queer kind of resigned patience. Certainly not people who would stand firm and defy the Duce; besides—his lips curled rather bitterly—'it isn't in their nature to oppose the man who holds the tommy-gun'.

He said nothing to Simeon, and the boy went off to school happily, still talking of his splendid evening the night before.

Emmanuel sat at his desk, writing necessary letters, when the telephone shrilled. He lifted the receiver.

'May I speak to Mr. Gollantz?'

'He is speaking . . .'

'Oh—yes. This is Cynthia Crawley. I'm still very much ashamed of my behaviour last night. No, please—let me admit that I was unkind, and ill-tempered. I don't often apologise—I'm doing so now.'

'But'—he was confused and touched—'this is very sweet of you, but quite unnecessary. It just happened to be an unsuccessful party.'

'Which I didn't attempt to make more successful!'

'I'm a conceited fellow,' Emmanuel said; 'I like all my efforts to be successful. So for this reason—alone—that party is forgotten. And today do you go back to Dimstoke?'

'I'm going shopping this morning, and going down by a train at half past two.'

'Then you would perhaps have luncheon with me?' He was surprised at the sudden sense of excitement which gripped him.

'I should love to—where and when?'

'The Berkeley at one? Will that suit you?'

'Admirably! I shall be there—and in a really good temper. Goodbye.'

Emmanuel waited to hear the news at one o'clock. There was no actual mention of Italy and the war, merely a statement that it was believed that Mussolini would make an announcement which would be reported in the news at six o'clock. The news from France was no better—they were slipping, giving ground, their vaunted Maginot Line a failure.

'Thank God,' Emmanuel thought, 'that I'm going out. This waiting would have been too much for my nerves.'

Cynthia was charming to him. She spoke with admiration of Simeon, his good manners, his obedience, his looks. He was grateful that she made no reference to the war—to Italy or to France.

'When does your leave end?' she asked.

'In two days' time, and then I hope to be sent to an O.C.T.U.'

She watched him, and, smiling a little, 'You don't like being a soldier very much, do you?'

'Of course I don't—I don't want to fight, certainly don't want to kill; but now this huge machine has begun to move, and it must move forward to a successful conclusion. There is nothing for any decent man to do except join one of the For-rces. But, I don't pr-retend that I like it! Not for one moment.'

A voice behind him said, 'Good morning, Miss Crawley —and what is it that you don't like, Emmanuel?'

He turned, as Cynthia cried, 'Mr. Gollantz, how are you?'

Julian stood smiling down at them, immaculate in a uniform which contrived in some way to have achieved a

117

greater degree of smartness than any other in the room.

Cynthia answered for Emmanuel, 'Your brother has just been telling me his opinion of soldiering.'

'Really,' Julian's eyebrows were raised, 'this scarcely is the place to deliver yourself of opinions of that kind, is it?'

Cynthia laughed. 'Oh, it was nothing even approaching Fifth Columnism, I assure you!'

'No? Still, my brother knows that the airing of such opinions is not advisable.' Having watched Emmanuel paying the bill, he said, 'Are you going? Because if so, I am going to ask Miss Crawley to be very kind and tolerant and let me have five minutes with you, Emmanuel. It's rather important.'

'Of course—it all sounds mysterious—important. No, no,' as Emmanuel began to expostulate, 'I can manage very well. Simeon comes down next week, doesn't he? I'll write and tell you all about him.'

As her taxi drove away, Julian said, 'Come to my club, will you? I shan't keep you long. And don't scowl, my dear fellow, I only want to give you some advice—advice which I think is valuable.'

'Possibly I don't either want or need it.'

'I think that you certainly need it,' Julian returned.

Emmanuel shrugged his shoulders. 'Oh, ver-ry well.'

Seated opposite to his brother in one of the huge leather arm-chairs in the vast room at his club, Julian opened fire.

'Now, take all this as it's meant,' he said. 'I know that you dislike me, always make a point of distrusting everything I say and do. Believe that now I am trying to do you a good turn.'

'Please go on.'

'This chattering about your dislike of the Army . . .'

'Not the Army, the necessity for my serving in it.'

Julian made a gesture of impatience. 'That's a quibble! People recognise you, as they recognise me; they hear—at all events—part of what you say. They hand it on. It might damage you. Then again—this party you gave. At the Dorchester, wasn't it?'

Emmanuel said, 'Oh—you heard about that, eh? I felt certain that you would!'

'People talk!'

'People *chatter* and *gossip*,' his brother amended. 'And what did you hear?'

'That you were there with a party, most of them Italians, I gather. You and your son both speaking Italian, and finally one woman being led out in screaming hysterics. Frankly, it's not wise.'

'Wise? To have screaming hysterics?'

'Don't be a fool. You know perfectly well what I mean. Mixing with those foreigners, talking their language, allowing them to make scenes in public. Half London believes already that you're a Fascist!'

Emmanuel surveyed his brother calmly. 'What a ver-ry busy life you must lead! To gather so much information! Industrious fellow, you are. Now, for the last time—let me give you some advice. Mind your own business and leave me to mind mine. Half London believes! How many people are in the least interested in me? If I had been Fascist should I have r-returned home to join the Army? Understand, Julian, that I will not allow you to meddle with my affairs. If I hear of any malicious gossip concerning me, as having emanated fr-rom you—I shall act, and act very promptly.'

Julian scowled. 'All right—I've tried to be friendly!'

'Not with any marked success.'

'You choose to take that tone with me—the tone you've always taken—arrogant, conceited, so very sure of yourself, aren't you?'

Emmanuel rose. 'At the moment, very sure of myself; but if I allowed myself to r-remain in the same r-room with you much longer—I might lose that sense of sureness. I might do something for which—I hope—I should be profoundly sor-ry. Good-bye.'

Julian sat on after Emmanuel left. Why was it that Emmanuel always had the ability to keep calm and so score off him? Why was it that they disliked each other so intensely? Bill was bad enough—a dull, heavy fellow—but Emmanuel was worse, with his damned superiority, and his blasted air of self-satisfaction. What was he doing with Cynthia Crawley at the Berkeley? He'd only met her a short time ago—less than a week. That night at the Savoy.

'He's welcome to her, for all I care,' Julian thought. 'I remember I was fool enough to imagine that I'd got a crush on her, a couple of months ago. Damned expensive, and nothing to show for it!'

But the thought of Emmanuel lunching with Cynthia Crawley annoyed him. He, himself, had liked her more than he cared to admit. He had spent money on her, taken her to theatres, dances, dinners—those intimate, expensive dinners. Julian sat in his huge chair, in the big, rather gloomy room, and quite consciously worked himself into a state of acute resentment against his brother; he almost made himself believe that he was still in love with Cynthia Crawley, and that Emmanuel had stolen her from him. It was typical of Julian Gollantz that, while he would have resented it keenly had anyone accused him of being even mentally unfaithful to his wife, Amanda played a very small part in any of his schemes and experiences.

Someone said, 'Hello, Gollantz! Haven't seen you for weeks.'

Julian smiled pleasantly. 'Hello, Matters. Nice to see you.'

Captain Matters seated himself. 'I'm meeting the whole family today. Just passed your brother walking towards Knightsbridge.'

Julian said, 'Did you? Have a drink; we've time.' The drinks ordered, he added, 'Didn't know that you knew my brother.'

Matters nodded. 'Rather. He's in my company. Corporal.'

'Really. I'm afraid that the poor chap doesn't like the Army much. He was telling us so over luncheon at the Berkeley.'

Matters, a short man, with red hair and a very pink face, sniffed his disapproval. 'If he were less superior—if you'll forgive my saying so—he might like the Army better, and the Army'd think a good deal more of him!'

Julian stared, then set down his glass, and said nervously, 'Why, what's wrong with my brother, Matters? He's a great fellow.'

'I don't say that he isn't. Sorry I said that. Not the type of chap I really like in the ranks. However, he's going to an O.C.T.U. very soon, and after that he'll be outside my ken.'

Again Julian frowned, then said, 'He's going to work for a commission?'

120

'Yes—he and another chap—Mancini. That sounds a Wop name to me, doesn't it to you?'

Speaking very slowly, as if what he had heard carried no conviction with it, Julian repeated, 'My brother and Paolo Mancini—going to get commissions. Do you really mean that?'

'Certainly—why not?' Then, as Julian did not answer, Matters sat forward, his hands on his knees and screwing up his eyes as if to see more clearly; he asked, 'Look here, Gollantz, what's behind this? What's biting you? Nothing wrong with your brother, or Mancini, is there?'

Julian's response was almost violent. 'Good God, no! Of course not. Mancini's all right—married the soprano, Alfano. I believe that he's completely English, British, in his outlook. And my brother—I don't know what the devil you're driving at, Matters! He was a little—wild when he was young . . .' adding quickly, 'nothing very serious, not serious at all. He's lived in Milan for years. He's got a queer, almost Latin outlook on life—rather natural after all. But he's all *right*. Straight as a die—one of the best chaps I know.'

'Why did the idea of his getting a commission knock you sideways?'

'What *are* you talking about?' Julian's tone was nervously resentful. 'I was surprised—why I should have been I don't honestly know. I suppose that I was really most frightfully pleased. I am awfully pleased.'

Matters shook his head. 'I didn't—candidly—get that impression. You sounded—worried—to me. Sorry to appear to harp on this, but I hate mysteries, particularly when any of my men are involved.'

'Did I sound—worried?' Julian asked sharply.

'Yes, sounded worried to me . . .'

'Worried, eh? Look here, Matters, I'll be frank with you. I *have* been worried about my brother. He's never liked me much, I've always had a tremendous admiration and affection for him. Since he came back I *have* worried about him. But as you assure me that he's going to get a commission— well, that's grand!' With a hint of pathos in his voice, he said, 'The authorities must trust him if they recommend him, eh, Matters?'

'Of course, certainly. Why shouldn't they trust him?'

'That's exactly it! Why on earth shouldn't they? I must be getting rattled, choosing my words badly. Let's have another drink, shall we? Yes—do us both good. Forget anything I said, or seemed to infer, and get it clear—my brother Emmanuel is one of the best, straightest and most decent men I know.' He beckoned to the waiter, 'Charles—two more doubles.'

Charles leaned forward. 'Have you heard the news, sir?'

'What news? France?'

'No, sir. Italy's in the war. Or will be by the time we get the six o'clock news. Mr. Camber told me just now, sir.'

Julian whistled softly, and said, without turning to Matters. 'Whew! That's going to complicate things for some of us!'

Almost aggressively Matters said, 'How will it complicate things for some of us, Gollantz?'

Again that queer, nervous start. Matters reflected, 'By Jove, he's all keyed up about something! That's twice he's started like that!'

'Oh—I don't know. All right, Charles, thanks!' As the man moved away, Julian added, 'You see, my brother's got a lot of money out there—money and property. Hard luck on him.'

Two days later Emmanuel and Paolo returned to their unit. Emmanuel looked at the long lines of beds with their neatly rolled blankets and equipment. 'Change from being on leave, eh?'

Mancini nodded; his last two days had been spent in trying to console and comfort Iva. She had listened to the announcement of her country's entry into the war, her face drawn with horror. Since then she had cried incessantly, and not all Paolo's pleading had been of any effect.

'Iva, my darling, don't cry so—think of your voice!'

'My voice!' she had sobbed. 'I shall never, never sing again.'

'Yes, oh yes, you will. This war won't last for ever!'

'By the time it ends I shall be an old woman—a hag, with no voice, only able to croak that my heart is broken. Do not try to comfort me, Paolo. It is quite useless.'

122

He had protested in vain, and, when he left her, she flung her arms round him in despair.

'Now you go to become an officer—*tenente,* eh? Then they will send you out to fight, you will be killed—most probably by one of your own friends!'

Trying to speak lightly, he said, 'I might kill someone before they kill me, darling.'

'*Caro Dio!*' she almost screamed. 'How horrible! To think of you killing men, and men trying to kill you, when you have eaten together, drunk wine together! This world is a place only for imbeciles.'

A week after their return they were in the canteen when Herbert, a young corporal, came up to them. He was in high spirits, bubbling over with happiness.

'Just heard that I go off tomorrow—to the O.C.T.U. Who else? Oh, Carter and Blades, and young Fellows.'

Mancini said, 'And Gollantz and I . . .'

Herbert nodded. 'Yes—you, of course. I didn't see Gollantz's name on the list.' He called to a young soldier who was passing, 'I say, did you notice if Gollantz was posted to the O.C.T.U.?'

'No—I didn't see it. There's Blades and you, Fellows and me—oh, yes, and you're down, Mancini.'

Paolo frowned. 'That's queer. I can't understand it. Gollantz was told that he was going before we had our last leave—a week ago.'

Emmanuel rose. 'Let's go and have a look at the list. It's just possible that you missed my illustrious name, Carter, eh?'

'Might have done, but I don't think so. I should go and see Matters. He might know something. May have been a mistake in the office.'

They went out together, found the list, read it carefully. There was no mention of Emmanuel Gollantz. Paolo Mancini's name was there. Emmanuel stared at the list rather blankly. 'I suppose that I'd better try to see Matters. I hate having to do it, he doesn't like me.'

Indignantly Mancini said, 'Why the devil shouldn't he like you?'

Emmanuel smiled. 'Possibly His Satanic Majesty could tell you; being a conceited kind of fellow, I can imagine no

123

reason. Somehow my undoubted charm of manner hasn't been obvious to him.' With some difficulty he managed to see Captain Matters in his office. Matters looked up from the forms on his desk and asked what Emmanuel wanted.

'The list, sir, for the O.C.T.U. It's posted and my name isn't on it, sir. I was told that I was among the men who were to go. Told that before my last leave, sir.'

Matters' pink face changed to scarlet. 'Then it looks as if they'd decided that you were—more useful here, eh?'

'I should be grateful for the reason for that decision, sir.'

Matters exploded. 'Reasons! Your superior officers don't have to give *reasons*! Or do they in this war?'

'I couldn't say, sir. Might I r-respectfully ask for an interview with the Colonel?'

'I don't know . . .' Then suddenly, 'Look here, Gollantz, far better let sleeping dogs lie.'

Emmanuel forgot to behave like a lance-corporal speaking to his captain; he smiled, and Matters, watching him, thought that the fellow didn't *look* like a wrong 'un.

'Sleeping dogs,' Emmanuel said, 'have a habit of waking up sooner or later. For my own satisfaction I pr-refer their waking to be—sooner. I'm sure that you see my point, sir.'

Matters turned to his forms again. 'I'll see what I can do. Still think that you'd better let it alone.'

'Thank you, sir.'

Back to Mancini, he said, 'Something's wr-rong. What, I don't know. What I do know is that it is something that has happened since my leave—or dur-ring it. However, Matters pr-romises that he'll do his best to let me see the C.O.'

'I'm damned if I want to go without you!'

'Of course you'll go! Think how it will cheer Iva to know that you have some additional comforts—and that you're an officer!'

The next morning Mancini left with the rest of them for the O.C.T.U. Emmanuel was surprised to find how desperately lonely Paolo's going made him feel. Not that he didn't get on with the other men; on the contrary, they liked him, even admired him. They thought of him as an eccentric, something of an *original*. With his officers he had always had satisfactory relations; Matters had never cared much for him, but Matters was very much a regular soldier, and

124

made no attempt to conceal his dislike of 'gentlemen rankers'.

He knew that his work was up to standard, if not slightly above it. The Sergeant-Major had been almost complimentary about his going in for a commission.

'Goin' ter git a commission, Gollantz? So yer-rought. Got eddication an' brains—leastways as many brains as any pore bloody corpril ever 'as! Mind yer, one thing ter remember, an' never ferget—discipline—fust, larst and all the perishin' time. Thet's what the ruddy Army's bin built up on. Discipline an' the respect fer yer superiors in rank which they deserve. They've damned well *earned* it see? Must 'ave it, an' if they don't git it, then some poor b—— is goin' ter git it in the neck, and—ritely. Don't be soft wiv 'em. Treat 'em rough, an' they'll respect yer. Git soft wiv 'em, arsk 'em abart their wives an' mothers, an' Gor blimy, they'll stamp on yer fice! No, yer oughter do orlrite, if yer remember wot I've sed ter yer.'

And now—he'd been turned down. Emmanuel sat that night in the canteen, pretending to write letters, and thought hard. How, why, what? What could anyone have brought against him? Who had tried to do so; and lastly, why should anyone wish to damage his prospects? The whole thing was inexplicable and puzzling.

The solution evaded him; he went to bed still worried over the whole business. The next morning the Sergeant spoke to him.

'Luke 'ere,' said the stocky little Yorkshireman, 'what's tha bin oop tew? Gettin' the'sen inter bother or summat? Ah'll 'ave summat ter saay ter thee if so be as tha 'as. Message 'ere—Colonel wants ter see thee. W'at does Colonel want ter see a perishing corp'ral fur? Tell me that, will yer?'

'I asked if the Colonel would see me, Sergeant.'

The little man's eyes seemed as if they would bolt from his head. 'You axed if Colonel 'ud see thee! By gum, tha's gotten enoof brass an' conceit o' the'sen fer t'whole regiment!' More kindly he added, 'Not gotten the'sen inter bother, Ah ope?'

'I don't think so, Sergeant.'

'Tha shands a bit jubious—well, git along, an' see tha

125

remembers how ter speak ter commandin' officers. Respeck, mind that!'

Strange how the Army influenced you, Emmanuel thought as he made his way across the big square. There was nothing to make him nervous in having an interview with Colonel Leslie Bayliss. He had met men like him all through his life. That was where the Army changed you. In civilian life he was Emmanuel Gollantz; he could meet Colonel Bayliss, talk to him, even ask him to have a drink; in the Army all that went for nothing. And rightly, Emmanuel added. Here he was only Corporal Gollantz, with a number added for the sake of identification. A number which ran into six figures.

He was nervous, and his old apprehensions came rushing back. Bayliss was popular, reputed to be 'decent' and just, but—he was the commanding officer! Emmanuel pulled out his handkerchief and wiped his forehead.

'Whew! I'll be glad when it's over, and I know—the worst.'

12

He stood before the Colonel—a tall, lean man, with a strong jaw, and very keen eyes; the A.D.C. was busy with some papers at a side desk. Colonel Bayliss looked up, frowned and said, 'You wanted to see me?'

'Yes, sir.'

'For what reason?'

'To ask why I was not sent to the O.C.T.U., sir. Before I went on leave last time I was told that I was going. I passed the examination moderately well, I believe, sir.'

'Ye-e-s.' Then, turning to the A.D.C., 'Give me those papers, will you, in the green folder, Mr. Purvis. Thank you.' With thin, well-kept fingers Bayliss flicked over the papers, and closed the folder. 'Well, Gollantz, it was decided—rather late in the day—that you were not to go to the O.C.T.U.'

'Am I permitted to ask the reason for that decision, sir?'

The Colonel looked closely at the face of the man before him. Good-looking fellow, possibly too sensitive. Eyes too melancholy, mouth not hard enough. Obviously nervous. Too imaginative for the Army. The reports from his sergeant were good; there were no complaints about his work, his obedience. Yet, Matters—a sound soldier if ever one existed—had come back from leave with most disquieting reports. Bayliss remembered how he had grown scarlet as he spoke, how he had repeated his allegations with growing distaste for the job, which he evidently felt to be his duty to carry through.

Bayliss had asked, 'Did—this informant of yours actually make these allegations to you?'

'No, sir; the whole point was that he was so jumpy, nervy, when I mentioned Gollantz and his prospective commission. I've never seen a man more rattled. Kept assuring me that Gollantz was such a good fellow, straight, and all the rest of it. And yet, sir, I could see that he was struggling to overcome his distress, and yet not give away his brother. More than once he nearly jumped out of his skin.'

'You'd say that this brother was a level-headed fellow?'

'I've always heard that he's brilliant. He's got a special job, something to do with security, at the moment.'

'He didn't speak unkindly about Gollantz?'

'On the contrary, sir, in terms of the highest praise—and yet—there was this queer feeling that he was uneasy, desperately uneasy. He admitted with regret that Gollantz—our fellow—had never liked him much.'

Puzzling—as were the reports which had come in after his application for them. Confidential reports which bore out the fact that Gollantz had been closely connected with Italians, that he and his party had been speaking Italian in the Dorchester the night before Italy entered the war. One woman had been taken away crying bitterly.

Bayliss said, 'Mr. Purvis, be so good as to take down some remarks. Confidentially of course. Now, my man, I don't usually give reasons and explanations, but you're an educated soldier and may be able to clear yourself.'

'Against what charge, sir?'

'Whatever is said in this room by me to you, whatever

answers you give me, must not be discussed outside this room. Is that clear? On your honour, remember.'

'On my honour, sir.'

Bayliss nodded his acceptance of the promise. 'Ready, Mr. Purvis? Right! Gollantz, you can sit down, this isn't an official enquiry. Pass me those notes, will you, Mr. Purvis? Thank you. Now—Gollantz—you left England some years ago—why?'

'I had a disagreement with my father, sir.'

'Debt—the usual sowing wild oats?'

'A misunderstanding, sir.'

'Can you give me an idea of its nature?'

'I'm afraid not, sir.'

'You're attached to your family?'

'All of them—except one, sir.'

'Ah . . .' A long pause, while Bayliss turned to the sheaf of papers in the folder before him. 'Would it surprise you to know that the member of your family—whom you dislike—spoke most highly of you the other day? Spoke in terms of the highest praise and affection?'

He watched Emmanuel's long fingers twist themselves together, noticed how his jaw showed white under the skin, saw his whole figure grow tense and rigid.

When the reply came Emmanuel's voice was cold, even contemptuous.

'It would surprise me very much indeed, sir.'

'I see. Now, has anyone ever warned you against mixing too much, particularly in public, with your Italian friends?'

Emmanuel's face cleared, his figure relaxed, he drew a deep breath—it might almost have been a sign of relief.

'Yes, sir. The same person warned me against saying that I wasn't cut out to be a soldier, and that while I recognised it as my duty to do my best—which I have done and always shall do, sir—I didn't like the Army, and I should be gr-reatly r-relieved when there was no longer any necessity for me to r-remain a soldier.'

Bayliss nodded. 'Yes—I wish you fellows wouldn't make that kind of remark. I doubt if anyone likes fighting—not even the professional soldier. I once heard a man say that the regular soldier is the only actor who prefers the rehearsal to the actual performance. That kind of remark—

the one which you made—is so liable to be misconstrued. I should have thought that you had sufficient intelligence to realise that!' He turned back to the papers, making little clicking sounds of annoyance with his tongue against his teeth. He looked up suddenly.

'Are you a Fascist, Gollantz?'

Emmanuel, surprised so much that he forgot that he was a lance-corporal speaking to his commanding officer, said, 'I beg your pardon!'

'You heard what I said!'

Recovering himself, Emmanuel answered, 'Never, sir, and I never shall be. I dislike and distr-rust autocracy. No man in the world is sufficiently honest, str-rong or gr-reat to be a dictator.'

'And yet—I am told'—he tapped a paper with his fore-finger—'that you have defended Mussolini—if not actually in public, in a considerable company.'

Emmanuel rose. 'Forgive me, sir. You have been most considerate and courteous. I am deeply gr-rateful to you. These accusations against me are so utterly foolish—excuse my saying this—that I cannot contemplate you, a busy man, sir, wasting your time on tr-rying to pr-rove or dispr-rove them. They are fantastic, and they are malicious. If you wish to make further enquiries concerning me, my opinions, and my pr-rivate life, may I respectfully suggest that you apply to my fr-riend, Mancini—who has left for the O.C.T.U.—or to my solicitor, Sir Charles Wilmot? Would you be so good as to dismiss me, sir?'

Bayliss sat back in his chair and looked at Emmanuel in astonishment. He had rarely been so startled. Here he had been trying to straighten matters out for the fellow, who had suddenly dismissed the whole matter as if it were not only too trivial for consideration, but unworthy of his notice.

'Can't you see, Gollantz, that I am trying to sift this evidence against you?' he demanded.

Gollantz gave his chin that strange movement, as if he were lifting it to clear a high stock. Bayliss thought that the man was, in a queer way, old-fashioned. He didn't lose his temper or expostulate wildly, he didn't even say that he admitted he had spoken too much and foolishly. He only stared as if he were listening to something incredible and—unworthy.

Now he raised his fine eyebrows slightly and said, 'I beg your pardon—*evidence,* sir?'

'Allegations, then . . .'

Emmanuel smiled. 'Forgive me, but—*Non è vero è molto ben trovato.*'

Bayliss asked, 'Latin?'

'Italian, I'm afraid. Virtually—"this is not true, it is a happy invention".'

'You tell me that all these—these—reports are lies?'

'Distorted tr-ruths, might I respectfully suggest?'

Bayliss rose; he was losing his temper and he knew it. This lance-corporal was so very much master of himself. There had been some quite unpleasant suggestions made in the confidential reports which had come to him. He stood there, erect and completely unmoved; he even smiled a little.

'Look here,' Bayliss demanded with more heat than he really wished to display, but the fellow was rattling him, 'did you or did you not say—in company of several people —that there was only one real salute, and that—the Fascist salute?'

'Again, sir, might I suggest that—these people—may not have any ver-ry high r-regard for my intelligence, but they might cr-redit me with more than that implies. I remember the circumstance quite clearly.' So, Emmanuel reflected, all this came from Julian. 'I was—in the company of some people. One of them, I don't doubt, trying to be offensive, asked if they ought to give me the Fascist salute, and gave a —comic version of the Nazi one. I returned, and I think that I can trust my memory, "You're wrong, that is the Nazi salute; this is the real Fascist salute"—and demonstrated it. I remember one of the people present said, "It's the old Roman salute, I remember seeing Henry Ainley give it when he played at St. James' in *Julius Caesar*".' That had been Angela. 'One word deleted, sir, and the whole sense changed.'

Colonel Bayliss stared at him, frowning. 'Very well— there is no more to be said. You can go.'

'But not to the O.C.T.U., sir?'

Bayliss snapped, 'No, not to the O.C.T.U.—and learn to watch your words! That's my advice to you.'

Smartly, and with admirable precision, Emmanuel saluted and went out of the room.

Bayliss sat down and wiped his forehead. 'Can't make the fellow out, Purvis.'

'Too smooth, sir—has an answer for everything.'

'I know—but, damn it, if they're the *right* answers, what then?'

'But are they, sir?'

'God only knows! Mind, all that is confidential, Purvis.'

'Of course; certainly, sir.'

So Emmanuel went back to his hut, and sitting on the edge of his bed wrote a long and amusing letter to Simeon. He used all the phrases, flowery and grandiloquent, which he could count on making the boy laugh. He wrote to Vivian Mallet and to Cynthia Crawley.

Believe me (he wrote to Cynthia), *there is nothing that I want less than preferential treatment for my son, but I should be very grateful if you could spare him a word when you see him. It would make him feel that he is not quite cut off from his own small world.*

That letter finished, he sat with his hands hanging between his knees, thinking how cut off he was from what had been his world. The world he had once known, when his one search had been for beautiful things, lovely pictures and fine furniture; when Angela had talked to him of her own worries, and assured him that she always felt better and happier after one of their long talks. His grandfather, giving him advice, teasing him a little when he became too exultant over some 'find' in the salerooms, but never ceasing to be kind, wise and tolerant. Little Gilbert—who used to come and play to him, saying, 'Perhaps Bach'—or Chopin or Beethoven—'will allow me, my dear young man, to help to drive away the evil spirits and blue devils.' Gillie was in America, and likely to remain there until the end of the war. Guido—where was Guido now? Was he a small, rather insignificant Italian private soldier, in a badly fitting uniform made of very inferior cloth, with heavy boots, and an even heavier heart? Guido would never make a good soldier!

131

'And here I am,' Emmanuel reflected, 'in the war too. I believe that I could make myself an efficient soldier. Never —a "born soldier"—but able to do my work, and do it pretty well. But—Julian is against me, as he has always been. He's sown the seeds, and God only knows what the harvest may be. Bayliss is a good man, a grand soldier—so is Purvis —though he isn't used to this life any more than I am—he was a schoolmaster. Matters isn't particularly fond of me, he dislikes "gentlemen rankers"! But it will get round. "Gollantz was going to the O.C.T.U. Why didn't he go?" They'll be decent enough about it, they'll say that there was some mistake, that the lists were full, that this or the other thing happened. But they aren't fools, and they'll know that the rest of them aren't fools. Ah well, here I am, and I'm going through with it for my own credit and Simeon's. I must remember—*et in Arcadia ego*. What an Arcady, too, it was in which to live! Perhaps we didn't value it sufficiently.'

Pattison had entered the hut, and was standing near him; as Emmanuel raised his eyes he felt that he had been standing there for several minutes.

He said, 'Hello, Pattison. Want anything?'

Pattison shook his head. 'No, just wanted to say that I was sorry they'd messed you up about going to the O.C.T.U. It's a bloody shame; you'd make a grand officer.'

'Perhaps not, Pattison.'

Indignantly the other replied, 'Better'n Blades or Mancini.'

'No, they'll both be first-rate—in different ways.'

'Still,' stoutly, 'I will sai this, I'm glad as yer not goin'. An' lots o' chaps feel the same as wot I do.'

Emmanuel rose, and stood towering above the little, snub-nosed Cockney soldier, smiling down at him.

'That's very nice of you,' he said, 'and now, what about a visit to the canteen, and might I ask you to honour me in sharing a couple of pints of what passes in this unenlightened age for beer?'

'Blimy, you don't 'arf know some words, dontcher?' Pattison grinned. 'H'i h'offer you my 'umble thanks, Lord Whats-it. H'i shall 'eve very great 'appiness in being seen wiv yer 'Ighness in the marbil 'alls of the Canteen.'

They were grand fellows, Emmanuel thought, as he stood in the canteen. He never made the mistake of 'flinging money about', he knew when it was permissible to offer a drink, and when it was wiser to refrain from doing so. He would have loathed to have had the reputation of buying his popularity. These men—drawn from every class, trade and profession—were proud; they wanted nothing from anyone—except what they could 'win'.

Through the three months which followed, Emmanuel worked as he had always done, with efficiency, doing his best to bring his own intelligence to bear on such problems as entered into his daily life. He was not consciously unhappy; there was a certain sense of frustration when he heard from Paul Mancini, when he allowed himself to contraşt his life with that which his friend was leading. Not that he actually envied Paul, Emmanuel had never really envied anyone in his life; but the thought that Paul would very soon be an officer made him wonder again and again why his own promotion should have been shelved. Of course, Julian had given way to one of his fits of animosity, he had twisted facts, he had implied this and that, all with the knowledge that he was doing it to 'put a spoke' in his brother's wheel.

Once or twice Emmanuel had thought of writing to Julian, of asking him why the devil he still wished to injure him. He had rejected the idea. Julian would without doubt take the letter to Angela and Max, and . . . Emmanuel shrugged his shoulders. What did it matter? The Army was not his career; both Max and Angela were growing old, Max was increasingly delicate, and what good purpose could be served by adding to their worries?

'And apart from all that,' he thought, 'Julian's so damned clever, he'd make something, out of any letter of mine, which I never intended. Better leave it.'

The war continued—France had fallen, the world had swayed this way and that, ships and battles were won and lost on both sides. That silly song, 'Oh, what a surprise for the Duce' had fizzled out and died, as had another equally silly production from 'Tin Pan Alley' entitled 'Run, rabbit, run, rabbit'.

Pattison said, 'It 'ul be over bi Christmas, mate. The 'Uns

is short of oil and petrol and pretty well every blinkin'
thing.'

'That's good news,' Emmanuel said. 'I couldn't be more
pleased.'

'Well, wait an' see, china. 'Ow far's 'is blinkin' air force
got yet? One perishin' raid on Croydon. Nuffink more *'Im*
bomb Lunnon! Coo, I'd like ter see 'im try it!'

On September the sixth and seventh the Germans did try
it, and news came of blazing docks and shattered streets.
Pattison said that it was like their 'damn' nerve', and Emmanuel knew that his heart felt lighter because Simeon was
out of London. Hannah Rosenfelt wrote that she was all
right, adding: *Nothing to worry about. I don't like it, no one
does, no matter what they say, but here I am and here I
stay.*

Sergeant Dowson gave it as his opinion that there would
be changes soon.

'Can't expect to be kep' 'ere, coolin' yer bloody 'eels for
the duration. Gawd knows 'ow I've worked and sweated ter
make yer inter soljers, an' not what yer was when I first got
yer! Nah, sai what yer like, I've done wonders wiv yer—
wonders! Anyone sufferin' from delusions or weak sight or
softenin' of the ruddy brain might take yer *for* soljers. 'Is
Majesty ain't goin' ter let you lot 'ang abart for the rest of
the —— war. Not likerly. It 'ul be overseas for yer all before
long. Well, yer might 'ave a charnce against the Wops, but
it 'ul be Gawd 'elp yer if ye git up against Gerry. 'E may be
a —— 'orror, but 'e's a damn good soljer! B—— 'ul 'ave the
guts out of yer, unless yer all make yerselves suthin' very
diff'runt from what yer are at the —— moment.'

Changes were taking place as Sergeant Dowson spoke.

Colonel Bayliss said to Major Haversham, 'Here's a nice
thing. No need to talk about it, Haversham. Keep it under
your hat. The Westshires were due to go out any time.
We're second on the list. Now—the Westshires have a case
of spotted fever. Oh, they call it cerebro-spinal meningitis
—but it's the old spotted fever just the same. Beastly thing,
eh?'

Haversham said, 'Beastly, sir. Then—er—we ...'

'We're second on the list. So we go. Embarkation leave
starts at once. Three batches of them. We'd better get crack-

ing pretty quickly. Oh, yes, the men will have to know it's embarkation leave, but no need to tell anyone why we're taking the Westshires' place.'

So Emmanuel found himself in the third batch, and telegraphed to Simeon, and to Cynthia Crawley, that he was coming down to Dimstoke. He went to Heber Square and spent an evening with Hannah; the next morning he took the train down to Ordingly.

As he walked up from the station the beauty of the place struck him, as it always did when he returned to it after an absence. There was a wonderful clarity in the air, and the great trees were changing colour, showing themselves in all the late glory of their red and gold. Emmanuel looked at the trees, the splendid house, and smiled almost ruefully.

'I wish that I didn't love it so much,' he thought. 'After the war will anyone be able to keep up a place like this? I doubt it. And what's going to happen to it all? Shall we have to sell it, to see it cut up into building plots, the trees cut down, the whole place changed, altered?'

Tucker said, 'Why, Mr. Emmanuel, this is a very pleasant surprise, if I may say so.'

'Embarkation leave, Tucker.'

Tucker expressed polite astonishment. 'Really, sir. Going overseas. Well, well. They do say "Join the Army and see the world", don't they?'

Angela came rushing out to greet him. He felt her arms round his neck, her kisses on his cheeks, and realised that the love which he had for her had never changed. She still meant to him what she had always done. Her smiles were worth winning, her laughter worth working for, and nothing was too great an effort if he could insure her against worry or unhappiness.

'Darling, going overseas! Oh, Emmanuel, I don't want you to go!'

He smiled. 'My sweet, I don't know that I am altogether straining at the leash to get there.'

She sighed. 'Bill gone—and now you! Bill sends me letters which don't give me any idea *where* he is going to! Max thinks that it's Africa, I think that it may be India. Julian knows, I believe, but he's so circumspect that he tells us

135

nothing. Julian's doing so well! He looks better than he's done for years.'

'Then,' Emmanuel said, 'no one can consider the war a wasted effort, can they?'

He regretted the words as he spoke them, for his mother's face clouded, and he saw the little nervous frown between her eyebrows.

'Sorry, darling,' he said, 'I ought not to have said that.'

'I wish that you and Julian liked each other better. Oh, he always speaks of you with great kindness—even affection, but you don't really like each other, do you?'

He took her hand and stroked it gently. 'Don't let's talk about it. Let's talk about one another. Tell me all the news— real news, I mean. How's Father, and Viva and everyone?'

The moment of tension passed, and they sat talking as they had not done since Emmanuel's return to England. When Max came back from London—he had grown thinner, Emmanuel noticed, and limped more than he had done— the three of them seemed to have grown closer. There had been a sense of formality between Emmanuel and his father for many years; tonight it had vanished. Max was kindly, interested, and his voice was filled with warm cordiality.

'How long can you stay with us?' he asked.

'I must be off tomorrow. I'm going down to see Simeon.'

Angela said urgently, 'Oh, stay one more day—just one more.'

Max added, 'It would mean a great deal to both of us if you can.'

'Take me up to town,' his mother said, 'take me out to luncheon and let's pretend that there isn't a war!'

'No one,' Max Gollantz said, 'has ever been able to say "No", when Angela speaks in that particular tone, Emmanuel.'

Emmanuel laughed. 'I certainly can't say "no"! Another day, then.'

13

He had lunched with his mother. She had been gay and laughed at all his small jokes. Max had joined them rather later, and now he and Angela had left to drive back to Ordingly. Emmanuel made his way to Vivian Mallet's little house in Kensington.

Her drawing-room held a restful quality which soothed Emmanuel.

He said, 'This is what I miss in the Army, you know.'

'What? China tea and thin bread-and-butter?'

'No—not quite. All the small nice things—thin, old silver spoons, and cups with pleasant colours—these are Worcester, aren't they?—and fine napkins. Not of necessity luxurious things, but—all those little attractivenesses which make life so delightful. There isn't much charm in the Army —and why should there be, after all?'

'But you don't actively hate it?' Vivian asked.

'No, no. On the other hand, I don't actively love it. There will be a certain excitement in going overseas . . .'

'Quite a lot of excitement,' she said drily.

'Possibly. If I have a definite grouse against the life it's the monotony. Yet that's part of the system. And after all —as a system I suppose one has to admit that it's worked pretty well.'

As he watched her he thought how attractive she was, and how much he liked her. She never chattered, she talked well, and listened admirably. Her gravity never became heaviness, her laughter when it came was spontaneous and wholehearted. Her hands pleased him, they were well kept, they moved with sureness. He felt that she would never fumble nor drop things which she handled.

She looked up and found him watching her.

'You're looking very intently at me,' she said, smiling.

'I was thinking how much I admired you,' Emmanuel said.

'That's very nice to hear.'

'You're not annoyed with me for saying that?' he asked.

'Annoyed! Of course not; how could I be?'

He glanced at his watch. 'I must go . . . Vivian, write to me when I'm away, will you? Not only letters telling me about the latest play, or where you have been and whom you have seen and talked to . . .'

'Then what shall I tell you?'

'Oh, tell me what you're thinking and reading, and what ideas you have about things. Let me get really to know you while I'm away.'

He had not realised that he was holding her hands in his; now he did so, and raising one kissed it gently.

'Take care of yourself, Vivian—and—if necessary—if it seems wiser—leave London.'

'That's not very easy,' she said, 'I'm in the Fire Service. You'd not like me to run away, would you?'

He smiled down at her. 'I think if you ran to safety, I could find it quite easy to forgive you! There, I must go.'

'Good-bye, Emmanuel, and God bless you.'

During the journey down to Dimstoke he leaned back in the corner of the carriage and closed his eyes. He tried to look back to the past months, tried to see clearly and judge rightly. Cynthia Crawley had attracted him; he had liked her vitality, her energy, and her general air of complete smartness. Her attraction for him had, at one time, been far greater than anything which he had felt for Vivian Mallet. The thought of meeting Cynthia had excited him as no prospective meeting with Vivian had ever done. Yet now, after the lapse of a few months, he found it difficult mentally to visualise Cynthia. That she was tall, dark, that she moved well and dressed admirably, he knew; what were the tones in her voice, the colour of her eyes? How she looked when she smiled he could not remember.

On the other hand, when he had entered Vivian's drawing-room on the previous day, when she had come to meet him, holding out her hand and saying, 'Emmanuel—I'm so glad that you had time to come and see me,' his immediate thought had been, 'I hadn't forgotten! I remembered how she spoke, the way in which she smiled more with her eyes than her lips.'

His reaction to these thoughts was to make him wish vaguely that he had asked for Simeon to come to London, or planned to take him away somewhere so that the two of them might be together. He realised that he did not particularly want to meet Cynthia Crawley. The recollection of his unfortunate dinner party at the Dorchester returned to him. Cynthia had been bad-tempered, she had shown not the slightest sympathy with poor Iva Mancini. She had withdrawn herself, and become a slightly disapproving onlooker.

He had no sentimental feelings towards Vivian, but the memory of her brought a sudden sense of warmth. There was nothing—he sought for the word—unworthy about her.

He sighed, opened his eyes and stared out at the passing landscape. He wrinkled his handsome nose in slight disgust and faint annoyance.

'And you, Emmanuel Gollantz, were dangerously on the brink of making a fool of yourself over Cynthia Crawley. And now, when you know that you were lacking in judgment, you want to turn tail and run away! You're uncomfortable, because you're afraid that you've given an impression to Cynthia, and you despise yourself for having done so. Sheer pride, my man, and not the nicest sense of pride either!'

Cynthia, wearing well-cut country tweeds, met him at the station. He looked around for Simeon; his face showed his disappointment.

She said, 'Nice to see you. I hope the journey wasn't too bad.'

'No, quite a good journey.' He hesitated. 'You didn't bring Simeon?'

'No.' She looked surprised at the question, and he noticed a hint of sharpness in her voice as she answered, 'My father does not like the boys to be taken out during school hours.' Then, smiling, 'You shall see him at teatime. He's having it with us in your honour.'

'That's very kind of you'; but Cynthia knew that he was disappointed, and Emmanuel knew, too, that he didn't want to see Simeon for the first time in the company of other people.

As they drove away from the station, she said, 'So you didn't go to the O.C.T.U. after all?'

'No. I wish that I could tell you that it was because the powers that be decided that I was more valuable where I was, and that they gave me a very special and desperately "hush-hush" job. I can't—at least with any semblance of truth.'

'I was awfully sorry . . .'

She did not see the quick glance which Emmanuel shot at her. She did not realise that his tall figure had stiffened almost imperceptibly.

'Oh, then you knew all about it?'

'No—nothing. I mean that when I saw that you were still in that uniform, and—well, your letters still came from the camp. That was how I knew.'

Very smoothly he said, 'But you said that you *were* awfully sorry.'

Her voice was impatient. 'Of course, when I realised—as I say—that you were still in the camp.'

'I see . . .'

'Naturally I didn't write and ask why.'

'No, naturally.' Again his voice was very smooth and cool. They drove almost in silence to the school, Emmanuel wishing almost violently that he had never come. How had she known that he had not gone to the O.C.T.U.?—and yet, in common fairness, her explanation was quite sound. Only in his mind there was a growing sense that this visit was not going to be a success, that he would see less of Simeon than he had hoped.

George Crawley met them at the door; his greeting was warm, even effusive.

'Nice to see you, Mr. Gollantz. Would you like to go up to your room, wash, remove the stains of the journey? Yes, and shall I send the boy up to greet you there? Of course, he'll be with you in a moment.'

A pleasant room, with good windows overlooking the parkland. Some rather fine old furniture, and at least one print which attracted Emmanuel's attention. He took off his tunic, and began to wash his hands, when the door burst open and Simeon rushed in.

'Papa—oh, Papa! Never mind your wet hands. I don't care!'

Emmanuel took him in his arms, he had not believed that such a wave of emotion could sweep over him at the sight of his son after a three months' separation.

140

'Glad to see your ancient parent?' he asked.

Simeon beamed at him. 'That's not nearly a big enough word,' he said. 'It's marvellous.'

'Let me look at you.' He held the boy at arm's length. 'You're thinner—and taller, I think.'

Simeon nodded. 'I was too fat perhaps. And I take a lot of exercise—the H.M. believes in it for growing chaps.'

He was thinner, and to Emmanuel's fastidious eyes he looked faintly grubby. His hair—very dark and thick—was badly brushed. Probably he had been in too much of a hurry to make a straight parting.

'Come here, let me make a proper parting,' he said. 'Now, stand still—there, that's better. Let me see your hands.' Simeon held them out for inspection; his father whistled, 'Whew! Tomorrow I'll take you into the town and buy you a really first-class nail-brush. It's quite evident that you need one.'

The small boy grinned. 'Lots of things I want more, Papa.'

'You must learn to distinguish between the precise meaning of "want" and "need". You *need* a nail-brush, you probably *want* sweets and footballs . . .'

Simeon giggled. 'One would be sufficient, thank you.'

In the drawing-room Simeon seemed to Emmanuel to change before his eyes. He stood very erect, he addressed Emmanuel as 'father' and Sir George as 'sir'. He only spoke when spoken to, and then his answers were given to any question in the fewest possible number of words. Emmanuel, listening to his short, clipped sentences, felt a sense of dismay. They were changing him, changing him from an impulsive, amusing child to a stilted small boy, turned out to a pattern.

'Glad to see your father, Simeon?' Cynthia asked.

'Yes, thank you, Miss Crawley, very glad.'

'You'll have to show him round the place tomorrow.'

'Yes, sir, I should like to, sir.'

Emmanuel, trying to make him smile, said, 'Hey! What about that shopping expedition we promised ourselves!'

'Yes, P—Father. Of course.'

He ate very little, it seemed to Emmanuel, remembering the way that he and Julian and Bill had devoured food when they were allowed the luxuries of the drawing-room.

Pressed to have more, Simeon answered primly, 'No, thank you, Miss Crawley,' or 'No more thank you, sir.'

When he went away to do preparation for the following day Crawley turned to Emmanuel.

'How d'you think that he's looking, Gollantz?'

'Thinner than he was, I think.'

Crawley laughed. 'Oh, he can't keep his puppy fat for ever! He's very fit, I think. Gets on well with the other boys. Quite popular, I should say.'

'And his work? Or is it too early to give an opinion on that?'

'No, no. I see his marks and the form report every week. Well up to the average. Shows a strong liking for music. At least, so Dickenson—the music master—tells me. Of course . . .'

Cynthia said, 'Don't encourage my father to talk about the school and the boys, or he will never stop. You see,' she smiled at Emmanuel, 'I hear school talked all day and every day. It may be an absorbing topic, but it can grow deadly boring.'

'Then, obviously, it must not be referred to again,' Emmanuel said.

When Crawley left them she began to talk rapidly; he thought that she was intent on eradicating any possible bad impression which her reference to his missing a commission might have made.

Yet, again and again, he thought, 'She's nervous—now, why?'

A maid came to tell her that she was wanted at the telephone. 'Shall I switch it through here, miss?'

'No—I'll come immediately.'

Left alone, Emmanuel began to wander about the room. He had never lost his interest in old china, bits of fine silver, and all those things which had meant so much in his life. Anyone watching him moving about the big room, picking up one thing after another, holding them delicately in his long, well-shaped fingers, would have been able to judge the valuation which he set on each article by his expression. There were times when he glanced at the object which he held, and set it down immediately; others when his eyebrows were raised slightly, his head tilted a little to one side, and lastly, and most rarely, when he touched the thing which he held, delicately, almost tenderly, with the tips of his fingers. The gesture was almost a caress.

He came to a small glass-topped table, and saw a collection of old boxes—snuff-boxes, patch-boxes and the like.

He raised the lid, and leaned over the collection.

'Ah!' he breathed. Tortoiseshell—silver—*papier mâché*—gold and enamel. China—painted and ornamented with transfers, ivory heavily carved, and jade and malachite. Very gently he lifted them, examined them, sometimes smiling a little with pleasure. Then, as he picked up a jade box, inlaid with gold, his expression changed. He examined the box more closely, and at last raised the lid. On a small gold plate was engraved, 'Cynthia from Julian. September, 1940'. He set it down and picked up another, an elaborate gold snuff-box, beautifully engraved. Again he raised the lid, and found some initials, 'C. from J. April, 1940'. Carefully he closed the lid and went back to his chair.

Cynthia entered the room. 'So sorry to have been so long. A tiresome call from town. I hope you've not been too bored, my dear.'

'No—interested,' he assured her. 'I found your collection of boxes very fascinating.'

'They're quite pleasant,' she agreed. 'I know nothing of their intrinsic value, they appeal to me just as boxes.'

'One or two of them are very valuable.' He laughed. 'If ever you wish to—make capital out of them you will remember that I am still an antique dealer, won't you?'

'You want the first chance?'

'Assuredly. That chased gold box—it's charming. The kind of box which would delight my father. The inlaid jade is attractive too, though I am not really fond of jade. And really—forgive me for saying so—but my brother ought to know that it is almost a crime to add an extra plate to an old box!'

She stared at him, then said, 'Oh, you found that, did you?'

'My training has taught me to look at things—inside and out,' he said. 'The date interested me. September 1940. It's only September the thirteenth now. A recent present.'

'I have known Julian for quite a long time—we've never

been really friendly. From time to time we run across each other, and he is preposterously generous, and loves giving presents. My dear, you're surely not annoyed because Julian's given me a couple of little boxes! Really, how childish!'

'And so Julian told you that I had not got a commission?'

She shrugged her shoulders. 'He may have done. I forget. Does it matter?'

'Possibly not. Why did you never tell me that he was a friend of yours?'

Cynthia laughed. 'Emmanuel, I believe that you're jealous!' Her tone changed, she leaned forward and smiled at him. 'Would you like me to send him back his little present?'

'My dear Miss Crawley, what right could I possibly have to wish—yes, even *wish*—that you should return them? But —little presents! You mustn't underestimate my brother's generosity. Both very nice pieces, and with a very good value attached to them. And now, if you will excuse me, perhaps I might see Simeon before he goes off to bed. I should like, too, to talk to your father.'

'Of course . . .'

As the door closed behind him, Cynthia sprang to her feet. Her face furious, she walked over to the glass-topped table and stared down frowning at the little boxes which lay there.

'What infernal luck,' she thought angrily, 'to leave him alone for five minutes—and to forget that curios and the like would draw him to them automatically. And while Julian was speaking to me from town too. It's fantastic! Something has happened to Emmanuel during the last three months. Before, in town, he was eager to see me; I was confident that he liked me—was on the verge of doing more than—like me. Now, he's changed. Comes here absorbed in his wretched brat—and . . .' She swung away from the table, and went back to her chair.

She had been attracted to Emmanuel; he was the eldest son of a baronet; after the war he would take up his work again. There was still something to conjure with in the name of Gollantz. They had dignity, they were quoted as authorities on matters relating to art. Cynthia had been certain that Emmanuel would, sooner or later, ask her to marry him. With Simeon at her father's school, there would be many opportunities to see Emmanuel, to win him by her interest—simulated or real—in Simeon.

She had known Julian for some years; there had been a time when she found his charm irresistible; then he had asked her to be his mistress and she had refused indignantly. For months she had not seen him, until they met by chance in Bond Street. He had stopped, smiling and insolent.

'Ah, Cynthia, how pleasant—or it may be pleasant if you have forgiven me.' That was what he had said, and she had known that once again she was conscious of his charm, the fascination of his smile, the attraction of his dancing, impudent eyes.

He had bought her the gold box, 'to mark the termination of hostilities', he said.

For a week she had thought of nothing and no one except Julian Gollantz, then he had 'taken her for granted', had become neglectful, had continually put off engagements with her, and the whole thing had terminated in a quarrel. They met again when she was lunching with Emmanuel, and the following morning Julian had telephoned to her. He was penitent, he protested that he had been the world's greatest fool to let her go.

'. . . and then,' he said, 'to find you lunching with my oaf of a brother!'

'But I like Emmanuel—like him very, very much,' she told him.

'How much? Enough to marry him—if he asks you?' That was characteristic of Julian—'*If* he asks you.'

'Perhaps.'

'Good God! I'd hate to think of any woman that I *like* marrying Emmanuel! What idiots women can be! My dear, he's no good. I know if anyone does.'

From that day he had seen her constantly. He had telephoned, had met her in London and given her long, intimate luncheons in small, intimate restaurants. He had made her laugh, had teased and petted her alternately, he had gained her confidence, and she had confessed that she found Emmanuel attractive.

'Not nearly so attractive as I am,' Julian told her.

145

'Perhaps not—he'd wear better!'

'He'd bore you to tears.'

'I believe that he'd be very good to me—to any woman.'

'Very good,' he mimicked. 'What a miserable, dreary prospect!'

Cynthia Crawley had no greater scruples than Julian Gollantz. She listened to him, laughed with him, gave him everything for which he asked, and mentally decided that Emmanuel should know nothing of the friendship which existed between them, Julian would scarcely dare to admit that he had a mistress; both his official position and the fact that he was married would prevent that. Neither, she reflected, was her affair with Julian likely to last very long. They were both changeable, and only the fact that Cynthia realised that her youth was passing made her willing to contemplate marriage.

Now, Emmanuel by this mischance had discovered that she was—at least—friendly with his brother. How far that would affect him, Cynthia did not know; Julian had said that he was 'one of those fools who have ideals and standards'.

So while Emmanuel sat talking to Simeon in Sir George's study, which he had left so that father and son might be alone, Cynthia tried to make plans as to how she should greet Emmanuel when he returned. How much could she make him believe, what could she make sound credible? Julian might call his brother a fool and an oaf, but Emmanuel was capable of being completely cold, logical and hard.

At the same time, Colonel Bayliss was imparting news to his officers, in the camp which Emmanuel had recently left.

'I've just had news,' he said. 'The Navy wants a convoy, and wants it quick. It appears they've made a quick turn round, and are itching to get off. Mr. Matters, those men in the last batch, on leave now, must be got back immediately. Notify that official embarkation leave is cancelled, they return at once. Lose no time, please.'

'Very good, sir.'

Back in his office Matters went through the lists of names, and the habitations of all men on leave. They were mostly Londoners and Sussex men. The police must be informed, they must make immediate announcements in the cinemas and music halls.

The orderly checking the lists said, 'There's Tole, sir. Lives in Manchester. The only one who does.'

'Telegraph to him.'

'Billstoe's from Bristol, sir. Telegraph to him, sir?'

Matters nodded. 'And'—he hesitated—'Gollantz, where's he?'

'Twenty-four Heber Square, Kensington, sir.'

Matters pinched his lower lip between finger and thumb. He had worried about Gollantz; it had been hard luck about that commission and he'd taken it damned well. There had been no sulking, no air of hardship. No, he'd come out of that pretty well. Somehow he didn't seem the kind of chap who'd automatically gravitate towards a cinema—or music hall for that matter. Better send him a telegram as well as the other two fellows.

'Send Gollantz a telegram,' he said, adding more from habit than anything else, softly, 'And damn these gents in the ranks!'

Later the Colonel sent for Matters and gave him instructions.

'I want this to get to the Brigadier. It's important, and you'd better slip up to town as quick as possible. I can't possibly go. Get back as soon as you can, give my compliments to the Brigadier, go into Marsh and Hendersons and get me some socks, if you'd be so good. They know my size, the type I prefer. Can you get up tonight? By car? Yes, yes, certainly. Deliver the letter as early as you can in the morning, and come back. Drive like the devil.'

Eleven o'clock found Matters walking into his club. He was hungry and thirsty; the car had behaved like a fiend all the way up. In the dining-room were empty tables, and a general air of the place having gone to bed for the night. Only one man was eating a belated meal, the light from the little table lamp shining on his fair hair.

Matters walked over to him. 'Hello, Gollantz. You're late.'

Julian said, 'Hello, Matters. If it comes to that, so are you.'

'Business for the Colonel. We're off. Oh, by the way—all

147

leave's stopped. They'll have bawled it out in all the cinemas tonight. Your brother's on leave. I told them to send him a telegram. Didn't seem a very likely chap to find in a cinema. Twenty-four something-or-other Square. I suppose he's at home? Telegram should be delivered first thing in the morning.'

Julian smiled delightedly. 'I say, that is decent of you. I'm awfully grateful. Have a drink, have a couple of drinks. That's touched me, Matters, it has honestly. He's at home all right. I was talking to him on the telephone—when?— why, this afternoon.'

'Well, he'll get it first thing in the morning. Thanks—all the best.'

'And good luck to you, Matters! Again, thanks and my gratitude.'

Matters beamed back at him. It was pleasant to find Julian Gollantz so cordial.

'Not a bit of it. Now—the next's mine. You staying here?'

Julian nodded. 'Yes, I've got to be out and about early tomorrow. Gosh, we're all rushed off our feet!'

14

Vivian Mallet, walking home after a long night spent on Fire Service, passed through Heber Square. She felt cold and tired, and the thought came to her: 'How pleasant it would be if I could call at Emmanuel's and ask for hot coffee, sit by a small bright fire, and talk to him—and have him talk to me!'

She was not a woman given to sentimentalising, but she had to admit to herself that Emmanuel Gollantz filled her thoughts very often, and that with thoughts of him came a sense of security, of deep contentment. She had repeated his last words to her very many times. 'I think, if you ran to safety, that I could find it quite easy to forgive you.'

Was he back from the country, she wondered. Dare she stop at his house and ask? Better not, perhaps. Anyway, she felt tired and dirty, as one does feel dirty after a long night without sleep. Then as she drew nearer to number twenty-four she saw a tall figure in uniform, and knew that her heart missed a beat. She walked slowly, narrowing her eyes, for she was short-sighted, in an effort to see more clearly. The tall figure in uniform had stopped to speak to a telegraph boy who had flung himself from his bicycle. Dimly she saw the lad hold out an orange envelope, saw the tall man take it, and immediately the boy remounted his machine and rode away. The soldier turned and began to walk in her direction. It was as he drew nearer that she realised this was not Emmanuel, but Julian.

She said, 'Good morning, Mr. Gollantz—you're out early.'

'Why, how nice to meet you!' he returned. 'Yes, I'm one of the world's little workers in these days.'

'Have you been to see Emmanuel?' she asked conversationally.

'My brother? No, this is a pleasant way to my office.'

'I thought,' Vivian said slowly, 'that I saw you collect a telegram for him.'

Julian's face was blank. 'Collect a telegram? Oh—I know what you mean! Apparently the boy's new to the game, wanted to know if this was Trevor Square. Yes, he showed me the envelope—some strange foreign name, house in Trevor Square. No, no—I believe in allowing telegrams to be delivered—one of my little rules of life. Well, I must get along. Nice to have caught a glimpse of you. Good-bye.'

'Good-bye.'

Julian walked quickly to the end of the square; having turned the corner he took a telegram from his pocket, and without opening it tore it into pieces, which he dropped carefully down the grating of a drain.

'On its way to the sea,' he said softly, 'or at least, that's what one likes to suppose.'

At the same time, Emmanuel was lying in bed in a small country inn, to which he had taken Simeon for the remaining days of his leave. Dimstoke had proved uncomfortable. After Simeon had gone to bed, he had rejoined Cynthia Crawley in the drawing-room. Her manner was cold, and vaguely he felt thankful that it should be. The fact that she knew his brother Julian intimately was sufficient to disturb im. More than that, he felt that his first estimate of her character had been wrong. She was not the frank, rather impulsive, kindly creature he had, at first, believed her to be. He felt that her frankness was assumed, her apparent impulses often degenerated into little bursts of bad temper and irritability, and her kindliness went for very little.

After dinner he said to Sir George, 'I wonder if you would let me take Simeon away for the three remaining days? There are so many things which I want to say to him, and—although your kindness to me has been wonderful—I feel that it might be good for us to—spend these days together.'

Sir George replied with enthusiasm, 'Of course, of course, my dear fellow. Excellent idea! Yes—now let's see where there is that would be pleasant for you both?'

Cynthia said crisply, 'I thought, Father, that you disapproved of boys going away during term-time?'

'In theory I do! Emphatically disapprove. But, my dear, we're in the middle of a war, and our own little ideas have to be—er—adapted. Discipline must give way to—er—compassion. Now, Gollantz, let's see. There's the Bear at Lessford—no, too noisy. I have it—the Royal Crown at Bilmore. That's the place. I'll put a call through myself. They know me there. My man can drive you over in the morning.'

Dinner over, he bustled away to telephone, and Emmanuel was left alone with Cynthia.

Emmanuel said, 'That's most astonishingly kind of your father.'

'I'm afraid that I can't return the compliment,' she said.

He asked, 'What exactly do you mean by that?'

'I hate and detest people who sulk!'

'So do I,' warmly, 'but what has that to do with—this conversation?'

'Simply that you're sulking because you discovered that I know—slightly—your brother Julian. Because you and he don't get on, is that any reason why your friends should be forced to treat him as something—outside the pale?'

'Of course not. If I gave you that impression, please forgive me.' Never had Emmanuel been more suave. 'Please take this wish of mine to have a few days alone with my son —on its face value.'

Cynthia lost her temper; she saw Emmanuel Gollantz retreating, saw her possible marriage to him disappearing into the realms of extreme improbability. Julian was amusing, exciting, but she knew that tomorrow, next week, in a month's time, Julian might forget her when he embarked on some new adventure. Julian was unstable; Emmanuel—she had felt from the first—was reliable. Now, thanks to those damned snuff-boxes, he was skulking behind his son, and using him as an excuse to get away from her.

She said, 'I think that you have behaved disgracefully. You made yourself a perfect nuisance to me when you were in London, you did your best to monopolise me, and now because your insane jealousy is aroused, you—sulk! Julian always told me how much you hated to see anyone except yourself in the limelight.'

For the first time Emmanuel smiled. 'How clever of my brother—because, you know, he has never seen me—in the limelight. However, there is no more to be said, I think. If I have—in any way—appeared to be tr-troublesome, then I can only offer you my ver-ry sincere apologies.' Then, as the door opened and Sir George entered, 'Yes, sir—what news?'

'All arranged. The Royal Crown at Bilmore. I've told them that they must look after you—that you're a friend of mine.' He chuckled. 'They know me there.'

They had left the following morning. Emmanuel had not seen Cynthia again, she had sent a message by a maid wishing him a pleasant time. As he drove away, he shrugged his shoulders.

'Another enemy,' he thought. 'Well—what of it?'

Simeon had been entranced at the thought of an unexpected holiday. He asked gravely if Emmanuel didn't miss having his batman with him, and on being assured that batmen were luxuries unknown to lance-corporals he elected himself to the post.

'I'll show you how I can clean boots and buttons!' he boasted. 'I'll make you say that your clothes have never been so well taken care of, Papa.'

Emmanuel asked him, 'Remember our last holiday—on Como?'

Simeon nodded. 'Yes, when *Zio* Casimero came and took

151

us away, back to Milano. It was like a song Guido used to sing: "How lovely it was!" ' '

'But,' anxiously, 'you like England, English people?'

'I like the boys at school. I thought they might not like me much, but—they're very nice to me, and'—he smiled—'I can help most of them with their Latin and French, I tell you, Papa, I should like England if we could bring Lake Como and the sunshine, and things like that over here. It is just a little cold, isn't it . . .'

'Try living in a camp, my son!' Emmanuel advised. 'Your school is tropical by comparison.'

'I expect so.' There was a long pause, during which Emmanuel blew smoke rings with immense care, and Simeon worked busily with a button-stick and metal-polish. Presently he laid down the tunic on which he was working, and asked, 'Are you really—going abroad?'

'I believe so.'

'To fight Germans and Italians?'

'That's the idea, my son.'

Simeon frowned. 'It's very difficult to understand—for me at least,' he added politely. 'You see, all my life Guido and *Zio* Casimero and Signor Tolini have been friends to me. Then one of the boys—Gilbert Mason—explained to me that after July 10th all those people became enemies, and, if I could, it would be my duty to kill them—and theirs to kill me. He said that I must hate them all. It's difficult to understand, isn't it, Papa?'

'It's very difficult,' Emmanuel agreed, 'so difficult that some of us can't quite grasp it yet. Shall we say this—it's not the *people* we hate, we hate the things to which they subscribe—agree.'

'Fascismo—Nazism—those things?'

'And what goes with them, yes,' Emmanuel said.

Simeon sighed deeply. 'It's getting worse,' he said, 'because Guido was never in the Party—he didn't like it, and the Party didn't like *Zio* Casimero, or Signor Tolini. They all thought that the Duke of Aosta would be better than Mussolini. Then there was the Baron Brockmann—he wasn't a Jew, but he didn't like the Nazis a bit; they threw him out of Germany. Herr Kalish didn't like them either. But they were Germans both of them. Now what I want to know is—do you hate all Italians even if they're not Fascistis and hate all Germans even if they're not Nazis?'

'This is supposed to be a holiday,' Emmanuel told him, flinging back the bedclothes and preparing to get up. 'I will not be dragged into your political arguments, Simeon. I don't know how much of the Bible you learn at school, but there was one occasion when God promised to save a certain city if five just men could be found there. Maybe there will be five just men found in the countries against which we are fighting. They may save their countrymen.'

Simeon considered gravely. 'Well, *Zio* Casimero, Guido and Tolini are all just men. So in Italy we've only to find two more. That shouldn't take long, should it? Oh, and there's the Pope! That only leaves one!' The thought seemed to cheer him a good deal, and Emmanuel was thankful that he asked no more questions. He talked quite freely, and showed no trace of shyness; he was kind and affectionate and his father felt a sudden tightening at his heart when he remembered that he must leave him so soon. He was to go direct to London, and Simeon was to be driven back to Dimstoke by the car which Sir George was sending.

On their last morning together, Emmanuel said, 'I suppose that I ought to talk to you seriously, Simeon—but I don't think that I shall. It's been a grand three days, and I feel we're very good friends. I shall always try to be worthy of your friendship.'

'And I will of yours too,' Simeon assured him, 'and of my other friends too. I have Guido's photograph in my room, and I always smile at it—to show that I am friendly. A boy saw it the other day and asked who it was. I said, "My friend, Guido." He said, "Oh, he looks like a queen!" I said, "Ah, but if you saw him in his smoking in the evening, you would say that he looked like a king!"'

'What did your friend say to that?'

'He said, "Don't be cheeky, young Gollantz, or I'll smack your head." I didn't think that I was being cheeky, do you?'

The boots put his head round the door. 'The car's 'ere, sir, for the young gentleman.'

Emmanuel saw Simeon's face lose its colour, watched his hands clench, and his small jaw stiffen.

'Everything ready, Simeon?'

The boy's throat worked painfully, but he answered steadily, 'Everything is ready, Papa.'

'Come here . . .' He took his son's hands in his. 'Remember that you matter more to me than anything or anyone in the world. Never be afr-raid to come and tell me things; I shall always tr-ry to understand. No need ever to be fr-rightened of me, because I love you so much. Now, this separ-ration is hard for us both, and you've got to help me not to—be weak. I r-rely on you for your help.'

'No—I mean yes, yes, you can. It's all right for you to kiss me "Good-bye", isn't it?'

Emmanuel caught him in his arms, and holding him closely kissed him again and again. He felt Simeon shudder, and once he made a small smothered sound as if he were choking. Emmanuel let him go.

He managed to smile. 'Listen, we never say "Good-bye" in the Army, we just say, "See you soon" or something like that. So—bless you, the God of Our Fathers have you in His keeping always. Now let's walk to the car, and don't let us show anyone how much it—all matters to us. It's our own pr-rivate business.'

Simeon walked steadily to the car, nodded his thanks to the boots who opened the door, climbed in and leaning forward said: 'Good-bye, Papa.'

Emmanuel kissed him. 'See you again very soon.'

'Yes, see you again very soon,' the boy repeated, then added as an afterthought, 'Papa—give my love to Guido, if you should meet him.'

'Indeed I will. *A rivederci.*'

'*A rivederla, papa mio.*'

Emmanuel caught the train which was to take him down to rejoin his unit. The journey was long and tedious, and again and again Simeon's face, white and strained with the effort he was making to remain calm and controlled, came back to him. He could remember seeing the same look on Juliet's face when she was leaving him to go on one of her tours. The boy was growing very like her, Emmanuel thought, and instinctively he put his hand in his tunic pocket and pulled out the little leather case which held Juliet's photograph.

He stared at it intently, then smiled faintly.

154

'I never thought to carry your picture, my dearest, in the same pocket as railway warrants, identification papers and a soldier's pay-book!'

Carefully he slipped it back.

Two changes, a long wait at the junction, and at last Bursterleigh. He trudged rather wearily up the long hill, along the High Street, past the small villas and into the country. He was tired, and it was a relief to know that he had reached the camp. He made his way to the Guard Room; an orderly who was unfamiliar to him glanced up from the paper which he was reading.

'Hello, what is it?'

'Just back from leave—Gollantz, E.'

'Jest back from leaf!' the other repeated. ''Oo d'you want?'

Half impatiently Emmanuel answered, 'I'm back from leave. Come back to rejoin my unit.'

''Oo the ruddy 'ell is yer unit, chum?'

'Hundred and twenty-fourth Southlands.'

'Gor, luv us! They're 'arf way to the flamin' East by this time.'

'They've gone!' He frowned, rubbed his eyes with the back of his hand, and repeated, 'They've gone—you mean that?'

'Left three days ago, china. Suthin' 'appened; reinforcements wanted in a 'urry—that was the tale I 'eard. Chaps was all recalled. Lef' from Avonmouth.'

'No chance of catching them up?' Emmanuel gasped.

'Not unless yer was a better swimmer nor any Channil swimmer as was ever born. 'Ere, where are yer goin'?'

'That's all right, thanks. I'll manage somehow. Good night.'

He turned and walked rapidly to the Orderly Room. He knocked and went in. A sergeant was sitting at the table, he looked up as Emmanuel entered. A strange face; Emmanuel felt as if he had wandered into a new and unfamiliar world.

'Good evening, Sergeant,' he said.

''Evenin'.' The man had a plump, round face, with small twinkling eyes, and a mouth like a wide gash in his freckled face.

'I want you to do something for me, if you will.'

'Let's 'ear what it is first, eh?'

'Certainly.' He was trying desperately to keep his tone light, as if the whole business were a trifling annoyance but in no way serious. 'I belong to the 124th Southlands, Sergeant. I've been on embarkation leave, and through some mischance—because I had to go down into the country—to see my son—I missed the message recalling me . . .'

The Sergeant leaned forward and tapped Emmanuel's hand with the end of a pencil. ' 'Ere, this is on the dead level, isn't it?'

'On my word of honour. I knew nothing about the recall. I get back here to find the battalion gone. I hear they left three days ago.'

'That's right—three days. Well, I can't catch 'em for yer, can I? What can I do?'

Emmanuel leaned nearer to the round freckled face; he spoke very quietly. 'Give me a warrant for Avonmouth.'

' 'Oo? Me?'

'Yes—once I get there I might find some means of going after them. If I try to travel under my own steam I shall only get hauled up by the Red Caps. Once I get to the embarkation port, I may wangle some way of going after them. Anyway—one fence at a time.' He slipped his hand into his pocket. 'I'll—make it all r-right for you, Sergeant. I can keep my mouth shut, and will.'

The Sergeant was gaping at him, his face purple, his mouth lolling open a little; he panted and the smell of stale beer reached Emmanuel.

'What's it worth to you?' the Sergeant whispered.

'Name your price,' Emmanuel whispered back.

'Lor, 'ow do I know—never done this before.'

'Couple of pounds?' The other nodded with such emphasis that Emmanuel realised that he could have got the warrant for half the money. 'Then—under this letter tr-ray you will find the money, and perhaps the warrant might flutter down so that it is close to my foot—you see no money has passed.'

The Sergeant was busy with the warrant; breathing deeply, at last he let the paper drop to the floor, and Emmanuel retrieved it. As he straightened himself he met the Sergeant's eyes filled with unmistakable admiration.

156

'Whew! Clever, thet. No bees an' 'oney parst. Goo' night.'

He left the camp, and hurried down to the station. He was terribly tired, his pack and equipment seemed to weigh a ton. He was more than tired, he was shocked to think that he had missed the battalion. He was no eager soldier, but he wanted to do his best, wanted to be a credit to the people who were fond of him. He had no idea what the punishment for overstaying his leave might be, he only knew that he had heard it referred to as a serious offence. The station was dark, and only after rapping at the ticket office for several minutes did a sleepy face appear at the opening.

'Is there a train for Avonmouth tonight?' Emmanuel asked.

'For Avonmouth?' the voice sounded as sleepy as the face looked. 'For Avonmouth? Why, you can get as far as Winchester and change there. You'll not get to Avonmouth until morning. Better wait until the morning—best train's the 10.15.'

'No, no, I can't wait.'

'Have it your own way.'

A long, dark journey, with a tedious wait at Winchester, then another change, and he arrived in Avonmouth at half-past eight in the morning. He walked down to the docks, his pack was unbearably heavy. He remembered that he had eaten nothing since breakfast the day before. Breakfast with Simeon in a bright hotel dining-room! The dock police stared at him. Unshaven, dusty, and unutterably tired, he puzzled them.

'But the 124th sailed four days ago, soldier!'

'I know—I overstayed my leave. I want to know if there is any way of catching up, of following them.'

One huge policeman peered at Emmanuel's unshaven cheeks and his heavy, bloodshot eyes. 'Not been on a blind, have you?'

'Good heavens, no! I've been travelling since yesterday morning, not had anything to eat.'

'You're not a deserter then,' the policeman said with pleased conviction.

'If I were I shouldn't be trying to chase the battalion!'

'No more you wouldn't. Better report to the A.P.M., I reckon.'

They told him where to go, and one of them advised him to get something to eat first. 'Might as well be hung for a sheep as a lamb,' he said. 'Feel a lot better with something inside you.'

Emmanuel shook his head. 'No, I want to get it over.'

Sergeant-Major Albert Baker was a relic from the war of '14-'18. He boasted that he knew how to handle men, that he stood no nonsense from anyone, and that his god was—discipline, 'fust, larst an' all the time'. He regretted bitterly the passing away of Field Punishment Number One, as he had known it in pre-1914 days; with its savage roping of the delinquent to a wagon wheel, there the soldier remained out under blazing sun or in pouring rain; all part of the outmoded brutalisation, that the early days of that earlier war had seen—so sensibly—swept away. He declared that the present Army was scarcely fitted to knock off slices of bread-and-jam. He still clung to that type of hairdressing known as a 'quiff', and wore his reddish moustache stiffened with soap so that it stood out in sharp points on either side of his scarlet face.

On this particular morning Sergeant-Major Baker's temper was not of the best. The A.P.M. was away, and he was in charge. While usually this might have been a matter for congratulation to Sergeant-Major Baker, on this particular morning he resented it.

Something had been wrong with the beer last night in the 'Lamb and Harp', he had risen with a headache, and his wife had given him the rough side of her tongue because she said that he tried to give them all hell; also he was suffering from the effects of last night's 'booze-up'. He had already given the corporal, who was serving in the capacity of clerk, a few particulars regarding his parentage and general home life. The little soldier had tried to treat the remarks as amusing, but his ears were still red, and a nerve at the corner of his mouth twitched nervously.

Into the bare and ugly little room entered Emmanuel Gollantz.

Baker stared at him with bloodshot eyes. 'What d'you want?'

'Lance-Corporal Gollantz, sir. 124th Southlands. Inadvertently I overstayed my leave. My unit has sailed, and I wish

158

to report and ask what means I can possibly take to rejoin them.'

'Gollantz! What are yer? Polish b—— or what?'

'British, sir.' But the chin had tilted a little, and there was a faint tone of disgust in the voice.

Sergeant-Major Baker heard it, he heaved himself out of his seat and came round to where Emmanuel stood.

'Oh, yer—"British, sir"—are yer? Educated, too, I'd not wonder. *And* yer've missed yer ruddy unit, *through* over-stayin' yer leaf. I'm not satisfied, let me tell yer. Let me see yer perishin' papers. Come on now. I haven't got all day ter waste.'

That was when Emmanuel began to fumble. His hands, which had been used to handling the most delicate china, the most exquisite lace, the finest jewellery, seemed sud-denly incapable of taking out his papers.

Baker said, 'Gawd love us all! 'Ere's a soldier—educated soldier—can't get his perishing papers out! Nice 'andy feller ter ave in action! Pore blarsted England, if you're what's goin' out ter defend 'er!'

Emmanuel steadied his shaking hands a little, pulled out the papers and handed them to Baker; as he did so Juliet's photograph in its little leather case, with the strip of mica in place of glass, fell to the floor—face upwards. Emmanuel saw it fall, and bent to pick it up; unfortunately the Ser-geant-Major had seen it too, and a huge foot was placed firmly over the photograph.

Breathlessly Emmanuel said, 'Let me have that back, please.'

'In a minute, in a minute.' He stooped and picked it up, and gazed at it. 'Very nice—very nice indeed. Overstayed yer leaf, eh? Listen, you tell that square-pusher of yours ter kick you outer bed a bit sooner in the morning, that's what you'd better tell that tart! Overstayed ...'

That was when Emmanuel swung out his fist, caught him on the jaw and sent him sprawling to the floor. He lay there breathing heavily, Emmanuel regained Juliet's picture and stuffed it back in his pocket. The little corporal sprang to his feet.

' 'Ere, don't 'cher dare ter run awai. That's a ser'us
159

offence, thet is. Striking a superior. An' don't you damn well try ter 'it me.

Emmanuel said sharply, 'Shut up, you silly fool! Who wants to run away or hit you? Help him up. No, I certainly shan't help you—or him.'

He stood feeling curiously detached, as if he had no place or part in the scene. It had been sufficiently serious, he supposed, that someone called Emmanuel Gollantz should have overstayed his leave, that he should have missed his unit, but far more serious was the fact that he had struck a superior.

The Sergeant-Major was being assisted to his feet, groaning heavily. He sat slumped in his chair, holding his head.

'Don't let that barstard escape,' he panted. 'If 'e escapes b' God—I'll 'old you responsible, Corp'ral.'

'Not likerly that I'll let 'im escape.'

Emmanuel said coolly, 'Make your mind easy, Sergeant-Major, I've no intention of trying to escape. Take your time.'

The Sergeant-Major lifted his head from his hands for a moment. 'You b——!' he said with feeling.

Emmanuel was under close arrest. By the morning of the following day he had been marched, under escort, to a Reception Camp; there to remain while a report on the act of 'gross insubordination' was forwarded to be dealt with by the authorities.

15

Charles Wilmot, tall, silver-haired and immaculate, said, ' 'Pon my word, how you fellers stand this life is incomprehensible to me!'

'It's very nice of you to have come down, Charles,' Emmanuel said. 'How are the family taking it?'

Charles stretched out his long legs, and stared at the toes of his excellent shoes.

'We-ell, on the whole very well. Y'mother—angel that she is!—says that, of course, there is some mistake. Max—well,

Max is inclined to be irritable, and swears that one or other of the family is always in some trouble or other. That's because Julian's been outstripping the constable lately, Max has had to foot the bill—as usual. Julian . . .'

Emmanuel said quickly, 'I don't give a damn what Julian thinks.'

'No, don't altogether blame you. By the way, a Miss Mallet came to see me. Nice woman. You'd written to her, I take it?'

'Yes, she's a good friend of mine.'

Charles flung back his head and laughed. Emmanuel thought how strange it was to hear anyone laughing. He felt that he had heard no laughter for days. Here was Charles behaving as if they were sitting together in his exceedingly comfortable office, discussing the ordinary things of life. Instead of which, Emmanuel Gollantz—under close arrest—was meeting Sir Charles Wilmot, K.C., in order to get the facts marshalled for the former's Court Martial.

'M'boy,' Charles said, 'it's my private belief that she's more than a friend. But, I repeat—a nice woman. She'd got some story about having seen Julian stop a telegraph boy otuside your house, and take a telegram from him. Now, that might be of value, but if she's right in her facts it won't affect the main issue, which is your taking your fists to this Sergeant-Major feller. Let's keep the whole thing as clear as possible. We don't want complications—and particularly family complications. Do you agree?'

Wearily Emmanuel said, 'Oh, for God's sake let's leave Julian out of it. But I should like to hear what Vivian says.'

Charles told the story; Emmanuel nodded.

'Sounds quite probable. Apparently some telegrams were sent. But—let's leave that. One day I shall have time to deal with my charming brother. Now, do I brief counsel?'

Charles laid his finger-tips together. 'I think not. No, I think not. There's a man here, friend of mine, a soldier man. I've known him for years. Able, got a sense of humour . . .'

'Most necessary at a trial,' Emmanuel interpolated.

'More than you think. He'll act as soldier's friend, if I ask him. He'll come and have a word with you. Major Cuthbert. Let him run the whole thing in his own way. You will? Very well, I'll see him as I go, and give him such information as he needs. Now, don't worry, the whole thing can be cleared up, I don't doubt, and as for catching the Sergeant-Major bloke a tu'penny one—good luck to you.'

That night Major Cuthbert came to see him. He was a tall, thin man with a long upper lip and wearing glasses. He looked vacant and not a little vague. Emmanuel thought, 'I don't think a great deal of Charles's selection.'

Emmanuel said, 'This is really very kind of you, sir, and I am very grateful. I may tell you that I haven't the faintest idea what is going to happen, what the procedure is like, or what kind of punishment I'm likely to get.'

Cuthbert blinked behind his glasses, removed them and polished them carefully on a silk khaki handkerchief.

'For striking a superior,' he said, 'or, as they put it—personal violence to a superior—that of course means that it is someone who is your superior in the Army sense of the word—the sentence to which you are liable is—death,' he grinned happily, 'or any lesser punishment. It's *usually—invariably*—the "lesser punishment".'

'And the "lesser punishment"?' Emmanuel asked.

'Depends upon how clever your "soldier's friend" is. Didn't old Charles speak highly of me, and my mental attainments?'

'Then how much need I worry?'

'In your shoes—I don't think that I should a great deal. But then—and why will you force me to make these admissions?—I am a very remarkable man. Nothing else you wish to tell me?'

'I don't think so. Oh—one thing. You probably know why I hit the "S-M.". Over a photograph—yes. Will there be any need for the identity of that photograph to be made public?'

He spoke so calmly that Cuthbert smiled, saying, 'Well, we'll do our best to keep her name out of it. Engaged to her?'

He watched Emmanuel draw a deep breath, then he answered, 'No, sir. It's of my wife. She died nearly thirteen years ago.'

Cuthbert gave him a little bow of apology. 'I beg your pardon.' Later, as he walked back to his quarters, he thought a good deal about Gollantz. Charles Wilmot had told him that he had 'gone through a rough time', had added, 'regrettable misunderstandings, and somehow this poor devil always got caught like the toad under the harrow.'

'But,' Cuthbert reflected, 'it's not the bad times and the misunderstandings that have given him that particular look on his face as a legacy. It's the loss of this wife of his. I wonder if I can get him off so that he could come out with our lot. I'd like to have him with me. Now—one last look at this evidence.'

Later word was brought to him that the Deputy Judge Advocate General had arrived and wished to see Major Cuthbert. He walked over, was presented to the D.J.A.G., and found with him the Senior Major who was to preside over the Court in the morning.

The President had received papers of a confidential nature. There had been some doubt concerning Gollantz, and his political beliefs, his friends, and so forth.

The D.J.A.G. interposed. 'Let me remind you,' he rapped out, 'that no man shall be convicted because he has a bad name. We—you—gentlemen are only concerned with the present charges against him. Let us keep that very clearly before us all. Another point of which I should like to remind you is that courts martial are actually definite, organised attempts to—get the man off as lightly as possible. Particularly in times of war. This man, I gather, is not a professional soldier. The Army is not his career. No, I thought not. Therefore, so far as the Army is concerned, once the war ends the Army is done with him, he is no further concern of ours. On the other hand, at the moment the Army needs him. I cannot stress those points too strongly, gentlemen. He's not habitually overstayed his leave, I take it?'

'Never done so before, sir,' Cuthbert said.

'Educated man?'

'Well educated, sir. One of the best antique and art dealers in the world, I should say.'

'Not *the* Gollantz lot?'

'The same, sir.'

'Really, really! This is a coincidence. I picked up an old French watch last week, at Wildmans in Edinburgh. Know it? Oh, very honest, nice fellow—Wildman. He says that I've got a bargain. Probably I have. I wonder if this fellow

Gollantz would have a look at it for me? Irregular, but interesting to know what he says.'

Cuthbert said, 'I'll take it over to him, sir.'

Emmanuel sat reading, wondering why the fact that you were not allowed to go and come at will made you long so violently to take exercise. He was still tired, he was worried concerning tomorrow, and yet he wanted nothing so much as to go out into the September dusk and walk for miles through the woods, inhaling the scent of the pine trees, feeling the softness of the needles under his feet.

Cuthbert came in, and said, smiling, 'It's been decided to give you an intelligence test, Gollantz. Ready?'

'Intelligence test—what on earth for? Oh, very well.'

'What do you make of this?' He held out the watch.

Emmanuel stared at him. 'Is this a joke? I don't follow it at all. If you want me to tell you about the watch—it's French, date—oh, pr-robably about 1700 to 1720. This type wasn't made after then. It's astonishingly small for its period. They are usually ver-ry large and rather clumsy. The diamonds are excellent, beautifully set. One has been replaced, I see. That's not quite so good as the originals. The works . . .' He flicked open the case, and slipping his hand into his pocket brought out a little leather case, which, when opened, Cuthbert saw, held a magnifying-glass. Emmanuel screwed it into his eye. 'The works,' he continued, 'seem very fine. That exquisite cover—what a charming piece of work! I think that we can safely say that the owner has found something—ver-ry, ver-ry nice indeed.' He closed the case and handed the watch back to Cuthbert.

Queer, Cuthbert thought, how the man changed. He had switched from being a rather apprehensive lance-corporal to the complete specialist. He had assurance, certainty, and poise.

He said, 'What is it worth?'

Emmanuel smiled. 'I didn't realise that you wanted a valuation—I fancied that you merely wished for an expert opinion.'

Cuthbert said, 'I don't see the difference.'

'No?' the smile widened. 'You see, a fee is charged for a definite valuation. I should be pr-repared to offer forty pounds for the watch. And, of course, there is ver-ry little market for things of this kind—at the moment.'

Cuthbert flung back his head and laughed. 'You'll offer forty! Which means . . . ?'

'Which means, naturally, that it is worth a trifle more.'

'How much more?' Cuthbert grinned.

'Thirty-three and a third for overhead expenses, and then —a small pr-rofit for me.'

They both laughed, the difference in military rank had slipped away, and they were two equals laughing over the small joke which they had perpetrated. Cuthbert, watching Emmanuel, thought, 'The fellow looks suddenly younger, less tired. He's a good chap; I'd rely on him in a jam! If I can help it, I won't lose sight of him.' 'Thanks,' he said, 'and don't worry about tomorrow. It's going to be all right. Don't *feel* like a prisoner, or a culprit. Don't let it worry you that you can't come before the Court wearing either side arms or your cap. That isn't to mark you down as something criminal; it's in case you lost your temper and flung your cap at the Presiding Officer. Then the fat would be in the fire! It's just one of those queer examples of the way military law tries to play fair. Good night, and get to sleep.'

'Good night—and many thanks, sir.'

Cuthbert took the watch back, and handed it to the Deputy Judge Advocate General. 'There you are, sir, and Lance-Corporal Gollantz will offer forty pounds for it.' He laughed. 'As he, very honestly, explained to me, it is worth a trifle more'

'How much more?'

'Thirty-three and a third per cent, so he explained, and' —he mimicked Emmanuel's speech—'a small additional tr-rifle of pr-rofit for himself.'

'Astonishing fellow! Rather amusing,' he chuckled. 'He'll offer forty pounds! Gosh, this is a funny war!'

Emmanuel awoke the next morning with the sense that something difficult and unpleasant was impending.

He dressed and shaved with his usual care; his guards were kindly fellows, who kept assuring him at intervals, 'Don't cher worry, china!' and, 'All over in no time, chum.' 'Don't you b'lieve they gets art the Firin' Squad if they can

165

possibly 'elp it. It's a 'ell of a job ter git a bloke shot by verdict of Court Martial. You'll be orlrite!'

Marching into the room, five officers seated, the Senior Major and Cuthbert, who sat a little apart, turning over some papers.

The charge read by a lieutenant who stammered a little, and pronounced the name 'Gollantz' incorrectly. Once or twice Major Cuthbert made pencil-notes on a pad.

Then questions regarding his leave. 'It has been conclusively proved that a telegram to recall you was sent to your address—24 Heber Square, Kensington. You never received it, you say.'

'No, sir.'

'Had it been delivered at your house, would anyone there have opened it and sent on the message to you?'

'Yes, sir. Without any doubt. My housekeeper knew where I was staying.'

'You have no idea what happened to the telegram? The boy who delivered it says that he handed it to a man in uniform outside number twenty-four. You were not that man?'

'No, sir.'

'Have you any idea as to the identity of this man in uniform?'

Emmanuel's face was unmoved. 'Not the slightest, sir.'

He was questioned about his return; he recounted how he had got to the camp to find that the Southlands had gone; he had gone to the Guard Room, then on to the Orderly Room.

'What was in your mind at the time?'

'Dismay, sir, and otherwise only a wish to—catch up with the battalion.'

'Can you remember whom you saw in the Orderly Room? The man you asked to let you have a railway warrant?'

'I might recognise him, sir. I think that it is doubtful.'

'How did you persuade him to let you have the warrant?'

Cuthbert interjected, 'Well, we all know how that is done, don't we?'

The President snapped, 'I take a very bad view of bribery!'

'But,' Cuthbert insisted smoothly, 'this incident proves the determination on the part of the accused to rejoin his unit, don't you think?'

'Did you bribe him?'

For a split second Emmanuel's lips twitched. 'No money changed hands, sir, between us.'

'Very well—and then . . . ?'

He gave his account of the long journey to Avonmouth, of his reporting to the Dock Police, and how he followed their advice and went to the Military Police.

Cuthbert interpolated, 'I think this is all additional proof of his determination to rejoin, additional proof that whatever—er—mistakes he may have made, he had not the slightest intention of deserting.'

The Sergeant-Major was called. Watching his beefy face, with its reddish moustache twisted into sharp points, seeing again his 'quiff' of greased hair, Emmanuel felt a sudden spasm of fury sweep over him. The Sergeant-Major gave his evidence with what Emmanuel knew that he regarded as 'military precision'. His replies came rattling out like machine-gun bullets, his voice was loud and almost mechanical in its complete lack of any emotion or expression.

'Seated in the office on the morning of the 17th inst., I saw the prisoner . . .'

The President interpolated, 'Accused—not prisoner.'

'Accused, sir, enter. He told me that he had missed his unit, which 'ad gorne overseas. I arsked him to let me see his papers; he fumbled about and finally produced same. I was examinin' same when he hit me—knocked me down, sir.'

Cuthbert said, 'Just like that, eh?'

'So far as mem'ry serves me, yes, sir.'

'Your story doesn't exactly tally with the accused's.'

'What did you actually *say* to him?' the President asked.

The Sergeant-Major gazed at the ceiling as if making a tremendous effort to recall the exact words. Finally he lowered his gaze and after clearing his throat said, 'I told him that it was serious for anyone to overstay their leaf, that the matter would 'ave to be reported in full to the A.P.M., who was absent at the time. So far as mem'ry serves me, that is the grist . . .'

Cuthbert asked, 'The *what*?'

'Grist, sir—the account of what took place. Then he hit me, sir.'

'And knocked you down?'

'That is correct, sir.'

Cuthbert asked, 'But in your evidence you say that you were seated in the office.'

'That is so, sir. I was going through some papers—forms and the like, sir.'

'At the desk, I take it.'

'Correct, sir.'

'The accused came in and stood opposite to you at the desk?'

'So far as mem'ry serves me, that is so, sir.'

'Is it a biggish desk, Sergeant-Major?'

'Well—it's'—for the first time the big man began to fumble for his words—'I should say that it's an ordinary-sized desk, sir.'

Cuthbert said, 'Let's get this scene right. You are seated at the fairly big desk, in a chair. The accused is standing facing you. He hands you his papers, and you deliver him that little homily of yours about the gravity of what he has done. He then hits you, and knocks you down. But you weren't standing up, were you? Did he really lean over the desk and lift you bodily out of your chair at that distance—at least several feet?'

'I might have stood up, sir—during the conversation.'

'Oh, you might have stood up. But the accused is still on the far side of the table—or did he nip round and deliver his blow?'

'Well—as a matter of fact, sir—I was so taken aback that I'm not certain where the accused did acherly stand at the moment of the attack. I was engaged in reading and examin-in' his papers, sir.'

'Not speaking at all?'

'No, sir.'

'Then when did you deliver this little speech of yours?'

'Before he hit me, sir.'

'I thought you said that you were examining the papers, and not speaking. Come, come, Sergeant-Major . . .' He turned and, smiling, said to the President, 'I think that's all I want from this witness, thank you, sir.'

168

The Lance-Corporal who had been in the office was called. He was a small, nervous man who spoke with a strong Lancashire accent. He told the same story as that already given by the Sergeant-Major, though his manner was less assured.

'The accused actually knocked the Sergeant-Major down?'

'Aye, 'e did, sir.'

'Was the Sergeant-Major sitting or standing at the time?'

The little soldier flushed. 'Ah'd scarcely like ter saay—'e might 'ave bin sittin'—or 'e might 'ave bin standin'. Ah'd be inclined ter say 'e were standin'.'

'On which side of the desk?'

'Why, sir—theer agean, that's bad ter saay. Ah wasn't reely payin' mooch attention, sir. Ah was gettin' on wi' me work, sir.'

'Did you hear what was said to the accused?'

'Why—t'Sergeant-Major axed fur t'papers, and t'chap up an' 'it 'im.'

'Didn't the Sergeant-Major say anything in addition to this courteous request for the papers?'

'If 'e did, sir, Ah didn't 'ear 'im, nor yet wot 'e said, sir.'

'Why—does he whisper?'

'Not what you'd call whisper, sir, no.'

'You're not deaf?'

'No, sir, Ah'm not deaf, sir.'

'Did you see the accused drop anything while he was handing over his papers to the Sergeant-Major?'

With an air of pleased confidence, the Lance-Corporal beamed at Major Cuthbert.

'Ah did see 'im drop summat, sir. A photer I think it was.'

'Ah, then you *were* watching and listening?'

'Ah just 'appened ter see that, sir.'

'Then the accused up and hit the Sergeant-Major, after dropping this photograph? During this time the Sergeant-Major never spoke, never made any remarks of a pleasant or unpleasant nature?'

An expression of complete blankness passed over the Corporal's face, he answered, 'No, sir—'e never spoke at all.'

Cuthbert turned to the President. 'Really sir, I don't think we can have that. I submit that neither of the two last witnesses are reliable. They have both contradicted themselves, their story is palpable rubbish. Far too much of "it might have been this" or "it might have been that". We're wasting our time.'

The President nodded. 'I'm afraid that you're right.' He turned to Emmanuel. 'Your contention is that you acted as you did under extreme provocation?'

Emmanuel answered, 'Provocation which I felt to be extreme, sir.'

'You dropped this photograph—what happened then?'

'The Sergeant-Major put his foot on it, sir, and made remarks which I felt to be—fr-rankly—insupportable. The photograph was of my wife . . .' He hesitated, then added, 'Of my late wife, sir. May I venture to put it to you what the effect would have been on you, sir, under the same circumstances? That is all I have to say.'

The Major watched him intently as he spoke. The quiet voice, the rather stilted phraseology, made him realise that this man was still suffering from some incident which had made an indelible mark on his mind. He thought, 'I should like to see what this fellow would do to that same Sergeant-Major if the world were at peace.'

The President said, 'The Court will adjourn, gentlemen. March out the accused.'

Emmanuel, between his guards, was taken from the Court Room. They marched him to an empty hut, and with a certain kindliness told him to sit down; one of them added with a grin, 'Make yer miserable self 'appy, chum!'

The other asked him, 'Not frightened, are yer, mate?'

'No, only ver-ry tired, thanks.'

'That Cuthbert didn't 'arf cane the old S.-M., didn't he?'

The other soldier answered, 'It's b——s like wot that S.-M. is that makes the 'ole Army git a rotten nime. B——y old sweat.'

The President glanced round, watching the faces of the officers around him. The junior officer was chewing the end of a pencil, his face was flushed, he was obviously nervous; the President remembered that he stammered a little, which probably added to his diffidence.

'Well, gentlemen,' he said, 'we've got to admit that in an Army like that we have today, you can't have all the soldiers cut to a pattern. I happen to know something about this man—his wife was Juliet Forbes, a celebrated singer. Apparently, he adored her. Now, when this S.-M. put his foot on the photograph, Gollantz saw red. Any of us would have done, I think, exactly what he did . . .' He stopped, smiled and said in a tone of apology, 'Of course, that is only my personal view. But it *is* as well for me to remind you that the punishment which a court martial awards should be the *minimum* consistent with the proper maintaining of discipline. Let's face it; we want the *use* of this man—as we want every other man—as a soldier in the field.'

He listened with satisfaction to the little murmur of approbation which ran round the table.

He continued, 'I think that—as Major Cuthbert in his role of soldier's friend pointed out—neither the tales told by the S.-M., nor his little henchman, were particularly convincing. But of course we must have a formal verdict.' He turned to the junior officer and said encouragingly, 'Well, Symington?'

'It's g-got to be "G-guilty", of course, sir.'

The President nodded. 'As a paper transaction, of course. But to a temporary soldier what do entries on an A.F.152 matter! Then it's agreed, "Guilty"?'

The others nodded their agreement; the President went on briskly: 'It is now a question of the *sort* of punishment we award.'

It was Captain Campion, the only Southland officer to sit on the Court Martial, who spoke, and made what the President hailed as a particularly sensible suggestion.

He said, 'F.P. Number Two, sir, is my opinion. Sixty days, just to show that we have a proper respect for discipline and its maintenance.' He grinned. 'But we can be pretty certain that will be cut down to thirty. Most of it will be worked off during the voyage out, since I take it that he'll be given orders to proceed with the next ship-load of "details". He'll rejoin his unit. I happen to know, sir, that there's a transportful leaving within the next ten days, since I'm under orders to travel in her myself. So, if the reviewing authorities don't hang things up, his sentence can be promulgated in ample time for him to sail.'

The President nodded. 'Very good. And now, gentlemen, if you are agreed—we'll let it go at that.'

16

Long days at sea, days which to Emmanuel were precious. Cuthbert kept him fairly busy, he was kindly and sympathetic, he allowed himself to unbend, to cease to be the officer and became a pleasant, friendly person. He talked easily, and Emmanuel gathered that he was an unconventional soldier. It was evident that he had done well, but that his successes had been gained by his own methods, which were not always those which were advocated by the Higher Command. Emmanuel enjoyed those long talks, and felt that he was gathering a certain amount of military knowledge. The Army began to hold new interest for him, it ceased to be a mere matter of routine, orders and exercises; it began to appear as a huge machine which, for all its mechanisation, still relied on the efforts and intelligence of the individual for its best results.

'It must be tremendously satisfactory to pull off something really good, do something really important,' he said one evening.

Cuthbert nodded. 'Yes, it tastes fairly sweet in the mouth,' he said. 'There's only one way to get things done—that's the ability to work to a split second. That's where young men so often have a pull. They may make mistakes—but at all events they make *something*. I dread the time when I shall be conscious that my brain is beginning to work slowly, ponderously. Oh, that time will come, it comes to everyone sooner or later.'

That night Emmanuel stood on deck, staring out over the dark sea. The phrase 'it tastes fairly sweet in the mouth' had stuck in his mind. It was long since he had known that anything tasted sweet in his mouth. A few hours with Simeon, the consciousness of Vivian Mallet's friendship, Hannah's thoughtful kindness, his mother's smile—those things, yes. But they were fleeting and transient. He had, of his own free will, flung himself into a world which was new and strange to him. Not a bad world, he reflected; he had found kindness and friendliness in the Army. His fellow soldiers might, and probably did, regard him as a queer fellow, but they had never done anything to make him conscious that they thought so. It had been left to Julian to attack him wherever and whenever possible.

Vivian had written that she was certain that she had seen Julian take the telegram from the telegraph boy; Charles Wilmot had written asking where the 'confidential information' regarding Emmanuel had come from. Emmanuel felt certain that Julian had been determined to take Cynthia Crawley away from him. He smiled.

'The one thing over which Julian need not have concerned himself. Perhaps one thing for which I ought to be grateful to him. I was perilously near making a fool of myself. Whew! What an escape!'

The quiet of the sea soothed him; as the voyage passed he knew that his nerves were becoming steadier, that his whole outlook was growing calmer. He had resented the court martial more bitterly than he had even admitted to himself. Not that he had any quarrel with the way in which justice had been administered, he had nothing but respect for the men who had dealt with his case; but to have found himself in such a position was abhorrent to him. The thought of the red-faced Sergeant-Major still had the power to distress and disturb him. Power—what a wonderful thing to have, and what a terrible weapon against humanity—whether the mass or the individual—when abused! Then the realisation came to him that this was why the Allies were fighting, this was why men were ready to give their strength, their health, even their lives, this was why the factories all over the world were working day and night! Men had seen the result of the abuse of power, the sight had horrified and infuriated them, and—the Allies had gone to war. Hitler, Mussolini, the red-faced Sergeant-Major, Palumba—all men with power which they had abused.

'Perhaps,' he mused, 'it was that realisation which made me come back to England to fight. Not entirely from a sense of complete patriotism, but because there is something in me which loathes, hates and fears—fears desperately— the unwarrantable use of power. The power of Dictators, the power of the financiers, of the aristocracy, of the people, of the bureaucrats. All power which is allowed to become completely vested in one class, or in one individual. Against

173

whom it is directed matters less than that it should be directed completely against any party, any people, any class who happen to be in temporary disfavour.

'Men—whether individual or in parties—cannot bear the weight of too much power and remain sane. And when this is all over, shall we remember that? Shall we really visualise a new world, or shall we only attempt to remake something on the lines of the old, which will suit *our* requirements better?'

A voice at his elbow made him start. 'Hello, Gollantz, thinking unutterable things?'

He saw the tall, thin figure of Cuthbert looming up in the half-light, as he made his rounds.

'They may be unutterable, sir, because I haven't the ability to utter them.'

Cuthbert chuckled. 'Dreaming of the years when the war is over, I'll be bound.'

'More or less, sir—yes. Puzzling, isn't it?'

'"Dreams of a remoter world",' Cuthbert said. 'I wonder what ingredients will go to the making of a "remoter" and —finer world? Ever thought that bit out, Gollantz?'

'I've tried to, sir. It's difficult without growing ponderous, I find. Compassion must be one, I think, and justice another.'

'Can they go hand in hand?'

'I don't know—it ought to be possible. Justice isn't a cruel thing—or it isn't justice. It may not be a very *pleasant* thing, but though it may hurt, smart for a time, it doesn't really leave a scar, the kind of scar that aches and throbs.'

Cuthbert glanced at the tall man beside him, his arms folded on the rail, his eye staring seaward. Again he had the impulse to ask this soldier for his story, and, as he almost spoke the words, something warned him that to do so would to be make Gollantz retreat into his shell.

'I wonder,' he said, 'how many of us have got complete justice from life?'

'That's no reason why we should not have had it, sir.'

Impulsively Cuthbert asked, 'Have you had—complete justice?'

The voice in which Emmanuel replied was studiedly even

and unmoved. 'In my pr-rivate opinion, no; I may be wr-rong.'

'You never talk about yourself, do you?'

'Not if I can avoid doing so. Human documents can be so desper-rately bor-ring. If you tell them with any r-real dr-ramatic effect they sound like "hard luck" stor-ries. Otherwise they're like second-rate farces.'

'Eases things sometimes to talk, y'know.'

Emmanuel's reply was almost arrogant. 'I have heard people say so, sir.'

The long golden days passed, the convoy stood well out to sea, for days no land was visible, one day merged into another, nights followed as a kind of interval between the acts. To Emmanuel it seemed that time was lost, that it had become non-existent. They might sail on and on for ever like this, through quiet seas, with bright skies overhead. Daily tasks were only imposed to mark the passage of time. To carry on with endless chores, for the nature of the 'punishment' he had been awarded reduced him, in effect, to the position of being unendingly at the beck and call of anyone with an unpleasant or arduous job of work which might be allotted to hands other than their own. This, Emmanuel reflected, was what the said 'punishment' consisted of—filling every four-and-twenty hours with the maximum of dreary and mind-dulling labour.

Meals were occasions when one ate automatically, escaping from the hot lower decks to the bright sunlight as quickly as possible, save when the strident notes of 'Defaulters' were followed by the despatch into the very bowels of the ship to carry out some 'fatigue'.

'It's a visual existence,' he said one day to Cuthbert. 'Don't you find it so, sir? The look of the sea, of the sky at night, or the oily shimmer of a rifle bolt when you've given it a really good cleaning, even the food is something which you see, and realise that you must eat. One doesn't feel anything particularly except the heat of the sun, or the coolness of the little breezes at night. We might be going to sail on for ever. I remember once reading a story where a crew sailed and sailed and believed that England had sunk at her moorings. Queer if we should find that wherever we are going to had sunk at her moorings.'

175

'Fantastic idea—you're a queer fellow, Gollantz.'

Emmanuel smiled. 'Incur-rably r-romantic, I'm afraid, sir.'

Land at last, and a few days to be spent on shore. It was a relief to walk long distances, to breathe this new and very clear air, to stare at new sights and listen to new sounds. The splendid flat-topped mountain, the bright blue sky, a concert arranged for the troops where a woman, very fair, with kind eyes and a ready smile, sat and played, sang old songs which brought back vague, half-forgotten memories.

'Oh, I am a soldier in a little cocked hat and I ride on a tin gee-gee' and 'Just a little bit of string—such a tiny little thing'. And a man, who told them stories—some of them not even very good stories, but, thanks to his inimitable fashion of telling them, they became the best stories in the world.

'I sore 'im yeres and yeres ago,' a soldier whispered to Emmanuel, ' 'e was actin' in a plai called "Sleepin' Partners". Not 'arf good it wasn't neether—spicy, too, in bits, I mind 'ow 'e sed, "Tell yer wot, I wanted ter be yer lover, an' blimy all I can be is your ruddy nite watchman." Coo, didn't arf mike yer larf.'

Another man said, ' 'E's gotter title—so 'as she. Clarse.'

The first man sniffed. 'None o' these 'ere actors an' actresses is reely clarse, 'sept w'en they marries inter the nobility like wot José Collins did.'

Then the little holiday was over and they were on their way again, living through hot nights and blazing days. Again and again Emmanuel had that feeling that this life must go on for ever, that they would never reach a port. The voyage ended as suddenly as it seemed their holiday ashore had done. Trucks with their special 'desert camouflage', then what seemed to be thousands of small, brown-faced grinning boys, crowding round, shouting, gesticulating, fighting one another. Every one of them anxious —for a consideration—to supply anything under the sun, from sticky dates, black olives, and boxes of dubious-looking cigars, to the addresses of even more dubious lady friends. Then long hours of boredom and waiting about— that interminable waiting about that, in retrospect, seems to be a good two-thirds of a soldier's life. Everyone hot and

176

dusty, everyone speculating as to what was to be their destination.

At last, when it seemed impossible that such a thing could happen, they had come to their journey's end, and everyone was saying, 'Rest Camp outside Alex. . . .'

Emmanuel sat half dozing, wondering idly where Mancini might be, if they might meet before the war was over; where was Guido, were the Germans still bombing London, when would he hear from Simeon and Vivian Mallet?

Cuthbert said to Emmanuel that night, 'Well, I might be selfish and try to keep you. But "ships that pass in the night" must have been written by someone who knew the life of the poor unfortunate soldier. I don't know where I shall be posted, or when; but I do know the Battalion your lot of reinforcements are marked down for. I've also a pretty shrewd idea who'll turn out to be your Platoon Commander. I hope that I'm right, for if you get in with the man I'm thinking of—well, he's a pretty dam' good sort of man to be with. He ought to appeal to you, he's a good leader. Well, good luck to you.' He added, 'I hope one day we may meet again.'

'I hope so sincerely, sir, and many thanks. I shall always look back on those nights when you were making your rounds, and used to stop for a word with me. I can't tell you how much it meant to me. And what you did for me at the Court Martial, sir.'

'Nothing, Gollantz, nothing. Perhaps I wanted to prove to you that the Army isn't a great, soulless machine. That's why it's lasted so well. Again, good luck.'

'And to you, sir.'

That was how things happened, Emmanuel reflected. For weeks he had seen Cuthbert several times every day; they had talked, discussed most things under the sun, and had often forgotten the difference in rank which existed between them. Now, in all probability they would never meet again, most certainly not merely to talk as they had done during the voyage out. Vaguely the thought depressed him; and on its heels followed his old nervousness at the thought of meeting his new Platoon Commander.

Camp, and then, after posting in record time to the Battalion, his first sight of the desert, which did nothing to raise his spirits. He thought that he had never seen anything so dull, so dreary, as the vast expanse of sand which lay before them. He had imagined that the desert was a tract of bright yellow, with pleasant undulations and a possible dotting of palm trees and brilliantly green oases. Instead he looked out on a sea of greyish sand covered with stones; above the sun beat down fierce and unrelenting.

That night he heard men talking of his Platoon Commander—one said that he was 'crackers', that he had 'bloody bats in the belfry'; another, a quiet fellow, gave it as his opinion that Sinclair was a 'marvel, and the Heads know it, that's why they give him so much rope'.

An elderly man with a soft drawling voice said, 'He's the last of the gentlemen adventurers. Six hundred years ago he'd have been a mercenary soldier, he'd have followed fighting wherever he could find it. He'd have captured kings and dukes, and squandered their ransoms on wenches in English ale-houses. He'd have known as much Latin as a priest, and have been at home with all the unprintable curses of the Army. He'll ask you—order you—to risk your life twenty times a day, but he'll always risk his own twenty-one times. And always two jumps ahead of everybody else. I've heard him called everything from a pig to a dog, and from a brilliant leader to a foolhardy idiot. Those of you who know him realise that I'm right, those of you who don't know him will probably hate him on sight, and at the end of a week he'll almost make you feel that you're glad you're in the Army, and in this part of it in particular. Sort that out!'

The quiet youngster said, 'I think you've hit it, Nobby.'

A little chap with small bright eyes added, 'Say it with music! Blimey, you don't 'arf talk loverly, china.'

Emmanuel tried to imagine what this man might be like, and it was a complete surprise to find, on seeing him the next morning, that he was short, with yellow curling hair, very bright blue eyes, and a roundish, curiously youthful face.

'Been everywhere, seen everything,' the man with the drawling voice whispered to Emmanuel. 'Shaves twice a day, and washes with scented soap. He's rapidly becoming a legend. The men call him "Reggie". Yes, his real name is

Reginald Mostyn Waldo Sinclair. Can you beat that?'

The small officer stared angrily in their direction.

'Can't you keep those damned chattering fools quiet, Sergeant?'

The Sergeant yelled, 'Si-lence there!'

'Can you hear me? Listen, you're just out. Raw. Completely and entirely *raw*. You may make soldiers, with the help of myself and Almighty God. We're not out here to spend time in the brothels in Alex, or to hang round the junk shops buying fancy bits of jewellery for our girls at home. We're here to do a job of work, and the sooner it's done, over and finished, the sooner we can all get home. Don't get any bright ideas about dying for your country—make the other chap die for his! Be careful what you drink, and how much you drink. The secret is—not *too* much of anything. I don't want a bunch of Sunday-schools lads, but I certainly don't want a crowd of knock-kneed, pimply-faced, sour-stomached ineffectuals. Beer isn't very good, and it's a shocking price. Ten piastres. Used to be three. A piastre is just under three pence. You'll learn to call them "Akkers". That's all I've got to say.'

He walked off with that queer characteristic strut which was to become so familiar to them all. Emmanuel learnt from his friend of the drawling voice, whose name was Clerk, that Sinclair was a specialist in patrol work, and that he was given a good deal of licence. It appeared that more than once he had embarked on raids which 'by all the rules' ought to have failed disastrously, but which thanks to his extraordinary resource and complete lack of wishing to spare himself—'or,' Clerk added, 'any other poor bastards' —had been brilliantly successful. 'Something of the high-light of the place. Rather a pet of the Big Noises, but never puts on airs on the strength of it.'

Life settled down into its accustomed routine. There were rumours that Rommel had done this, that the Italians had done that. We had sunk a convoy, the Germans had only three hundred tanks. That was a lot of lies, another rumour implied. A convoy of ours had been sunk, the Germans had recently had a huge consignment of armour, of a new and tremendously efficient type. We were falling back, we were advancing, we had fallen back to 'lead 'em on'. Every day

Emmanuel realised the truth of the statement that the ordinary soldier knows nothing of the progress of the war except the small piece which comes under his immediate notice.

He took part in several small but spectacular forays. Each time Sinclair grinned and said. 'Off we go—the Forty Thieves.' He referred to his men, quite openly, as bandits, and they grinned back at him, and tried to imitate his swagger.

The platoon had its ordinary complement of Bren-gun carriers, and to these Sinclair had added what he always described as a 'Wopgut', his name for an Italian General Utility Truck, which, together with an assortment of Spandau, Fiat, Breda and Schwarzloso machine-guns, a Zolothern anti-tank rifle, with their appropriate 'ammo', he had captured during the course of his raiding activities. As he had never officially reported the existence of his 'spoil of war', authority was careful to avoid all official knowledge of it. Sinclair had 'won' it, and since he continued to employ it with great effect against its late owners, the 'Powers that were' turned a blind eye on Sinclair's 'circus' on such rare occasions as they came its way.

As a great concession Emmanuel was permitted to replace the erstwhile driver of the Buick, who had recently 'returned to Base', by kind favour of the R.A.M.C., with a neat little label on the top button of his tunic marked— 'G.S.W.—right deltoid'.

'Can you drive?' Sinclair had asked him.

'Yes, sir. I've driven for nearly twenty years.'

Sinclair screwed up his eyes. 'It's an Italian truck.'

'I've been used to driving Italian cars, sir.'

'Umph! Didn't you get into some spot of bother before you came overseas? I heard something about it. Don't blame you. If a man—sergeant-major or C.C.—said anything about my girl, I'd be wearing his entrails now as a collar. Now, back to this truck. Look after her, I've an affection for the thing. Mind, if you make a mess of it, there's no second chance. And'—with considerable weight—'don't blame the engine.'

So Emmanuel drove the Utility Truck, with its reliable Fiat engine, and grew to share his Commander's affection for the thing. In it, trailing the Bren-gun carriers behind so that they got his dust, he made many expeditions into the desert. More than once he met little groups of Italian soldiers, footsore, parched with thirst, their uniforms unbelievably shabby. Their sunburnt faces were thin and downcast, Emmanuel felt that they were men who had no heart left in their cause.

At the sight of him up went their hands, and in a tone which was far from despondent they would cry in chorus, 'Un prigioniere!' Their delight when he bade them climb into the truck was almost pathetic. Most of them had thrown away their arms, and seemed glad to sit in the truck, their hands hanging idly, their dark eyes staring out onto the desert.

Once when they entered a village which had been fought over again and again, where the British had been in occupation, and later the Germans, then the Italians, and now the British again, Sinclair said, 'Care to have a look round? Might be a few of 'em lurking about. Go and have a look-see, Gollantz.'

Emmanuel found no lurking enemies, but what he did find was something which made his eyes dance with excitement. The room had been used as an office, he surmised, and there in a corner stood a small table of walnut wood, with a scrolled pattern of some lighter wood to which he could not put a name. Dust lay thick on the polished surface, the handle had been torn off the front of the drawer, but the thing remained—a piece of unexpected loveliness in its strange environment. Prising open the drawer, he found a small, leather-bound book, an obviously early Missal, its covers beautifully tooled, its edges retaining their worn and faded gilt.

He stood staring at the table, when he heard a step behind him.

Sinclair said, 'What the devil have you found here?'

'This table, sir, and a Missal. Both early, and both—good.'

'How the devil do you know they're good?'

'I'm an antique dealer, sir—in civvy street.'

'Let me have a look at the Missal. Furniture doesn't interest me.' He took the little book and as he turned the pages Emmanuel noticed his sensitive fingers and well-kept nails. He smiled as he flicked over the pages, and Emmanuel remembered that Clerk had said that he might have 'known as much Latin as a priest' had he been a soldier six hundred years ago.

He read in a curiously soft and even tender voice:

'*Nihil proficiet inimicus in co: et filius iniquitatis non nocebit ei.*' He looked up and met Emmanuel's eyes. 'Grand stuff; I think I shall keep this, Gollantz. Probably has no value, eh?'

'That would depend on who wanted it, sir. Some people might pay a fancy price. The market value—when the covers were cleaned a little—would be about four pounds. Do you want the table, sir? It wouldn't take up much room in the truck.'

Sinclair laughed. 'You're hoping to God that I say "No", aren't you? No, I don't and you do. Go on, take it, only you must be responsible for it. I mean if anyone "wins" it from you, don't come to me wailing about it.'

The little table was carried back to the truck, and Emmanuel, with great care, covered it with a piece of gunny-sacking. All the way back to camp his mind kept turning back to the table. When he had some free time, how he would wash the dirt from its surface, later he would try to 'heal its scars', he might even pick up a handle for the drawer in Alex—when he went there on leave—if ever. Slowly and carefully he would produce a polish on the wood, and he smiled with pleasure at the thought of this small piece of beauty which he had salvaged. He would beg 'Reggie' to let him take the Missal; that too should be cleansed and restored in so far as possible to its original state.

How had they come there? he wondered. How came it that his little table had been left stranded in a village in the desert; how had it come there in the first place? Had some priest brought it, and knelt before it while he recited his Office from the old Missal? Had he perhaps written letters for the men to their homes and families, seated at the table writing in his fine, clerical sloping handwriting?

Just another of the queer mysteries of the war! Fine furniture, an old book, a little fire-eating buccaneer of a

182

soldier, and Emmanuel Gollantz. A strange collection. But then all war was strange; even now, taking part in desert warfare, Emmanuel could never think of himself as actually 'taking life', killing and wounding other men. He had fired the Bren guns very often, but it was never in his mind that he fired at 'men'; to him it was 'the target' at which he aimed, which he either hit or missed. He wanted to get 'a bull', but there was a disconnection in his mind between that 'bull' and the fact that it was the vital part of a man's body. He tried to explain this feeling to Clerk.

'But you want to see us win the war?' Clerk asked.

'Of course, because I believe that we're on the side of justice.'

'Then you want to kill as many of the enemy's men as possible.'

'I want to score as many "bulls" and "inners" as I can.'

'Yet one's heard that it adds to a man's efficiency if he gets a kind of lust for blood, a killing sense, a concrete hate for his opponent.'

'I doubt it, I doubt it very much,' Emmanuel said. 'To me, in allowing any lust or longing to kill to *possess* you is to rob yourself of the ability to be cool and calculating. It's no use, Nobby, I'm not a soldier. I have no soldiering instincts. As little Watson says, "I want to see the job over and get home to my tea".'

Book Three

17

Watson, peering into the truck, whistled. 'Our "Reggie" hasn't 'arf eased some stuff from somewhere, 'asn't 'e? Bet the 'ole lot's unauthorised.'

'Like your nosing round my truck,' Emmanuel responded.

'Wot's like me nosing round yer truck, mate?'

'That and the ammunition and "Reggie's" play toys are unauthorised.'

Watson grinned. 'One o' the funny things of this bloody war,' he said, 'finding two chaps like you an' old Nobby in the same platoon. "Reggie" calls us "the Forty Thieves"— no one ter look at you, nor listen ter you, nor old Nobby 'ud picksure you as two of the thieves! Yet, I'd not wonder if both of yer got yerselves promoted or decorated or what-not before this ruddy show's over.'

'Not me, Watson,' Emmanuel said. 'You can take a bet on that.'

Two days later the platoon went out on a raiding expedition. Sinclair, shrugging his shoulders, said in a voice which implied that he was bored with the whole business, that they were after an advanced petrol dump.

'Nothing which is likely to lead to anything amusing, or even interesting. Just—one of those things. Get cracking.'

For once he was wrong; they engineered the raid on the dump with complete success, though he kept grumbling. 'Lot of unnecessary noise and commotion. I like a nice clean get-away. This is going to be messy if we're not hellishly careful and very clever.'

For the first time Emmanuel saw his little Commander anxious and frowning. 'They're after us!' he grumbled, then followed a series of strange oaths. Emmanuel imagined that some of them were Hindustani, or culled from the dialect of African tribesmen.

187

'Mixed bag coming after us,' he said at last. 'Jerry and the "Itis" both taking a hand. We've got to fight it out. They're stronger than we are, but, of course,' with a grin, 'not nearly so good or so courageous.'

The rest of that blazing afternoon was merely a series of almost disconnected impressions to Emmanuel. Sinclair still grumbling. 'Rotten position—beggars can't be choosers'; and wiping his forehead with a strangely clean pocket-handkerchief. Then a sudden exclamation from him, 'Mortars, b'the Lord Harry! Oh, damn them!' Clerk suddenly rolling over on to his face, making a noise like a camel, then lying horribly still. Little Watson, shouting as he danced with pain, 'The b——s 'as got me finger!' Someone shouting that 'summat's hit t' Bren-gun carrier', and another voice adding, 'An' got the old truck!'

Everything changed. Emmanuel had felt that the whole thing was indefinite, like something seen through a gauze curtain, that it was unreal and improbable. Clerk wasn't dead—couldn't be dead. Watson had only been fooling; young Patterson, who was lying there holding his leg and whimpering like an unhappy dog, he, too, was fooling. But —his precious truck, 'Reggie's' pride and joy, the truck which held his only piece of 'stock'—the inlaid table. He was galvanised into life. He heard himself talking rapidly, in a hoarse whisper.

'Not going to get the carrier. Neither are they going to get the truck—or my table. I'll show them. They shan't get Watson or young Patterson either. Now, Emmanuel, do a little sprinting.'

The truck was on the extreme left, the disabled carrier in the middle, the still serviceable carrier on the extreme right. He sprinted, running as if he had been on the racing track, cursing when he slipped, cursing when the sweat ran into his eyes and obscured his sight. He reached the carrier, started it up, muttering, with a quick glance towards the rest of the platoon, who were grimly holding the advancing enemy. 'Oh, don't make so much *noise*!' Then laughed because, of course, noise was necessary.

He drove the carrier forward, halted it, and flinging himself from the driving-seat rushed round to the side for the drag rope. Swiftly he hooked it on to the out-of-action carrier. Back into the driving-seat, starting again, reaching the precious truck. Again he repeated the process with the drag ropes. He'd done it, and felt a glow of achievement. The cars were saved—and with them his precious table.

He stood for a moment staring over the desert. Over towards the left of Sinclair and his men something was happening; men were moving forward, slowly and very steadily, Germans—putting in a stealthy and beautifully timed attack on flank and rear. Sinclair and his men threatened from the left as well as in their front. Emmanuel felt that the sun had been removed from the sky, leaving the day astonishingly cold.

'A German raiding party. Probably returning from the same kind of job that we've been doing. Hearing the row of our "party" like the good soldiers they are, have headed towards it! And there are just enough of them to tip the scales! And they've got that confounded "element of surprise", damn them! Come on, do something!'

He fancied that he heard little Watson's voice saying, 'Our "Reggie" 'asn't 'arf eased some stuff from somewhere.

That stuff—ammunition, guns all stored away in the truck, and, like the truck—unauthorised.

He never remembered running round to the back of the truck, the whole thing was a blurred recollection; the first clear picture was of himself working a machine-gun, swearing under his breath, and laughing suddenly and unexpectedly at the obvious astonishment of the party advancing on the flank. He saw them waver, halt for a moment before they began to go forward again. Sinclair had realised what was happening, seen the new danger which threatened him; he was bringing his men back in short rushes. The engine of the carrier was running when he reached Emmanuel.

'Nice work—oh, very nice work. In you go—yes, we've managed to get Patterson—you got him in, Gollantz? Yes, O.K., Sergeant. Go on, Watson—what's a finger? Make for that fold, Gollantz. There—go on, man, step on it, step on it!'

It was over—they had outdistanced the enemy, they chugged along over the desert, the cars rattling and shaking.

Sinclair said, 'You did damned well. I'll send in a report that ought to do you some real good.'

'Very kind of you, sir.'

'Kind—be damned!'

'Rotten luck about poor Clerk, sir. Good fellow.'

'B——y bad luck. He *was* a good fellow.'

Back in the camp they were swamped once again in the routine bustle. Emmanuel felt desperately tired; not even the sight of young Patterson being lifted out of the truck was sufficient to affect him. He stood leaning against the side of the truck, thinking only how much he longed for a hot bath, for some of that scented soap which the men declared that 'Reggie' used. A cup of good tea, a whisky-and-soda, clean under-clothes, socks, an immaculately ironed and laundered shirt. A soldier called Culver offered him a cigarette.

'Thanks, nice of you.'

'It's a bit bent,' Culver explained; 'just straighten it out. It will smoke all right.'

Conscious that he longed for sleep, Emmanuel said, indistinctly, 'Thanks—yes—smoke al' right.'

It was only when Emmanuel woke the next morning, while the sky was still streaked with trails of primroses and brighter orange, that he realised fully and completely that they had left Clerk behind, lying face downwards on the desert sand.

During the morning Sinclair sent for him. The Platoon Commander sat bolt upright in his folding chair, beautifully shaved, and, Emmanuel fancied, exuding a faint—a very faint—aroma of excellent scented soap. He might have been posing for the advertisement of some outfitters who sold kit for the desert war.

He nodded to Emmanuel. 'How's the old truck this morning?'

'Nothing that can't be put right by the mechanics in no time, sir.'

'That's good. Well, I've sent in my report. Good deal of "cheering" and "hand-clapping" for you. Apart from which the Old Man's been badgering about names to put forward for recommendation for a commission. He's pretty certain to include yours now—if you want it. And you *ought* to want it. Educated sort of bloke, don't lose your head when

190

a "party" starts, and not,' he smiled, 'completely unintelligent.'

'Very good, sir. I hope that the recommendation goes through.'

'Reggie' leaned forward, and asked in a confidential whisper:

'And the—table?'

'Intact, sir.'

'Now as a matter of interest—between us—what gave you the idea of that hitching up the truck and the carriers?' His eyes were dancing as he spoke.

Emmanuel smiled his grave smile. 'I knew how attached you were to the truck, sir.'

'True devotion—when a man risks his life for the—unofficial—property of another. And no other motive?'

'Perhaps you'd give me the benefit of the doubt, sir.'

'Nothing could give me greater pleasure than to do so. Help yourself to cigarettes.'

Later the C.O. himself sent for Emmanuel and questioned him, made him give a full account of what had happened. Emmanuel felt that he was growing a little tired of repeating his story, for earlier in the day the chaplain had spoken to him. A stout man who prefaced every sentence with a rich, 'er'. He had said:

'Er—you're Gollantz, aren't you?'

'Yes, sir.'

'Er—I—er—heard of your exploits yesterday. Admirable. C. of E. are you?'

'No, sir.

'Er—not a Roman Catholic, I trust.'

'No, sir, officially a Jew.'

'Officially—er, yes of course, difficult to observe the dietary laws in the Army. Quite. But—er—a Jew.' He laughed pleasantly. 'We can't have that, no no. When you get leave we must get you facilities for visiting the Holy Land. I think the sight of that, the wonders, the holy places will put an end to your Jewish Faith. Most conclusive, most interesting. Remind me, when you get some leave. Let me have your impressions when you come back. Er—yes, most edifying.'

Emmanuel pondered over those remarks all day, and wished that he might have discussed them with 'Nobby'.

There was something, he felt, distinctly wrong with the reasoning which argued that a Jew visiting the land of Palestine would come back shaken and disturbed in his faith. Not that Emmanuel had any very strongly developed faith. At Ordingly they had always been what old Emmanuel used to stigmatise as *'link'*; as a boy Emmanuel had talked to his grandfather of the Jewish Faith and listened to his pronouncements.

'My dear boy, I em afraid thet I em, end alvays hev been, a ver-ry unsatisfactory Jew. Maybe we—my family—hev moved about the world too much, lived in too many countries, known too many cities, and been too inter-rested in what they had to show us, to pay ver-ry much thought to our religion.

'That is not, my dear boy, an extenuation, it is merely how I r-reason it. I hev never been *untr-rue* to the Faith, I hev neffer indulged in mockery of it, saying that in these days it is too difficult to be a Jew. I hev made time for many t'ings, I could hev made time for my religion—if I hed wantet to do so sufficiently. I r-realise that. I hev only one t'ing to say which may help me, in the day when I shell need help. I hev neffer denied help to people who needet it and were Jews. I hev tried to be charitable, and to be charitable with *kindness,* with the wish to give in my heart. I ver-ry well r-remember an old fr-riend of mine saying, when both he and I hed given large amounts to a certain Jewish charity: "Emmanuel, you're paying the Fire Insurance, eh?" In a way he was r-right. I was—deep in my heart—hoping and believing—that if I were charitable—if I gave a little more than might hev been r-reasonably expected of me —that one day—someone might be charitable to old Emmanuel Gollantz.

'Thet there is thet gr-reat Someone I hev never doubted. Someone who is incapable of meanness, vileness, cr-ruelty, unworthy passion, and capable of complete and absolute forgiveness. If at any time you wish to follow the Jewish Faith closely, carefully, then—I shell be very happy. If not, then r-remember that nothing can alter the fect that you *are* a Jew—half a Jew—by birth, and do your duty to that race which hes suffered so cr-ruelly through the ages, and never make it possible for men to point at you and say—

with tr-ruth—"There goes a bed Jew, a disgr-race to the race to which he belongs". Thet you owe to the Jews, my dear boy. Jews are picturesque people, they hev colour, often genius, ver-ry often excellent br-rains. Perh'eps,' he shrugged his shoulders, 'men are jealous of them, it may be that Jews are not always ver-ry wise in their behaviour. Jews are always *watched* by other nationalities. Be certain that when the eyes of men watch *you* they find nothing unworthy. There, I hev explained not'ing, I hev only been able to tell you how I have tr-ried, with indifferent success, to run my life.'

Watson and the quiet fellow—whose name, curiously enough, Emmanuel had never learned—were the only men with whom he really enjoyed talking. There was a soundness in Watson's Cockney outlook, and in the other fellow—Emmanuel always called him in his mind 'the quiet lad'—he found real kindness and sensitivity. Again and again he would bring Emmanuel papers and books, saying: 'I thought that these might interest you. I have a friend who sends them out to me whenever he thinks there is anything which will appeal to me.'

Emmanuel always took the papers, always read the books, though, from the number of papers which arrived for him, he felt certain that Angela had placed a standing order with some shop. He was seated outside the canteen one day when Watson came up to him, evidently excited.

' 'Ere, seen orders?' he demanded.

'No, why?'

'Yer down fer a D.C.M. Thet's all.'

Emmanuel stared at him, dismay in his expression.

'Me in for a D.C.M.!' he repeated. 'What the devil have I done *now*?'

Watson uttered a great shout of laughter, and made an appealing gesture towards the other men seated round.

' 'E arsts wot 'as 'e done now! Shows yer what a confirmed crim'n'l 'e is. Always expectin' trouble. Thinks as D.C.M. means—probably does fer 'im—District Court Martial! Whatcher know abart it; carnt 'elp larfin', can yer?'

'When you have finished being amused at my expense, you wretched little nitwit,' Emmanuel said, 'perhaps—since you know all the answers—you'll tell me what those mystic letters DO mean.'

'It means—in addishun to what you, pore blarsted idjot, think it means—Distinguished Conduct Medal, an' you've got it! 'Ere, *an*' "Immediate Award" an' all. Let me tell you, pore 'arf-baked barstard that you are, that "Immediate Award" means suthink.'

There was a chorus of 'Thet's right!' 'You sed it, chum', for they had that deep appreciation of the soldier for the world of difference that lies between 'Immediate Award' and the 'Rooti Gongs' which periodically 'come up with the rations' with the publication of the New Year's and King's Birthday Gazette.

They were all pleased. That was one of the delightful things about these men, they never grudged their fellows promotion or decorations, if they were of the opinion that they had been honestly and honourably earned.

Soldiers came up to Emmanuel who were unknown to him, to say, 'Congratulations, mate,' or 'Glad to hear the news.' 'The quiet lad' beamed at him, and said, 'I wasn't there, but I'm certain no one ever deserved it more.' 'Reggie' said that he supposed they had a few extra medals and didn't know what to do with them so 'picked you, because of that astonishing name of yours'. Then he smiled, held out his hand, and said, 'Glad to know that I wasn't wrong in my estimation of you.'

Emmanuel felt warmed and happy. Things were going better for him than he had ever dared to hope. And then came the news that the recommendation for his commission had been approved. Soon he would be on his way to Alex and the O.C.T.U., where they would give him a white hat-band to mark the transitional stage on the journey from 'The ranks' to the dignity of a commission in His Majesty's land forces. Presently he would have a pip on his shoulder-strap; and he would have to face the necessity for taking responsibility, and giving orders. He felt satisfied that he would give those orders with increased authority because he had first gone through the school where he had himself learnt to obey them implicitly.

He had the delight of having achieved something. True, Angela wrote that Julian had now three pips, that Julian was thought of very highly, that Julian was doing wonderful work—these things did not affect Emmanuel. He felt that whatever the Army had done to him, it had done this for him—he no longer feared or suffered apprehension as to what Julian could do to him. Julian had done all that mortal man could do. He had engineered that scandal should touch his brother, had estranged him from his father and contributed to what was virtually banishment. Yet in that banishment he had found Juliet, he had lived in a country which he loved, he had made a not undistinguished name.

Again, on his return to England, Julian had done all that he could to discredit Emmanuel. It hadn't really mattered. Even the Court Martial had been nothing more than a temporary and transient worry. Through it Emmanuel had gained Cuthbert for a friend. True, he might see Cuthbert only at rare intervals but the sense of friendship was never affected.

Emmanuel sat smoking, thinking, trying to form correct estimates. Julian had failed. Emmanuel wondered if, deep in his own heart, he did not feel at that moment a strange sense of pity for his brother. He must have planned so carefully, he must have suffered agonies of fear when he fancied that his plans had gone astray. He must even have feared that Emmanuel might fling his promises to the winds and give him away.

'I don't like him,' Emmanuel thought, 'I never wish to see him or talk to him again, but I am damned sorry for him. He's allowed jealousy to grip him, and fling everything out of proportion. Even Cynthia Crawley, and my apparent friendship with her, inflamed his mind to such an extent that he had to take endless trouble to assure himself that he had—queered my pitch. No—I was wrong. I used to think that I had been given a rough deal. I probably needed it. I've had more complete and absolute happiness than any man had a right to expect. I'm fairly young, I've a son who loves me, and whom I love. I've friends—and the war can't last for ever.'

He turned to find that 'the quiet lad' was standing before him.

He said, 'You're off tomorrow, Gollantz?'

195

'Yes—what shall I bring you from Alex, young 'un?'

'Nothing at all. It would be different when you came back, if you do come back here, which isn't likely. They don't post a newly commissioned officer back to the Battalion where he served in the ranks. Not if they can help it, anyway. It saves—well, difficulties all round. But even if you were back with our lot—you'd be an officer, and I should be a lance-jack. I wish that you'd have a photograph taken in Alex and let me have one. Not in your officer's uniform, but—as you are now. I'd like that more than I can tell you.'

'But we'll see one another sometimes,' Emmanuel expostulated.

'It isn't so easy as that,' the other said. 'Perhaps one day, when we're back in civvy street, we might meet. Do you think that we might?'

'I think that—emphatically—we shall. All right, Q.L., you shall have your photograph. Bless you, you're a good scout.'

Alexandria seemed unadulterated bliss to Emmanuel. There was a considerable draft of money waiting for him, a letter from Max urging him not to econimise, but to be comfortable and to 'do yourself really well'. Letters from his mother, from Hannah, from Simeon and from Vivian Mallet.

'The Majestic'—he had determined to spend the few days' leave which had been granted to him, before he joined the O.C.T.U., at this hotel. It might be expensive, but how well worth it! After the austerities of the desert, Emmanuel felt that he might permit himself a little additional luxury. His bed was so comfortable that he felt he never wanted to leave it. He bathed at every possible hour, he even managed to buy some expensive soap, and hoped that he smelt as 'Reggie' did. He visited the 'Rameleh' and sat drinking good coffee and staring out over the sea; he met some people and was invited to the Greek Club, which he felt was like the Byzantine dream of some Hollywood producer. Best of all, he wandered down towards the docks, where he found dozens of little shops, the vast majority containing what he stigmatised as 'junk', but others where it was still possible to find odd pieces of jewellery, and curios which appealed to him. It gave him the greatest joy to handle again these things

196

of beauty, and for hours he would stand examining them minutely, revelling in their workmanship, their loveliness, their antiquity.

He was down in this quarter one afternoon when he heard shouts from the natives and saw them rushing for such shelter as was near. For a moment he stared after their retreating forms in surprise, wondering what on earth had frightened them. Then the hum of aeroplanes reached his ears, and looking up he saw the machines come over the town. Heard, too, the crash and scream of the anti-aircraft battery, saw one 'plane heel over, quiver, leaving a trail of smoke behind her, as she dived into the sea. Somewhere further along the dockside he saw a house burst into flames, watched the orange tongues of light licking the roof of the building.

A voice near him said, 'You bloody fool, what do you think it is—Brock's Benefit? Get some cover, for God's sake!'

Taken completely by surprise, Emmanuel exclaimed, 'It's "Reggie"!'

Sinclair smiled. 'That's what they call me, is it? Come on, man, I don't like this display of air supremacy, not at all! In fact I'm damned frightened. Get cracking!'

Together they walked rapidly down the street; the bombardment was in full swing, and everywhere they turned they heard the crash of bricks and mortar; again they watched an aeroplane dive into the sea, and heard the anti-aircraft boom and thunder.

Sinclair whistled. 'Whew—that was a near thing! Lord!— a bit of their damned nonsense has ripped my sleeve! Confound them!'

Emmanuel slipped to the paved roadway. 'Sorry, sir, they've got me in the leg! It's nothing—really nothing.'

'Reggie' was down on his knees beside him. Show me where. Oh, Lord—the knee. That's nasty. Oh, shut up, don't worry about me, it's only torn the cloth! Look, we must get you back somehow. You can't walk.'

Emmanuel said, 'Oh, I believe that I could . . .' and fainted.

He remembered nothing more except the jolting of the ambulance, and the way in which the pain ran right up his

197

leg as if someone were driving a jagged sword into the flesh. He came round to find himself in a hospital cot, in a room with a wide-open window, through which a cool breeze drifted. Someone who had been sitting in a chair rose and came to the side of the cot. He had an impression of a very white cap, and a pink, pretty face with eyes which smiled down at him.

'Hello,' he said, 'could I have a drink?'

Nothing in the world had ever been so delicious as that iced drink. He felt the cold liquid trickling down his throat, it was ecstasy. He sighed.

'Marvellous. Where am I?'

'In hospital. You hurt your leg, you remember.'

'*I* didn't hurt it!' he was indignant. 'Blame the Jerries for that. I say—how bad was it? You're not going to lop my leg off, are you?'

'Of course not. It's doing beautifully. You've had a touch of fever, but the temperature's down and you'll soon be able to hop about, sit on the balcony, and generally enjoy life.'

He said, 'It sounds—most—attractive,' and went to sleep again. He slept a great deal, and woke feeling hot and heavy; restless too and without appetite. Again and again his nurses assured him that the leg was better, and that he must be patient; again and again Emmanuel protested that he felt 'like death', and asked how they accounted for that. They were kind, soothing, and utterly self-sacrificing; nothing was a trouble, and everything they could do for him was made to appear as a positive pleasure to them. Sinclair's leave had ended long ago, he had returned to the regiment before Emmanuel had fully regained consciousness. Emmanuel was very lonely, longed to have friends with whom he could talk.

One morning the Matron came to visit him; she was stout, elderly and benevolent. She stood with her hands clasped before her and looked down at Emmanuel.

'Well, young man, you've given us a great deal of trouble.'

'Sorry, Matron, I didn't intend to.'

'So much trouble that we're tired of you.' She smiled, showing beautifully white teeth. 'And so we're going to send you back where you belong.' Emmanuel stared at her. He was still conscious that his mind did not work very clearly.

'Back where you belong.' What did that mean? Not the O.C.T.U., because he'd not been there after all. She must mean to his old Battalion, back to 'Reggie' and 'the quiet lad' and Watson and Culver.

He said, 'Back to the desert. Back to my own crowd. That's unusual, isn't it? But I'm awfully glad. You see, I'll have a room of my own—not a "room with a view".' He laughed and thought how silly his laugh sounded. 'I might even get back to driving the truck. It's an Italian utility truck with a marvellous Fiat engine. And I've got a table there—it's rather a good table . . .'

Very quietly, the Matron said, 'We fancied that England might suit you better,' and she smiled at him.

Emmanuel started, sat upright. 'England! The war's over? Is it? Really over and finished?' His eyes filled with sudden tears, he was conscious that his voice shook. Awful that weakness could rob you of self-control. In another minute he'd be crying like a child.

The Matron shook her head. 'I only wish it were. Now, try to listen and don't talk. You've been talking too much.'

Carefully she explained that, while his wound had healed, he had contracted some kind of blood poisoning which rendered further service in Egypt and the desert impossible. 'You might start it up again, and be more bother than you're really worth! Now—we've actually found a friend for you, you'll travel back together. Can you guess who it is?'

'Not the faintest idea—tell me.'

'A Captain Paul Mancini. Poor boy, he's been in here for weeks. He's coming in to see you, but you mustn't let his appearance shock you—he's been very ill.'

She did not add that half an hour earlier she had said almost exactly the same thing to Captain Mancini. Both of them were gaunt, both had the yellowish pallor of pro-longed illness, both had eyes sunken deeply in their heads, both had the same brittle-looking hands, and strange, weak, hoarse voices.

Emmanuel said, 'Mancini. That's nice—and we're to go home together—that's even nicer.'

18

Long, warm days which Emmanuel neither enjoyed nor disliked. He was still very weak, and though he and Paul Mancini were able to walk slowly on the deck, they had a mutual feeling that talking was too much trouble.

From time to time Mancini would say, 'Grand to be going home.'

Emmanuel would reply, 'Pretty good, yes.'

Emmanuel felt queerly homesick. Not that he had ever actually enjoyed soldiering, but he had grown used to the routine, the consciousness that he acted under orders given by his superiors, orders which it was not his business to question. The sensation which he felt during the first part of his journey was that of a schoolboy who leaves school in the middle of the summer term. He was continually wondering what Watson, 'the quiet lad', Culver and the rest were doing. Was Sinclair all right? How was Cuthbert?

During the first ten days he made his only real effort and wrote long letters to them all, letters which were posted at the first port of call. That done, it was strange how they receded in his thoughts; they were people who belonged to another world, who lived lives in which he would never again take any part.

News trickled through to them by air. Hess had landed, though no one seemed to be able to discover the real reason which had sent him flying to Scotland. Greece had fallen after a magnificent fight. She had been able to hold the Italians, but when Hitler flung his highly trained, splendidly equipped troops into the struggle, it had turned the scale. Stories of the air raids on London sent the colour flying from Mancini's lips.

'They say these are the heaviest raids yet,' he said to Emmanuel. He shivered. 'There must be miles of devastated streets. Makes me dread what I shall hear next. Iva in the middle of London through all this horror! God knows I've tried to persuade her to go into the country!' Then with sudden irritation, 'She says that she'd rather be bombed than bored! Iva's only attempt at a joke since I've known her—and it's a damned poor one.'

'See where they send you when you get back. She'll go with you anywhere.'

Mancini was in no mood to be either soothed or reasoned with.

'Where they'll send me! Pleasant if it's some place that is going to get it hotter than London.'

'They won't. They'll probably let us both down pretty lightly for a time. That's one of the things that makes me slightly apprehensive—not having enough to do. Having to plan one's day, find amusement, decide where to go for a meal, which play to go and see. I've lost the knack of ordering my own life.'

Paul nodded. 'I felt like that when there seemed a chance, in the hospital at Alex, that I should be slung out of the Army altogether. I was dismayed. That was the feeling—blank dismay. What the devil was I going to do? No work to do for Iva, no stout impresarios to argue with, or contracts to "vet". When the doctor told me that I was making progress and that I should only be sent away from the East, I nearly cried with relief.'

Emmanuel nodded. 'Without beating big drums,' he said, 'I suppose it's true that the only way to live—provided you're neither too old nor too young—is to be in one of the services, or doing some kind of vital, essential work which is controlled—and where you are controlled too.'

The days were growing warmer; both he and Paul were stronger, looking less like ghosts, their eyes less sunken and their jaws less lean. With increasing strength Mancini grew less apprehensive and lost his hunger for any scrap of news. Emmanuel, watching him, thought how strange it was that the difference in their ages never affected their relationship. Yet he must be ten years Paul's senior. There had been a time when he had—because of that additional ten years—become Mancini's unofficial guardian. When it had seemed that the rift which had formed between Paul and Iva Alfano could never be bridged. Emmanuel remembered how he had argued with Mancini—argued as an older man with a youngster; there had been occasions when Paul addressed him as 'sir'. Yet now the difference in age seemed non-existent. Queer, too, to remember that Mancini had first come into his life as a very poor, very shabby student of singing. Now—he was Emmanuel's superior officer.

A good fellow, a plucky fellow who had faced the loss of that lovely singing voice of his bravely and without whining. It couldn't have been easy to realise that never again would there be the slightest chance of his attaining to the heights in his career that the Alfano had reached in hers. No career at all in that direction for Paul Mancini. He had set to work to make some real work for himself, to justify himself completely as Iva's manager-secretary as well as her husband.

As he lay in his deck-chair, his eyes watching the gently undulating sea, feeling the soft caresses of the little breeze on his cheeks, conscious that health was returning to him, that he could afford to draw on his store of physical energy, instead of conserving it because that store was so pitifully small, Emmanuel tried, as he did so often, to order his thoughts.

Mancini did not indulge in long arguments and speculations on the future. In fact—Emmanuel smiled gently—Mancini had grown very like Alfano and so many of the singers and musicians with whom they mixed. None of them did bring much thought or speculation to anything except their art. That was sufficient for them. They were kind, lavishly generous, open-hearted and hospitable; they could be amusing, though their anecdotes were usually restricted to matters connected with the musical world. How both Paul and Iva had laughed—laughed for days—over the story of the famous composer and his hideous Viennese mistress!

He could still hear Paul recounting the story.

'. . . and as you know he was no longer very young . . .' Iva had interrupted as she always did, 'I shall tell this—you are too slow! Emmanuelo, listen. His wife heard of this. Immediately she wrote, *This is very well, I do not mind. Have your amusement, only how strange it is that your friend*—I forget the name, but she gave it—*should have done the same thing. He was a year younger than you are—as you remember, a very strong man. He too took a young mistress. He died last week and was buried on Sunday.* That night the mistress was sent back to Vienna!'

She had laughed until the tears had poured down her

202

cheeks, and her mascara had got into her eyes and made them smart.

What was going to happen to all these kindly musicians and singers after the war was over? Would they be able to command huge salaries? Was it not probable that salaries would drop to something which would not permit of a villa on one of the lakes, a huge house in Rome, Milan or Turin, high-powered cars, and expensive hotels? In France, in Germany as well as Italy, were all artists going to be too poor to live in any comfort? In Russia, the State would arrange their lives for them; Russia had always regarded art and artists as necessary to the spiritual health of the community. Perhaps they would go to America, and leave Europe without music and singers.

He had said as much one day to Mancini, who shrugged his shoulders and said, 'Oh, these things arrange themselves. I only hope the climate in England won't affect Iva's voice.'

'But doesn't the idea disturb you?' Emmanuel persisted.

'I suppose it might—if I thought about it a lot. Only what's the use of worrying about it. I can't do anything, can I?'

'I think that we shall all have to—do something.'

'What do you mean? Work harder—or what?'

'That is just what I don't know, and for that r-reason it is something which I wish to find out, if I can,' Emmanuel said.

Paul advised him, 'Don't you get headaches trying to solve problems, old man? There have always been wars, and things have been sorted out afterwards. The same will happen this time.'

'But don't you see, Paolo, that what happened last time must not be allowed to happen again? People will have to— or let us hope that they will have to—keep their heads, and,' with sudden gentleness, 'their hearts.'

Paul glanced at him sharply. 'You don't mean put on kid gloves to deal with the people who are responsible for—all this!'

'Not kid gloves, though they might be better than mailed fists.' Now he lay in his long chair and wondered. His mind wandered to the places which had been near and dear to him. His fine, rather melancholy face was very grave as his

203

thoughts took possession of him. He looked much older than he had done two years ago. Apart from his illness and his wound, new lines were graved deeply at the corners of his mouth, and between his eyebrows. His hair at the temples was grey. Only yesterday he had heard two young officers comment upon his appearance. They had not imagined that their words reached him.

'... chap with the D.C.M.?'

'Yes, elderly bloke to have only one pip, isn't he?'

Elderly. Emmanuel smiled. He supposed that he was growing elderly, and yet there was so much he still longed to do.

'I would r-rather that instead of pursuing adventure,' his grandfather had once said, 'that you indulged in the pursuit of beauty. All beauty is good. People who say "evil beauty" are ver-ry ignorant. They speak in terms which ar-re con-tr-radictory.' He had pursued beauty, and young Emmanuel had tried to follow his example. Years ago, when he had first read Rupert Brooke's *The Great Lover,* he remembered that he had laid down the book and tried to decide what things he had loved—would always love.

There had been the beauty of fine lace—whether he found it slowly yellowing with age folded away in some old carved chest; the lace of the spider's web spun during the night, to be discovered early on an autumn morning; the lace of a faded leaf from which all substance except the skeleton had decayed. The clear, pale yellow of old gold, the clear, bright, rather hard yellow of the spring celandine, the primrose of a calm sunset. The gleam of good wood, the dignified darkness of mahogany, the solid durable quality of oak, the delicacy of rose and walnut, the beauty of Italian, Dutch and French inlaid work—*l'intarsiatura.* His lips twisted wryly. 'My poor little table! Will you remain for the duration wrapped in a piece of gunny-sacking, or will "Reggie" perhaps rescue you?'

Yes, he had loved those things, as he had loved the beauty of materials—the softness of fine old velvet, the richness of silk, of brocade, good linen and exquisite cambric. Glass from Murano, china from Meissen—he remembered his delight when he first saw the china peal of bells hanging in the church tower at Meissen—the rather hard but enchanting blue of Sèvres, the pale, cloudy tinge of blue in Waterford glass. The picture galleries with their incredible cargoes of beauty—Dresden and 'The Courtesan', laughing and enticing the robust men whom Vermeer painted, that small and exquisite Van Eyck of the Virgin with a glorious red robe; the Louvre and the Mona Lisa, past which he had always hurried because he disliked the creature so, and preferred to remember his beloved Leonardo as the creator of the Last Supper and the Head of Christ.

London and an El Greco to which he always turned, and in the Portrait Gallery that pathetic picture of the dead young Monmouth, and the gay, gallant flamboyance of Rupert of the Rhine. The Edinburgh Gallery—small and like a jewel box filled with treasures. The Finding of Moses —was he dreaming or were the two side pieces in San Giorgio in Verona?—and the best Monticellis he had ever seen. A Giorgione he had seen in the collection of Prince Giovannelli at Venice; a Bellini in the same town; a terracotta head of the dead Christ in the museum at Padua—he had once taken Juliet to see it, and with tears in her eyes she had bent and kissed the tired, suffering mouth.

Music, too—but he had always been a little afraid of music since Juliet died, it affected him too deeply. Only when little Gilbert played to him, when they sat alone in his apartment in Milan, could Emmanuel listen with real happiness. Sometimes when Iva Alfano sang he heard with pleasure the lovely quality of her voice, and her operatic arias had nothing in common with the songs Juliet had sung.

All these things had demanded his love, he had loved them dearly, and to that was added his love for Juliet. Strange that someday there would be a new world, a world built out of the horror and cruelty of war—a world in which Juliet had never lived, in which she had no part.

What would it be—that new world? Would men still have time to look for beauty, or would they be too immersed in reconstruction and the rebuilding of their fortunes? Would it be still possible to visit Paris and to meet the eyes of Frenchmen steadily and kindly and greet them? Would it be possible, in the new world, to hear music in Munich, and to wander along the bank of the Elbe at Dresden and watch the barges come drifting past with their loads of timber? Should we be able to talk and exchange ideas with Germans without their remembering the exploits of our Air Force or our recalling the Battle of Britain and the scarred City of London? And the Italians—could he go back and meet the glances of his friends and the expression in their eyes when he asked for news of their sons, and received the answer, 'He was killed in a raid on Turino', or, 'He died, signor, in Africa.' Could we refrain from hinting how much wiser they would have been to remember the curse of Garibaldi?

He sighed; the sun was beginning·to set, the sea had lost its air of sunny gaiety, even the breeze had grown a little chilly. Emmanuel shivered and pulled his rug more closely around his knees. There must be a solution, a master-key which would open all the doors of the new world; but where was it to be found and who would find it? There must be so many people who held, as Paul did, that 'things could be sorted out afterwards'; many people who would be content to leave the whole of the planning to politicians, once the war had reached a satisfactory conclusion.

Surely that wasn't and never could be enough. The end of the war must be regarded as the beginning of Peace; Peace was the first and most important thing. He moved restlessly, he felt that he was going home, having been rendered useless for the effort to which he had grown accustomed—scrapped so far as his original sphere of usefulness was concerned. He had grown into his work, he had overcome his natural shrinking for mixing with his fellows en masse. In England it would be impossible to forget those problems, which distressed him and caused him to speculate.

He rose, folded his rug and walked to his cabin. There he sat down with his head in his hands. Paolo was right, he had given himself a desperate headache. Violently he wished that he might have had old Emmanuel to talk with him, that he could have sat and listened to 'Reggie's' common sense, his sane historic references which always had some bearing on the present. Sinclair, Emmanuel reflected, never saw history, never saw matters political as belonging to any particular decade, much less year. To him events were all part of a historic pattern. He stood well back, viewed happenings in perspective, and with his store of knowledge—

military, political and social—saw things as a whole.

'Facts,' 'Reggie' had said to him once, 'facts—proven and reliable—are there for our use. The facts of 1066, the facts of the Reformation, of the Civil War, of the loss of the American colonies; of the Council of Trent, the Test Act, the Act of Uniformity—are not separate things. They all fit into the *pattern* which is history. Seen in that light, history ceases to become something which is taught, it becomes a plan for our guidance in this stage of the world's un-civilisation and underdevelopment.'

Emmanuel suddenly found that he was contrasting himself with the little soldier for whom he had such an admiration. Sinclair might indulge in small affectations, but Sinclair had always faced facts. He had never tried to escape from them. Difficulties had been things which must be fought, problems were there so that he might solve them, battles—mental or physical—were contests into which he was ready to fling himself.

Emmanuel raised his head and stared at the reflection in the glass before him. The dark, rather sunken eyes, rimmed with shadows, stared back at him.

Speaking very softly, he said, 'And you? How have you faced your problems, Emmanuel? Have you faced facts, fought difficulties, and gone into battle? Haven't you always tried to escape? Right back to the time when Julian dragged you into that affair of the night-club until the time when—thanks to the idea, which you had possibly implanted in his mind, that you might be used as a whipping-boy—he involved you in a particularly nasty and cheap scandal. You have always sought refuge in escape. Oh, I know that you told yourself that Angela must be spared any shock.

'You remembered that Nathan Bernstein said that she must suffer no shock. But you ran away. It was not only Angela, it was that you hated the thought of unsavoury discussions, of arguments, of seeing the disintegration of your family. It was for Angela's sake—but not entirely. Again, when you came back to England—after Juliet died—you found that you could not face facts. You gave yourself no time to live down your father's—rather difficult attitude towards you. This immersing yourself in beauty—face it, a form of escapism! What have you in your life? Simeon, left

207

in trust to you by Juliet. Isn't it your concern that he shall live his life in a world which will be a better, safer, kinder place than the one which you are seeing now battered to pieces?

'There are problems to be solved—immense problems which will be left to the Prime Ministers and Presidents of the world; there will be—are already—small problems which can be solved by small people. Either you can enter the arena or stand outside. Either you can face facts—such as come your way—or prove yourself *to* yourself as someone unworthy and recalcitrant. If the individual tries to solve the problems of individuals, then the solution of international problems will have begun—before the war ends.

'How, where, in what manner, I don't know. Sufficient that they will come, and you—must not try to escape.'

He sighed. He was very tired, his head was throbbing unbearably. He had not even come to any very definite conclusions; only to vague and ill-defined thoughts and aspirations. Yet, his heart was comforted.

Mancini, coming into the cabin, found him lying in his bed, so still, with his face so white that, for a moment, he was frightened.

'Emmanuel!' he whispered. 'Emmanuel!'

The dark eyes opened. 'Hello, Paolo.'

'You're ill?'

Emmanuel smiled. 'On the contrary, I think that I am very much better than I have been for a long time. Don't wor-ry about me. Only I don't want anything to eat, please.'

Mancini said, a week later, with that sudden irritability which was characteristic of him, 'I told you not to worry yourself about all kinds of problems. That's what I'm certain that you did. You were all set for being introspective that afternoon. Now you see the result. Ill for a week—more than a week. Running a temperature, and making people anxious!'

'But now I am ver-ry well. You see, on that particular afternoon I contr-rived to get something out of my system. How soon shall we get to England, Paolo?'

Mancini grumbled. 'You know what they are—never commit themselves. Might be tomorrow, might be next week. Oh, here's some news for you. Germany has invaded

Russia. No formal ultimatum or declaration. Goebbels told the Germans that their country was at war with Russia. That was all! Now we shall see things move! Hitler won't get it all his own way with Uncle Joe Stalin.'

Nearly a week later Emmanuel, standing on deck, saw the big transport nose her way up the Clyde, past the shipyards, to anchor. They were home, they had come through all the dangers which the ocean held for them, and here was a new life ready to begin for most of them.

He still felt weak and a little uncertain after his bout of fever, but Paul's delight and happiness at being home infected him. Together they made their way to an hotel— one of the huge station hotels, where page-boys still ran about calling names and the numbers of rooms.

Paul said, 'I can't understand a word they say!'

Emmanuel grinned. 'You should hear what they say of the way *we* talk!'

Paul writing telegrams to Iva, Emmanuel more soberly writing his without the endearing expressions which positively peppered Paul's. Paul making enquiries regarding trains and sleepers, while Emmanuel leaned back in his chair watching and listening to the talk which went on around him.

'Nine o'clock tonight, and I go to pick up the sleepers. It's evidently rather a special concession—or they're pretending that it is—probably someone has turned two in. London tomorrow morning early! It seems impossible. Do you feel that you could face coming out to do some shopping, I want to buy Iva a thing called a haggis. What the devil is a haggis?'

'Nothing that Iva can wear round her neck as a pendant.'

Paul rushed from one shop to another, he was like a schoolboy with plenty of pocket-money. Emmanuel followed him, feeling suddenly old and almost out of tune. Not that he was not glad to be home, but Paul's gaiety and excited pleasure was something in which he felt that he had no part. In his cases he had the things which he had bought in Alex, and except for a few books for Simeon, and a magnificent dinner service of Coalport and a Rockingham dessert service, which he ordered to be sent to his London address, he bought nothing.

It was a relief to be on the train at last, to undress and lie down on the comfortable bed, conscious that the morning would bring Euston station, his own home and Hannah's delight at his return. As sleep overcame him he wondered vaguely if Vivian Mallet might come in as she left her fire duties in the morning. He would spend most of the day at home, telephone to his mother, and possibly walk down to Bond Steet, and drive out to Ordingly with Max. The train had begun to move, the wheels seemed to beat out the words: 'Nice to be home, nice to be home.'

His last waking thoughts were that Egypt and the desert, Watson, Culver and 'the quiet lad' were all very far away, and—for the first time since he left Africa—strangely unreal.

19

He woke, having slept soundly. He had not realised how much the voyage home had tired him. Not that he had been afraid, but that probably the unconscious strain had taken its toll. In the next sleeper Emmanuel could hear Mancini whistling. He smiled, thinking how much that whistling of '*Morro, ma prima in grázia*' must be annoying some passenger in the sleeper on the other side of Mancini.

Paul was coming home to Iva, and his heart was filled with thoughts of her. Her rôle of Amelia in *Un Ballo in Maschera* was one of her best efforts. Automatically Paul's mind turned to music which represented his wife's triumphs.

How often had Emmanuel heard Iva sing that rôle? In Bologna, in Navarro, in that lovely little opera house in Venice—La Fenice! Her other rôles might have been successful, but this was supreme over all her other characters. There was a tenderness, a sensibility in her singing of 'Amelia' which she never reached in any other opera.

He listened to the clear, liquid notes, whistled by a man who had once been a great singer, and who would never sing again. That lovely music, the music of Verdi, possibly less touching than that of Puccini, but greater and grander. They knew something, these musicians; they not only wrote music to fit good, dramatic stories, but into those stories they wove something which was imperishable.

'I die, but first in mercy'. Emmanuel wiped his chin with the rather inadequate towel which represented the railway's concession to the war effort. 'I die but first in mercy'. Couldn't that be applied to this war—to the conditions and rules which must be laid down once the war ended—by the victors over the vanquished?

To die—what did that mean? Not of necessity the end of life on this earth, but the ending of life as you had known it. No matter in what country, in what state of life, there must be a change, a great and certain change. That was a minor death, surely. Many people must die before the end could come—some to die finally, definitely, irrevocably; others to die in that the world which they knew must end . . . 'But in mercy'.

How often had he heard people say, 'I almost died'; but they had lived, and so the nations of the world must live. Such nations as were conquered must realise that they had offended—been anti-social—had transgressed against the 'law of the jungle'. There must be justice meted out—hard, cold, stern justice, but that justice must contain the element of mercy.

Because in his mind were thoughts of that whistling in the next sleeper, which automatically linked up with Italy and Venice—the city which he had always loved so dearly—his thoughts turned to that play of Shakespeare, that typical Britisher who yet voiced truths which were international.

> A stony adversary, an inhuman wretch,
> Incapable of pity, void and empty
> From any dram of mercy.

Sufficient to condemn a man that he was 'void of mercy'! Mercy—'it is an attribute of God Himself'.

Spenser, another complete Englishman, had written of mercy:

> Who will not mercie unto others shew,
> How can he mercie ever hope to have?

211

How they had harped on mercy, these old poets! Otway—Emmanuel remembered how Angela had stigmatised him as 'an old brute, with his silly fulminations against women'—had, for all his bitterness, held mercy high. 'The attribute of Heaven' he had called it.

The whistling had ceased, and Paul was hammering on his door.

'We're in—we're home!' he cried when Emmanuel opened it. 'Just running into the station.' His face was all alight, his eyes shining, he sounded a little breathless.

'You look the picture of the Happy Warrior,' Emmanuel said.

'And why not?' Paul demanded. 'In half an hour at the most I shall see Iva again. She might even'—he hesitated—'have come to meet me.'

He saw the sudden shadow cross Emmanuel's face, and laid his hand on the elder man's arm. 'Sorry—I forgot. We're selfish brutes when we're happy.'

'No, no,' Emmanuel protested, 'I must learn not to be always looking back over my shoulder. Come—get to the window!' The grimy walls slid past them, slowly the long train drew into the station.

Mancini shouted suddenly, 'Iva—Iva—here I am!' and Emmanuel saw the Alfano waving wildly; and beside her the stout, heavy figure of Hannah Rosenfelt. Paul flung himself from the train into Iva's arms; Emmanuel, following more slowly, found himself clasped to Hannah's ample bosom.

'Ah, it is good that you have returned!' she panted.

Iva cried, 'Emmanuelo, and imagine that Paolo did not think that I should be here! Think of that! I have scarcely been to bed, in case I might be too late. You will come back and breakfast with us, Emmanuelo. Yes, of course, you must both come back.'

He shook his head, laughing. 'No, later in the day, *the week,* I will come and pay a visit to the wife of my superior officer.'

'If there was any justice,' Alfano declared, 'you would both be generals—at least, at the very least.'

'Emmanuelo's got a medal,' Paul told her. 'Look!'

'A medal—very nice, and how clever! I shall go out and

212

buy all the ribbons and sew them on your coat, my Paolo.'

Remembering the old joke, Emmanuel said, 'And get him the D.C.M. at least, only this time it *would* mean District Court Martial.'

He drove back to Heber Square with Hannah, her small, fat hand clasped in his. She had so many questions to ask, needed so many assurances that he was really well again, that the house was reached before he had an opportunity to ask any questions himself.

Only when he was seated with a cup of fragrant coffee before him did she allow him the chance to speak of things which he wanted to know.

Simeon—she beamed, he was well, and had grown. He was longing for the holidays; she had been down to see him a fortnight ago. No, Miss Crawley was not there. Hadn't Emmanuel heard? Her bright dark eyes looked at him keenly.

He smiled. 'I have heard nothing. Miss Crawley took a sudden dislike to me, I fancy.'

'That didn't worry you?'

'Not very much, I'm afraid,' he admitted.

'She's gone to Canada. Some kind of work, I don't know what. Simeon didn't seem very interested.'

'And my mother and father?'

'Sir Max,' she paused, 'he grows old, Emmanuel. Old even for his years. He misses his annual "cure"; and though your mother made him go to Harrogate, he told me that he missed the gaiety of Aix. Poor Aix—it must be a sad place now. The gaiety will have died—like so many other things. Your mother,' she smiled, 'has telephoned to me five times since she heard that you were back. Was I certain that the sheets were aired; had I sufficient food; was I certain that there was some wine for you? "Remember," she said, "that he loves his wine, that son from the wars." She was like a child, so pleased, so excited that you were home again.'

'And Julian?'

Hannah scowled, she had never attempted to conceal the fact that she loathed Julian.

'Oh, his brilliance has become more brilliant than ever! He has been sent abroad with Lord Morforth, first to America, then to Canada. There is no doubt that he will

213

settle all the problems in his usual masterly fashion. That *gonof*! Now, Bill—there is a different man. There is nothing spectacular about Bill, but what did the old song say?—"he gets there just the same". He is in Scotland, doing work which is very secret and important. Imechine, we do not know even the name of the place where he is!'

Emmanuel pushed his cup forward for more coffee. 'It's good, this coffee, Hannah, thanks. Well, everything seems most satisfactory. The Gollantz stock is evidently rising!'

Hannah returned, suddenly sour, 'The Gollantz stock—with one exception—has always been high.'

How good it was to go out into London again, to visit the hair-dresser, where he had gone since he was a boy at school, when Max always used to say, 'There's the money for your hair-cut, and there is the tip for the man who cuts it.' Good, too, to order new shirts, to be measured for a new uniform, to go into his club, and have the porter exclaim, 'Why, Mr. Gollantz, this is a pleasure!' He nodded his greeting. The porter asked, 'How's things out there, sir?'

'It's so long since I *was*—out there,' Emmanuel said, 'I was in hospital for so long. Then the voyage home—it seems years since I saw the desert.'

Darkly the porter said, 'When this is over—let's hope that we shan't be so *soft* as we were last time, sir.'

He went along Bond Street and called in to see Max. His father sat there behind the big desk which had been old Emmanuel's, with the familiar inkstand which had belonged to Napoleon before him. As Emmanuel entered Max rose, exclaiming, 'My dear boy, this *is* good!'

How thin he had grown, Emmanuel thought; there was an air of fragility and even transparency about him. He stooped more than he had done, and his hair was quite white. The fine eyes looked tired, and were shadowed heavily. Even his voice seemed to have lost some of its resonance.

'When are you coming down to us, my boy?' Max asked.

'I thought perhaps that you'd allow me to drive down with you, tomorrow.'

'Allow you! Your mother will be delighted. We're both delighted about the decoration, and the commission. You've done well.'

214

'Then you've forgiven me for that wretched Court Martial?'

Max frowned. 'Poof, that business! I told Charles Wilmot at the time that he should have pursued the matter of that telegram much further. This friend of yours, Miss Mallet, was prepared to swear that she could have identified the man—the soldier. Very well then, Charles had no right to let the matter drop.'

Emmanuel said easily, 'Oh, I don't know that it materially affected the issue. They were able to prove pretty conclusively that I did my best to get back. That I was in no way trying to desert. That cleared me. No use dragging in a lot of red herrings, Father.'

Then came the inevitable question, 'How do you think things are going?'

'Well, as you know the soldier knows nothing of the war; all that he knows is how things are going in his very small bit of it. We're better equipped than the Italians, and, I should say, not *quite* so well equipped as the Germans.'

'Ah!' Max leaned back in his chair, and laid his finger-tips together. 'I was in the last show—as you know—when we sent a boy to do a man's job—and b'God, he did it. Then the politicians ruined the whole thing. Breathing fire and slaughter at Versailles, and doing nothing in Germany—except allow our men to fraternise far too much, and marry German girls! It will be very different this time. Turn them over to the Poles and the Russians if we're too lily-handed to deal with them ourselves!'

'How would you deal with them—when we've conquered them?'

'Deal with them!' Max sat suddenly upright, his eyes hard. 'How should I deal with them? On the principle of "an eye for an eye, and a tooth for a tooth". Bind them hand and foot—make it impossible that they should ever rearm, and even if they did, ensure that they could raise no army to fight! Make them pay—not only in money, but in prestige, in freedom, in everything that makes life tolerable.'

'I see,' Emmanuel said quietly. 'Yes, I see what you mean.' Later in the afternoon, when he walked away from his father's office, he called to see Vivian Mallet. She greeted him warmly, and he was conscious that he was glad to see

215

her; that her voice still held a certain music for him, that he enjoyed watching her hands, her deft movements.

Again questions about the war and the progress which was being made, the quiet conviction that, whatever setbacks the Allies might suffer, the end was inevitable. 'Peace with Victory'.

'And then?' Emmanuel asked.

'Then—accounts will have to be settled.'

'How?'

'I don't know. When I go out and see devastated areas, when I see the churches which are shells, ruined houses, and remember other things which I have seen—then I think that I *know*. I'm not given to hating very much, but—I admit that I find it perfectly easy to hate the people who did those things.'

'There are cities in Germany which we have—devastated.'

'Only after they had bombed our cities!' she challenged him.

'Were all our air raids only reprisals?'

She moved her head impatiently. 'Emmanuel, how can I tell? I don't know; these people were the aggressors, transgressors—and we're told that the way of transgressors is hard. I only hope that it *will* be—very, very hard indeed. You're not going to make me believe that you want to be gentle with these people!'

'No, no, I don't think so. I don't quite know what I do want. I only know that I want a lasting peace when it comes. I'm trying to find out what—other people think. I asked Hannah; she glared at me, and asked if any punishment could be too harsh for a people who had organised a system for the persecution of the Jewish race. I reminded her that the Russians had never been very gentle towards that same race. Now, Hannah is a sensible, very sane woman. Her reply was that "that was a long time ago. Russia has re-organised everything since those days". Frankly, I am desperately puzzled. On board ship I tried to argue it all out, I thought that I saw a gleam of daylight. Now—and I have only been home, in London, for a few hours—I don't know.'

Vivian's eyes met his troubled ones, hers were gentle and very kind.

216

'Poor Emmanuel, try not to worry too much. Let's win the war, and the rest will settle itself.'

He laughed. 'For a reasonably clever woman, Vivian, that remark isn't wor-rthy of you.'

She tried to tell him of what she had seen on the morning when the telegram disappeared. He shook his head.

'No, no, my dear, it's over and finished with. As a matter of fact the whole affair turned out to be most fortunate for me. Thr-rough it I met a man who was my good fr-riend— Major Cuthbert; and again thr-rough him I met a man I shall love and admire as long as I live. Who took the tele-gr-ram, what they did with it—is ancient and speculative histor-ry.'

'You're hopeless!' she exclaimed. 'Are you always going to take everything lying down?'

That startled him, he sat upright. 'Ah, you think that I have done that always?'

'Not always, perhaps, but very often.'

'I think that you are wr-rong, or partly wr-rong. I have not lain down, I have r-run away, done my best to escape. Not from what I have done, but from the consequences of what other people have done. By consequences—I do not mean actual r-results. I mean those things which would have to happen, in which I should have to be involved in order to pr-rove that they had done wr-rong. Arguments, explanations, disillusionment for people dear to me, and so on.'

'Sometimes I don't believe that I understand you at all!'

Emmanuel laughed. 'Then we are in the same boat, for ver-ry, ver-ry often I do not understand myself—or many things.'

She still had the power to soothe him, and he went away to dine with Paul and Iva Alfano conscious that his nerves were less on edge, his outlook less tense and disturbed.

The Savoy—Emmanuel stood looking round him for a moment. How unchanged it was; not quite so many flowers, scarcely anyone in evening dress, a preponderance of uni-forms—both men and women; but the same air of prosper-ity, of extreme comfort, and efficiency. If there were fewer flowers in the public rooms, there were as many as ever in Iva's sitting-room; the air was heavy with their scent. She

217

herself looked magnificent; wearing a wonderful dress and a good deal of jewellery. She embraced Emmanuel warmly.

'Look!' she ordered, 'tonight we make the great *festa*, because the two most important soldiers have returned. Tell me, beloved Gollantz, how many German pigs did you kill? Many, I hope.'

Emmanuel said, 'I don't know. I don't like to think that I killed anyone. I like to forget that part.'

'But,' she screamed in her surprise, 'that is what for you go to war! To kill as many of the enemy as possible, no?'

'How would you like me to tell you that I killed many Italians?' Emmanuel asked.

'Oh, the Italians—*poverini*! Dragged into the war by that big fool Benito! He and Hitler between them have ruined that poor country. I don't believe that either you or Paul would kill any Italians. Germans are all pigs; only a country inhabited by pigs could have produced Wagner and his hideous music!'

'And Mozart?' Emmanuel said. 'What of his music?'

'He is the exception to prove the rule—Mozart and one or two others. Hitler only enjoys Wagner—pah! *Scellerato.*'

'And how would you deal with these *scellarati* after the war?'

Calmly Iva Alfano, one of the kindest women Emmanuel had ever known, replied, 'There is only one way—*castrare tutti li!*'

Paul laughed. 'Nice, civilised wife I've got!'

'Iva, you don't mean it,' Emmanuel cried.

'But I do mean it—of course I mean it. I am a patriot, I love my country. These *porci* have dragged my country into war, to the verge of ruin. They must be punished; they will be punished if there is any justice in the world! I, Alfano, tell you this, my dear.'

Emmanuel made a little gesture of bewilderment. 'But, Iva, did your country—which I love, as you know—resist *very hard* being dr-ragged into the war?'

'How could they resist?' she demanded; 'the infiltration had begun, the Black Shirts were armed. Please, Emmanuel, talk sense! How can you resist men with machine-guns when you have only a stick? Don't let us talk any longer about the war. I am sick of the war. It is a stupid business.

Paul, give Emmanuel a cocktail, and for the rest of the evening remember that the subject of war is prohibited. I shall not allow Paul to go back to fight again. I shall make friends with generals and brigadiers, they shall find him a beautiful position in what they call "War House". He will wear little bits of scarlet cloth on his tunic to show that he is working there. I see many of them here, I think that all dine here. I shall ask them to have wine with me—the rest will be easy.'

Paul winked at Emmanuel. 'Be careful, Iva, we don't want any scandals. I should take a very poor view of them!'

'Poof!' she retorted. 'I am far too clever to make scandals.'

Of course, Emmanuel reflected, Iva was not a clever woman; she was not even particularly intelligent, except where her singing was concerned; neither was Paul given overmuch to thinking seriously about anything except his wife's business. Iva's declaration had shocked him. True he had heard soldiers of the rougher type declare that 'if I had it my way, I'd castrate all the bastards. But he had only believed that the expression was used as a kind of defiant verbal gesture. When Iva left them, and he and Paul were talking together over a last whisky-and-soda, Paul opened the subject again.

'Iva's very bitter about Germany, eh?'

'She wasn't serious?'

Paul frowned thoughtfully. 'Yes, I think so—oh yes. You see, like a great many Italians, Iva is not frightfully developed. She's the greatest darling imaginable, she'd die for anyone she loved, she's generous to a fault, but as far as actual civilisation is concerned she's not much in advance of those ancestors of hers—the women of Brescia. Those women who—in the absence of their men during the wars—fought and defeated the enemy, when their town was attacked. Both men and women from Brescia have always been good fighters. Look at the present war—the Brescia Division are damned good. Iva may be indolent, luxury-loving, extravagant, but that's only superficial; underneath she's got the same fighting spirit, and the same passionate resentment. I doubt if those women of the Middle Ages from Brescia were particularly gentle with the men they

219

captured in battle, or after attacks on their town. I think that you'll find plenty of women—not only women like Iva, but ordinary, average British women—who would subscribe to what Iva said tonight. Women are often far more vindictive than men! They always have been, don't you think? "The female of the species", you know.'

Emmanuel chose to walk home, through the soft darkness. He would go down to his much-loved Ordingly tomorrow, and the next day he would visit Simeon. He smiled at his own relief that he would not find Cynthia Crawley there. Strange that she had gone to Canada, and that Julian should be going there in the future. Yet he knew that he felt little or no actual interest in either of them. He had no affection for his brother; on the other hand, his acute dislike of him had grown tempered, had become indifference. Julian's path was unlikely to cross his, at all events so long as the war lasted. Then—he sighed—what profit was there in speculating what would happen then?

His attempts to discover other people's ideas regarding the ultimate peace, and the conditions of that peace, had distressed him. It seemed that there was no medium road. Either they hoped for vengeance, or for the destruction and degradation of the enemy. His father had talked of 'an eye for an eye'; there must be many others who thought the same. Yet this was a Christian country, and even Emmanuel Gollantz—registered in his Army papers as a Jew—remembered other words, which began, 'But I say unto you, love your enemies, do good to them that hate you . . .' Again, 'Vengeance is mine, saith the Lord, I will repay.'

Was there no middle course—something which lay between violent and uncontrolled bitterness, and a complete readiness to shrug one's shoulders and say, 'It's over, things will sort themselves'?

Surely there must be some way, a way which could be discovered now. Some method which might prove even to the vanquished that while punishment must be meted out to the aggressor, that punishment should hold no vindictiveness, no unnecessary bitterness, only sane—cool—considered—in his mind he fumbled for the word which he wanted, and it came to him—Justice. That was what the world wanted, what the nations needed, what must be maintained throughout the ages if the new world were to be built on a solid foundation.

What was this thing—Justice? Again thoughts and recollections came crowding into his mind. 'Justice—but has regard only to truth', *Justinian* said—what was that? *'Justitia est constans et . . .'* he had forgotten so much of his Latin, but the translation came to him. 'Justice is a firm and continuous desire to render to everyone what is his due'. Justice and with justice mercy.

Only that morning Paul had whistled 'Amelia's' lovely aria, 'I die, but first in mercy'. He turned off the main road to the quiet little square where he lived, a backwater from the noise and the traffic, the dull thunder of heavy lorries, the rush of dispatch riders in their crash helmets mounted on swift motor-cycles. The square seemed filled with intense peace. Softly Emmanuel began to whistle, *'Morro, ma prima in grázia'*, when through the darkness came the clear sound of someone who was joining in his whistling. Emmanuel stopped; the whistling continued, and drew nearer, then stopped.

A voice said, 'Pardon me, but it was so pleasant a thing to hear that aria whistled!'

A tall slim figure in uniform, a voice which he recognised. He cried, 'Louis, my dear Louis Lara!'

The tall officer shouted, 'Emmanuel—my beloved cousin!'

'But this is wonderful,' Emmanuel exclaimed, 'to find you walking out of the darkness, whistling that music! And in uniform! I had feared you were still in France.'

'I was in France—a long story—a veritable history how I escaped, and my wonderful Olympia also. I am Free French, dear cousin, I am with General de Gaulle, at Carlton 'ouse Terrace. There is so much to tell . . .'

'Then come and tell it. My house is here. There will be good coffee and cognac.'

Together they entered the house. Emmanuel turned and grasped his friend's hands. 'If only Guido were here!' he said.

'Indeed,' Louis replied. Then added—being eminently practical—'but if Guido were here the war must be over—in which case—none of us would be here. So . . .'

20

Ordingly! Seated beside his father in the car, while Max kept grumbling that he would not be able to use it much longer, and then qualifying his assertion by adding, 'And quite right too! Time we all had it brought home to us that the country's at war. Only, it will mean that I shall have to stay in town and only come home at weekends.' He smiled. 'Right, I know; but it's going to be hard on an old man.'

Then the first sight of the house which Emmanuel loved so much: the tall trees, slowly changing their colouring from the green of summer to the glory of red and orange which heralded the autumn; the lawns, perhaps not quite so well kept as they had been, the flower-beds denuded of their blooms and planted with vegetables. Max pointed to them. ' "Digging for Victory! Don't depend on others." We're carrying out those slogans.'

Tucker—did his clothes fit him less tightly than they had done six months ago?—opening the door and saying, 'This is a very pleasant occasion, Mr. Emmanuel. And congratulations, sir.' Then his mother—holding him tightly in her arms and whispering: 'Oh, my dear—how good this is! My dearest, you're so thin!'

Max went off to change and wash, and Emmanuel found himself in his mother's own sitting-room, where a small but very bright fire was burning.

'I know that we're told to save fuel,' she apologised, 'but this is only wood from our own trees—and I'm growing too old to suffer cold gladly, or to find that patriotic fervour warms my thin blood.' Then her flood of questions. How was he, what had the voyage been like, and how did he gain his decoration?

He lay back in his chair and smiled at her. How attractive she was! Even though her hair was turning grey and there were new, fine lines at the corners of her eyes, her skin was still beautifully smooth and clear, her eyes as brilliant as ever, and she still retained her eagerness.

'I am very well,' he assured her; 'in three days I go before a Medical Board. The voyage was pleasant but boring, and

I gained my decoration because I remembered that I was—in spite of war—still an antique dealer.'

Gravely he told her of the little table, carefully making light of the whole incident, and suppressing altogether the fact that they had left 'Nobby' Clerk lying face downward in the sand.

'And they gave you a decoration for saving a little table!' she cried.

'No, no, I left out that part. I pretended that I wanted to save the utility lorry.'

Angela laughed. 'Darling liar!' Then suddenly, 'Emmanuel, are you going to marry that nice Vivian Mallet?'

'One half of me wonders that very much indeed—always supposing that she will marry me; the other half knows that I don't want to marry anyone, that I'm far too occupied.'

With apparent irrelevance, Angela said, 'She came to see me—after your court martial, you know.'

'I didn't know when she came—I don't blame her for coming, anyone with sense would want to come and catch a glimpse of you.'

'Emmanuel, be serious. Most of my life I have hated being serious, and now fate has been too much for me—I have to be. She—Miss Mallet—was quite frank, she told me that she knew who intercepted that telegram.'

Emmanuel leaned forward. 'My dear, I don't want to talk about it. It's ancient history. Trivial and uninteresting. I told my father the other day, the loss of that telegram didn't mater-rially affect the case. Can't we forget it?'

She watched him, her face very grave, then rose and came to sit on a low chair beside him, taking his hand and holding it in her own.

'Listen to me,' she said, 'and don't interrupt me. I hate to admit that I've been wrong. I remember years ago when your grandfather attacked me—oh, a verbal attack, but an attack none the less—how furious I was. He was right—he always was right, I think. I had behaved meanly, unkindly, unjustly. Max—my dear Max—hasn't old Emmanuel's strength or courage or clear sight. Max has been through a great deal of trouble. The last war, he was wounded, then he went through a terrible time, and after that was over I didn't help as I might have done. Max very rarely probes;

223

his father did. Old Emmanuel would dissect anything, dismember it, delve for motives, weigh arguments. That was why his judgments were sound, based on facts, on logic.

'I want you to be truthful with me, my dear. There is no need to "spare me", for I have come to my own conclusions. Do you remember years and years ago when there was some fuss because you had been to a disreputable night-club?'

Emmanuel nodded. 'Yes, indeed. One does these stupid things.'

Angela leaned forward and laid her finger on his lips.

'S-sh, don't pretend. We've done with pretence. Was your name ever taken by the police, were you ever at that—that *beastly* place?'

'No, darling, never.' Then he added quickly, 'But I don't doubt that I have been to many other night-clubs just as disreputable.'

'Julian gave your name?'

'Well, you see, he was on the point of being adopted as parliamentary candidate for . . .'

'I didn't ask you for explanations. Julian dragged you into a mess which might have been very unpleasant? You need not answer. I know the truth of it all. Julian tried to get Viva away from you—oh, Viva has no scruples—and one night when you were having to face that court martial, Viva was here. Julian made some disparaging remark. I forget what. "My brother in trouble again!" or something of that kind. Viva was here with Toby, who was on leave. There was an awful scene. Thank Heaven that Max was away. She sprang to her feet, with that nice Toby shouting as if he were following hounds, "Go on, Viva!" And,' she wrinkled her lovely nose with a kind of reminiscent disgust that anyone should have made a scene at Ordingly, 'Viva—told us all she knew.' She paused, the disgust had gone, and Emmanuel saw the marks which disillusionment and suffering had left on her face. 'It wasn't nice, Emmanuel,' she said appealingly. 'I suppose it never is nice to be shown that one has been a blind, selfish, crass fool! You see, Viva knew everything. Oh, my dear, my dear, why didn't I know?' she asked passionately. 'Why was I so stupid, so lacking in knowledge, in understanding, that I didn't *see*?'

He lifted her hand to his lips. 'Angela, dearest, need we

224

talk about it? I don't want to—it's over.'

'Yes, yes,' insistently, 'We must discuss it. I must show you that at last I do understand. Viva is young—modern, she has learnt not to mince words. Ugh!' she shivered, suddenly, 'it was horrible. Julian stood quite still, his eyes very hard, and yet—yes, afraid. Once he started forward and said to Viva, "Be quiet, do you hear, be quiet!" Toby leapt to his feet and said, "Be quiet yourself. Viva's spilling the beans, isn't she? And you don't like it, do you?" Darling, it was like a nightmare. There was Emmanuel's portrait looking down on what he would have called—a brawl!'

The door opened and Tucker entered with the tray.

Emmanuel, trying to break the tension said, 'Oh, good, Tucker—cocktails.'

'Very difficult in these days to obtain the correct ingredients, sir, but'—Tucker smiled—'I have done my best to—er —rise to the occasion. I think that you may find my "African Desert" quite a pleasant mixture, sir.' He poured out the liquid, handed one to Angela and another to Emmanuel, saying, 'With my compliments, if I may be allowed to say so?'

As the door closed behind him, Angela set down her glass.

'You must listen,' she said. 'I've had too many sleepless nights since Viva—talked. I daren't write it to you. Say that you understand, my dear—tell me that, please.'

'Of course—don't distress yourself.'

Like a lioness she turned on him. 'Don't distress myself! How can you say that? Didn't you distress yourself when you accepted—what was virtually—banishment? Did you enjoy leaving England, conscious that your brother—and my son, God help me!—would hint that you had "left your country for your country's good"? Viva said all that there was to be said, Viva told me that you had—done what you did—accepted the weight of that very unsavoury scandal, because you feared that if I knew what had really happened, I might suffer. Julian and a nasty second-rate young man! Pah! Listen, Emmanuel, if there had been love—yes, real love, devotion—I would have *tried* to understand. Oh, again and again Julian tried to stop her, and each time Toby Tatten turned and shouted at him, "Shut, up, d'you hear, shut up!'' I felt frozen, my dreams—yes, I admit that I have always had dreams about Julian—all smashed to pieces at my feet. Viva talked and talked—recounted everything. How Walter had made admissions, how he had recounted to her the truth about Julian, and how Julian had signed letters with your initials.' She paused and dabbed her eyes with a little handkerchief. 'How stupid of us to give you names with initials so alike—E.J. and J.E.! Only,' pitifully, 'we didn't know then that one of our sons was—lacking in decency and moral integrity, did we?

'The whole wretched story ended, with Toby standing with his back to the door so that Julian couldn't get out. Darling, it was dreadful. It was like watching someone whom you have loved degraded and spattered with dirt. I'd been so proud of him—I needn't tell you, my poor one, you *know*. And to listen—and I listened half horrified, half fascinated to the whole dreadful story. When it ended, Viva said, "Have a brandy, Angela, you're all in." I laughed because it seemed so amusing that anyone should suggest brandy, when you really wanted to die of shame.

'I think that I went mad. I turned on Julian—I was so afraid that Amanda might hear anything—she's a very dear person, you know. Not clever, but very sweet.' She sighed. 'Poor Amanda!—what was I saying, oh yes—I turned on Julian. I don't remember what I said, everything was blurred. I couldn't really see him. I only knew that every bit of resentment flared up in me, that I felt that I must—at last—range myself on the right side, *your* side, my dear.' Tears were pouring down her cheeks, and yet so great, it seemed to Emmanuel, was her anger, even in retrospect, that she was not shaken by sobs. She had risen and stood facing him, her hands clasped as if she craved his forgiveness.

'My dear, my dear,' he said, 'it's all over and done with—can't we forget it all?'

'No, no, no!' she cried passionately. 'I still must explain to you. My sons are my sons; I love them all—my fault was that I loved one of them too much. That was a fault, that was how all this misery began. One son—you—giving, giving, giving; the other—taking, taking, taking; and their mother such a fool, such a misguided idiot, that she could not tell—could not differentiate between gold and pinch-beck. And yet—even now'—she came closer and laid her hand on his arm—'because I am the mother of all of you—you, Julian and Bill—I can't have it in my heart to *hate* Julian for what he did, what I know he would do again if opportunity arose. Can you understand, can you make allowance for the fact that—that he is my son? You see—this is all so new to me. I am seeing you clearly for the first time. I'm realising what you've done—believing that you did it for me—not once, but so often. Oh, my dear—you've been through so much—suffered—you've been patient. . . .'

He caught her in his arms, and held her shaking body to him.

'*Mamina*—mother darling, don't, don't. I don't want you to hate Julian, I don't want you to hate anyone. There's too much hatred in the world. That's why it's in this mess and muddle. I should loathe it if you were to be any different towards him . . .'

'But how can I help it? Emmanuel, it's impossible that I should feel the same towards him!'

'Yes, yes,' soothingly as if he were speaking to a child, 'but you must never show any change—not in affection. Perhaps you can be—what shall I say?—wiser, and never again make incredible sacrifices for him. I'm thinking now of your own money, comfort . . .'

'And Max's'—quickly.

'You can be wise for Max,' Emmanuel said; 'and as for me—well, apart from the fact that you have been dis-tr-ressed this is a ver-ry gr-reat day in my life. I have always wanted you to know, I have never dared to speak openly to you. Now—thanks to Viva, everything has been made clear and pulled str-raight.' He laughed. 'I am ver-ry fond of Viva, she is such a nice, downr-right person. Now, another of Tucker's "Afr-rican Desert" cocktails, and—here is my father to join in the *festa*.'

Max entered, eyed the cocktails with disfavour, and muttered that they were poison. He added, 'And when I have ordered Tucker to open a 1919 Montrachat and an 1889 Romanée Conti! You pair of Goths try to ruin your palates with that rubbish! Ah, well, have it your own way. No, no, not for me. Tucker is bringing me a glass of sherry.'

227

Emmanuel felt that evening that in some strange way he had reached harbour. His father had never been so sympathetic, his mother never so adorable. All his old admiration for Max came rushing back; as for his love for his mother—that had never waned. Five minutes before dinner was due to be served, the telephone rang, and Emmanuel's delight was complete when he heard that it was the voice of Louis Lara speaking to him.

'But where are you?' he asked.

Louis's voice emitted a chuckling sound. 'I ventured to come to Ordingly, I am now at the village—what you call it —public-'ouse.'

'Then come along—and be quick about it!' Emmanuel ordered, and to Angela, listening, it seemed that he sounded younger, happier, more hopeful.

Louis replied, 'At once—quick as greasy lightning—I come.'

'Louis Lara!' he told his father and mother, 'I met him last night. He's with the Free French and de Gaulle. Wishes to pay his respects.'

Max said, 'And, I don't doubt, have a very good dinner!'

Emmanuel beamed at them both. 'I am so happy to have met him again. I was afraid that he might have been caught in France. He's my favourite relation.'

'He's not really a relation at all,' Max said; 'he's not really a relation. A connection if you like. Your grandmother, Juliana, married her cousin Count Leone Lara. This lad is the son of one of Count Lara's brothers—Louis.'

Louis arrived, incredibly smart in his uniform, into which it seemed that he must have been poured, so perfectly it fitted. He bowed, with clicking heels, before Angela, kissing her hand; he bowed with deference to Max, and he embraced Emmanuel with fervour.

'Last night,' he said, 'we meet each other in the darkness. Ah, what a truth is this! In these days always we all meet in the darkness. We enter the bijou house of my dear cousin, and talk for many hours. We mix our tears—ah, how we weep!—but,' he smiled, showing brilliantly white teeth, 'we do not mix our drinks! You see, Emmanuel, I am still as you knew me in afore-times—a joker!' Not that he joked all the time; there were moments when he spoke of his country, when his voice vibrated with passion, when his dark eyes grew hard, and his anger almost choked him.

'Sold—sold everywhere,' he told them. 'Greed in every place. Greed for place, for power, for superior positions. Dirty men, playing dirty games. I was a soldier—ah, *mon Dieu*! were there ever such soldiers? "Captain, where do we find ourselves?" I answered, fighting down my shame, "I do not know." I try to be discipline officer. I say, ver' stern, "Where is your rifle? Tell me!" The soldiers shrug their shoulders. "Ah, Captain—they were no use. The date of them was 1916 . . . 1914 . . ." Yes, and before that! I saw a general stand leaning against the wall of a farmhouse, his arm thrown over his face, crying like a small baby—only much louder. He cried, "Judas, Judas, he still lives! He has sold France for thirty pieces of silver!" These things,' Louis said, turning with respect to Max Gollantz, 'are not ver' nice for a man to remember.' Olympia, to whom he referred as 'my beloved and magnificent wife'—though Emmanuel could never remember whether they were legally married or not, and had never felt it worth while to find out—had escaped to England.

'There she wandered, like poor little lost dog—I beg your pardon, I forget all my English—like a little lost bitch. Imagine the distraction of this wonderful creature—all heart, my dear cousins, all heart. She imagines that I am dead, dreams that she sees my bloody body lying in some bloody field. The stays in hotels—lying in her lonely bed, thinking of the days when the arms of her Louis embraced her, when his lips . . .'

Max said, 'Yes, indeed, terrible! And when did you get away?'

Louis spread his hands wide. 'A miracle! Nothing less. In my pocket is a small medal—of no actual value. It is of Saint Hedwig . . .'

'Who was Saint Hedwig?' Max asked.

Louis blinked his eyes rapidly, then recited in parrot-like tones: 'Duchess of Poland; after the death of her husband she retired to a convent and practised the greatest virtues and austerities.'

Watching him, exquisite as regards his clothes, obviously the product of a life of the greatest possible comfort, remembering the many occasions when Louis had practised many things but never austerity, Emmanuel chuckled. Louis turned to him, and grinned like a schoolboy.

Emmanuel said, 'Now, Louis, don't make a good story out of it! How did you get away? Never mind Saint Hedwig!'

With the greatest good-humour Louis nodded. 'How right you are! Always, in those happy and ever-to-be-remembered days when we were together—Emmanuel would pull Guido and myself on to the solid ground! I escaped, I walked miles and miles, I almost died of thirst, I nearly starved. I hid in ditches, in stables, under straw. I was dirty, fleas and other creeping beasts bit pieces from my most tender places. Then—like the films—I get away in a little boat, in the deadest of the night! England and British coast! I knelt down and sent up a prayer to Saint . . .' Then catching Emmanuel's eye, he went on hurriedly, 'We landed—I cried "London", and there, when I go to the Free French, I find that my Olympia—with that cleverness which is almost incredible—had been asking for me. I described her. Tall, magnificent, well formed, of a fascination which—ah, well, our beloved Emmanuel knows her, and when you have a few hours to spare, no doubt he will recount to you the wonders of this astonishing creature. We were united! Oh, the tears of Olympia—tears of joy, you understand—at my return. My tears at having returned! Again tears of joy! It was touching and beautiful. There you have my story.'

Angela said, 'You must bring Madame Lara down to see us here.'

Louis rose and bowed. 'Madame, I am grateful. But—my Olympia is a shy, delicate flower. Like the violet, she loves best to hide her beauty.'

To Emmanuel, remembering Olympia making a progress through the Galleria at Milan, the description seemed scarcely the most exact. She had been more like a three-masted barque in full sail.

'And was it all—as easy as it sounds?' Max asked.

'Easy! Sir Gollantz, nothing was easy, but am I like the beggars in Casablanca who show their sores? It is over and we laugh, my wonderful Olympia and I—we laugh because we have cried so much that we fear to cry again.'

'And after the war?' Emmanuel queried.

'After the war? Huh! Pétain will die—Laval will die—Blum will die—and all their army of filth will die with them. The Germans—ha, ha!' he laughed with a ferocity strange in such an exquisite product of civilisation, 'you will see. Yes, you will see. On the day when France rises again'—he tapped his chest with his forefinger—'Louis Lara will be there! For every tear shed by his wife, for every sleepless night spent by her, for each fear in her brave heart, Louis Lara will demand payment! They have said that the French are mercenary. Good! So we shall be when we demand the payment of debts. Not money, you understand, madame, but in things more valuable than money. This is how mercenary we—the Risen French—will be! What is the name of the small beast which works in the darkness—very quietly, with small, clever hands? Not a rat—a vole—no? Ah, a *mole*! France is a nation of moles. Digging, working in darkness, silently, stealthily, and so cleverly.'

He sighed deeply, and Emmanuel, rising, brought him a drink. He took it, and was about to drink it when he got to his feet and, raising the glass high above his head, cried, *'Vive la France!'*

Max, embarrassed and yet completely sympathetic, said, 'Yes, of course, *Vive la France*! But out of compliment to her—to a great nation—why drink that toast in whisky? Surely we can give you the wine of your own country in which to drink her future. Emmanuel, ring for Tucker. Yes, yes, I insist. Louis, you're a fine fellow. I'm proud to know that you're one of the family. Yes, Tucker—a bottle of wine. *French* wine, you understand. For a toast.'

Tucker stood fingering his lower lip, then bent and whispered discreetly in his master's ear. Max smiled and nodded. 'Yes, yes.'

Emmanuel, tired both physically and emotionally, leaned back in his chair and smiled at his mother. This evening had, he felt, marked the end of his banishment; tonight had seen those doubts and clouds which existed in his mother's mind removed and dissolved. She had been brave and frank, she had admitted her—Emmanuel scarcely liked to use the word, so deep was his affection for her—shortcomings. He

231

was closer to her now than he had been for years, and his content was almost complete.

He was back at Ordingly, sitting in a room which he had always loved, a room which held many memories for him. There was the portrait which Sargent had painted of his grandmother, Juliana Lara, who had married old Emmanuel. There were the two immense glass chandeliers which had been brought from Venice; the delicate—and yet comfortable—furniture, with the brocade seats, and beautiful lines—so typically French. Max Gollantz, sitting silent yet with a little smile touching his lips. Emmanuel knew that smile; it indicated that Max was waiting for the promised bottle of wine, that he was preparing a small surprise for them all. Louis chattered gaily to Angela; he looked so immaculate, so vivacious, that it was with difficulty that one remembered that he had suffered, had spent days and nights in danger.

Max said, 'And how much leave will they give you, Emmanuel?'

'I have to go before a Medical Board next week. One can't tell, but I should think that I shall get two or even three weeks. Always supposing that they consider me sufficiently fit. The second Board will decide that.' He smiled. 'Frankly, I'm in no hurry to get back into harness!'

Tucker entered; he walked with the dignity of a high priest, bearing a tray on which stood the immense goblets which Emmanuel remembered from the time he was a child, and which he had come to associate with ceremony. There was the tiny spirit lamp, the flame of which Tucker allowed to lick the glasses very delicately.

Max said, '1812, eh, Tucker?'

'1812, sir.'

Turning to Louis, Max said impressively, 'I toyed with the idea of drinking to the future of your country in champagne. The suggestion that this *fine* was more suitable came from my good Tucker. I hope that you will think that it is worthy to be used for such a toast.' Tucker handed him the goblet. Max inhaled the aroma delicately, glanced round to see that Emmanuel and Louis were ready. 'I give you—the France of the Future, a France which will be worthy of that country in the past.'

232

Louis put down his brandy-glass, and walking over to Max embraced him warmly. Max looked startled and disturbed, but retained sufficient control to pat Louis warmly on the back, saying, 'Ah—yes, oh, it will be all right! In our hearts we know that.'

When Louis had departed in his small, rather noisy car, Emmanuel returned to the drawing-room and stood looking down at his parents.

'A nice fellow, Louis Lara, eh?' he said.

Angela assented. 'Charming—quite charming.'

Max said, 'Undoubtedly—oh, undoubtedly. A little disconcerting being embraced, but I don't doubt that he meant it kindly.'

Angela laughed. 'My ultra-British Max. There, good night, both of you. Sleep well, Emmanuel.' Then taking his hands in hers, she leaned forward and kissed him. 'Welcome home, my dear,' she said.

21

Emmanuel went down to see Simeon. The boy had grown, broadened, and was wild with delight at meeting his father again. He spoke English more easily, rarely said 'Papa', seldom used Italian words, and when talking—even excitedly—moved his hands very little.

Emmanuel said, 'You've forgotten most of your Italian.'

The boy frowned, then said slowly and with evident thought, 'No, not really, Father. Only it's difficult to belong to two countries, 'specially when they're at war. It's like trying to play on both sides of a game, you see. At first, when other boys made fun of the Italians, I used to think of Guido and Uncle Casimero and the Alfano, and get furious. Well, now I don't, because it isn't any use. I didn't do them any good by saying that Mussolini and the rest might be swine, but that lots of them were grand. So I just tried to concentrate on the British. Do you understand?'

'I think so.' He sighed. 'It's a mad world, Simeon, eh?'

Simeon nodded. 'I expect so. P'raps only mad for a time.

You know, like George the Third used to get. Then he'd get all right again. We're doing the Hanoverians this term. Whew—it's difficult! Somehow, further back, it was easier—when we did the Stuarts.'

'The complications of advancing civilisation,' Emmanuel suggested.

Simeon never mentioned Cynthia Crawley, and Emmanuel asked no questions. Sir George was kindly, offered him hospitality, but Emmanuel felt again and again that the elder man was on the point of asking questions, and that always he decided against doing so. What did it matter? The thing was over and done with. He had felt a certain attraction for Cynthia, but recalling it in perspective Emmanuel realised what a transient thing that attraction had been.

Simeon was the person who brought his problems regarding Vivian Mallet back to him very vividly.

He said, 'Where shall we go for the holidays, do you think? Fellows—he's a friend of mine—is awfully excited because his father's going to be married in the holidays. It must be funny for your father to get married again, don't you think?'

'By "funny" do you mean amusing or strange?' Emmanuel asked.

'Oh, strange. No, not amusing!'

'Then I take it that you would not willingly give me your blessing if I contemplated matrimony?'

'Father—what rot! As if you could! I mean,' earnestly, 'she might not fit in with Guido and Hannah and—our friends. And . . .' his face became scarlet, and Emmanuel saw that his eyes were filled with tears—'and—it would be so difficult for Guido to talk to me about—well, about my mother, if another lady was in the house and might hear. Then all those pictures—you know, of your real wife—my mother—it wouldn't be very nice for this other lady; because she'd know that she wasn't as beautiful, and it's not likely that she'd sing awfully well.' He had mastered his emotion and said with sudden defiance, 'I don't believe that Guido would like it, or *Zia* Iva, or "Gillie" when he gets back from America—and I shouldn't like it!'

'All right, old man,' Emmanuel said, his voice carefully

calm, 'there isn't anything to wor-ry about. We're doing very well as we are.'

Simeon answered in his studiously rough voice, 'You bet that we are, and after the war—everything will be just the same!'

He went back to London, sensible that Simeon had been right. True, he pictured things in his own childish way, but that way happened to be right. Photographs, Guido's stories, Iva's laudatory stories of Juliet's voice, 'Gillie's' tender and loving respect. These things would make life difficult, might even make it insupportable. In addition, there was Emmanuel Gollantz—what had he to give any woman? Love—yes, a love which would be sound, but— desperately sane! To marry again would be an attempt to dispel his own loneliness—and yet, thinking calmly and logically, did he want to dispel that loneliness if it meant putting another woman in Juliet's place? However good a companion she might be, however charming, kind to Simeon, would there not always be a comparison? He had lived with his memories of Juliet too long, some of those memories had grown to be more real than actualities.

It was strange, he felt, that in these days he could meet Viva Tatten, laugh with her, let her tease him, make fun of his serious outlook; he could meet her husband, conscious that he liked him enormously. It was with difficulty that he remembered that Viva had ever been his wife. Juliet had been dead for many years, and she still remained real to him.

He knew that they had all conspired to 'keep her alive'. Not by remembering the days which had been important in her life, but by keeping her memory bright and clear in their own lives. They had never spoken of her as someone who was dead; rather they had assumed that she was merely away—away on a long tour.

'Perhaps we've been wrong,' Emmanuel thought, 'perhaps it is a rather false and artificial thing—this memory which we have kept alive. Who knows? But it's too rooted, too clear, to be effaced by the entrance of another woman into my life. I had a warm affection for Viva—she's been a wonderful friend to me. I like Vivian; there have been times when I felt that she and I together might make something

235

very good of life. Now I see that I like her too much to offer her—a second-best affection. I have monopolised her, I have enjoyed sitting and talking to her, but . . .' he closed his eyes as if to shut out something which was too poignantly beautiful to be borne—'but when I remember those days on Lake Como with Juliet, the first time she came into my little shop in Milan—to buy a chicken-skin fan—days in Munich when she sang there and I went to meet her, those days before Simeon was born—dear God—I could never marry any woman and feel honest about it.'

That night he went over to Vivian Mallet's flat. She greeted him, as she always did, with warmth. She asked questions about Simeon, about the decision of the Medical Board; she was interested in his doings, and he remained grave and very serious.

'Emmanuel,' she challenged, 'what is depressing you?'

He raised his eyes and met hers, then said, 'If I express myself very badly—very badly—will you tr-ry to understand and forgive me?'

'Of course. Get yourself another drink first.'

He walked over to the table where the drinks stood. A nice table, oak and beautifully polished, the glass well cut, and shimmering softly. What a pleasant room it was! Not very large, and containing no piece of furniture, no picture, of outstanding merit, but the whole effect charming and harmonious. Those old samplers, the rather inefficient water-colours of Cannes and Nice, the china in the tall cabinet gleaming softly and full of quiet colour. A room in which one could be—if not happy—at least at peace. For a moment Emmanuel experienced a sense of acute temptation. What a fool he was being! Why not ask this woman to marry him, why not catch what happiness there was left? He might never be able to return to Italy, his business there might have been ruined through the war. Simeon would grow up, in his turn he would marry—there were possibly years of loneliness to be faced. Guido might be killed, Louis Lara had his Olympia and his own interests. 'Gillie' was old, Paul Mancini and his Iva had their own lives to live. Bill would come back from the war—if he did come back—and he too would marry and settle down. Another marriage might not be 'the glory that was Greece, and the grandeur

236

that was Rome', but it could mean companionship and kindness, warmth and a certain content.

As he stood there, pretending to be busy with the glasses, he remembered Juliet's villa on the shores of Lake Como. 'Gillie' had played for her to sing, it had grown late and he had gone, saying 'as he always did, 'Good night, Juliet—good night, my dear young man.' Together Juliet and he had wandered into the sweet-scented garden, she had leaned against him and laid her cheek against his. He heard his own voice saying, ' "Hang philosophy! Unless philosophy can make a Juliet." '

She had answered, 'I can quote too. "Yet I should kill thee with much cherishing." Isn't that enough?'

No one could find twice in a lifetime such love as theirs had been. One mustn't go looking for love; if it came—ah, that was another thing altogether. He walked back to where Vivian sat, glass in hand, and stood before her.

'Please listen to me,' he said, 'because I am very conscious that I have been—less admirable than I should wish to be. I may also be filled with unwarr-ranted conceit. If I am, then I ask your pardon. Vivian—we have been ver-ry good friends—the best of friends. I know how loyal you have been to me, and I am gr-rateful. I have thought that perhaps you were fond of me, and I have known that I was gr-rowing very, very fond of you. Two days ago my mother spoke to me about you. She has a gr-reat affection for you. I thought that I would come back to London and ask you to marr-ry me; I don't know what your answer would have been . . .'

She held up her hand to interrupt him. 'Before you went to the East, I should have said that my answer would have been "Yes". I should have had not the slightest hesitation. I like you, we get on splendidly. Then when I went to see your mother at Ordingly, we talked. She told me something of your life. Made me understand—though, believe me, she was not trying to—made me see clearly. She achieved that quite unconsciously. I came back here, having come to a conclusion.'

'Which was?'

She raised her eyes and met his squarely. 'That even if

you asked me to marry you, Emmanuel, I should say—
"No".'

'You decided that?' Emmanuel said. 'Could you—would
you tell me why?'

'Because—and forgive me if I say anything which hurts
you—because so long as you live, Juliet will always be in
your heart, because to you—she will never have died. You
were right once when you said that you went through life
looking back over your shoulder. Only,' she smiled, 'I don't
think that you need look back very far, because I think that
she walks beside you.'

He came forward and took her hand in his, then raising it
to his lips he kissed it.

'And I—decided that I dare not ask you to marr-ry me,
because I could only offer you the second-best, and—only
the best is good enough for you.'

She shook her head. 'Very, very nicely said, Emmanuel.
Now, shall we forget all about that—rather difficult conversation—and never mention it again.' She laughed. 'Oh
no, I have no intention of letting you go! You're much too
pleasant a friend for that!'

After he had gone that night, Vivian Mallet sat in her
room, which Emmanuel liked so much, and fought down
the disappointment which had come to her. She knew that
she loved Emmanuel Gollantz, knew that she would have
been willing to take risks, to begin a new and completely
strange life with him. She would have adapted herself, could
have adapted herself, to everything—except one: the knowledge that Juliet would always remain alive in his heart.

That realisation had come, as she had told him, when
Angela had talked to her. The elder woman had spoken with
real feeling, with a tenderness which was essentially beautiful.

'There was no one quite like her,' she had said; 'I had
known her, and my husband had known her, for many
years. My father-in-law—old Emmanuel—loved her dearly.
There was some quality in Juliet which was unique. She had
looks, her voice was magnificent, she had charm and person-
ality—but all those things mattered less than this—*quality*
which made her—Juliet. They were married for a year—she
had been married before, as Emmanuel had been. They had

faced difficulties, and they overcame them. That year . . .' she had paused, and rested her chin on her hand, had stared out blankly as if her mind were turning back to her memories of that year, 'must have been the one memory which has helped Emmanuel. The one precious thing—except his son—on to which he could hold.' Then she had laid her hand on Vivian's and said gently, 'I do so terribly want happiness for him.'

Vivian rose, and shivered suddenly, for the room had grown chilly. She squared her shoulders, met her own eyes in the Chippendale mirror, and nodded.

'I'm right—and I know it—but it wasn't easy. Poor Emmanuel, but he at least has his memories—I have nothing.' She smiled, and said softly to her reflection, 'Well, I am spared the regrets which would have followed—if he had asked me to marry him.'

Emmanuel went before his second Medical Board. He was better, his strength had returned, and he was growing faintly bored with having so much time on his hands. The novelty of roaming about London had long since vanished, and again his old disquieting thoughts returned to him. Again he talked with people, always getting back to the question as to how the world should be remade when the war was over. He had talked with Louis, who for all his emotionalism had a very admirable and practical side. Emmanuel found his practicality almost too much for him. Louis might be an exquisite, Louis might laugh and weep with an ease which was startling to an Englishman, but in Louis's heart there was a quality which, as Emmanuel told him, was harder than the nether millstone.

Louis shrugged his shoulders. 'I am Frenchman. I have seen my country invaded twice in my lifetime. No, I do not remember the first time with great clarity—but I *was* alive when it happened. You, my cousin, have not known invasion!'

Olympia screamed. 'But 'e 'as! The Germans—I like better this word—'Uns—'ave invasioned Italy!'

Louis laughed, as one might laugh at an over-intelligent child.

'Tell him what you think of the Germans, Olympia,' he said.

239

Olympia made a gesture which, though, as given by Mr. Churchill, might have a patriotic appeal, as given by her had nothing in common—or very little—with the Victory V. She enunciated a word which when followed by '*alors*' may indicate a hearty wish for good luck, but without '*alors*' has a meaning which is distinctly unpleasant.

Emmanuel said, 'Just a *gamin*, Olympia! That's all you are!'

She nodded. 'A French *gamin*—and so content.'

His depression grew. He read books on 'after-war planning', and found no comfort in them; his mother shook her head and said that he looked less well than when he first came home. Max grumbled that Army doctors didn't know their business, adding, 'Go to Nathan Bernstein. That's the only man who is worth his salt.'

July came, and he went away with Simeon and Hannah to a village in Cornwall, and for one glorious week forgot that war existed. He only knew that the sands were yellow, the water very blue, and that the rocks were colourful with their lichens and seaweed. Emmanuel lay on the hot sand, and felt the sun bathe him in its rays. This was the oasis in the desert. The quiet, broken only by the cry of a sea-bird, or the soft thudding of the waves as they broke. Far out on the horizon he could catch sight of the grey shapes of ships, and feel that war had suddenly drawn closer. Felt that keenly, when one sunny morning he turned over on his face in the sand, with his head in his folded arms. He sat up so quickly that Hannah, who was sitting near him reading, glanced up and asked if something had bitten him.

Emmanuel nodded. 'Yes—that's it—something bit me!'

For the remainder of the day he carried about with him a mental picture of 'Nobby' Clerk lying face downward in the sand.

One morning Simeon came running in with a telegram; Emmanuel opened it, while his son stood near watching him anxiously.

'They're not going to send you out again, are they?' he asked.

'No, but they've found some work for me, and I've got to go back.'

'Oh!' Simeon's face betrayed extreme disgust. 'Oh, I do

240

think that it's a rotten war! Can't you telegraph to tell them that you're having a holiday?'

He travelled to London, and that evening went out to wander about the town. Uniforms everywhere, girls and men; British, French, Norwegian, half the countries of the world who had dared to refuse obedience to the oppressor. He heard the babble of foreign tongues round him, and wondered if these men and women were reasonably content to be living and training in a foreign land. Through the dark streets he went, scarcely knowing where he was, only walking on, vaguely conscious that he was growing hungry. He hesitated. He might hail a taxi—though they were difficult to get—and drive back to dine at the club. Somehow the thought of the vast and rather gloomy place chilled him.

No good going to the Savoy, for Paul had been sent to Bradford, and Iva had gone with him. Louis and his Olympia had taken a little house in Hampstead. His own house was closed until the end of the week, when Hannah would return with Simeon. On he went through the dark streets, each street seeming darker than the last. Surely those two buildings were theatres—which theatres?—the St. Martin's and the Ambassador's. He was staring at them, wondering where he could get some food, when a door behind him opened and two men came out.

One said, '. . . it's always full. Good meal, though.'

'Even in wartime!'

They laughed, and disappeared into the darkness. Emmanuel pushed open the door and went in. He wandered into the restaurant, and stared about him. Of course, he'd been here before! Every table occupied. It would have to be the club after all!

The head waiter shook his head. Tables were booked early in the day. Yes, a pity—if he cared to wait a moment or two—perhaps something might be arranged.

Emmanuel nodded. 'I'll wait.'

Looking round, wondering if he might find someone he knew, he caught sight of a small figure dining alone. Emmanuel's first thought was that it was astonishing to see a boy of such a young age dining alone. What would he be? Fourteen, fifteen—not more. Suddenly the diner glanced up

241

and their eyes met, and he pointed to the empty chair; then, calling the waiter, spoke to him.

The waiter came over to Emmanuel. 'The gentleman who is dining alone will be glad if you care for a seat at his table.'

'It's very good of him.' Feeling diffident, Emmanuel walked over to the table. Not a boy at all, but a man, who smiled up at him. A man with thick, soft brown hair, a tie which Emmanuel recognised as admirable, a dark suit, and eyes which were at once keen and very kind.

Emmanuel said, 'This is more than kind of you . . .'

'No, no—only too pleased. Sit down. My name is Birch.'

'And mine—Gollantz.'

Looking back, Emmanuel never knew how he came to talk as he did. There was something about this little man which broke down all barriers. There seemed no need to be on one's guard, no fear that any conversation could bore him. He was alert, capable of nodding to half a dozen people without ever losing the thread of what he was saying. He had a queer way of saying, 'Yes—yes, of course,' when you began a discussion with him. Emmanuel realised that he had been talking and talking for quite a long time, as if he had known this man for years.

He said, in sudden confusion, 'I don't know why I am telling you all this. I hope that you're not bored.'

'If I am bored,' Birch said, 'I ask for my bill, pay it and go home. The fact that I've done none of those things proves that—I am not bored. Now tell me more about "Reggie" and Culver and "the quiet lad". Yes, please, I insist.'

Emmanuel talked; the little man laughed—laughed immoderately when it came to the history of the table—and gave it as his opinion that it would 'turn up one day, probably bringing "Reggie" with it'. Then, his laughter dying, he watched Emmanuel with kindly yet grave eyes.

'And now?' he asked. 'What now?'

'I'm to have my second pip, and—I only heard this morning—I am to go to a camp for prisoners of war.'

'Not being yourself a prisoner of war? No, no, I'm joking, of course. Which prisoners of war—Germans?'

'Italians, I imagine, on the strength of my Italian.'

'Ah!' Birch leaned back and laid the fingertips of his delicate hands together. 'Ah—well, you've got your chance, haven't you?'

'I shouldn't indulge in favouritism because some of my friends happen to be Italians!' Emmanuel said with some indignation.

'No, naturally not. But you will have the opportunity to make them understand that they—and their allies—are very sick people. Greed, the belief that might is right, oppression, cruelty—these things are a mental sickness. For the sake of the world people who have believed in these things must be cured. Cured, remember—not merely forced to change their ways and opinions. The first thing to do—and it will have to be done in all these misguided and misdirected countries—is not only to make the people understand that they have been ill—very, very will—but to make them *wish* to be cured. Now, cures are not always very pleasant, or comfortable, things, but they are *necessary*. Don't let me talk too much, will you?'

'No, go on,' Emmanuel urged.

'The doctors who are going to effect cures must be people with strength of will, the power to direct, and the possessors of knowledge. Now, where this madness, which leads people into wars of aggression, differs from other illnesses is that they *could* have prevented themselves from being dragged into this—horror. People, however imbued with ideas and creeds, still retain free will. Therefore their actions need never have happened. No person, no community, no nation can escape from the result of their actions. Once these nations return to sanity they will, they *must*, realise that. It's not a question of whether those results are pleasant or unpleasant, the only question is that those results are inevitable.

'When this war ends, the doctors—we call them that for want of a better name—must have time to study the case. Some of these patients may begin to recover more quickly than others, some cases may almost cure themselves, some will need constant attention and rigid discipline. The moment the war ends there will still be too much bitterness, resentment, in men's minds. There must be no precipitate rushing into Peace Terms until our minds have grown attuned to thoughts of Peace again. The flame of resentment must have died down, and there must exist the clear, steady light of determination glowing. That—as I see it— will not happen for at least a year.'

He smiled at Emmanuel, one of the kindest, most friendly and understanding smiles Emmanuel had ever seen. He wondered vaguely how old this man was. He looked so young, and yet when he smiled there was something which could only have been born of suffering, and great and acquired tolerance.

Emmanuel nodded. 'Yes—and those terms, what of them?

Birch pursed his lips thoughtfully. 'I have my own ideas,' he said, 'and they may be entirely wrong. I believe that if a family get into mischief, become a menace to the rest of the community, they must be separated. They must each be given—responsibilities. They must each—each branch of the family—have an opportunity to work out their own salvation, to make their own way in the world. "You have broken windows", "You have refused to obey the by-laws—in other words you have *offended* against the social state".'

'But not—I mean that you do not suggest that these— families—should be taught by violent methods?' Emmanuel asked.

'Violent methods! Tut, tut! Surely you don't regard me as a savage, do you?' He laughed. 'As a matter of fact I am a "Savage", but it's as a member of the Club, not as holding a certain type of belief. No, violence does nothing but beget violence. As I said some time ago—and I am afraid that it is a long time ago, and that you must be very weary of me —the patient must be convinced, wherever possible, that he is very, very ill. He must *want* to be cured. So, when you tell me that you are going to a prison camp—I reply that you have great opportunities. Not for pandering to the prisoners, not for fussing after them, but for convincing them that you are just, and sane and kind. You will have authority—*use it*. You don't want men to tremble at your voice, but you do want them to respect it, and to know that you mean what you say and demand obedience. They will take away with them the conviction that—however little they may enjoy the "cure"—yet it is right they should be cured. You will be paving the way for the international cure that will come—later.'

244

He sighed. 'I am so tired. I have done two immense railway journeys in two days, and worked in between. I must get home to bed. It's been so very pleasant to meet you.' He called for his bill, and though Emmanuel protested he insisted upon paying for them both. When he rose he laid his hand on Emmanuel's shoulder for a second. 'Don't worry too much,' he said; 'remember that Peace on earth will come to—and only to—men of good will. Good night!'

22

The Captain held out his hand. 'Glad to see you, Mr. Gollantz.'

'Thank you, sir.'

He was a tall, thin man, with blue eyes and a long, rather melancholy nose, but the eyes twinkled and the corners of the wide mouth turned up. Emmanuel thought, 'I don't know what age you gave them, but I'll bet any money you're older than you said.'

'Nice camp, eh?'

'I haven't seen much of it, sir.'

'No? Well, it's a pleasant spot. The prisoners are taken off in lorries to work on the farms. Taking them by and large, they're not bad fellows. There are some rank Fascisti among them, turbulent chaps who have to be kept in order. Have a cigarette—sit down. I've known Italy for years—Rome, Milan, Turin, Genoa, Civita Vecchia, Naples. Decent people until this Fascist bug got hold of them. But then,' he leaned back, tilting his chair on to its back legs, and blowing cigarette smoke towards the ceiling, 'you can say that of most of them. The Germans—never met nicer people than in the country round and about Munich, in Dresden, and so on. Frightful shock to me when I went there and found—a change. No more cheerful greetings when you met peasants walking through the fields, only this awful, "Heil Hitler". Dam' silly anyway. Imagine if we met a chap in Bond Street, and shouted, "Long live Churchill". Couldn't be done.

'Y'know, Gollantz, most people in the world *are* decent. It's these superimposed doctrines that spoil them. We've got a chance here. Understand me, there must be no pandering to them. No "Oh, the poor, misguided, badly led Italians. Let's be kind to them." I'll never have that attitude. Never. They're grown people, they have brains of their own, and if they don't take the trouble to use them—let 'em take the consequences. Mind—I'll have no fellow manhandled or knocked about. I'll tell you why. That's not the British way of doing things. Old Kipling said, "Ye were led by evil councillors, and the Lord shall deal with them". That's all right to a point. I've a great respect for the Lord, but it's not always possible to wait for Him. He works very slowly. Time moves on! No, that's not the quotation—time *marches* on. Got it! Marches dam' quickly. But let's face it. Barring the French—who, whatever they are, or may have done, have a marvellous sense of proportion—these chaps are awful sheep. The old bell-wether, call him Mussolini or Hitler, goes ahead of the flock and they follow him.

'Now's our chance to teach 'em to think. I was talking to a fellow I know who is in charge of the Germans not far from here. I said to him, "Easy does it, in everything except discipline". Let 'em sing—why not? Let 'em play their game with their fingers—you know—*uno, tre—quatro—otto* and all the rest of it. Who cares? Certainly I don't. *But . . .*' he paused and thrust out a nicotine-stained forefinger, 'make 'em understand that *we've got something.* Understand that democracy isn't always standing on its toes looking out for slights, and getting ready to punish mistakes. We're not a new idea—we've got tradition behind us, and we can afford to be kindly and wise and even tolerant towards our enemies.' He glanced at his wrist-watch. 'I've talked a lot; time that we had a drink. Come along.'

Emmanuel followed him; his tall spare figure half rolled, half slouched towards the Mess. There were only two other officers present. The one a medical officer—red-faced, with small, twinkling eyes, and a nervous-looking youngster who kept looking over his shoulder, as if he feared that at any moment some Italian prisoner might fling a bomb into the hut.

The Captain said, 'This is Mr. Gollantz. He'll be here tomorrow to receive the new draft. I shall be away. Got to go to town—"War House". He speaks the lingo. Don't worry, Carter.' He grinned pleasantly at the young lieutenant.

That night they played poker. Emmanuel thought that he had never seen anyone bluff so persistently and so successfully as the Captain. The stakes were very low and the amount of money that anyone could possibly lose was negligible. But Emmanuel trembled to think what might have changed hands had the stakes been of any importance.

That night he slept soundly. He woke in the early hours of the morning, when the sky was changing from dull grey to soft pale silk shot with orange and vivid red. Flinging on a dressing-gown, he went to the door of his hut and stared out at the landscape. The country was changing, the bright green of summer had gone, and its place had been taken by deeper and richer tints. The trees which surrounded the camp were gorgeous in their red and bright yellow, made more brilliant, it seemed, by the dull green of the fading grass.

The early air had in it a new chill, a kind of promise that winter was following in the steps of autumn. He sniffed it with appreciation, an appreciation which he knew was only due to the fact that it was still a new sensation. No one hated cold and winter frosts more than Emmanuel Gollantz.

He drew his dressing-gown more closely round him, and looked towards the 'cages' where the men were housed. He saw the smoke of their kitchens begin to rise in thin, delicate spirals towards the sky, heard the distant clatter of dishes, subdued and indistinct, and the voices of men reaching him from a distance. Another day—another day in a life which was new to him. He remembered what Birch had said—'What an opportunity!' Again he recollected that old Emmanuel had always said, with that smile of his which so often had a hint of cunning in it, 'Neffer neglect an opportunity.' Well, if this prison camp should offer any opportunities, he would try to take them; to take them in the best possible way. Not with sentimentality, but working on the advice which people, in whom he had trust and faith, had given him.

Emmanuel dressed, and walked over to the mess for breakfast.

Captain Geraldson was there; he looked up, nodded, and said: 'Huh! 'Morning. Sleep well, eh?'

'Thank you, sir—very well.'

'I'm off in a few minutes. The draft ought to be in any time today. Take their names and particulars. Keep a sharp lookout for any of the real "Dago" type—you know, the sort who can hide a knife anywhere. Keep your ears open for any rubbish about "Il Duce" and all the rest of it. Squash it. I'll see you when I get back. The lorries have all left for the farms. Right! That's all.'

He was off, his long legs with their queer loping stride taking him swiftly over the open yards.

Emmanuel spent the day going over papers, trying to get some idea of the men who were imprisoned in the camp. He was interested, for here and there he found an entry regarding some man who came from a town which he knew—this street in Brescia, another in Verona, here someone who came from Milan. The morning passed rapidly; at luncheon he met the doctor and the nervous young officer once more.

The doctor was full of the exaggerated heartiness which Emmanuel detested. His voice was loud, he even ate noisily.

'Think you'll like our little home of rest for the Wogs?' he asked.

Emmanuel answered a trifle stiffly, 'Wogs? I don't follow you.'

'Itis—ice cream merchants. Otherwise Wogs.'

Still speaking coldly, Emmanuel replied, 'Ah, I didn't follow you. That epithet "Wog" wasn't applied to the Italians, but to the Egyptians many years ago.'

The nervous young lieutenant said tentatively, 'The men were singing this morning when they went off to work. Did you hear them?'

'No, I'm afraid not.'

The youngster had blushed at his own daring in entering the conversation, and was surprised at the readiness of Emmanuel's smile.

'What were they singing?'

' "Donna è mobile"—that's from Rigoletto, isn't it?'

'It is indeed. I had a friend—he was my officer when I was in Africa. He had a short leave—forty-eight hours at Durban—and stayed at a friend's house so long to listen to a recording of *Rigoletto* that he nearly missed the boat. He drove down to the docks in a hansom cab—yes, they still have them there!—scattering pedestrians right and left. He caught it by three minutes.'

The doctor looked up. 'You in the ranks?'

'I was.'

'Damned unpleasant, I should say, eh?'

'On the contrary, on the whole, very good fun.'

The day passed slowly for Emmanuel, he felt that he had little or nothing to do. Perhaps when Geraldson came back he would arrange for him to visit the farms, to see that the men were working well, that they were doing their utmost. Emmanuel frowned thoughtfully. That was part of—the cure—of which Birch had spoken. Could he—might he be one of the doctors, in however small a way?

He went on a round of inspection, talked to the various orderlies, cooks and sergeants. Nice folk, ready to be interested and also ready to be amusing at the expense of the prisoners.

One Lancashire cook said to him: 'It's a reit gaame, sir. Them Itis talking theer lingo and uz talking ourn. Still— some'ow we mak' each uther unnerstand all reit. Not bad chaps, sir. In fac', Ah dean't b'lieve, sir, as *onny on 'em,* as indivijuals that is, is reit bad. Misguided, thet's what they are. Nassi's—as the French saay—Ah was in France in the last show—*ong masse* is reitly naamed nasties. But 'Ans an' Fritz an' Ludwig, takin' 'em as indivijuals, is proberly decent enoof. That's 'ow Ah luke at it, sir.'

Emmanuel was in his office when the sergeant entered.

'Noo draft jest comin' in, sir.'

Emmanuel nodded. 'Line them up and bring them in— one at a time.'

'Very good, sir.'

The sound of voices outside, sudden orders, once a shout of laughter, and the first of the men entered.

Emmanuel looked at the man before him—short, stocky, ill-shaven, wearing a shabby uniform, threadbare and dirty.

He asked, *'Come si chiama?'*

The man answered sulkily, *'Mazetti Rudolfo.'*

'Dove suo patria?'

'Milano.'

249

Emmanuel tried to speak to him kindly. 'This is a camp for Italian prisoners. You will have work to do, and it will be well if you do it well for . . .' he hesitated, 'for the honour of your country.'

The man scowled at him. 'The honour of my country! *Dio!*'

Emmanuel nodded. 'Indeed, yes, think over what I have said.'

Others, boys who smiled nervously as if to gain favour, men who stood stiffly erect as if they defied the soldier who was in authority over them, others who were obviously nervous and apprehensive. Emmanuel tried to deal with them all firmly, kindly, always remembering that the people who had been dragged into these autocracies were sick people, people infected by a germ which must be exterminated, before they could be whole and sane again. He was writing busily when the sergeant admitted the next prisoner. Without looking up, Emmanuel asked mechanically, '*Come si chiama?*'

'*Maroni Guido, signor tenente.*'

The pen fell from Emmanuel's hand, he lifted his head and stared at the man before him. Small, with a face which had once been round and was now very thin, and which had lost all its cherubic contours; the curling hair overlong and untidy, the large eyes—seeming too large in his thin face— fearful and disturbed.

Guido—the perfectly dressed, the sybarite, the gallant friend who had—so many years ago it seemed—defended him against the allegations of his brother Julian.

For a moment the two stared at each other in silence, then Guido stammered, 'Emmanuelo—my master—it is not possible.'

Emmanuel stretched out his hand. 'Guido—my dear Guido.'

The Italian seized the outstretched hand and held it tightly.

Emmanuel thought, 'My poor little Guido, he is very frightened!'

He said, 'Have no fear, Guido. You are safe—quite safe. It is a very wonderful thing that you have come here. You understand that we shall not be able to talk to each other

250

very much. That is what war does, my dear friend—separates those who *are* friends. But you can help, Guido. You have never failed me yet, you won't fail me now, will you?'

The large eyes had overflowed, the tears were pouring down Guido's cheeks. 'Fail you!' he said. 'If I do, please kind God let me die. I have been lost. Caught first in the war which Mussolini made—*mi, mi, mi* the people, Emmanuelo. Oh, the Black Shirts—who cares for them? The financiers—the men who made shells, and aeroplanes and guns! Ah, for them—what amusement! Money for them; for us—the people—nothing. There are some—I have heard men speak as we came over in the ship—oh, that ship and that sea!—saying that Italy must fight for her place in the sun. I, Guido, said, "Place in the sun! *Ma Dio!* Place in hell upon earth!"'

Emmanuel said, speaking very gently, 'But they don't all think as you do, Guido *mio*, no?'

With some of his old intolerance, Guido contrived to swagger a little and answer, 'Not all—but these are Gawdam fools.'

'Listen, I am here to help you all,' Emmanuel said. 'Not to make life easy, Guido, but to try to show you people that this is only the beginning. It is difficult to say what I feel. You must not imagine that life here will be easy—soft—delightful. There will be work, and hard work. In r-rain, in sunshine, in cold—but it must be done. Mistakes have been made, quarr-els have been made, forced on some of us, accepted with joy by others. It might so ver-ry easily have been that I could have been a pr-risoner in an Italian camp. The fates have had it in their hands. Will you believe that we shall treat you as we should wish that you would treat our men who are prisoners? Guido—let us make this a time when you and I work together. We've worked together before, *mio amico*—we can work together again. Try to make these other men understand that the future must . . .' he struck the palm of one hand on the other, 'must be different. Italy loved freedom, followed Garibaldi—and then sold herself to a régime which could end only in disaster. What we take we must pay for. We British may be slow, stupid, lacking in imagination; but when we see other nations, smaller nations, attacked . . .' he smiled, 'we see red.

If the Negus had represented a great nation we might have shrugged our shoulders and said, "He's got all he needs to defend himself!" If, when the Germans attacked . . .'

Guido said eagerly, 'Yes, yes, I know, the sight of the below-lying dog rouses you always. It is commendable, Emmanuelo, my master and friend—I have always said that, *non é verro?*—what you look for is a new world, eh?'

Gravely Emmanuel replied, 'A new world, Guido.'

'And I can help in talking this way to the other men? I shall say, "It must finish. Things are rotten. We all know this. Let us start a new work, making a new world." How is this?'

'Not quite, Guido. It's that we must get together, we must want to see the world made different. No hate, no envy, just the determination that we're all here, we've all got a right to live—but to live without fear of oppression. It's not a bad world . . .'

'Not a bad world indeed,' Guido agreed eagerly; 'but there are—now I shall speak real English—so many bloody-minded devils in it.'

'Make these men who are with you understand,' Emmanuel said; 'I'll try to do my part. I'll try to show them that justice doesn't mean cruelty or bestiality. Tyrants and the systems which make tyrants must go! We've all got a right to a place in the sun, but no nation has a right to take —all the sunshine. Work with me, as you did for so long, *mio amico*—you're young, you can talk easily and with sensibility. Make them understand.' He took Guido's hand in his and held it. 'In this camp there are nearly six hundred men. If between us—you and I—can make them understand —that will be a start. Eh, Guido?'

Guido said, 'Six hundred. A start—from an Italian prison camp. Ah, and why not? Emmanuel, as always, whatever you do, whatever you order, I am at your backside.'

For the first time Emmanuel laughed. 'How often have I told you that you must not say "backside"? Behind you, that is what you mean. Yes, be behind me always, we've been together before, we'll be together now. I shan't be able to see you often, Guido. You'll understand. Won't you? But sometimes we'll meet, and talk and—plan.'

The little Italian smiled, his eyes were full of tears, his

voice charged with emotion as he answered, '*Sì*—yes—*Tu duca, tu signore e tu maestro*. Good night, I shall sleep very happily with my task before me.'

Emmanuel sat down at his desk, his head in his hands.

The sergeant, entering, said, 'Excuse me, sir—that's the lot.'

Emmanuel nodded. 'Very good, Sergeant.'

Rising, he went to the door of the office and stood looking out into the night. A clear, lovely night, with the sky spattered with stars; tranquil and deep blue.

From the prisoners' quarters a high tenor voice sang with almost unbearable pathos the song which Emmanuel had heard Gigli sing so often—'*E lucevan le stelle*'. How often had he heard that aria, sung on the stage at one great opera house after another? The quietness broken by Gigli's golden voice, the light slowly breaking over Saint Peter's, the day beginning. These men were prisoners, men who until the end of the war must remain to do the bidding of their captors, yet this lovely night had impelled one of them to sing 'When the stars were brightly shining', and, in that gentle music of Puccini, to forget their present state.

Was that, he wondered, the solution of all the problems? Not that men were so different when they were born in different countries, but that they were fundamentally the same?

Beauty, tranquillity, love and devotion—surely these things were common among all peoples. There must be common ground on which all men could meet, ground upon which they could share the good and lovely things of the world. These emotions were understood by them all— Frenchmen, Germans, Italians, and British. If they were suppressed by some superimposed system—that was artificiality, that was something foreign to mankind as one knew it.

The essential things of life must always exist, they must be worked on, claimed as a common meeting-ground, developed and even exploited. The love of a child for its mother, of a man for his sweetheart, a girl for her lover, husband and wife for one another, and for their children— these were the loves upon which the world must be built. Not with greed and ambition as the impulse to go forward,

253

but with a determination that—because of love—men and women wished to leave the world a better, safer, more contented place than they had found it.

'From the individual love to the love of humanity,' Emmanuel said softly. Then remembering what the little man had said to him in the restaurant, 'Peace on earth—*to men of good will*.' Good will—what, after all, was 'good will' but kindness? He stood staring out into the darkness; the singing had changed, they were indulging in that nostalgic ballad—he couldn't remember all the words—'*Santa Lucia —limpida mare*'—then something about 'coming back again'.

'This is happening everywhere,' he thought. 'In Germany —in Italy—British prisoners are singing—some song which means home. All the world is making prisoners, holding them until the war is over. But however unhappy they are— they sing. But the real prisoners are those who are bound down by—*what was*. Freedom lies in realising—what *may* be, what *must* be. Life will never be the same—why should it be? We've stood still for too long, we've lost strength. Only those systems which had a great, fanatical idea behind them made headway. Benito Mussolini with his ideals, Lenin with his, Hitler with his. Right or wrong, they took ground, gained ground, and held what they gained. Some of them grew upwards, some downwards—but none of them stood still. Nothing can—to stand still is stagnation, and stagnation means death. If we're sincere, if our aspirations are high, and our spirits clean—then we can launch a greater system than the world has ever seen. Here's a beginning— six hundred men. Dear God, how some of them hated me tonight! They saw me as someone who was there—to remind them that they were prisoners. Prisoners! If only Guido can help me—he and I may be saviours of at least six hundred. "For the sake of five just men . . ." Well, for the sake of six hundred men, if Guido and I can do our work—well, the city—no, the world—might be saved.'

He sighed and straightened his shoulders. In the dusk he could see the orderly waiting to lock up the hut.

'That's all right. Sorry to have kept you waiting,' he called.

The man hurried forward. ' 'Sall right, sir. Loverly night, sir.'

'It is indeed.'

'Them chaps sings nice, sir, don't they?'

'Who—the Italians? They're always singing. Good night.'

'Goo' night, sir.'

He walked slowly towards his own hut, his feet crunching on the cindered path. A queer life, he thought, living here in a prison camp miles away from anywhere. But then his whole life had been strange. He had possessed everything that any man could want. A successful business, a beautiful home and—Juliet. Now—he might or might not see his home again—that was on the knees of the gods. He reached his hut, opened the door and sat down on the small camp bed, leaving the door open so that he could look out at the stars. He had some things left, after all—his son, the complete understanding of his mother, the affection of his father. Bill, who would come back one day—'Gillie', who would return from America—Hannah, that plain, elderly woman who had always given him so much devotion and affection. No, life might be worse.

But his whole body stiffened instinctively, he had work to do. Simeon, his son, must not grow up in a world where peace was a thing which might last, or might end at any moment. Simeon's future must not be spent in a world where the destinies of nations were held in the hands of politicians and financiers, aggressors and tyrants. He might not be able to fight in an extensive field, but fight he would, and with the only weapon which he understood.

He stood up and walked to the door, again he stared out at the starlit sky. He reverted to his old trick of finding quotations to suit his mood. The night . . .

' "Make the floor of heaven so bright . . ." "Night's candles . . ." ' A little stab of pain when he remembered what Juliet had said—'That I should kill thee with much cherishing.' 'Ah, Juliet! If only . . .' Then throwing back his head with that movement which was characteristic of him, Emmanuel said softly, 'You shall be proud of me—my dear —you shall!'

He stood looking out into the night, standing very still. He sought for some words which should seal his dedication to what he believed and trusted in. They evaded him, then his face cleared. Words from some poem which he scarcely remembered—not a very good poem, he fancied—the author's name he did not know—but the words were there.

He said, ' "Write me as one that loves his fellow men".'

London,
November 1942

If you would like a complete list of Arrow books
please send a postcard to
P.O. Box 29, Douglas, Isle of Man, Great Britain.